D1521969

Now or Never:
The 11 Secrets of Arimathea

The Greatest Story Never Told

By

Joseph Rocco Cervasio

www.xulonpress.com

In Memory of ...

Michael Geltrude of Nutley, New Jersey, ... mathematician, teacher, coach, philosopher, believer, family man, athlete, and friend. Michael taught many of us how to enjoy the gift of life. He lived in every moment. The thing I remember best about him was that whenever anyone expressed the wish to do something good for other people, relative to the timing of the deed, Michael would always respond:

"What about now?"

Dedicated to ...

The many who shared the secrets of destiny-living in their sometimes overlooked acts of kindness, service, achievement, and love. From the classroom, to the playing field, at the pulpit and podium, in the board room, and by spoken and written words, ... they each in their own way revealed priceless revelations that are shared in the book.

Books by Joseph Rocco Cervasio

Bad News on the Doorstep

Now or Never: The 11 Secrets of Arimathea

Acknowledgements

My wife Maria has been a true partner in every respect, particularly supportive in my efforts to share through the written word. Corrine, our younger daughter, has always been an objective and analytical force driving me back to reality. Her loyalty to all she commits is a beacon of inspiration. Our first daughter Tina demonstrates daily her resilience to achieve in sports broadcasting. She and her husband Kevin McKearney are always ready to serve their families.

Dr. Ken Atchity, Chairman of Atchity Entertainment International, continues to oversee my work as literary manager. He just never gives up, always supporting with his encouragement to believe in what you are doing and to expect a worthy conclusion. His assistant Brenna Liu persists in orchestrating our communications with the publishing world. At Dr. Atchity's suggestion, my life changed when he introduced me to two writing coaches and editors, Rudy Yuly and Dawn Grey, both from his Writer's Lifeline subsidiary.

My first editor and publicist Mike Finley has become a good friend. Honesty, even when it hurts, has been his trademark with me, as well as his magic pen which helped craft my original manuscript.

My brother Alan Cervasio liked what he read, so he insisted he would assist on the project. His introduction to Gerhard Gshwandtner, publisher of *Selling Power* Magazine, eventually led us to the energetic Rick Frishman of New York City publicist fame, and then to Dr. Atchity.

The Kormanicki and Komarnicki clans of Chester, Pennsylvania have been priceless in their sincere support as fellow believers and writers. Dr. Michael Kormanicki is my dear friend and mentor from our days at Marriott Vacation Club International; his Uncle Dave Komarnicki is the Reverend of Reverie in my life with his sensitive and artful glances back to the times of our lives, from the Big War to the return of his brothers from overseas, written regularly on his precious blog; Uncle George still records his conversations with the Almighty daily; and his son Todd Komarnicki honored me with reading this work—himself an acclaimed screenplay writer, novelist, and movie producer.

The early readers of *Now or Never: The 11 Secrets of Arimathea* were chosen because of their own employment of the Secrets. Award-winning sports writer of *The Boston Globe,* Dan Schaughnessy, talked to me about his own writing projects; Pete Watzka, Chief Operating Officer of Ritz Carlton Club, and always my Psi Upsilon fraternity brother at Cornell, took the time to add this book to his prolific reading list; Deacon Sam Costantino of the Metuchen (NJ) diocese, reacted with his astute Catholic spirit and his uniquely Silver Lake section of Belleville perspective; my personal "consigliore" from the great Belleville Class of 1960, Ron Sanfillipo, critically reacted like the true coach and teacher he still is. And Sam Stellatella, former Penn State and Nutley High School immortal, gave me hope with his uniquely Jersey blurb: "Hey, Jo-Jo, where'd ya find the Fifth Gospel?!"

Dan Vitiello and his Printing Techniques family in Nutley are still there to read, study, print, and argue all that I write. How priceless to have his parents, brothers, sister, and employees always ready to help when I begin a writing project.

Ed Marinaro, "... perhaps the greatest player in Ivy League football history ..." and Hollywood actor, but more than that, a loyal friend, still reminds me, "Never, never, never give up." Also at Cornell, Pete Noyes and the Cornell Football Association guys just keep running interference. Dr. George Arangio, a couple years ahead of me at our alma mater, continues to inspire with his life and love of family and the Lord.

During my days as President of Bluegreen Institute in Boca Raton, Florida, Stephen Wilke gently introduced me to the metaphysical aspects of Christianity like only a former seminarian could; and my assistant Marisela Sanchez daily demonstrated the power of rebirth in the Christ.

Pastor Anthony Ventola at Agape Worship Center in Bloomfield, New Jersey, allowed me to "test" the Secrets on his Adult Sunday School classes. His Superintendent Nick Frannicola, former Olympic fencer, would constantly remind me from his regal sitting position of my "call" to write and teach—both men could not be closer friends.

When my childhood friend John Senesky introduced me to the Fellowship of Christian Athletes, our lives changed forever. How can I forget Bishop Peter Bruno, Sr. and the dynamic young Pastors he developed back in the eighties and nineties for the Abundant Life Worship Centers? All are still spreading the Gospel around the world.

The writings of Oswald Chambers, Joel Goldsmith, Og Mandino, and Eckhart Tolle have reconfirmed my faith in the empty tomb in Jerusalem; the brilliance of Joyce Meyers and Chuck Colsen have given me strength to speak the truth; the Holy Bible and the wisdom of my Jewish, Buddhist, and Hindu friends have proven that God is still on the throne, and prayer and meditation on that Higher Power still changes things.

Back home in Nutley, New Jersey, the spirit of my late friend Mike Geltrude is still alive in his beautiful widow

Judy and his powerful sons John and Daniel. Indeed, Mike employed all the Secrets.

Of course, I cannot forget my parents Rocky and Marietta Cervasio, as well as my wife's, Angelo and Sally Corino. Without much formal education, these wonderful members of the Greatest Generation set examples that fueled the research to discover the Secrets.

I pray each reader of *Now or Never: The 11 Secrets of Arimathea* will apply every Secret daily. In the changing world we live in, I have found my own peace and destiny in each of them.

And so, I encourage you to begin the journey back to Jerusalem 2000 years ago to meet some friends of mine. I can guarantee your life will change for the better, just as mine did.

Do it Now.

Joseph Rocco Cervasio

Chapter I.

Yesterday Was a Long Time Ago

Joseph awoke to the scent of lilacs. The rich drapes that separated him from the early bustle just outside his lush walled garden fluttered restlessly on a light breeze.

All Jerusalem was blanketed with the warmth of early spring. The temperate, fragrant air should have been a balm, but Joseph's wounds went too deep. The troubled man gingerly struggled upright. The subtle bouquet reminded him of a life—a much sweeter life—he'd led not so long ago. As he swung his stiff legs off the bed and put his aching feet on the cool marble floor, the searing pain in his lower back deepened. Yes—perhaps he was becoming an old man. He was certainly much older than his years.

Joseph's deeply lined face lit up slightly when Duca entered. The lean eunuch, though much younger than Joseph, had been a loyal servant—and even more, a friend—for many years.

"Master, your bath is ready. I know it will refresh your spirits," Duca said, hopefully.

Joseph rose from the bed and shook his graying head slightly. "Duca, you know how it is with me. My heart aches, my body follows suit, and my spirit pines for answers. But they never come."

Duca assumed a familiarity with his master that not many slaves were allowed. And today he had a secret—and more hope than ever before that he could finally rouse Joseph from the dark clouds that had so deeply oppressed his master.

"You've dwelt in sorrow too long, master. Your Lord would expect more. It's time for you to go forward."

Joseph accepted the elaborately embroidered silk robe Duca held out. An Arab merchant who hoped to gain the influential Hebrew businessman's favor had given it to him many years ago.

"My Lord is crucified. My beloved Sarah passed without warning. Now, this latest news from Persia. I fear I am ruined."

Once again, Duca was reminded of the stream of events that had cast down Joseph's spirit. Almost more than the remarkable events of Jesus' departure from the earth, the sudden passing of his wife of many years was a sharp shock Joseph could not seem to come to grips with. Death was common in Jerusalem. It often came cruelly and without much warning. But the grief Joseph felt for his departed wife still overwhelmed him.

Even on this gentlest of sun-drenched mornings.

"Master, I have a plan," announced Duca. "A plan to make you whole again."

Joseph looked at Duca indulgently, with something almost like a smile. He had little faith in his servant's ability to heal the wounds that were dragging him down, but he was touched by the man's faith and devotion.

"Duca. Why haven't you given up on me?"

"Because until this day, I've failed you. I can't change what has occurred. But I must beg you, master—let me help you move toward the vision you said your Lord had revealed especially for you. If your precious wife were here she would not stand for you so sad and forlorn, wasting your precious days."

Joseph plodded ahead of Duca to the bath. The thought of Sarah's not-always-gentle encouragement was strangely comforting.

Duca was right, as usual. Sarah would have given him a short while to lick his wounds and then used every tool of a wise and loving, no-nonsense wife to get her husband moving again.

"You must begin to sing a new song to chase this despair away," Duca said, as Joseph lowered himself into the pleasantly warm, richly scented water. As though bidden by his words, a thrush in the garden began to sing its sweet song. It was a rarity, and Duca took it as a sign. He looked at his master with renewed hope that his plan would succeed.

"Today will be different. The sad days are behind you. Today, a new direction will be revealed. We'll make yesterday what it's supposed to be—a mere memory. By the end of today you'll see the truth. Yesterday...was a long time ago."

Chapter II.

Fragrant Mystery

For weeks Joseph of Arimathea had been aging visibly, day by mournful day. His quick wit, creative mind, and boundless energy were now only memories to his friends, family, and colleagues.

His craggy face mapped a lifetime of adventures. Persia, Greece, and Egypt—his weathered skin bore the marks of endless travels. He had set foot in Spain in the far west of the known world, and splashed ashore in the Arabian Gulf to the east. Buying and selling. Prospering. It had been an enviable, even glorious life.

He'd spent his youth in Arimathea, in the rolling countryside of Ephraim northwest of Lydda. Growing up just a day's journey from Joppa had prepared him well for a career at the crossroads of the Roman Empire. Trade and the whole bustling world of ideas was his arena. He proudly witnessed his people's daily, yet restrained, resistance to Rome. As a young man, his own adventurous, vibrant spirit jumped at the first opportunity to participate in trade caravans—traveling to unknown lands to find wealth and excitement.

Joseph had always lived passionately, and lived for two things. There was his pleasure at achieving—at doing new things and seeing new things, forging bravely into the unknown. But more than that came his devotion to the God of Abraham, Isaac, and Jacob. Among the trading class, he possessed an uncommon reputation for high integrity, guaranteeing reward for those who walked with him. All knew him as an honorable and faithful counselor as well, one of seventy-one judges of the Sanhedrin, the supreme court of all the Hebrews. He was also a Decurion of the Roman Empire, a position that had greatly helped his business as a metal merchant who had diversified into fine linens and clothing.

Joseph winced slightly as Duca poured warm water down his back. "I'm like an arthritic old dog," Joseph told his manservant as he replaced the pitcher of water before him. "All my life I've served my God, my family, my friends and associates faithfully. But now I see how wrong everything has gone. I'm just an old dog, broken down and confused."

It was true. It seemed everything Joseph had worked for was crumbling. Only weeks since the shocking series of events in Jerusalem, he was weakening daily. Duca sighed. Joseph's reputation as a balanced man, devoted to family, business, and the Temple, was uncertain, and even his oldest friends had begun to look at him with skepticism.

Since his boyhood, Joseph had prayed for God to send the Messiah to restore Israel to its glory and rekindle in the hearts of Jews a hunger for God's truth. He also prayed for guidance and for personal success in his business dealings.

Many of his dreams had come true, and he had a deep belief that anything was possible. Often he talked of signs, which seemed to point to the coming Messiah. Maybe not in his lifetime, but soon.

One day his friend Nicodemus, a fellow elder on the Sanhedrin, beckoned Joseph aside. His face was flushed with excitement. He had spoken with Joseph many times about his beliefs.

"I've seen him!" he whispered excitedly.

Joseph thought Nicodemus might be speaking of a long lost friend. "Who? Who have you seen?"

"I have beheld the promised one!"

"Nicodemus, my friend," responded Joseph affectionately, joining in on the joke. "Finally—you've heeded my words to open your mind to new possibilities!"

"Joseph, all you've ever spoken of is new possibilities," Nicodemus said. "Yes, I know—if I'd heeded half of them I'd be a much wealthier man today. On the other hand, I might be teetering on financial disaster every couple of months, like the wandering caravan master *you* sometimes seem to be."

Joseph laughed. The old friends had teased one another since boyhood.

"Nicodemus, you sound like the Pharisees. They remind us daily of our tithes, but wilt at the thought of striving or risking for gain. You know me well. Life is all about possibilities. I see the glow on your face. So tell me about your Messiah. Will he rid us of these Roman leeches who want as much of my wealth as the High Priests?"

Nicodemus became serious. He leaned close to his old friend. What he had to say was dangerous, especially for two respected elders of the Sanhedrin.

"I tell you truly, Joseph—the young teacher seems to be from God. I've heard him speak, and I'm moved. In his every word I hear faith, hope, and love.

"And he does miracles."

Had it been anyone else, Joseph would have laughed in his face. Instead, he looked deeply into his oldest friend's eyes.

"What is the man's name?" he asked.

"His name is Jesus."

"Jesus, the young rabbi from Nazareth?"

Little did Nicodemus know that Joseph had known Jesus, the son of his cousin, since the Nazarene's boyhood.

He hadn't seen him in years, but he remembered him well. Even as a child, experiencing the world from the caravans of his distant relative, the wealthy Joseph of Arimathea, Jesus had shown wisdom far beyond his years—and something else; something hard to define.

Once, the boy was found missing from Joseph's caravan and servants were sent to search for him. If he had been another the caravan might simply have moved on, but there was something about the radiant youth that made such a thought unthinkable.

The servants found the child not too far away. He was praying. A strange light seemed to glow around his head.

When Jesus was brought before his elder, instead of punishing the boy, Joseph was suddenly overcome with relief and gratitude that he was safe. He embraced Jesus and sent him on his way. He remembered feeling unconditional love for the boy. As if Jesus was his own son. And more—much more.

But the Messiah? That was a big leap; even for a self-made man who believed almost anything was possible.

"He is preaching today, not far from here," Nicodemus said. "Will you come with me?"

Joseph hesitated only a moment. "Of course, my old friend," he said. "I will come."

Jesus had changed utterly, yet he had much in common with the boy Joseph remembered. The strange, penetrating young man commanded attention by telling simple stories, asking pointed questions, and advocating the idea of a heavenly Father who rules over the world with a heart, spirit, and mind of infinite love. The rabbi's knowledge and learning seemed to have no bounds. Yet even now he was young, so much younger than Joseph and Nicodemus.

That evening, Nicodemus and Joseph spoke for hours over their wine about what they had heard. Even more than the words, Jesus seemed to exude an energy that inspired confidence and hope. There were many eloquent and learned men on the Sanhedrin, Joseph and Nicodemus not the least of them. But Jesus was different.

"Surely the kingdom of God awaits us after this life," Nicodemus said.

"Yes, I agree," Joseph replied, thoughtfully. "Listen, though. Jesus talked about this life, too; about having God with us every moment."

And I believed him. The preaching had moved Joseph to his very core. *Had it been the words? Or something more? How can this be the carpenter's son—someone from my own family? He claims that heaven and earth might be the same place, just seen through different eyes; that all we seek in the future may be ours … here and now.*

From that day on, Nicodemus and Joseph followed Jesus.

In the early days of their discipleship, the elders tried to sort and parse all of Jesus' teachings, so practical in every way, and yet so fragrant with mystery. But before long the sophisticated merchant humbled himself, analyzing less and simply putting every atom of hope and trust in his young kinsman. Soon, he began to believe as Nicodemus did—that this could truly be the longed-for Messiah.

Joseph began to pray differently, too. Rather than reciting the established prayers of his fathers, he sometimes spoke directly to God.

I offer you my heart and my faith. Accept my service. Let me live in the light of the teachings of Jesus. I knew him then—but I'm only truly discovering him now.

21

Chapter III.

The Cataclysm

On the night of the Passover celebration, one week to the day after Jesus entered Jerusalem like a humble emperor, riding a white ass as the adoring people placed palm fronds in his path, soldiers of the Sanhedrin took the prophet prisoner in an olive garden on the outskirts of the city.

Joseph and Nicodemus had just finished breaking bread together when the news came. In an instant, Joseph's dreams of heaven on earth came crashing down.

He wasn't surprised, exactly. He'd heard plenty of muttering and much more from his fellow elders about the young upstart who seemed intent on undermining their absolute authority. Nicodemus and Joseph weren't the only ones who believed Jesus was Messiah—and many of Jesus' disciples were much less discreet than the two wise old counselors. But the shock of his arrest was incredibly painful.

"On what basis could they try him?" a heartbroken Nicodemus asked.

Joseph dropped his head in disgust. "I knew this day was coming."

"Yet our fellow Counselors aren't stupid about the laws of the Court," Nicodemus groaned, pushing away his wooden plate in frustration.

"Indeed," added Joseph. "It'll be 'blasphemy,' of course. A false prophet dividing our people—an imposter who'll bring the wrath of the Romans on Israel! Oh, I've been hearing it for weeks, watching their envy rise. And now the High Priests and Elders are presenting him to the Governor, I know it! They want our enemy to judge one of our own. I warned Jesus about all of this!"

"But he wouldn't listen," Nicodemus said. He knew Jesus well enough to know the answer.

"Never."

Jesus had been taking too many chances; causing too much hatred for Jesus in the halls of the High Priests. Joseph had seen them cringe and redden when the Galilean calmly claimed, "My kingdom is not of this world."

"He thinks he's a king!" they cried out.

"Worse than that," the Sanhedrin objected, "he speaks of being the I AM. Abraham, our father, and our God Himself must be as outraged as all of us!"

"He's another false prophet, like all the rest—a leprous plague upon the people of Israel!"

"Lord, you must be careful with these men," Joseph had said to Jesus. "They're proud, angry and powerful. They are dangerous—and I know they mean you harm."

But his warnings went unheeded. Joseph cursed himself for not being more persuasive.

In my business, everyone heeds me. Why has Jesus ignored my counsel? Why no respect for his elder?

Joseph was, first and foremost, a merchant. He saw it all too clearly: Jesus had reached a peak the moment he entered Jerusalem's gates. For a brief and shining hour, the common people were on his side, cheering the Messiah's entrance to the Holy City. They believed he would surely deliver them from the Romans. Many claimed to have witnessed his healing the sick and restoring sight to the blind.

But that was the high point—the time when a smart trader sells.

There was no doubt in Joseph's mind that the arm of the pendulum was about to swing sharply back.

Fearing condemnation from other Jewish leaders, Joseph and Nicodemus had both resolved to keep their devotion to the young evangelist a secret from most. They would be private disciples of Jesus.

Yes, it was the proper way for me to serve Jesus. I defended him from time to time, but all I could accomplish, at best, was to make them pause and think. If I had only been as persuasive and forceful as I've been in the past, bargaining with Persian traders!

Joseph tried to convince himself his strategy was a good one—that there was virtue in prudence, that he could do more for his kinsman when the time was right if he kept in good standing on the Sanhedrin.

But he felt a sting remembering just a few days ago when Jesus peered deep into his eyes—deep into his soul.

"No man can serve two masters," he had said.

"Let us rush to the Temple. I fear his life is at stake," Nicodemus said.

Joseph called for his wife.

"Sarah, we must leave. Nicodemus is right. We must stop this insanity erupting in the Court."

"Joseph," she said, "you are right. His life *is* in the balance. But it's too late for you to help. The High Priests and your fellow judges know of Nicodemus' nighttime conversations with Jesus. And don't be so foolish to think they've discounted your family connection. My love, I fear for your safety—and what will happen to your business? Who will be served by a futile gesture?"

An uneasy silence engulfed the room.

Duca could be heard running up the marble hallway. Breathing hard, he broke the silence. "A messenger has delivered the news—Jesus is already on his way to crucifixion!"

"The horses, Duca—prepare them now!" ordered Joseph. "We must go!"

Joseph's silent support had proven worthless. While it had kept him safe, that consolation paled to nothing next to the fate that awaited Jesus. As the horses sprinted to the execution site, neither Joseph nor Nicodemus could speak.

The Sanhedrin didn't want the Romans to see their ineptitude in controlling Jesus. Wise like foxes, cowardly like jackals; they dumped their case in the lap of the Romans. Of course they feared Jesus was disrupting our people, turning them against each other, attracting too much attention from the occupiers.

They want him dead, knowing only the foreign rulers can legally sentence him. This Roman Governor Pontius Pilate has proven to be the perfect dupe. The Pharisees tricked him into thinking Jesus was a threat even to Caesar and his insatiable empire.

And maybe they were right.

Oh, my God, I should've been at the Temple to quench this madness! I was absent when Jesus needed me most.

Joseph saw it all exactly as it had unfolded. The Sanhedrin convinced Pilate the Procurator that Jesus was Rome's problem. Pilate hesitated to announce a guilty verdict upon the tortured prophet, so he evoked an ancient Hebrew custom. At Passover, if two citizens are sentenced to death, the ruling powers can allow the people to choose one to be released. For Pilate, this was a convenient means of extricating himself from the distasteful duty of killing an innocent man.

Surely the local rebel Barabbas will be executed, Pilate assumed.

But even the people of Jerusalem turned against the peaceful man of God, screaming for his death.

"He's no Messiah! Give us Barabbas!"

"Jesus does the works of the Devil. He's an imposter!"

"Barabbas is one of us!"

Pilate's hands were tied. His bluff had been called. He reluctantly delivered Barabbas to the Jewish people. His sentence for the silent Jesus: death on a Roman cross.

By the time Joseph arrived, it was too late. He could do nothing but witness all that was to transpire on the tiny hill called Calvary, the rugged site of the crucifixion.

It happened in slow motion.

The weather turned. The light of day was chased away by a tidal wave of darkness, cold black clouds rolling across the graying sky like a demon corps rushing to witness the execution. A biting, heavy rain pelted everything in its path like the worst sandstorm in the desert. Joseph's vision blurred, his body chilled, and the weight of his heavy cloak pulled him down into the muddy earth at the base of the cross.

He suddenly recalled his past caravan rides.

My body fully covered, I felt the daggers of the wind-blasted desert sands—yet I gloried in the challenge to survive. I knew I would survive. Now, only water assaults me, yet my skin, my bones and my spirit are cracking.

The thunder frightens me now. Before, the most blood-thirsty robbers could not disturb my peace.

I feel all the good on earth has left, leaving a space that's filling with evil from all time: past, present, and future. I look up at my cousin's son, and evil surrounds him and takes his life. And the foul malevolence rains on us all.

The ground now quakes. Where is the peace of my Lord? Where is the victory? What can I do?

Nailed to a cross between two thieves, the weakening Jesus struggled to speak to those at the foot of the cross. As the young rabbi gasped for his last breaths, Joseph stood transfixed; his very soul was battered by the shrill, evil wind, as he tried to convince himself that Jesus' life had not been in vain.

Jesus cried out and died.

The realization took a minute to sink in, but when it did it snapped the enterprising merchant back to reality. Joseph had to act.

Without a thought, he approached the centurion in charge.

"When Jesus is taken down from the cross, I'll bury him myself. Yes. That's what I'll do." And he gave the man a piece of gold to cement his authority.

The single image in his mind was of Jesus lying dead and deserted on a garbage dump. That was something that must never happen. At the moment of Jesus' death, he felt himself taken over by a higher power. His grief must wait. The flood, the lightning, the quaking earth must be overcome. Only one thing mattered now. And time was of the essence.

Joseph ordered Duca to escort him to Pilate. The centurion agreed to accompany them.

"Is he mad?" commented a heckler as Duca positioned the horses for the trip to Pilate. "The criminals all get dumped by the Romans."

In the midst of pouring rain, lightning, thunder, and the moaning and moving ground, Duca, the centurion and Joseph mounted the horses, and they exploded into a gallop as mud sprayed all nearby.

Striding purposefully up the stone stairs and into the anteroom of the Procurator's chamber, the centurion did his job well.

"It's most advisable that the Governor sees his caller. A favor is needed."

When Pilate grudgingly appeared before Joseph and the centurion, he was perplexed. "What's this all about? Centurion, why should I allow this intrusion?"

"This is Joseph of Arimathea," answered the centurion, "a Decurion of the Empire, and distant family relative of the guilty man, Jesus of Nazareth."

Pilate looked up and down at Joseph. Soaking wet and exhausted, the businessman was not much to look at. Yet Pilate was familiar with his name, and he stood erect, purposeful and dignified. The official then stared curiously at the assertive guard. He quickly turned back to Joseph.

"Centurion, you may leave us alone. I'll call for you shortly."

"Sir, as you command."

Pilate wasted no time. "I perceive you have an urgent need. Speak, and speak quickly."

"I respectfully request the dead body of Jesus, so I may place him in a suitable final resting place."

"That's all you wish?"

"Yes."

Pilate had endured a difficult few days. Ever since his condemnation of Jesus, he had experienced the strangest sensation that his hands were not clean. Although it was impossible, when he looked at his hands he could sometimes almost swear they were stained with blood. He called for the attendant. "Some water, quickly!"

As the servant returned with a basin, Pilate washed his hands quickly. He studied Joseph, but seemed distracted, rubbing his hands together as if in pain. Then he pointed his finger at the businessman.

"I know who you are. Our roll of Decurions in the province has you at the top of the list—your fortune from metals and clothing?"

"Yes, I've been blessed," answered Joseph, masking his impatience with humility.

"Well," Pilate pondered, "this thing you're asking would be a break in policy, you know. After all, your relative was just a common criminal—convicted by his own people, I might add."

Joseph interrupted. "Sir, the reason he's now dead and who's responsible is no longer a concern of mine. I wish simply to honor him with a proper Jewish burial. You've respected our customs in the past, and even during his trial. Please, I beg of you—grant this last wish."

"Not so simple, Decurion. And not so quickly. Why should I satisfy this request?"

"From what I've heard at Calvary, there are those who believe you thought Jesus an innocent man. If so, allow him and his family the dignity of a proper burial."

"My wife thinks him innocent. I? Well, many of his followers turned on him in the end. My people say he may be more trouble dead than Barabbas alive!"

Joseph had faced tougher negotiations than these. And he had an uncanny ability to be calm, forceful and convincing when the situation seemed most desperate. In this case, he appealed to Pilate's boundless Roman pride.

"Please, your honor. This is a chance for you to show your wisdom, your mercy—and your strength. Many say that you had no desire to condemn Jesus, and certainly no desire to set the murderer Barabbas free. But the Pharisees and the Sanhedrin manipulated you unfairly. Surely you thought the people would choose to release Jesus. But the fickle masses had been bribed, cajoled and tricked into a ridiculous and unjust decision!

"There are those among us who feel what my fellow leaders did was wrong. Nothing can bring the innocent man back. But there is no need for the final indignity. By allowing Jesus a proper burial you can show that you make the decisions in Jerusalem, not them."

"You are quite the politician, Decurion!" Pilate said. "I can see how your routes have prospered. You're somewhat convincing. But only somewhat."

"Honorable Pilate, you know a peaceful and innocent man has died on a Roman cross because the Jews forced you into a corner. At least let Roman justice be served in my taking his body to a suitable place."

"Listen to me now, Joseph," Pilate said. "We're alone, and I've a request of *you.*"

Pilate walked away from Joseph to study the courtyard, still whipped by the sudden, treacherous storm. Dozens of soldiers scurried about, fighting wretched gusts to assess the earthquake's damage.

With his back to Joseph, disturbed by the storm, Pilate continued with raised voice.

"My term as Procurator, you know, cannot come to an end soon enough. Pardon me for my revulsion for your Holy City, but look at this disgusting place! In the end, my wife and I plan on enjoying life somewhere far removed from Jerusalem. It would be easier to grant your wish if you were to make a more…tangible show of appreciation."

Very well. This is something I know all too well.

"Continue, honorable Pilate."

"Caravan routes into the East have always been an endeavor that would be a worthy investment." Pilate turned to Joseph. "It's a rich frontier, and with my patronage and partnership, it could be even richer.

This was dangerous territory. Joseph must tread very carefully. Pilate's "partnership" could devolve into something little better than slavery if Joseph made a wrong step.

"Pilate, you honor me deeply with your most compelling offer. However, such a momentous arrangement is not to be entered into in haste. And time is very short for me to bury Jesus, if I am to follow the laws of my people. I beg for time to consider—and the honor to simply make a generous contribution to your personal treasury now."

"But that is not my request, Decurion," Pilate said, slightly exasperated. Still, ready money was not to be scoffed at. And there would be time for the rest later.

"On the other hand, I could not expect a different response from such an experienced trader. I will accept your donation. The rest, we will discuss later. But I warn you—I do not take well to rejection of my generous offers."

Relieved, Joseph bowed low. He had barely heard Pilate's response. Time was slipping away.

Anything. Anything to get out of here with permission to bury Jesus.

Pilate gestured for his attendant to come forward. "Retrieve the centurion!"

The guard quickly returned. "Your command, sir?"

"Your name?"

"Longinus, having arrived in Judea from Rome just thirty days ago."

"More information than I requested, young man. And more than I needed. Your unscarred face and new Roman-issued dress clearly advertises your lack of experience."

The centurion shifted uncomfortably under his superior's hard gaze. He was young for a leader of 100 men, it was true, but he had earned his rank with as much blood and hardship as any other centurion—more than many, in fact.

"Return to the site," Pilate continued. "And put that shiny, unstained spear to use—into the heart. Confirm the criminal's death. Then allow this man to take the body where he may be buried. Joseph of Arimathea is an honorable and trustworthy supporter of the Empire." Turning to Joseph, Pilate nodded, "My assessment is accurate, Decurion, is it not?"

"Always—and never more than at this moment, honored Pilate."

"Then go," Pilate commanded. "Our business is done—for the moment."

The mad gallop to Calvary did not take long. The raging winds had diminished, and the torrential rain had settled to a steady shower.

Jesus, lifeless, hung between the two groaning thieves.

"Thank goodness you have returned, centurion!" exclaimed one of the guards. "It's time to break their legs and be done with our work. This worthless ground's still quaking beneath our feet, we're soaked to the bone, and we've been dodging lightning for the last hour."

"You have nothing to complain of, legionnaire," Longinus said sternly. "Proceed with those two. I have orders from Pilate regarding the middle one."

The Romans saw their centurion was in no mood for complaints. They quickly went to work, killing the two convicted criminals with brutal blows to their legs. The cries and screams of the women at the foot of Jesus' cross seemed to reach the heavens.

Longinus, meanwhile, seemed to hesitate. It was not like him. Despite the newness of his gear, Longinus had earned his centurion's rank in the blood of many enemies. Never before had he been so hesitant to use a spear.

Joseph saw, and once again acted. Clearly, the force that emanated from Jesus, even in death, moved the burly centurion. He went to the soldier's side to offer his encouragement.

"Don't fear doing what you've been told. The prophet is dead. Your thrust cannot harm him. His blood won't be on your hands. He's already in the presence of the Father. The blood and water to be shed will merely prove his demise so he can be properly buried. Do it now!"

With Joseph's assurance, Longinus carried out the confirming thrust. The blood and water flowed instantly from Jesus, giving testament to his death.

To Longinus's shock, Joseph reverently captured the liquid in an oversized goblet, or grail, he had taken from a leather pouch.

For the next several hours, the rain now a haunting mist, Joseph, Nicodemus, one of the women, Duca, and Longinus did what they had to do to bury Jesus in Joseph's own tomb.

The burly centurion moved slowly but gracefully as he personally removed the nails from the broken body. The woman assured Joseph she would go ahead to his garden tomb with the burial elements to prepare the body in Jewish tradition. Joseph and Nicodemus would wait for Duca and Longinus to place Jesus in a cart for the short ride to the garden tomb.

Time was short. The eunuch and the centurion gently carried Jesus toward a finely-made two-wheeled cart hastily provided by Joseph. The cart was to be pulled by a black Arabian horse far finer than one would ever expect to see in such a place, and though the storm howled, the well trained animal stood patiently, with only his wide eyes and flaring nostrils showing his distress. This was the animal Joseph had rushed to Calvary on. They had wrapped the corpse in swaddling clothes to preserve Jesus' dignity in death, and as they passed the horse, Persian Prince by name, it snorted violently and leapt upward, his powerful hind legs pivoting in the muddy terrain. As if shrieking in grief, the magnificent steed could only be calmed by Joseph's experienced touch.

Once inside the cart, the body lying covered with several of the women's shawls, Longinus glanced to Duca for assurance it was the proper time to proceed. The servant couldn't help but let his own glance turn into a stare.

Are these tears streaming down the soldier's face—or merely the wetness of the storm?

The centurion turned away, leaving Duca and the body alone. The Egyptian was overwhelmed at the horrific suffering Jesus had experienced. He could not recognize the man he had first encountered as a fellow teen. Sympathetic, he rested his hand upon the preacher's heart.

A flow of peace, like a steady stream of warm water, emanated into Duca's very essence. He nearly collapsed in a euphoric state, reaching out to balance himself. An instant later he found himself at the head of the cart. The moment of tranquility had transcended time.

With Duca enroute to the tomb, Joseph and Nicodemus hurried to a shop owned by one of the Arimathean's partners. His own burial shroud was stored there. It would be put to use before its appointed time.

Joseph had almost completed his assignment.

It was one he would soon question.

But for now, it was enough.

As his plan unfolded, he had moved, walked, talked, and acted as if he were in another realm, under the control of an unseen authority. He was a Joseph of Arimathea few had seen before, with no interest in collaborating with others. He simply had to complete the mission. Although he was accustomed to authority, this was different. Even if no one had listened or helped, he would have found a way, and no power on earth short of death—not even the power of Rome—would have stopped him.

Later that night, the gruesome task accomplished without a second to spare, all Joseph's strength was gone. He hid himself in his bedchamber, unable to speak to anyone, locked away from Sarah and Duca. He was horrified—and ashamed to have done so little.

His entire world had cracked to its foundation. Kingdoms were clashing in his mind. Jesus' words echoed without ceasing.

"No one can come to the Father, except by me. Those who look upon me, look upon the Father."

Then Jesus' blood ran in rivulets down the Hill of the Skull! He was my cousin's first born, just the son of an ordinary carpenter! How could he claim to be one with the Lord God Almighty, creator of heaven and earth?

But my time with him in his youth, my hours with Nicodemus, Jesus' family; we all had the sense that his outrageous, preposterous, and unthinkable claims just might be truth! But why did he have to be radical and offensive to others' beliefs? It could've turned out so differently.

I must stop thinking. I sense my thoughts aren't my own. They're foreign. Even on my most dangerous routes over the years, I'd find peace by contemplating God.

But tonight the spirits are battling in my very soul! My God is not present to win this fight for me!

Eventually, Joseph's tortured thoughts turned to Pontius Pilate. What did it mean that he had given up his own personal tomb to a known blasphemer? Had the ever-prudent Joseph made an incredibly imprudent decision? He did not want the Sanhedrin to see his gift of a sepulcher as a gesture hostile to them. And yet surely they would see it as a great betrayal.

And what did the pompous Pilate really want? He would pay dearly for Pilate's favor—that was certain.

Shock, sorrow, and confusion reached a pitch in Joseph's mind. He was not alone. He was wrestling with a horde of spirits. Some were good. Many were not.

In forty-eight hours, his personal cataclysm would widen.

Chapter IV.

Aftershock

J oseph's sprawling fortress of a home had always protected him.

For many years, Sarah, Duca, a small army of lesser servants and countless guests had enjoyed Joseph's peaceful sanctuary of luxury and plenty. Flowers, fruits and vines from all over the known world graced the gardens and wound gently around the bases of noble columns, while the playful splashing of fountain waters kept the hubbub of the outside world at bay.

But not now.

Three long days after Jesus' horrific death, the numbness of shock was not enough to dull the grief that hung over Joseph and all who were connected to his household. The silence was tangible and not peaceful. It was full of dread.

The dread was well founded. Early in the morning of the third day the oppressive silence was shattered by the clatter of horse's hooves, the marching of hobnailed sandals, and an urgent pounding at the gate with the butt of a sword. Romans—soldiers from Pilate's personal guard.

Duca, as usual, was at Joseph's side. Without waiting to see his master's reaction the servant rushed to the ornate brass gate just beyond the courtyard. There was shouting and the metallic clang of swords being drawn.

Duca protested, but he might as well try to stop the tide as to prevent the band of legionnaires from advancing through the house and invading Joseph's seclusion. The faithful eunuch bravely followed at their heels but was restrained as they invaded the mournful privacy of Joseph at his untouched morning meal.

A short, thick centurion strode up to where Joseph sat, Sarah at his shoulder.

"Where is he, Decurion?" the centurion demanded of Joseph. "Joseph of Arimathea—tell us now! Where's the dead man?"

Sarah fearfully gasped for breath. "No," she pleaded. "My Joseph's an honorable man. He's a member of the Sanhedrin!"

Sarah's words had as much effect as though they had never been spoken. Joseph looked at the centurion confusedly.

"The dead man?"

"Where is he?"

"Do not waste our time, Decurion. You have abused the special favor of Pontius Pilate."

Joseph rose, holding his hand to an aching forehead. He had no idea what this imperious soldier meant.

"I...I do not know. Do you mean Jesus?"

"Legionnaires. Take this man away."

Duca was released, and he immediately positioned himself in front of Sarah as the Romans whisked her speechless and confused husband out of the house.

"My lady, the Sanhedrin will not stand for this," the servant assured her, although he could barely raise his voice above a whisper. "All will be well with my master."

Duca said the words, but in his heart he was far from certain about Joseph's fate. So much had happened so quickly. What was coming now?

Joseph felt he was being swept along in a terrible dream that wouldn't end.

Was Pilate angry about their agreement? Did the Roman ruler feel he had given too much? Were they going after the followers of the false Messiah now? Was he heading to his own crucifixion?

Once Jesus was properly buried, Joseph felt he had survived the worst experience of his long and eventful life. True, when the huge stone was rolled in front of Jesus' tomb—just moments before sundown—he had not felt any real sense of relief. But he had felt a powerful sense of accomplishment.

He had done his duty against all odds.

The forty-eight hours since had been a blur of nauseating, exhausted grief punctuated by fitful, restless sleep. Joseph's mind would not be still, and the doubts, self-recrimination and fears came at him like a rain of arrows, wave after wave from every angle.

I followed Jesus as a disciple—but in the shadows. I told myself it was best for him, but I was afraid. I feared for my life, my business, and my place in the Court. Or was my belief in him only a shallow expression of what I wanted it to be—because I really couldn't really imagine it all to be true?

The priests, the rabbis and my peers in the Sanhedrin must be glorying in the success of their scheme. Their mission is accomplished. Their joy at ridding themselves of Jesus is matched only by their glee at getting the Romans to take a hand in his death.

Perhaps that's what this is about. Even with Temple guards hovering over the tomb, Pilate may feel he'll look like a fool to his own people and to the Hebrews for allowing me to care for the body.

I only pray my death will be quick—oh God, put me out of my misery. Your servant has failed you!

It was not far from Joseph's compound to Pilate's official residence. The soldiers quick-marched the old man around the Roman's palace and down, down into the dungeon. They slammed shut the door and left him in the ringing silence, where his thoughts raged even harder.

Frightened and hungry, his aging bones chilled by the stone bench, floor and walls, Joseph languished for three days and nights in Pilate's foul, dark cell. He was far from anything that was fresh and pure, worlds away from the light. It was a perfect environment to poison his spirit.

As he awaited his fate, Joseph continued to lament. What a fool he had been, thinking he would not give himself away as a follower—and then trying to gain the confidence of the unpredictable, all-powerful Roman official. Joseph felt reckless for obligating himself to the occupying enemy. He was ashamed of the duplicitous way he had negotiated for the body of the man who preached love, peace and freedom from guilt.

That last part, the part about guilt, was a teaching Joseph longed to believe in now. He was filled with a nagging sense of responsibility for Jesus' fate. Was he really any different from those he was silently judging? Had he not offered coins to Pilate for Jesus' body? Was his spirit really much cleaner than the soldiers who cast lots for Jesus' cloak?

And he had done nothing to save him from his fate.

But I had to honor the Rabbi in his death! Revealing myself would have done no good then. If only he had listened to me! And yet I did so little for him when he was alive. He needed more than my money; he needed my presence. I should've stood by him in his early days. Maybe then I would not have had to arrange his burial. Maybe he would be preaching today!

The idea of Jesus dead was horrifying. But the idea of his body left to the crows, thrown onto a garbage dump, sickened Joseph even more.

That he had spared the Rabbi that fate was the one bright spot in all this. He had done his duty. Yes, there was that one thing. It had been hard and dangerous. At first it had seemed he had accomplished the nearly impossible.

But now…perhaps now he would pay the ultimate price for doing this one duty, even though it was too little, too late. Jesus was gone; his destiny as Messiah unfulfilled.

I still want to believe in him. I don't know why. I still want to believe.

After letting the rich merchant suffer for three days, Pilate finally granted the increasingly broken man an interview.

He was relentless in his questioning.

"Outrageous!" the Roman raised his normally urbane voice to something approaching a scream. He rubbed his hands together incessantly.

"I do your priestly friends and you a favor, and what do I get in return? They called me back from Caesarea before I even arrived—back to this despicable province of capricious Jews! Why? Because the body I allowed you to bury is now missing! You will regret withholding this information from me!"

"I swear to you, honored Pilate," Joseph pleaded. "I know nothing of this!"

The sincerity in Joseph's voice was real. He had absolutely no idea how Jesus' body could have disappeared. It seemed beyond even the malice of the jealous Pharisees to take a dead Jew from his grave. Such sacrilege was unimaginable. But who else would have disturbed the sanctity of the tomb?

After his ordeal in the dungeon Joseph had difficulty standing, and found it challenging to even speak. Pilate, too, seemed a different man, shaken by what had happened. It had taken three strong men to roll the heavy stone in front of the tomb. As far as Joseph knew, the Sanhedrin's men had zealously guarded the tomb day and night since then. His confusion was growing by the moment.

"Were you aware of Jesus' prophecy to rise from the dead?" Pilate asked, trying to calm himself with a goblet of wine handed him by the attendant.

Joseph had no idea of what to say. He did know, vaguely, of Jesus' promise to return, but he had never had the faith to take it literally. Was Pilate saying he believed a man had risen from the tomb? Joseph's silence seemed to egg him on, and the questions came flying out.

"Were you privy to a conspiracy?

"Who among the Rabbi's disciples did you know?

"Were there any capable of conceiving a grand hoax against the Empire?

"Are you a tool of the Sanhedrin to make me look foolish in front of my superiors?

"Do you know the whereabouts of the followers of this weakling of a revolutionary?"

Joseph kept his head down and answered each question carefully—as if his life depended on it. It was clear, now, that Pilate believed Jesus' followers had stolen his body. This was something Joseph could not imagine. Jesus' truest followers were the ones who worked the hardest to see he got a proper burial. He was honest about his shock and confusion, but he continued to downplay his personal connection to Jesus, claiming the merest of family ties while clinging for safety in his status as a Roman Decurion, wealthy merchant, and member of the supreme Hebrew court. He also cast his answers to minimize the conflict between the Hebrew Judges of the Sanhedrin and their Roman occupiers.

"He was just the son of a Galilean carpenter, one of dozens of cousins of mine. And yes, there was power in his words, which made him a threat to the Pharisees. As I told you on the night of our Passover, he did speak of life, and even a life hereafter. But these were mysteries, not facts.

You know he was a humble man—caring for the sick and infirmed! Noble Pilate, we discussed your wife's feelings. In my opinion, despite his preaching to the Jews, Jesus was not dangerous—how could he lead a revolution? He never carried a weapon in his life."

Joseph stopped and closed his eyes. *Could Jesus have led a revolution?*

It was more than possible.

The pause was too long for the impatient Pilate.

"I don't want to hear about his wretched life again. All I care about is where his corpse is right now! You'd better continue, sir, and continue quickly, before I jump to unfortunate conclusions about your own well being."

"My august associates of the Jewish Court and the Temple were concerned with one thing. They said that allegedly he...he was proclaiming himself...the Son of God."

Normally, Pilate might have laughed at such a conceit. Now, though, he was dead serious. "Continue, please."

Joseph resumed, but slowly, as if swallowing each word, tasting it, judging its potential ramifications for his own future.

"It seemed he believed he had come from God—perhaps was equal to our Almighty. And they, the judges and Pharisees, understood the troubles that claim could bring to our people...and even to you Romans."

"Decurion, you are overdramatic. First of all, I do not need you to tell me if he was or wasn't a threat to Rome," Pilate confirmed with sarcasm. "He was not. That was obvious. Son of God, on the other hand? Well, we've got lots of those in our own Roman Senate. But the fact of the matter is I didn't need him disrupting my office then, and I don't relish the idea I've been drawn so deeply into this controversy now! Are you saying the Sanhedrin is responsible for the disappearance? That's the question, Decurion. It's as simple as can be: Where is the body?"

"Pilate, I do not accuse the Sanhedrin. In fact, I cannot imagine in my wildest dreams why or how they would do such a thing. True, they wanted Jesus dead—but no Jew would disturb a tomb. He was my distant relative. I only wanted to do my duty for the peace of my family. I saw him wrapped for burial. I helped place him in the tomb. I watched the stone as it was rolled. Everything was as it should be. The Sanhedrin even placed guards to ensure no one meddled with the tomb.

"Every moment after that—every long moment—until your soldiers came to my home I was in my chamber observing the appropriate mourning of my people. Your soldiers know he was dead on the cross! I stood inches from the centurion as he thrust the spear into his side. Ask your guard again! He saw the water and blood flow out of the dead body. His corpse must be somewhere! You know his followers. Right now I'm sure they're as dismayed and confused as you are. They loved him—they would not have wanted his tomb disturbed."

"Then you accuse his rabble of stealing the body?"

"No! Most definitely not! I only swear I don't know and can't imagine what happened. I can see no profit in it for anyone. Ask yourself, honored Pilate—why would anyone want a decaying body, anyway?"

Waving in disgust, the exhausted Pilate proclaimed, "You Jews are a superstitious lot—you put your faith in some single, faceless God, and then become so excited about a false prophet! Better to consider the Gods of the Romans. Ridiculous to place all your faith in one God when there are so many!

"You know, my wife *did* think the Galilean an innocent man," reflected Pilate. "She's spoken to others about it. But she was wrong! Even the masses wanted to see him crucified, and the barbarian Barabbas released to freedom. What an exchange!"

Pilate seemed to realize that Joseph really didn't know where Jesus' body was. But he could not resist taunting his fatigued captive.

"You people still don't know what you want. You wait for a messiah so you can kill him! A bit double-minded, I'd say. And your High Priests—quite an auspicious group. Oh, most definitely. Pleased to see Barabbas back in the streets killing Romans, and Jesus hanging on a Roman cross? Well, I hope you're ready for the scores that will die now for this missing preacher. It's only just begun. And, somehow I'm in the middle of it!"

"My people only seek peace and truth, Pilate. And that's what Jesus preached."

"Apparently he didn't do it well enough. Your people rejected what he had to say. Don't defend your Court. I've never seen such a rush to injustice. And they will get what they deserve—Barabbas, to keep inciting the masses against the glory of Rome. Final result? More Jews killed in rebellion! Never once did I think the people would scream for that thug's release. But I must tell you, Joseph," Pilate continued, suddenly contemplative, "Jesus was like no other accused I've ever tried."

The Roman paused, studying his hands, seemingly perplexed. Joseph waited for the Procurator to continue.

"You know, Decurion, I asked the captive preacher if he was a king. Do you know what he said?"

"No."

"He said, 'I am.'"

"Is that all he said?"

"No. He also said, 'I bear witness to the truth.'"

"And?" inquired Joseph.

"And then I asked him, 'What is the truth?'"

"What were his words?"

"No words. Only silence. And that penetrating gaze.

"That silence spoke to me, I admit it. It was more of a rebuke than if he had defied me directly. It convinced me I should send him away to be flogged, and taught a lesson. But not crucified. I do not relish injustice."

Joseph's senses snapped to attention as he realized how close Jesus had come to surviving his ordeal. Clearly, Pilate had not wanted to send the Rabbi to his death.

"To be honest, the man's silence filled the air. It filled my head with thoughts that could not possibly have been my own."

Pilate seemed far away, as if remembering something long ago. "But then I pondered that for him to not answer me, the supreme Roman official over this province—that took much stupidity. Or perhaps it required much conviction—conviction in his belief…that he *was* a king. And strangely, so very strangely, *truth* could be found in his silence.

"I felt no threat to Rome." Pilate looked at Joseph, but it was as though he was looking through him. "Because in that quiet, in that silence, I became convinced his kingdom—if it exists—is not of this world."

Joseph stared at Pontius. Was this Roman actually saying out loud that *he* believed Jesus to be more than an ordinary man?

"For a moment, that silence set me free of the burden of my duties here in this wretched Zeus-forsaken hellhole Judea. Somehow, he lightened my load. Indeed, for a moment I felt at peace. Because if *his* kingdom exists, it is you spiritual Jews who should be concerned, not us practical Romans.

"What do you have to say for yourself?"

Joseph was silent for a long time. His words now might seal his fate.

"I grieve that my kinsman, one of our innocents, is dead. And I deeply regret the violation of his tomb, that I labored hard to put him to rest in."

"Joseph, you are no fool. I see you are wisely concerned about yourself—whether *you* live or die," replied Pilate, as he reentered his role as Roman Procurator, finishing his wine. "That is as it should be. So here's what you will do—be gone out of my sight, before I send you to your promised land as well. And feel grateful that I have an unfulfilled agreement with you. When you leave this earth, then you can join this Jesus, wherever and whoever he is! I am choosing to believe you do not have a part in the removal of his body. So great is my generosity.

"But do not travel. I neither trust you nor your religious officials. I also don't think your people are as wise as they claim. They have behaved very foolishly throughout this whole ridiculous ordeal. See that you do not emulate their bad behavior. Now return to your home and trouble me no more."

Three days of agonizing discomfort followed by two hours of interrogation and intimidation. Pain and suffering to no purpose. Confusion and darkness.

It was over as abruptly as it began.

Chapter V.

Going Home

Duca and Nicodemus were waiting at the gate to escort Joseph home. A faithful, devoted—and strikingly beautiful—follower of Jesus was with them. She was the one who had so ably assisted them at the tomb.

Her name was Mary of Magdala.

There were no open arms or joy at the reunion. The three looked mournful and avoided his gaze—but Joseph himself was too dazed, weak, and lost in his thoughts after his ordeal to notice much. Not a word was spoken on the short, plodding journey home.

When they arrived at the compound, Joseph entered the gate in silence. His only wish was to sit a while with Sarah, have a quiet meal, and retire for a long sleep.

But his wife was not there.

Joseph called for her, but she did not come.

Duca prostrated himself on the floor. Mary began to weep.

Joseph's heart turned to ice as Nicodemus took him by the arm.

"Joseph. Joseph—my oldest friend. Sarah…is gone." Silent tears streamed down Nicodemus's face.

"Where. Where is she?" Joseph's voice was flat and his shoulders slumped, but his eyes were wild and far away.

"She has passed, Joseph. She died shortly after you were taken to Pilate's dungeon. We had to lay her to rest yesterday."

Joseph tried to stand, but he felt his legs would not support him, and he slumped hard against his old friend.

"Tell me this is not true." There was no inflection in Joseph's voice.

Duca let out a sob. "Master, forgive me—but the mistress has gone to her rest. It was her heart, my Lord. I fear—I fear she couldn't stand to see you taken away."

"Help me, Nicodemus." Joseph voice was now barely audible, and his friend led him to his seat.

Mary continued to weep quietly. Duca could not contain his sobs. Joseph heard them as though they were miles away. He stared through an open window off toward a cloudless, inscrutable sky above the rusty hills outside the west wall.

My duplicity has recoiled on me. It failed to save Jesus. And now it has killed the person I loved most. I could have sold everything and followed Jesus. Others did so. Or I could have worked harder and channeled my fortune to the Rabbi's work.

Jesus' words haunt me. I have been lukewarm. Neither hot nor cold. And what has happened? Just as he predicted, I've been spewed out of the mouth of God—so despicable has been my double-minded indecision.

You have failed your God.

The thought hit Joseph with all the force of a physical blow.

A guttural scream burst from deep in his chest, echoing into the courtyard.

He collapsed to the marble floor as Duca, Nicodemus, and the Magdalene rushed to his side to console him, to surround his grief. His body shook uncontrollably, primal screams coming in wave after wave.

Every regret, every fear, every pain of his long life came up and out into the world. The things he had truly valued, more than gold, more than his position and fame, were gone.

Forever.

The release was violent. After what seemed like hours but was really a short time, Joseph's already exhausted, aging body could take it no longer. His voice became harsh, then hoarse, and finally faded to a weak, irregular sob that seemed to come from the very bottom of his soul.

When it was over, what remained was silence. Deep and profound. A stillness as deep as eternity.

Joseph couldn't move. He didn't want to move.

Because in that strange, still moment, he felt some sense of relief.

What was this uncanny, peaceful feeling?

His friends had not left his side.

Was there any more agony, sorrow, unhappiness, or regret left in him? Was he still overwhelmed by this avalanche of destruction of all he deemed precious and of value?

No.

In the moment, after the release, it was as if an enormous burden had been lifted.

Joseph had been delivered into a moment where he had come face to face with his eternal existence. He felt no need for what had been of such worth before.

He was alone, yet connected to everything. Alone to simply be.

Where does this tranquility come from? I feel I have lost everything. And yet at this moment I feel peace.

Joseph was losing more than he realized.

With his reputation equally bruised with the Sanhedrin and Pilate, another conspiracy had been launched.

No longer was the Procurator thinking about a partnership with the Arimathean. Pilate had called for the High
Priests as soon as Joseph was released. He would make
sure others—others more compliant and open to his own
patronage than the broken-down merchant, would now
control the Arimathean's rich caravan routes.

The grave-faced Pharisees of the Sanhedrin summoned
to Pilate's chambers offered just enough dignified hesitation
at the prospect of their brother's ruin to satisfy the barest of
appearances.

Chapter VI.

Consolation

W hen the storm of grief ended, Duca embraced his grief-stricken master and helped him to his chamber. The servant was observant and sensitive. He felt that something—for now—had shifted in Joseph. There had been some release. It was time for his weary master to sleep.

Duca was holding remarkable news from Mary Magdala. She believed something incredible—unbelievable, really—had happened.

Something that might change everything.

But it must wait until Joseph was strong enough to take another shock.

"Master," Duca's voice was almost a whisper. "When you awaken you must not look back. Your wife was so proud that when the danger was greatest you risked all you had for Jesus. Yours is not a faith of backward glances.

"You must not give up now. My mistress and the Rabbi have not died in vain. Your God will bless you as you have always blessed others. Nicodemus is here, and Mary of Magdala. She has great news to share when you awake. Something beyond anything any of us could imagine. I promise you, master—it will resurrect your spirit."

After his ordeal and release, Joseph had never felt more tired in his long life. Despite his utter exhaustion, the words registered and touched him with a glow of hope as Duca settled the covers over him. Then he closed his eyes and was instantly asleep.

When he awoke, it was morning, and instead of thoughts for the loss of Sarah or Jesus' death or disappearance from his tomb, Joseph's thoughts turned to Mary Magdala.

What did she have to tell him? Had Jesus, before his death, done or said something she wished to share? Surely, this was a time when stories of the words and actions of the Rabbi were more precious than ever. And Joseph knew of the growing respect among Jesus' followers for the provocative Mary. She had spent much time close to him. Jesus' controversial casting of seven spirits from the Magdalene's body had stunned all who had heard of it.

Still, Joseph had lingering doubts about the woman.

Mary had an old reputation as a self-serving opportunist that was distasteful to the dignified merchant. And her alleged dealings with men before she had found Jesus had repulsed Sarah.

But after she met Jesus, over a short time the Magdalene's very countenance had changed before all of us, Joseph remembered.

After her deliverance from demonic possession, the Magdalene supported Jesus' ministry with all her time, passion and possessions. She was hardly recognizable to those who had known her before, shining with an inner light. Mary turned her entire being over to the Rabbi, and seemed such an entirely different person that her past was as close to being forgotten—or at least forgiven—as was possible in such a small and scandal-addicted community.

Was she not with us at the foot of the cross?

She had made it her mission to care for Mary the Mother of the young preacher.

And with Nicodemus, it was she who so selflessly and competently assisted me in the preparation of Jesus' body for the tomb; so many of the costly oils, herbs and spices bought with her own meager funds.

Joseph decided to listen to what she had to say. Any word about Jesus would be a balm to his battered spirit. And so, the four of them took a morning meal, as the one known as the Magdalene recounted her remarkable story.

A story that shook Joseph's world once again.

"Joseph, I am so honored to share this experience with you," Mary began. Her face was lit with anticipation at the news she had to share. "The gift of your tomb to Jesus was an act we who loved and followed him will never forget. I had visited the tomb every day. On the third day, when we passed the Roman centurions at the base of the hill leading to the garden, they simply nodded approval to proceed. As we passed, I could hear them joking about the sleeping guard of the Temple.

"When we reached the tomb we saw something very strange. The stone—that huge, heavy stone that sealed the tomb—was rolled aside. The tomb was open. A handsome youth stood by the entrance. It was as though he was waiting for us. At first I thought he was the guard."

"But he was not?"

"No. His garments were hardly those of the Temple elite. He wore a flowing, white robe."

"What did he say?"

Although Joseph did not intend it to happen, his tone was rather harsh. Mary, realizing how strange her words must seem, bowed her head. She seemed to anticipate a naturally dubious reaction from Joseph she would not be able to overcome.

"Tell him," encouraged the gentle Nicodemus.

Mary looked at Joseph, and seemed to find strength in the memory of what she had experienced. She inhaled deeply.

Her eyes brightened and a smile played at the corners of her lovely mouth,

"The youth said, 'Jesus has risen and is going ahead of you into Galilee.'"

Joseph started in confusion.

"Risen?"

"Yes. That was what he spoke. And he stepped aside so we could enter the tomb."

"Who was with you?"

"James' mother Mary—and Salome."

"Did you enter?"

"Yes."

"And?"

"The body of the Rabbi was not there."

"The other women were in the tomb with you?"

"Yes, just behind me."

"And then?"

"And then, we turned and walked out. The youth was gone. We were speechless. The others quickly returned home. I wandered about the garden, confused. I hungered to believe, but it was so strange—I doubted anyone would believe what I had seen."

"Who was the first you told?"

"Joseph, wait. There's more. Before I left, I saw a gardener on the ridge beyond the stone wall. I called for him and asked what he knew." Mary paused again.

"A gardener? That's my plot of ground. I have no one working that ground."

"The man had a hoe, and he was scratching the dry land, gathering the lose stones. And ... and soon, I was in *his* presence."

Joseph's eyes went wide as he began to understand what Mary was saying. Nicodemus rose and placed a hand on his shoulder in reassurance.

"What...did the man say?" Joseph asked.

"He said, 'Mary.' He called me by name."

"He was...an acquaintance?"

"No. It was the Rabbi. It was Jesus."

Although Duca and Nicodemus had already heard the tale, hearing the words out loud had an effect of all of them; but most of all Joseph. His eyes were hot and he covered them with his hands to cool them. His lips moved silently, repeating what he had just heard. Then he brought his hands down and spoke.

"How could it be?"

"It simply...was. I saw him. I tell you humbly, from the bottom of my soul. It is true."

For a moment, Joseph was swept away with belief in the miracle — then a wave of skepticism, the old trader in him, the man who knew every trick in the book, flashed forward.

"The Jesus I know was a carpenter, then a preacher," Joseph objected. "A hoe was not a tool of his — perhaps a staff, but never a hoe. Woman, I do not accuse you of lying. But you must have been mistaken."

"It seemed as though time stopped when I stood before him. I could smell and feel the balm of eternity flowing over me ... just like when he first healed me. I smelled a fragrance and felt a peace that evaporated any other thoughts but being in that moment. I was with him again. And the moment seemed to last forever. He was different, but yet ... the same," she continued. "What he looked like, his physical presence seemed unimportant as soon as he said 'Mary.'"

Despite his growing skepticism, Joseph was hungry to hear more.

The Messiah, after all, had always been predicted to rise from the dead.

"What else did he say?"

"He gently told me to tell the brethren what I'd seen."

The Magdalene began to weep with joy, overcome with the memory of what had taken place. But Joseph stared off into space. He had no more tears—of any kind—to shed. It was all too much. He didn't bid the thoughts to come; they simply started of their own accord.

I can't deny that Jesus' body has disappeared. My suffering in the Roman dungeon was all too real. Perhaps other followers of Jesus made off with his body. Was the Magdalene a party to the theft? She'd always been so dramatic—particularly before she met Jesus. So different from my Sarah. Was it a hoax? A way for this woman to keep attention focused on herself? Surely the followers see the power of this story. It would be a perfect way for them to rally the people against the Romans.

The thoughts invading his mind were quickly translating Mary of Magdala's account into doubt. Far from reviving him from his paralysis, the story drove him deeper into himself. It was partly out of disbelief, but mostly out of shame.

I don't deserve to believe this.

Joseph's short-lived peace of the evening before was evaporating. As he looked backward and started to think of all the things he should have done, his heart began to refill with dread, guilt, and fear.

The Magdalene could sense that Joseph was suffering. She must make him believe. She had seen Jesus and felt his power. He had truly risen from the dead!

Mary beckoned Duca to retrieve what she had placed on the stone lion guarding Joseph's home, just inside the entrance.

Duca came forward and handed the tightly folded object to Mary. She knelt before Joseph and offered it to him, her head bowed in supplication.

"It is the shroud you provided for him. It was lying on the ledge in the tomb where his body had been and is no more. You should have it. Is it not proof enough?"

Clutching it, Joseph wept.

The days and weeks that followed presented an emotionally wrenching challenge for Duca for which he felt hardly prepared. Joseph's moment of peace after his emotional release did not last. He was torn by a desire to believe the Magdalene's word that the Rabbi was indeed risen, but he was completely mired in regrets for the past and fear of the future—literally paralyzed with remorse and guilt. All he could think about was the many types of support he could have and should have offered Jesus. Worst of all, he believed the loss of Sarah was divine punishment for his lukewarm support for the Messiah.

I could have lived a different life—a better life. My belief was weak. I doubted and wavered.

It pained Duca deeply to see his master in a slow and steady decline that would surely end in his death.

But Duca was not one to sit idle. He had a plan. It had emanated out of his very first attempt to communicate with Joseph's God.

If there truly is a Higher Power, one God, perhaps He'll help me restore my master: Oh, Sir, unworthy and deformed as I am, I only wish to serve. If you hear me, you'll guide me. Forgive my years of bitterness, envy, and ignorance. These sad situations must be replaced by hopeful ones.

Duca heard no audible response, but he felt something. It was similar to, but much more powerful than, how he felt when he received an appreciative nod of assent from Joseph. He felt he had received divine permission to prepare his rescue effort.

He began to search the markets, the bazaars, and loiter at the Temple gates, convinced his actions were being approved by a higher power. As he continued, the feeling grew, until he felt that his actions were perhaps actually being directed by Joseph's God.

If Jesus could rise from the dead, surely Duca could find help for Joseph.

Chapter VII.

Duca's Story

There had been a time, many years before, when Duca had been in dire need of assistance. Back then, it was Joseph who had rescued him.

The Arimathean's long camel caravan had been laboring its way by the cool of night across the Arabian Desert. The lead driver signaled that a human lay in the drifting pathway ahead. It was a young eunuch. He had wandered for two days in the fierce sun. He was near death.

Duca was ravaged by fever. In and out of consciousness, he was raving.

"Sirs, I made a petition to the carrion birds, 'Don't wait for me to perish.' I begged, 'Kill me now, and bring to me my peace!' But alas, the birds ignored me."

"Save this poor fellow," commanded Joseph to his camel drivers. "May God have mercy on his soul!"

Unable to walk, Duca was carried by two slaves in an improvised litter and attended to by Joseph's personal physician. By the time the young boy showed signs of recovery, the caravan was just a day's journey from Jerusalem.

Duca had drifted in and out of consciousness, until one day he rubbed his eyes and looked into the face of a young man about his own age, in his early teens.

"You've survived your ordeal," the lean boy said softly to Duca. "Your God has plans for you. Rise up and receive your blessing."

It was that simple.

Duca could not speak, but miraculously, he sat up with ease, staring into the deep eyes of the youth attending to him.

"Don't speak. Your strength will return," assured the stranger. "But you must use wisdom. Here, drink this water and remain still in this moment."

Bewildered, but feeling a profound peace enveloping him as his companion offered the water skin, Duca sipped the cool drink.

"We'll arrive at our destination shortly. Then you'll be in the service of the most honorable man in all of Judea. Joseph will look after you and help you as he's done with others. Rest assured, he is a far better master than those you have served before. Listen to him, remain humble, and learn all you can."

Duca hadn't spoken in days, and his voice was hoarse and ragged, but the pain that had driven him alone into the desert came pouring out.

"We must be the same age, yet you speak so assuredly. This future you promise sounds like a blessing—but truthfully, I feel unsure if I want to live. I am a eunuch, less than nothing, not even a man. I have been beaten and reviled at every turn."

"My friend, selfish men have maimed you. But you are whole for the work before you—and nothing more will be stolen from you."

"Nothing?" protested Duca. "Everything that makes me a man has been cut away."

"But why turn your loss into further *self*-destructive plans?" asked the young man. "Stop this senseless mental activity. Choose higher thoughts. Select those that will creatively drive you into this moment and the eternal opportunities it presents."

"I wish for this moment to disappear," Duca responded sincerely. "And you say look to it for opportunity. For what? Peace and comfort perhaps, rather than regret, fear, and torment?"

"Yes, my friend. But be aware. As your strength returns, I say live in the moment. Glory in it. It's the life you've been given by God. The past is dead. The future is a hazy, fictitious vision. Be at peace with this moment. Surrender to it. Accept it as it is. Then you'll feed your recovery."

"But ..." Duca weakly interrupted.

Quickly the visitor commanded, "Just listen as a child. Right now your body is restoring itself. Respect it. Don't be like those who abused you. Appreciate your remarkable being. Love it and yourself, for this moment is what has been promised you."

"Who has made me this promise?"

"God the Father, through the prophets."

"I know of no such prophets."

"Someday you'll learn of their messages."

"And then?"

"Every moment that follows will be the same—eternal. Cherish each one, each morsel of knowledge and each experience. By living this way, you'll enjoy the journey God has set before you."

"Enjoyment is not a word I understand."

"You will. This life of yours will not be rushed. You'll not lust for the future, but rather be content in the present.

"I say again," the young man emphasized, "learn from others, from ancient scriptures, and from the spoken word. Don't be dismayed by those who have more knowledge. Instead, learn from everyone you meet.

"But knowledge is not enough—understanding and wisdom are the keys to your life. Someday you'll teach others, and that's the ultimate calling."

"Will that someday ever really come?"

"Believe that 'someday' has already come. Be patient and do not lust for moments to pass." The young teacher chuckled, graciously continuing as he patted Duca's hand. "It's now. Your talent and proclivity to help others has always existed. Just walk into it. I know you *do* understand what I'm saying, and you want to receive it. It's merely your fatigue that pollutes your thinking."

Duca nodded in agreement, "My mind is confused, but I do sense a truth."

"An eternal truth, indeed," confirmed the youth. "One many will never grasp.

"Listen, Duca. You're being made whole for a purpose: the purpose of helping Joseph and others. By assisting many, you'll become filled with witty inventions and ideas that will aide the masses."

"I've always been a servant. Is that *all* that's promised to me?"

"Don't be disappointed in your role in life. Yes, you'll continue as a servant. But look upon that vocation as equal to the role as a teacher—and even a leader. This is the essence of your life—the one the mind of God has designed for you."

"But I feel sometimes I have higher ideas than even those I serve. And they don't seem to understand."

"Don't be disturbed by many who'll differ from your thoughts, actions, and deeds. Get into their worlds with love and respect—a love that demands no return."

"I find love hard to express because of my situation."

"The love I speak of is not physical, but rather spiritual. It's in your heart, in the mind of God where all things like love begin. There it's pure. Don't worry about its manifestation. Just love, emptying yourself each day for all you meet."

"That's a hard task, stranger."

"Yes it is. But in the end, live and love each moment as if it's the one selected by your Creator. Live fully in each moment and love unconditionally. At that point you'll be standing in a portal to eternity."

The brilliant young man paused and stared into Duca's eyes, then even deeper—into his very spirit. Duca tried to speak, but could not respond.

The visitor placed a hand on Duca's shoulder. Then he was gone.

Duca fell back. In what seemed to him like an instant he was quickened to rise again and peer into the landscape to behold his caller one more time. The lean teen in the flowing silk robe was trudging deep into the desert, away from the protected caravan. Duca squinted to focus. He felt as if his spirit was jumping out of his parched skin. He could see the dry, unfriendly wind lifting the hem of the young man's garment as hot sand swirled around him in the distance. The mysterious visitor's body appeared to have been swallowed in an all-consuming desert cloud.

Then there was calm. Had the caller plodded over the drifting dunes? All that was left were his footsteps, which had somehow resisted the devouring desert gusts.

Has this all been a dream—a delirium-induced vision?

For many years, Duca was never entirely certain. But the words and the promise stayed with him always.

Duca lived under Joseph's roof in the days to come. At first he was assigned to menial tasks, helping other servants in the kitchen. Still, it was far better than what he had left behind. No one beat him, or treated him badly in any way. In fact, everyone in Joseph's household seemed kind, efficient, nourished, and content. He did his work to the best of his ability, and fit in well.

One day Joseph summoned him, and Duca was finally able to thank his rescuer and benefactor.

"I wanted to die in the desert, master. You found me and restored me to health. But I wonder if this is a mixed blessing, mutilated as I am. My life will never be like any other man's."

Joseph reassured him, "No creature of God is meant to perish like an animal in the desert. You should consider yourself blessed. You are a comely and intelligent young man. The other servants speak well of you. And despite your great loss—in fact, because of it—you can be trusted where others cannot. I will give you a better place in my home. You will serve my wife and me personally.

"And if you serve my family well, you'll one day become part of it."

Duca remembered the words of the young man in the desert. His fate was opening in this moment, and he must make the best of it. He was safe, in a wealthy home, serving a master who had already shown him more kindness and interest than he had ever experienced. He had heeded the young man's words by focusing on the present more deeply, and in so doing, he felt that blessings had flowed upon him.

For a moment, Duca relived a kaleidoscope of moments with that strange, articulate young gentleman in the desert.

Quickly returning to the present, he focused on Joseph and bowed low to his benefactor.

"Master," he said, "Command, and I will obey."

Chapter VIII.

A Member of the Family

Duca did his work exceptionally well. He was quick to learn and quick to obey; grateful for the new life he had been given. He moved up quickly through the hierarchy of servants. Eventually, Joseph and Sarah treated him almost like the son they never had.

Each day he welcomed his master's visitors and made them feel at home at the sprawling estate. Business associates, members of the Sanhedrin, and many others. When Joseph traveled, Duca usually stayed home and watched over Sarah. Over time, the gentle Egyptian earned a position of respect, authority and trust. Those who knew Joseph best knew that if Duca spoke on behalf of his master or mistress, his words could be absolutely trusted.

From the beginning, Duca showed his new family humility, love and respect. This was a very different kind of service than his earlier attendance on the feminine property of Arab nobles. There, compliance had been beaten out of him, and he had never been able to comply well enough to stop the beatings. He had been injured, belittled and humiliated until he could take no more. Finally, in desperation, he had escaped to what had seemed a certain death in the desert.

But a much kinder fate awaited Duca.

Duca never asked Joseph the identity of the boy in the convoy. Although he knew it was real, it had always seemed almost like a dream. Over time, Duca thought of the wise, mysterious teen less and less. But nothing could dim the memory of that first moment when his eyes had met the young man's and his head was filled with strange and powerful words.

Duca had done his best to take them to heart, and he had profited from them greatly.

One lingering benefit of that single profound interaction was that Duca unfailingly paid close attention to everyone he met—looking to learn whatever he could. Many times over his eighteen years with Joseph, Duca expressed gratitude at how much he had gained by simply listening carefully to Joseph's many well-traveled and well-educated visitors.

"Learn from all you meet, Duca. First comes knowledge, then understanding—finally wisdom!" Joseph would say.

Eventually, the young man from the caravan came back into both men's lives.

Duca had accompanied his master to go and hear a young rabbi, knowing nothing about him—except that people were beginning to talk a great deal about the compelling young preacher from Nazareth.

At first, Duca didn't recognize the man, but as he spoke, the connection became clearer.

"Master, that man—he spoke to me in the caravan when you rescued me! He was just a boy, then. He said words to me that changed the way I felt about life—from that day to this. Is it possible that he is the same man? What was he doing in the caravan? I almost thought he was a dream; he spoke to me and disappeared, and I never saw him again."

"He's grown—and become controversial," Joseph said. "Jesus is his name, and he is a kinsman of mine. The young rabbi is the son of my cousin—a carpenter who shares the same name as my own, whose wife is Mary. They're of the House of David. Jesus travels and teaches, speaking of a new kingdom to come.

"Even as a boy he was wise. But he has changed and grown, and I sometimes have a hard time believing he is my kin. I listen to his words and feel my prayers for our people are being answered!

"But I pray for him. His ministry is now under attack. He heals the sick and attends to the least of our fellow men. In fact, many who have come to my house, those you have learned from the most over the years, are his disciples today."

So it had been. For a time, it seemed that all was well with the world. Duca did not worship the one God of his master, but he listened and learned much from the words of Jesus. Joseph himself seemed different, even better than before, inspired with a new hope for the future. For a time.

Joseph and his business had never failed to prosper. But suddenly, since the events of the Passover, everything was coming apart—the trial of Jesus, his awful death, the haste in burying him, Joseph's imprisonment, and finally, Sarah's sudden passing.

And the Magdalene's incredible story.

Joseph had not been able to attend to business. And it seemed all the powers in Jerusalem had turned against him. His health was rapidly failing.

Now, if ever, it was time for Duca to attempt to repay his master. The moment had come when Duca realized *he* must guide his master back from the same kind of pit from which he was saved.

Just as I was delivered from the desert, so must Joseph be rescued from the oppression that has overcome him. I'll not sleep until he's well again. Now is the time to use everything I've learned in his service. We must turn this evil into good.

Chapter IX.

Dark Hope

It had been a very long month since Joseph's release from Pilate's dungeon. Duca's strategy to restore his master had yet to meet with any progress. Joseph was continuing his slow, steady decline.

The momentary respite after his emotional release had not returned, and though he had been moved by Mary's gift of Jesus' shroud, his faith had not been rekindled.

Duca had a plan, but it required help. And though he scoured the city, at first he could not find those he was seeking. Furthermore, the servant's naïve efforts to refortify his benefactor's businesses were anemic in the face of the invisible Roman and Temple conspiracy. No one dared trade with the Arimathean in the face of such powerful, hidden enemies.

Finally, it was an Ethiopian merchant, whom Duca remembered to have befriended Joseph in a heated market dispute years before, who conveyed the first glimmer of hopeful news to the servant.

On an excursion to shop in the heart of the city, a strong grip engulfed Duca's right arm as he reached for a handful of nuts piled before him. Frightened, he quickly turned to behold a smiling, giant Nubian.

"Young fellow, let me escort you to a fresher lot my workers just delivered."

A nod from Duca confirmed their past acquaintance. "I value your advice, good sir."

The dense crowd pushed against both men as the African led Duca to a peaceful alcove.

"Ah, yes. Now we can hear ourselves think," he said.

Duca was stunned by the man's next comment.

"Stop your attempts to discover the reasons for the Arimathean's disappearing routes. Pilate and his cohorts have forced Joseph's suppliers to channel all their goods to Roman-controlled cartels."

"I must work against this injustice!"

"Allow it to be for now, lest your life be the price of your curiosity."

"Is there nothing that can be done?"

"Yes," the trader responded sincerely. "I and my sponsors do not forget Joseph's integrity and fairness. At the proper time, we'll come to his aid. But the time is not now."

"But when? He may lose everything."

"Do not fear. In the mind of God, what is Joseph's will remain his. Be not discouraged. Tell him the Ethiopian and another are working together on his behalf. Now go about your business and be of good hope."

The handsome black giant turned quickly and left, parting people with bulging, scarred forearms to make his way deeper into the city.

Chapter X.

Woman by the Roadside

The Ethiopian had given Duca hope. But, despite the warning, he would not stop doing everything in his power to help Joseph on his own.

Maybe he couldn't do much for his master's business. But Joseph's sickness was spiritual, and that was an area where Duca had much more confidence in his ability to find meaningful assistance on his own.

It might have been better if he had listened to the Nubian more closely. Day after day, Duca made his way through the city to locate individuals who would take part in his plan, but all he found was frustration. He darted through the markets, around the Temple gates and into the Jerusalem countryside searching for rescuers. But it seemed the people he sought after most were in hiding since Jesus death. Others were too busy, or they were away, or they did not want to get involved in Joseph's personal affairs. Or they were leery of being seen with a man so recently released from Pilate's prison.

Everywhere he went, Duca heard the chatter of the faceless multitudes in the cluttered Jerusalem streets and the rutted highways leading into the city.

"Did they ever find the Nazarene's dead body? Or is that false prophet hiding in the hills outside Bethany with the rest of his frightened followers?"

"I hear Pilate still has that rich Arimathean in his dungeons. Now there's a smart businessman for you! Ha! The fool. You think he'd be content to live in such luxury. But no! He befriends this Jewish messiah who thinks he can rule the world."

"Maybe Joseph was Jesus' benefactor. How did a vagabond rabbi finance his way into such trouble in the first place?"

"Joseph of Arimathea? Of course he knows where the dead preacher is! He took the body, didn't he?"

"Ah, it's all a conspiracy—the Sanhedrin, Pilate and his Roman guards. Who knows, maybe even the God of Abraham, Isaac, and Jacob is involved. We're all just pawns waiting to be taken advantage of. We're the ones at fault— dying in rebellion sounds better for me these days. How about dying for Jesus, if he's really still alive? If he beat death, why can't I?"

One day Duca paused and sat down alongside the dusty road just beyond the Temple stairs. The city was bustling in preparation for the Festival that was only weeks away. Visitors, merchants, beggars, and worshipers roamed the cramped alleyways.

Wonder and confusion dueled in the young Egyptian's mind. The warmth of the springtime sun was a welcome balm to his tired body. Yet anxiousness plagued his spirit. He had expended so much effort, and it seemed he had not accomplished much for his master.

Duca remembered the words of Jesus. He focused on the present and looked for a blessing. He felt the sun on his face and felt his body relax. He concentrated on each breath, grateful for the fragrant air as it entered his lungs. By simply allowing himself to be refreshed and willing his constant, fevered stream of thoughts to be still, he began, slowly, to feel a sense of relief.

From behind him a familiar, gentle voice spoke to him and his spirit lifted immediately.

"Is this the loyal Duca of Joseph's house looking so forlorn?"

Duca sprang up and turned to face the smiling woman with flowing hair and peaceful, lovely features.

"My lady, it is I. I've looked for you everywhere! Your presence brings peace to my restless heart!"

"Let's find a quiet place where we may speak," she suggested. "Away from the unholy noise of our holy city."

The two walked a short distance and turned into a cool, quiet alley of farmers selling fresh fruit. The lady bought two oranges and offered one to Duca. Together, they peeled and ate the delicious fruit.

"I am so relieved to finally find a true friend of Joseph," Duca said, his voice full of hope. "He badly needs help—spiritual help—and I'm searching everywhere for rescuers. It seems the followers of Jesus have all but vanished."

"My Lord has ushered me to your side. Joseph of Arimathea will be healed," assured the confident woman. "We lovers of Jesus are all still here, although we have had to be cautious of late. Tell me exactly what you desire for your master. We will do our best."

"I wish to gather the wisest of those who had visited my master in the past—to comfort and advise him so that his strength of mind and spirit may return."

"I understand, my brother. I've but one request. I would like to be the first visitor."

"Oh—of course!" Duca agreed. "When Joseph just sees your face again, I feel his health will begin to brighten."

It had not been so long, but it seemed a lifetime had passed. Finally, Mary of Magdala was to be with Joseph again for the first time since that night of his release from Pilate's jail.

Chapter XI.

Now and Then

As he did on most days now, Joseph sat alone on the veranda, doing nothing, saying nothing. The veranda was a beautiful place, overlooking the terraced gardens and fountains dotting the good man's sprawling villa, alive with figs, dates, pine nuts, and the scent of rich spices. Lately, Joseph would often wave Duca away when his loyal servant tried to talk with him or raise his spirits.

Today, however, Duca was insistent.

"Master, you have a guest. She is coming."

At first, Joseph was going to protest, but when he saw the familiar, graceful form of Mary of Magdala walking toward him, his heart softened.

"Master," Duca said. "Forgive me. I have taken it upon myself to begin steps to bring you peace and restore you to health. I have had the great fortune of finding the Magdalene, who begs you to visit with her for a while. She has much she wishes to share with you."

Joseph's grace and chivalry, lately banished from his demeanor, reappeared quickly, although there was a great deal of weariness in his tone.

"This is good fortune. I am happy to see this visitor. You have done well, Duca." He rose and gestured for Mary toward a seat near his own. "I have thought of you often since we last met, and it does my heavy heart good to see you."

Joseph and the Magdalene embraced.

"Ah, Mary, with all the commotion about Jesus, your safety must be a concern. Yet you appear from the shadows of our holy city to take time with me!"

"Duca must have been mistaken," she said, smiling encouragingly. "He told me you were suffering to distraction with your grief and doubt. Yet the worthy member of the Sanhedrin finds the courtesy to open his home and heart to a humble handmaid of our Lord."

"Ah, it is good—I have fooled you. But Duca, as always, speaks the truth. It has gone very hard with me since the death of Sarah and Jesus. And so I ask, Mary—why has our world gone so wrong?"

Duca leaned anxiously against the serving table, flowers and luscious fruits and nuts gracing its surface. He had decided to act as scribe during these visits. Pen in hand and fresh papyrus scrolls before him, the curious, attentive servant was ready to record Mary's wisdom.

"My people are destroyed for a lack of knowledge, good Joseph," Mary quoted the lamentation of the prophet Hosea. "If I may, my friend, it's you who's inviting your own demise. The knowledge that can save you is close at hand."

"It does not seem so simple, Mary."

Joseph glanced at Duca beside him, writing down every word. He waited as Mary pondered her response.

"Your condition should not be fatal, but your countenance is deeply cast down. I warn you, my friend, without this vital knowledge, the spirit of destruction will ultimately weigh you down to your end."

"I do feel the weight, good woman."

"The force, the power that fueled your success, that made you an honored Decurion of Rome and respected judge of the

Sanhedrin, is still within you. But you've allowed it to dissi-
pate Have you forgotten? It was God's strength that fortified
you—never your own."

"Jesus' demise and the scattering of the followers have
made my heart heavy and doubtful."

Mary paused, as if to collect her thoughts.

"Joseph, I have many things to tell you. There are so many
things you need to know. But I'll begin with your perception
that events of recent days have destroyed your hopes. I can
tell you are transfixed by the death of the Master. I understand this. All who saw it were terribly hurt by it. I witnessed
it with my own eyes, and I'll never be the same. However,
once again you have forgotten—it was *you* consoling me at
the foot of the cross! You who took matters in hand so forcefully. You who stood up to Pilate for Jesus' sake!

"You must understand—the past is making you its prisoner more surely than Pilate ever could! You have bound
yourself like a prisoner to that awful day; it's a stone pulling
you to the bottom of the sea. But I say to you: what you saw
is not the truth!"

The Magdalene paused. The morning sun glistened in
her eyes as the shadows of the palm trees danced across her
lovely face. The busy, bustling everyday life of Jerusalem
could be heard in the distance. Yet its vibrancy was nothing
compared to that which she yearned to share with Joseph.

"The past," she began, "is a false idol. It is something we
should merely glance at. Never stare upon. Joseph, allow the
past to flow away, as it should!

"For God, past, present and future are all now, all here.

"But we are only here now.

"He exists in all time, eternal. He was in the past when
it was the present. When the future arrives, He'll be there.
But it's only in this moment, the moment at hand, that *we*
can experience God in His fullness. By focusing on what is
behind or what is ahead, we close our heart to him. By living

fully in the present we welcome Him in. This guarantees our futures will be fruitful, that the past will be behind us, and that He will be there when the future is ... now."

Duca's head had not risen since Mary's first words. He was scribbling furiously, gathering each of her offerings like priceless jewels.

Joseph resisted. The practical, always skeptical businessman in him responded. "Aren't you speaking in riddles?"

"No, Joseph, I'm simply reminding you of wisdom that you've forgotten. It was Jesus' greatest secret. When you were with Jesus, you always experienced life in this way, did you not? When he spoke, did you not feel it? That you were in the present in a way that felt like eternity?"

Joseph closed his eyes. The merest mention of Jesus caused him pain.

"It takes God's wisdom to recognize that the past will never happen again, and that the future is uncertain because of the tribulations in the world.

"This is one of the many gifts our Lord has given us— time. Jesus taught us, 'Be of good cheer, for I have overcome the world.' We need feel neither guilt nor shame for the past, nor anxiety and fear for the future.

"He's restored us to a single moment where we can dwell in peace. That moment is now. He recognized each moment as a gift," Mary smiled. "Maybe that is why our language calls it ... the present."

Duca raised his head and smiled at Mary. Hearing her words, writing them down, his ever-simmering unease seemed to melt away. He had never heard her speak with such authority. And with her every sentence, Duca was reminded of his visitor in the desert.

Joseph was moved. His resistance was high, but he had not felt this way since he had listened to Jesus himself preach. He felt Mary's words were coming directly from on High.

"Peace will come to you, Joseph. It will be the same peace you experienced as a young boy in the Temple, the same peace you felt in the presence of Jesus—even when he was a young man under your guidance. Have you forgotten the early days when he was permitted by his father Joseph to travel with you to your ports of call? The peace you experienced on those dangerous journeys—when you were fully alive in the present—you must wish to be that man again. You agree, don't you?"

"Yes," answered Joseph.

"Joseph, the best is yet to come for you. Even before Jesus' death, a current of worry ran deep within the stream of your soul. Blessed peace and accursed anxiety have always been at war inside you. They battle each other in your spirit because of the fears, tribulations, and heartaches of this life. Recent events have brought the battle to its highest pitch. But this agony, these regrets of the past and fears for the future, they only exist in your mind!"

Joseph protested. "But what about my secret support of Jesus, his crucifixion, the burial of his body, the accusations of my role in his disappearance, my Sarah's death...and the decline of my business? Are not these things real? Did I make them up in my mind?"

Joseph looked at his hands, and could not help but think of all that had slipped through them.

"How can I be at peace and be confident in a world of such horror, madness, and uncertainty?"

It was a question for the ages.

"Joseph of Arimathea, you must remember the peace and assurance you felt in God's presence, and also remember— that peace can only be found in the present moment. And you can never accept the present as long as you continually replay the past in your mind.

"It takes work. You must continually choose to gently return to the present when you drift into your dark worries and regrets.

"You've abandoned your peace because of many dark events. Yes, we all have doubted. Yes, we've all focused on our sorrows. But I say to you, my friend, there is a portico to eternity and all its peace and wisdom open to you. And that portico is the present moment. There is no other. Stand on that portico. Make it your abiding place. Be humble now in this time—and you'll know what it means to live eternally. You must make a decision."

"What kind of decision?"

"Join me and God as you know Him to be," Mary said, her words shimmering in the air. "Join us now...in this present moment. We may dwell with our troubles and hopes in the past and future, or we may join Him in the peace and humility of this moment, now!"

"But, Mary, as powerful as your words are, as a businessman, I fear it can't be that simple. Past and future are not figments of our imaginations! If I had not carefully planned for the future, I would never have achieved anything at all!"

"Wise friend, merchant, and religious leader, of course you're correct. Life is not simple. It must be lived, and that means we have many complex choices. But it is much simpler than you think. The present is the gift of God. What you attribute to your plans—could not all of it have simply been God's blessing?

"Has all your planning kept these difficult events from coming to pass? Honored Joseph, I implore you, stop dwelling where there is no roof...in the unchangeable past and the uncontrollable future!"

"Are you also saying the future is not real? As a Decurion in the Empire, accursed as the Romans may be, I've been able to look forward to a very real, very successful future."

"Yes, you are to be congratulated, Joseph," Mary replied. "But you must be honest. Much of what you call planning for the future is really...a present activity. What you call plans are often just correct actions taken fully in the present moment. And while many of your strategies have come to pass, I am willing to venture that just as many did not. Your success is attributable not to dwelling in the future, but in the present."

Joseph stared into the distance, lost in thought. Mary was content to sit and listen to the birds sing, and the faint bustle of life outside the walls.

The pause seemed eternal for Duca, but he welcomed it, catching up on his note taking.

At last, Joseph sighed. "There is truth in what you say. These thoughts strike me as divine wisdom, Mary of Magdala. How did you come by them?"

Mary smiled. "When Jesus was with us, did he not say, 'Before Abraham was, I Am'? Is not our Father in Heaven the great 'I Am'? Time is inconsequential to God. It is we who obsess over it. If with the Almighty there is no dimension of time, why do we spend so much of it in the immutable past and uncontrollable future? The great things of our civilization have been achieved through total concentration on the moment.

"Could God have created the universe, thinking about something else? Our friend Lazarus whom Jesus raised from the dead—the Lord was only focused on the love he felt at that moment for Lazarus, not the imminent betrayal of Judas or his prophesized fate on Calvary!

"One moment at a time was good enough for our Lord, dear Joseph; it should be good enough for us as well!"

"Mary, my mind tells me it's hard for mere flesh to grasp the intentions of God."

"Yes, Joseph, we simple humans must keep it simple," Mary agreed. "We know from the old writings and from

Jesus' teaching that God will never leave or forsake us. Over and over he pledges his faithfulness—in this moment.

"He did not say, 'I *will* be with you to the end of days.' His words were, 'I *am* with you, until the end of days.'

"He's with us where we live—in this place. The past is not a place. It was a place. The future is not a place. It will be a place. God is not in the past or in the future. God is the 'I Am,' not the 'I was' or 'I will be.'

"That is were you must be, my friend...here. Be humble and present. Overcome this one challenge, Joseph, and your life will be filled with renewed energy."

Joseph's face brightened slightly. "My spirit already feels lighter. My regrets of the past and my fears for the future have not served me well. I'm starting to see this. They have sapped the strength and joy from the present. But I must tell you, dear lady, my questions have only multiplied."

Mary glanced at Duca. She waited for the scribe to finish his writing. He looked up, and they exchanged smiles.

"You've been blessed, noble Joseph. You once saved Duca, and now he's committed to repaying the debt. His plan has been cast. My role has simply been to begin this mission and help him find others who will answer your questions.

"Other visitors will follow. Then I shall return. Within two weeks the secrets revealed will re-energize your life and you can again begin to fulfill God's purpose for you. Duca will record them. Then, these secrets will be your responsibility—to share as you continue your travels. I believe this to be God's will for you, Joseph."

"So your help will end just before the Festival begins?"

"Yes, Joseph. This is a divinely appointed schedule."

"How can you be so sure? I can't imagine feeling restored in such a short time..."

"You'll discover how and why after we meet again. In the meantime, I must depart. The Romans, the Sadducees, and the Pharisees watch Jesus' followers day and night.

They're determined to find the body that was in the tomb. And as you know, Joseph, you have always been one of the leading suspects."

Joseph rose and peered into his guest's eyes, reaching for both her hands.

"Mary, the things you told me on the night of my prison release—I could scarcely attend to your tale, so wild it seemed, and my body and spirit were so broken. Do you still believe all you said?"

A breeze gently lifted Mary's auburn hair, revealing her graceful neck. She smiled as she spoke more tenderly than during all their conversation. "I know what I experienced. I know whom I saw. We spoke."

She looked to Duca to assess his reaction, and then back to Joseph. "I'll see you both in two short weeks. By that time I expect to behold the honorable man from Arimathea fully restored."

Joseph and Mary embraced.

Duca escorted her to the gate. She turned to him to ask one last question.

"Has Joseph discussed the shroud?"

"No."

No further words were spoken. It was midday. Mary strode off onto the sun-splashed hillside sloping toward Jerusalem, her cloak over her head, destination unknown to all but her.

As he watched her depart, Duca felt better than he had in weeks. His plan had started well.

Joseph did not leave the breezy, idyllic veranda for some time. Sitting there, he could almost remember the peace Mary had spoken of. But it was hard to remain still. His mind would not stop racing.

What do I now do with this new wisdom? Could everything she said be true? God is the 'I Am'—there is no doubting she spoke the truth about that. It is written. But how do I stay in the present moment? And how can I move forward without planning for the future? And how can I learn without thinking about the past? So many questions!

As is the nature of urgent questions, they promptly pulled him out of the moment.

Duca had already retreated to his own chambers, leaving his master to ponder what he had heard. The Egyptian felt his duty was greater than simply finding those who could share their wisdom with Joseph. He would record the wisdom and prepare it for others who might be suffering like his master.

Duca simplified his notes:

The Magdalene's Foundational Secret:
God's Gift of the Present

- **Live humbly and fully in the present moment.**
- **The past and the future are unchangeable and uncontrollable illusions.**
- **The present offers a glimpse of God's eternity and escape from the dimension of time.**
- **A feeling of peace and timelessness will show you have entered the present.**
- **Living in the present takes work and practice.**
- **Knowledge is not enough—understanding and wisdom must follow.**
- **The power of focus will be released to allow for your magnificence to be revealed...in the now.**

Chapter XII.

A Glance Back

With her shawl covering her head on this warm spring day, Mary had reason to be concerned as she hurried through Jerusalem's crowded alleyways on her way to the home of one of Jesus' followers at the gates of the city.

Despite her words of wisdom to Joseph, she was herself surprised to find doubts creeping in and attacking her own peace of mind. As a well-known follower of Jesus, she was in danger from many quarters, and dealing with Joseph's obvious distress had tired her deeply. For a moment, she drifted back to the time before Jesus had lifted her up: a time when she was an utterly different person. A time when even raising her head to look at respectable Joseph, let alone speaking to him as though she were herself a rabbi, would have been unthinkable.

The thought of her awful past set off a wave of doubt.

How could I even imagine my ability to serve such a complete man as Joseph of Arimathea? What right do I have? It's he who was educated by rabbis. He who has traveled the world. He who sits with the high priests and judges in the Temple, and even in the garden with Jesus—always pleasing our God. But I, rebellious from birth, always wanted more. I, who gave permission to man to use me for his pleasures so that I could have a future far from the ghettos of this cruel city of hypocrites.

Oh my God! I'm in the past. It's judging me, drawing me to walk that road again, even attracting me to my desires of old. No, no! I'll glance back to when Jesus healed me. It was at that moment when peace flooded my spirit. It was then I first entered the moment.

It was glorious then, and it's glorious now. I do not need to feel shame at my past. Jesus told me to go and sin no more—and I have followed his command faithfully. I need not fret over my future. God is with me now. Just as I've shared with Joseph, it is here; it's now that I can experience the eternal wisdom and presence of the Almighty. I'm blessed, and I glory in this moment.

As the crowd pressed in on her, Mary stumbled, almost falling to the stone pavement. Suddenly, a strong arm grabbed her wrist. While the hand kept her from falling, fear overcame the Magdalene immediately.

She looked up to see who had seized her. An unforgettable face from the past drove her back to her youth. Nausea rose up from the depths of her being.

"Your disguise is insufficient, little woman." The oily, almost whispered words made Mary feel sick. She wanted to run, but the man still held her arm. "Your ugly garment could not fool me. Your form, even in that rug, your flowing hair, tell clearly what you really need—a man!"

Mary pulled away with difficulty. This man, squat and strong, had known her when she was twelve. He had taken her arm then, too, and dragged her to a dark and empty room. And though she had kicked, scratched, bit, and spit in his face, she had not escaped. He was Magdala's chief rabbi, and he had warned her of severest consequences, both to her and her family, if she ever told of the evil he had done to her young, unwilling body.

She knew of his prominence in her hometown, and had hid his abuse in her subconscious, fearful and ashamed. But it had changed the course of her life.

Now he was himself disguised as a commoner, no doubt looking for others to abuse. Only his victims most likely knew his double life.

"You're still disgusting, Rabbi of Magdala. Do you think your disguise is sufficient to cloud my thinking? Are you still hurting little girls?"

"You must be mistaken, whore. I'm just a lonely man, desirous of that which I know you can supply."

For a moment the Magdalene thought of spitting into the face of the smiling man, of striking out with anything she could get her hands on.

But the Spirit of God was suddenly with her. She entered the present and felt her heart fill with peace and forgiveness.

"Do you know Jesus?" she asked, perplexing the man.

"He's dead," he answered assuredly.

"Yet I see the old man's still alive in you, rabbi."

In the presence of God, there is fullness of joy and glory, she thought. *Greater is He who is in me than he who is in the world. No demon in hell can stand in the presence of the Almighty power.*

The man did not respond. He looked confused.

Mary calmly dressed her shoulders and head, smiled at the man, and left the market.

The surge of power she felt escorted her for the rest of her journey. She looked neither back to the encounter, nor to what lay ahead for her life. Rather, she marveled at her every breath and her every step.

She had walked into an eternal moment; confident once again that she had been worthy of delivering the first secret to Joseph of Arimathea.

Chapter XIII.

A Gift of a Fish

The pounding at Joseph's gate the next day was nothing like Mary's gentle tap. Duca smiled. His heart warmed at the thought of greeting the next guest. He pulled the hand-crafted mahogany entrance open. There the rescuer stood, tall and strong. He stretched out his arms and Duca embraced him in welcome.

"I'm honored, young Duca, to assist you and your master, who did such a great service to our lord!"

While the servant was himself tall and strongly built, the big fisherman dwarfed him. He engulfed Duca in his embrace — as did the pungent odor of the sea.

"Peter, it is my master and I who are honored by your presence."

"Yes, but move quickly inside, good Duca. I have urgent business in these pressing times." Still with arm around Duca's neck, Peter continued to smile. "It's amazing. The days are perilous, yet my joy abounds! And I wonder to myself, can I be any happier?"

Duca himself had not smiled this much since Joseph rushed home to tell him about the entrance of Jesus into the city of Jerusalem during the week of Passover.

"Joseph is on the veranda," the servant announced. "But may I first be so privileged to cleanse your feet from your journey from the shore?"

"Ah, good servant, yes, these feet do need some refreshing. *My* Master would be pleased with your commitment to service. But, another time. Let's not tarry."

Addressing him by his birth name, Joseph could barely believe his eyes as the big fisherman loped across the veranda toward him. "Simon, son of John, what a blessing it is to see you. How kind you are to visit a follower who has stumbled by the way!"

"Mystery man of Arimathea, you've not stumbled to God—only to yourself! I tell you this as one who cursed himself for his own stumbles.

"Did I not deny I even knew Jesus on the night of his arrest? Not once, but three times I did deny him! I could relive that sin a thousand times. I could curl up in a hole and die from shame! But I do not! I just listen, pray, and surrender to what is before me. Then I do.

"And then I pray some more!" The giant laughed out loud.

Duca pulled out the velvet stool for Peter. The huge man welcomed it as a relief for his weary body. His broad shoulders, massive hands, and peering eyes had new nobility about them. Even though his robe was soiled, and it was apparent from his aroma that he was still a fisherman, there was something new and wonderful in his demeanor. Joseph could not take his eyes off Jesus' impetuous disciple. Peter had clearly undergone a transformation as positive as his own was negative. Stunned at the presence of the surprisingly ebullient fisherman, Joseph remained standing and staring.

"Sit down, dear host," chuckled Peter. "Your loyal servant has me on a rescue mission, and his partner, the Magdalene, would want us to begin our business immediately. But first, Duca, from our bountiful sea I bring you a gift. Smelly, yes—but fresh as the morning breeze! Although perhaps not quite as sweet."

Duca received the large fish, wrapped in burlap, and went off to prepare it for consumption later.

"You are thoughtful, fisherman."

"Just a helpless *barbel*, boney but fleshy. Without coin in mouth, I must add, but with satisfying nutrition and delicious taste to promote your well-being."

Peter laughed again, and Joseph smiled as they recalled the miraculous event of Jesus' ministry. Jesus had once told Peter that the coin they needed to pay the temple tax would be found in the mouth of the next fish he caught. As usual, his prediction came true.

"Peter, forgive me," said Joseph, as he eased himself into his chair, with the help of the table. His back had been worse since his time in Pilate's cell. "Your appearance has addled my wits, along with my manners. I'm so honored to welcome you into my home."

"First off, Joseph, let me assure you your dear Sarah is in a better place. I can only imagine your grief, but I bring hope you will one day see her again."

"Your consolation delivers comfort to a grieving soul."

"And I rejoice to hear you finally address me as Peter. It's amazing, but even my cantankerous mother-in-law has abandoned my birth name of Simon. It's really quite remarkable! More her respect for the Rabbi, I know, but still, it's a major promotion for me to go from reckless son-in-law to my current august state."

Indeed, the thought of himself as dignified caused Peter to burst into a fresh torrent of laughter.

Joseph smiled. "How did that come about?"

"That's what I'm here to tell you."

"To talk about your wife's mother?"

"No, no, no. But, true to my instructions from Duca and Mary, I'm to share a secret with you—a lesson learned. And,

Jesus himself revealed this secret to me. Only it was filtered through the person of my mother-in-law!"

Duca had returned. Joseph softly reminded his scribe, "You must now be alert with pen."

The servant nodded, never to lift the writing instrument from the paper for the next hour.

"Let me explain," continued Peter. He reached for a ripened fig and continuing to talk while quickly devouring it. "Your disconsolate nature disturbs not only Duca, but all of us who have valued you over the time of the ministry. And, it was my dear—well, dear may not be the perfect word—the mother of my wife, who confirmed to me a powerful step in assuring strength for your challenging moments, restoring you to yourself."

"Mary of Magdala left me with heartening, wise thoughts yesterday. But the peace of her words turned out to be fleeting," said Joseph.

"I had no notion of peace, Joseph, until the Rabbi cursed the demon in me."

"You've lost me, Peter."

Duca lifted his eyes to the big man, waiting for the teaching to come forth.

Peter responded quickly, "The Lord revealed that his destiny was to be taken prisoner and to be executed. I could not accept this. As everyone expected, I objected violently. I would protect him, I swore. No one would hurt Jesus while I was around! I would never surrender!

"But the Lord's rebuke of me was sharp and swift. I was vain and ignorant in not surrendering to his truth—the truth of God's plan for him."

"Surrendering?"

"Yes, surrendering to a plan over which I had no say and no control."

"But, good man, before you lose me totally, you must please explain your mother-in-law's role in all this."

"Oh, right. I forgot that part."

Peter paused, smiled, and devoured a plump Persian date, seemingly savoring its feel in his hand, then its taste in his mouth. He gestured for Duca to continue writing.

"The more I was with the Nazarene, the more I forgot my cares, my past and future. It was only after he healed my wife's mother that my hard head realized the gift of her life to me. I know it's unbelievable, but true.

"Ever since, to please my wife and to honor her healer, I've listened to my mother-in-law," added Peter, staring into the garden just outside. "In fact," he laughed, "I've surrendered to her every wish." Turning back to Joseph, he became more animated. "Almost every wish, anyway. But in the old days we fought like a cat and dog. Not over anything of importance, just my own foolish orneriness. I resisted this good woman out of my own pride!

"And then, I discovered something."

"What?" asked Joseph, leaning closer to Peter. "What did you discover?"

"I felt her love for me. She appreciated my service to her. She accepted me. It opened me up, I tell you. And so, I surrendered right back to her. What lambs we became!

"In my surrender, I gave up a war I had no hope of winning. She had done the same. Instead of willfulness, I found peace when I was around her. It was the most wonderful thing—a feeling of love for my wife's mother—someone I'd hardly acknowledged as human, much less lovable.

"And I tell you, Joseph, this was the same tranquility, the same rest I experienced whenever Jesus was nearby."

"So...surrendering subdued your anxiety?" Joseph asked.

"Aye, and the like demons that afflict a soul—the fretting, the fear, the regret. Oy!" Peter slapped his forehead. "My motto was always 'never surrender!' What a fool I was! I tell you truly, sir—the only victory is through surrender!"

There is no doubt this is a good soul—but he is naïve.

"My friend," Joseph began, "I've lived in a complicated world of ruthless competition. You cast your net upon the water, surrender to fate and reap your living. As a businessman, I'm not in a position to surrender so easily. Honest Peter, surrender would have meant ruin in my business and life a thousand times over. Success is the result of conviction, of planning to change the world around me, to prosper and to share those blessings with others! Not all traders are as honest as I pride myself on being. Even now, it seems my enemies wish to steal what I have worked so diligently to build. I constantly have to fight for fairness and to make a profit. Giving in as you say to the slightest resistance, surrendering to the moment, as you call it—will that not only paralyze my operations?"

Peter looked levelly into his friend's eyes. "Joseph, you make a good point. I do not suggest you blindly surrender to the wishes of those who wish evil upon you—although our Lord himself commanded us that if a man strikes us we are to turn the other cheek. And he gave himself up as meekly as a lamb when the time came.

"But surely, you should surrender to that which you know is right.

"I do not suggest you surrender to confusion. But I do believe that to find the peace you are seeking you should fully surrender to that which you understand. And to that which it is out of your control. Even to painful events like the death of your wife—your surrender will rob them of their power to harm you.

"There are many contrary thoughts and situations in life. You're correct. But don't be so emotionally bound to resistance. These teachings are true wisdom from our Lord.

"I tell you Joseph, I have never been happier! I feel I can fly like an eagle. When he beholds the storm about to consume him, he simply sets his sights higher, spreads his wings, and allows the winds to lift him to safety! By forgetting to resist, he follows the laws of nature and allows the compassionate hand of his Creator to carry him. And you know what ultimately happens?"

"No. Please tell me."

"Those deadly winds lift the eagle so high that his face feels the soothing warmth of the sun—the sun that was there all the time, behind the dark storm!"

"A calming thought, Peter," Joseph said. He meant it. There was something deeply comforting in the words of this childlike giant.

"Too many times in days gone by, Joseph, we resisted. To the point of exhaustion! How disagreeable I was over the years, fighting everything, resisting everything," said Peter, pounding his chest. "But it is what it is— that's what I learned. True power comes through acceptance.

"And I learned something else. Much of my resistance sprang from my desire for control. But I learned, thanks to Jesus, that the desire for control was really something else. Something much better: a desire to do the right thing.

"And I felt truly blessed when I realized that surrendering does not mean doing nothing. Quite the contrary—when we surrender, we *always* do something. Something appropriate to the moment. Simply spread our wings! This invites God to lift us, to allow His plan to be applied to the situation. When we can just do that, the rays of the sun will greet us in the most unexpected times and places."

"The imagery is most pleasing."

"Indeed, Joseph. But don't forget: surrendering also means giving up the desire to always be right, always win out. So be careful what you surrender to."

"More examples. Please." Without realizing it, Joseph had actually begun to enjoy himself, for the first time in many days. These moments with Peter were rich, and Joseph found himself savoring the enthusiastic words, feeling the sun on his face, and listening to the busy scraping of Duca's quill on the parchment.

"Do you want to be a beggar in this life? Then surrender your every thought to the past or the future. Focus your attention on past glories or future success, and you're doing no more than begging for the scraps of life. Less than scraps: illusions!

"I can see it in you, Joseph, and I grieve for you. You have become trapped in regrets of the past! I know how hard it is to let these terrible events go. But answer me this, good sir: How has it profited you?"

"Not well, I must admit."

"Not well? It is dragging you to your premature grave! Don't give in to the illusion of reliving the past and wishing for what can never be, my precious friend. If you seek fulfill-ment of your destiny in this life, then you must find a force under which to stand, believe in, and cast your cares upon— in the present!

"Yes, Joseph, life's full of earthly complications. As a businessman, it's true you can't always simply ignore them. But don't become one of those who think the world is theirs to control. They ignore God who created everything. His mind alone directs this world's comings and goings. This ignorance is the road too often traveled. In fact, it is more than ignorance. It is a great sin!"

"I struggle to see what you're saying, now," Joseph said. "Can you please explain?"

The giant's smile faded, and he became very grave.

"I mean, Joseph, if you pursue this vision of your own control, you're an idolater—for you put your judgment and planning above God's! This attempt to control everything shouts to the heavens, '*I* am the master of my affairs, not *You*, Father!'

"Second, I say to you in all seriousness: the very thing you seek to control is the first thing you will lose."

Joseph was exasperated. He had felt so close to under-standing, but the old resistance was stubborn. There was a strange, sick comfort, almost a security, in clinging tightly to grief and regret, in playing over and over in his mind what might have been. He wasn't quite ready to give that up. He sighed, "Peter, you make some sense. But this word 'surrender' repels me."

"Joseph, you and I are more alike than I thought."

Peter paused, and reached for a goblet. Savoring the fresh water, he closed his eyes as if in thanksgiving. Slowly wiping his wild beard with his hand, the giant stood. He looked down on his host, pondering.

Then his face lit up and his smile returned. He had a new insight to share.

"Merchant and counselor, God has given me new words for you to consider. Perhaps they will help you accept this secret. Can you live with 'acceptance'? Or perhaps 'submission'? Yes, that's it. Accept what is before you and don't struggle. Submit yourself to *reality*. Surely, businessman, you of all people must accept that the facts are the facts! Only a fool would try to stop the tide."

"Accepting reality is surrendering? Submission…"

"Better yet, Joseph, consider this!" Peter began to pace in front of Joseph's seat, waving his arms in enthusiasm. "Yes, listen up, both of you." He pointed to Duca. "In surren-dering, or accepting the circumstances, you don't even have to be concerned about your survival anymore! No, you don't have to be consumed with yourself again from that point on. Why? Ah, ha! Because when you accept, submit, and surrender, you die to self, and no one can kill that person anymore—your old self is a dead man anyway!

"Now, isn't that a soothing thought for some of us?"

Duca stopped his writing. Joseph looked dazed. This was all too much.

Jesus had said things like this, things that forced Joseph to ponder for days. *He always spoke about a rebirth.* The fisherman's words sounded a little like that strange advice of Jesus. Could Joseph's wavering fortunes, his reputation, his passion for life—could they really all be given up and then reborn?

Finally, Joseph spoke. "Can fortunes be made in surrendering—and dying to self?"

"Leave that up to God. Don't stray from the basic secret of surrender. If you seek fulfillment of your destiny in this life, then you must trust the only force worthy of surrender. Stand under God, and cast your cares upon Him.

"Don't argue with your Creator!"

"But what about results?"

"Joseph, you're as hard-headed as I was when this revelation came over me!" laughed the fisherman. Peter shook his head at Duca, and then became serious again.

"I'm not giving you advice, Joseph. I'm simply telling you the truth. It is indisputable. You're not in control, even of your trains of camels. In truth, you control nothing. Until you concede this truth, until you submit to the fact that the past and future are beyond your reach, you'll be a blind fool, groping in the dark, proclaiming you can see! A slave to phantoms!

"I do believe success is at hand for you, Joseph. All you must do is cease your selfishness—let that willful, self-absorbed old man die!"

Joseph's nostrils flared. Peter had hit a tender nerve. Joseph had always taken great pride in his generosity and concern for others. He thought of the tomb he had given up for Jesus, of the suffering that befell him as a consequence.

"My friend, Joseph of Arimathea has never been called 'selfish.' Sit down, please, and explain yourself on this point."

The big man obediently set himself back down.

"Joseph, do you know what Jesus threw at me when I denied his destiny? He commanded, 'Devil, get thee behind me!' Quite a bit worse than being called selfish, don't you think? Jesus knew my plans for him were devilish. I hungered for him to be successful and popular...so I could share in that glory. I wanted what I wanted!

"Ah, the old writings were so right: 'My people perish for a lack of knowledge.' I had my own greedy desire for Jesus' kingship to occur in this world. I wanted to overthrow the Romans. Yes, I had a sense of his eternal promises, but I also loved that he was looking to me as a leader, at least within our motley band. My selfishness tormented me throughout his arrest, trial, crucifixion, death, and burial.

"And yet, all I had to do was to stop, listen, surrender, accept the wisdom of his teachings, and allow God to craft the results. But no—with my fisherman's head as hard as the granite lion that greeted me at your door's entrance, I had to wait until the third day after the tragedy.

"If I had had more real faith in Jesus, I would have been comforted all along, and simply trusted he was fulfilling a destiny far more miraculous than anything I could have ever imagined!"

"We do affect results, to a degree, though, don't we, Peter?" Joseph asked, desperate for some kind of validation of the way he had always lived his life.

"Of course, good man. But take no credit for yourself. It's fine to work, to concentrate, and to strive. Do things, by all means. Do the things you feel moved to do, and do them with all your might! But don't worry about the results. Surrender to whom and what you believe in. Your humility will earn you riches exceeding your grandest ambitions.

"Just don't anticipate what those riches might be. Because they might be something you never imagined!"

Peter again lifted the goblet of spring water, dripping with condensation as the mid-spring day was delivering a hint of looming summer heat.

"As boys, we never craved for anything but what we were doing—playing, fishing, working with our fathers, reading the Torah, eating. Weren't we wealthy, then? We surrendered to our families, our siblings, and our friends. We submitted to our fathers. Was it not blissful, Arimathean?"

"It has been a long time for me, Peter." Joseph smiled ruefully. "While I know what you mean, it is very hard for me to remember."

"Joseph, did we know pretense or deceit? We didn't even know what pride meant. The real Joseph walked the earth in those days, happy and alive as each moment presented itself. Is that the case now?"

"I'm clearly not happy with the Joseph of today, my friend."

"That is why I'm here. Did not Jesus teach us, 'Unless you are as little children, you will never inherit the Kingdom'? Did he not say that 'It is of these little ones that the Kingdom is made'? Live life as a child, and all types of enchanting possibilities will open before you. Your life will become a blessed adventure, full of surprise and wonder—not unlike your many travels to the east!"

"Surrender, submit, accept—then receive great rewards," Joseph pondered.

"It is true, Joseph. But that's the wrong spirit. Surrender not to get what you want, but what God knows is best for you—that which is destined by His hand. Your life will yield much fruit, because you've given control back to where it properly belongs. It may not be the fruit you imagined—but what fool would put his imagination above that of the Creator of all?"

"What about those who did not follow Jesus? How about my Duca, who's been respectful even in his disbelief—his lack of knowledge?"

Duca looked up, surprised at his master's comment.

"Yes," Peter answered. "There are those who did not walk with the Nazarene, and many did not have the benefit, as Duca did, to hear his words. Yet all they must do is yield their stubborn spirits for a cause, something they believe in—something wholesome, pure, honest, holy, edifying, and helpful. And in that humble state, they'll be open to the knowledge, understanding, and wisdom that have eluded them."

"Are you really so certain, Peter?" Joseph asked.

"The thrill of surrender lies in the uncertainty! Merely be certain of the goodness of what or to whom you surrender. The results will speak for themselves. I've learned this since Jesus' burial—and the incredible, unimaginable news that came forth three days later. I've been humbled by the impossible. It works. I've seen the ultimate proof of its working!

"Your conviction was that your way was the only way. You set a course for a journey you'd been on many times before, and you expected the same results. But if you surrender to possibilities beyond your imagination, your true adventure will begin!"

"Adventure? At my age?"

"Did not Jesus speak of eternity? Why burden yourself with concerns about growing old when you have so much to still discover?

"The greatest experience of my life almost turned into my death because of my refusal to surrender! Yes, I know you heard of my jumping into the sea that mysterious night when I saw Jesus approaching our boat. I was so excited to see the miracle of my Lord—imagine! Walking on water!— that I stepped onto the water to meet him. I surrendered to him, and the raging sea meant little to me ... at first! I was so encouraged to behold him that I bounded across the water! Then, fear overcame me. I stopped being in the moment. I remembered the past—that what I was doing was impossible. I thought of the future—that I would surely drown!

"And of course I began to sink! Thankfully, Jesus reached for my arm and pulled me to safety. Had I not lost my focus and listened to my fears, by the God of Abraham, I would still be stepping on those whitecaps!"

Peter stood again, stretching his long arms skyward. He could not seem to remain seated for long. He tilted his head back, eyes closed.

"Minds do not always change in an instant, Joseph. I understand you are clinging to a few shreds of doubt. But you've really listened to the knowledge I've shared with you. I can see that. Its truth will work its power over you as it has for me. It is a great secret and a divine truth. I know it will come alive in your understanding over time.

"Yes, I've done my work for our dear Joseph of Arimathea! I have such joyous anticipation for you, my friend." Peter pointed to his host and concluded: "Receive your restoration, Joseph. It's been delivered to you."

Joseph arose. He stepped forward, and the fisherman and the merchant embraced.

"I am grateful for the secrets you have shared with me, Peter. I do feel their power working on my spirit. You have done me a great service today."

"It's your Duca, with help from the Magdalene, who is surely being of service," Peter said.

Duca felt a rush of satisfaction. He looked up from his notes and smiled at the wise, joyful fisherman, knowing progress had been made.

Peter departed as quickly and energetically as he had arrived. Although he had as much to fear as the Magdalene, he would never hide himself or scurry through back alleys.

His trust was in God, and his every movement expressed confidence and inner peace.

Joseph watched Peter's figure get smaller as it kicked up dust from the well-traveled road connecting the estate to the city. Despite all the resistance he had expressed, a smile lit his face as he reviewed in his mind all he had heard.

Peter's message—and example—of surrender, submission, and acceptance had reminded Joseph of his own faltering obedience to the will of God. He had failed in so many ways!

Without realizing it, Joseph's thoughts began to be drawn in again by worries about his own shortcomings, replaying the mistakes of his past.

As Peter dissolved into the horizon, a gentle breeze coming from the city carried the pungent, disturbing scent of burning garbage from Jerusalem's public dump. It filled the old man with something like panic.

Try as he might to hold onto the good feelings, Joseph found his mind being pulled back to an awful place—to Calvary itself.

Despite the promise of Peter's words, the nauseating, sickly sweet smell of rotting garbage triggered the memory of the worst fear Joseph had ever experienced—that Jesus' body would end up food for carrion on that very garbage heap.

That thought triggered a hundred more.

I know I didn't do enough for Jesus. Perhaps Jesus would not have died at all if I had done more.

Did Jesus really rise from the dead? Perhaps the others desire for a miracle clouded their vision. If only I could have seen him rise for myself!

Did my stubborn standing up to Pilate cause Sarah's death?

The frenzied thoughts, like marauding robbers, were muscling Joseph back to his anxious, fearful state, trapped in replaying the past and worrying about the future.

It was exhausting, and Joseph retired to his chamber to rest.

Duca saw his master's doubt, and it troubled him. Still, he was hopeful. Such a powerful message must have an effect. Duca knew that there was a good chance Peter's message would stay with Joseph, and do its work in time—when the knowledge would turn to understanding.

For now, he was happy to have captured the essence of what the fisherman had to share. While Joseph took his rest, Duca summarized his notes.

The Fisherman's Supportive Secret: Surrender

- **Surrender to whatever you believe to be the highest good.**
- **Surrender concern for results to whatever you have surrendered.**
- **Submit to the present, focusing totally upon it, with no selfish, illusory thoughts of the past or future.**
- **Accept reality—it is the plan of God unfolding.**
- **In surrendering, there is no room for worry. Relax, for all is progressing as it should.**
- **Childlike joy and increased energy will be the signs of successful surrender.**

Chapter XIV.

Conditional Surrender

Peter had not been home in weeks. Despite his seemingly boundless energy, he was already tired before he visited Joseph. He had been traveling, avoiding the Romans and Pharisees, and meeting with as many of the scattered followers of Jesus as he could find. Trying to convince the deeply troubled, stubborn Joseph to correct his thinking had tired him even more.

As soon as he arrived at the outskirts of his modest dwelling, he stopped at the shed by the water's edge that held his fishing equipment. He felt a strong urge to go inside, to surround himself with his nets, oars, tools and the other gear he had so carefully collected and cared for over the years.

As he extended his tired arm to unlatch the rickety wooden door, he was nearly overwhelmed by the thought of how much he missed his daily fishing trips onto the Sea of Galilee.

He bent to enter the tiny shed and his huge frame seemed more out of place than ever. A yearning in his heart for the simple freedom of the past, a life of coming and going only as he dictated, gave him a sharp pang of regret.

I loved the freedom of my trade, yet I knew change was coming. I began to feel stifled as the Romans dictated to my profession more and more—the endless rules, taxes and obligations nearly drove me mad! I had to do something. It was the Lord who seemed to be the answer for me—to follow him and control my own destiny once again, through the power and wisdom of his teachings. If it weren't for him, my rash nature would've gotten me killed by the Romans.

It was glorious for most of three years. I'd fish when I had to, but as we wandered, all our essential needs were taken care of. I saw myself as his primary aide, protecting him from harm. My wife and mother-in-law were pleased Jesus had brought order to my life.

But then it all fell apart! Now, I don't even have a business, let alone a ministry. So many of Jesus' old followers have deserted him through fear, or they are in hiding, or demoralized by his crucifixion.

And did stubborn Joseph, once so sure and powerful, even hear a word I said?

Carrying on without Jesus is very hard! My wisdom is like a drop in the sea next to his, and I will certainly never accomplish the smallest miracle! Oh how I sometimes yearn for the freedom of the deep waters, the cool breeze in my face. I know what I've seen, but is this the way it was supposed to turn out?

I miss him so much. I hate this hiding, this waiting! And waiting for what?

Peter's frustration mounted. This impatient, exhausted, angry giant was, in the moment, reverting to the Simon of old, and he could not quell the anger welling up inside him.

He lunged for a tattered fishing net, fruitlessly trying to tear it as if it were mere strings wound together. Tangling himself in the cords, his hands began to bleed.

He threw it down in disgust and grabbed for an old oar hung on the wall. Clutching it, he swung wildly, like a caged animal in a battle against unseen tormentors.

He was about to swing the heavy thing at the entrance door when it opened.

Startled, he dropped both arms to his side and the oar clattered to the dirt floor.

His mother-in-law turned her tiny head to view the destruction. She surveyed his tattered and disheveled countenance, perspiration from his forehead dripping onto his splinter-covered beard, his breath coming in heavy gasps.

"Oh, dear. Is this Simon returning home — the cantankerous, violent, emotional, fisherman? I have not seen this unpleasant man for a while."

"Hello, Mother," was the giant's sheepish response.

"Ah, he addresses me as Mother. Perhaps to fool me? Or — just maybe — the dark force of the past has once again left us in peace?"

"I'm sorry."

"You are? Really? Well, perhaps it is our new Peter after all! Will you surrender to the reality of what is, rather than the illusion of what Simon thinks should be?"

"I don't know what came over me," said Peter, as he shuffled to sit on the three-legged stool that had avoided his onslaught. "We've all been hiding. I can't seem to adjust without the Master. The past seemed so much simpler. I yearned for it. I forgot what Jesus taught me over the years. His visits with us after Calvary — their memory just comes and goes like a ghost in the night."

"Have you become so fearful about your future that you've regressed to obnoxious Simon, the one I forbid my daughter to marry?"

"Mother, I'm truly remorseful," Peter said as he waved his arm, surveying the destruction he had caused. "I've just returned from Jerusalem where I did my best to encourage Joseph of Arimathea. His spirit is very low. Oh, my God, I spoke to him about surrendering to the moment. Can you believe that?"

"Yes, Peter, I can. I know the change in you is real. You are tired. Fatigue has temporarily robbed your new-found wisdom."

"But how can I avoid these lapses?"

The old woman smiled, reaching over to the big man to dust off the wooden chips and dirt from his robe. "Forget about yourself, Peter. And forgive yourself. Just begin again. Make the most of the present. Sometimes when we think we are surrendering, it's with the hope of gain—yes, and that is just another form of lusting for the future. I hope you made that clear to the poor merchant."

"I tried," Peter humbly reflected. "But I wonder: how can anyone possibly have my perspective without having seen the Master? Surrender because eternal life is possible? Even me—I beg the Magdalene to remind me of what she saw after Jesus rose every time I see that crazy woman."

"Peter, Mary of Magdala is the sanest woman you will ever meet. Just continue to listen to her. Ask her to repeat the words as many times as you need to hear them! There is no harm in repetition—if that is what it takes to penetrate that hard head.

"But for now, heed my words. Do you want to know how to make it simple?"

"Of course I do."

"Then—never forget the crucifixion."

"But mother, that's the one event in my life I've tried to bury!"

"Wrong!"

"But why?"

"Because it's the ultimate example of surrender."

"Speak clearly, woman, because I fear Simon is knocking at the door again."

"The greatest surrender of all time was by our Lord on that execution cross. He gave up his ultimate human right— the right to live. Even though he was totally in the right.

He surrendered to what the Father had orchestrated in the unseen world of the Spirit."

"But it was horrible! You weren't there. I was watching from afar with some of the others. No man should have suffered like my friend."

"Peter, of all people you should know the reward of his final acceptance. What happened three days later? The greatest miracle ever! Something that's never occurred before! And you can tell the story to all who weren't there."

Peter looked down, like a little boy corrected by his elder. It seemed so unreal, though he had seen with his own eyes and heard with his own ears the ultimate miracle of Jesus' rising from the dead. He was quiet for a moment, as if in prayer, and slowly a smile returned to his face.

"Yes, how can I forget his appearance after that horrific day? Like the smell of fresh springtime rain approaching, he walked into the room. Victory over death—because of his surrender!"

Peter rose and went out into the sunshine. As tired as he was, he stretched and turned his face to the sun. His smile grew as he was once again reminded that what he had seen had not been a dream.

"I'm sure the new Peter I know was a breath of spring-time air for the poor Arimathean! For the most part," his mother-in-law chuckled.

Peter nodded sheepishly. His good wife, still unaware of his presence, could be heard draping wet clothing to dry on bushes behind the stone home. As he thought of her, a far-away look crept into his eyes.

"One day I too will have to make the ultimate surrender," he said softly.

They were words the old lady wished never to hear.

"Peter, it is as the Lord prophesied for you. But don't be concerned. Just continue to act out your life. Your steps are ordered as long as you live righteously. When your final surrender comes, it, too, will usher in triumph for you and others."

Peter breathed deeply. "I'll glory to set the same example he set. The results of my surrender? I'll leave that up to the Almighty."

"One more thing, my son. The followers need you to be strong. Continue to show them you're wise enough to accept reality. But now you must go your wife! It is time for a moment of joy!" She reached into the pouch inside her robe. "Don't be offended, Peter. You know I love you, but my daughter need not be reminded of your fishing days. Here, anoint yourself with this scented oil. It will make a new man of you."

"Mother, you have grown so diplomatic. In years gone by, you might have thrown the scented container at me!"

"Ah, we were so alike," she laughed. "But, indeed— times have changed!"

Peter dabbed himself with the oil. His mother-in-law watched him approvingly.

"I am sad to say you can't stay long, Peter. The Romans and the Sanhedrin have been looking for you. You'll have to go into the hills of Bethany. We hear others are there.

"But first, be with your wife for a time." The old woman grabbed both his arms in assurance and pushed him toward the place his wife was working. "She has missed you greatly.

"Then follow your destiny. I know it will be an adventure."

Chapter XV.

Magnificence in Miniature

Duca could not sleep the night before the arrival of the third guest. In retrospect, their chance meeting in the bazaar outside the gates to the Temple seemed divinely inspired.

How did we find one another? How did that single voice leap above all the noise of the unruly crowd? I couldn't even see the tiny man. Yet he was drawn to me as if by a supernatural force.

Zaccheus had been debating with people in the crowd, businessmen like himself and ordinary citizens. The diminutive former Hebrew tax collector was forcefully espousing his belief in the Kingdom to come based on his recollections of the teachings of Jesus. His reedy, screeching voice and eccentric point of view cut like a knife through the marketplace—controversial, self-deprecating, mocking, with a flourishing, colorful speaking style unlike any other.

"Why do you even listen to me, good people? How can a man as puny and ugly as me even merit the attention of such an auspicious menagerie of the self-absorbed and self-pitying of our crumbling, occupied city?"

He glowed and grinned with pleasure, looking at the scores of people harking to his words from his slightly dangerous, strangely appropriate perch atop a chicken coop.

"Why, indeed, do you strange denizens of this city even give me this courtesy of attention? There is no doubt I offend many. Yet, you remain to listen. Why do you suppose that is? Could it be because there is infinite greatness in me ... and even in you, my dear sheep?"

Soon, the hecklers were drowning out Zaccheus' tirade, and the little man, satisfied with his own provocations, attempted to escape from the crowd with two companions. He leapt down from his makeshift roost, and made toward Duca in the shadows of a portico where he had been observing the scene.

As Zaccheus trotted on his little legs toward the eunuch, Duca's heart rose in anticipation. Suddenly, the merchant and the servant locked eyes. Zaccheus and Duca stared at each other amid the wave of people.

"Sons, stop!" demanded Zaccheus to his protecting boys. "The Lord bids me listen to this solitary soul. But I'm afraid you must be quick, young Egyptian! These poor ignorant souls are not at all ready to hear the exquisite wisdom I have so generously laid at their feet."

"I hope you can be of service to my master," said Duca. Something about the little man made him bold. "I sense great wisdom and power in you, sir."

"Your master's name?" inquired Zaccheus, as his much taller but not much better looking sons looked nervously over their shoulders.

"Joseph of Arimathea, Decurion of the Empire, and member of the Great Sanhedrin."

"The Magdalene was right!" Zaccheus shouted, startling Duca. "She told me I would find you here! The woman is uncanny, I tell you! I have been waiting for you for days, young man! You are Duca, are you not?"

The servant could barely speak. "You know of my mission to revive Joseph's spirits?"

"Yes—and I know Joseph of Arimathea personally! Although I cannot say for certain if he knows me. At any rate, I have already promised the Magdalene that I will do all I can for your cause. I feel I have a bit of a personal obligation to your noble master! We shall arrive tomorrow."

Duca marveled as Zaccheus disappeared into the crowd. This strange little man was unlike anyone he had ever seen. What gift of wisdom would he bring to the master?

Joseph was up early the next day, sitting on the protected veranda and gazing out over the city, inhaling the fresh morning air as a rare spring rain washed the dust off Jerusalem. The moist, green smell reminded him of his youth in Arimathea, when he and his friends would jump and frolic in downpours just like this one.

Eventually, the rain stopped, and Joseph began to grow impatient. Duca had prepared his master for a sunrise visit from Zaccheus. The day had long since begun.

When he finally appeared at the gate, sons in tow, the talkative Zaccheus insisted on endlessly examining Joseph's priceless statuary. He begged Duca for details about every single one of the unique brass, marble and copper oddments strategically positioned throughout the sprawling villa.

"Let us move along, kind sir," Duca said diplomatically, as he gently urged Zaccheus down the marbled hallway toward Joseph. "I'm sure my master will have even more details for your most inquisitive mind!"

"A thousand pardons, good assistant. My curiosity outpaces my manners. You're quite right. Joseph is ready?"

"I'm sure he is more than ready, sir," Duca said.

Joseph rose at the sight of the little man, and before Duca could finish making the proper announcement of his arrival, Zaccheus broke in with great enthusiasm.

"The Lord aptly taught that 'we shall know them by their fruits!' Indeed, Joseph, your success in foreign lands and your reputation at home abound—and they are perfectly manifested by this breathtaking abode! Your tales of the origins of your fascinating possessions would thrill my soul!"

"Well, yes. Naturally," Joseph responded, taken aback by the outlandish appearance and lively demeanor of Duca's latest guest.

"My master looks forward with much anticipation to your secret, which Mary has put such store by," reminded Duca.

"Ah, yes—I suppose my art history lesson must wait. That demanding, enchanting woman would certainly favor me with the severest of frowns if she thought I was wasting our dear Joseph's precious moments. Forgive me again! I am dazzled by my surroundings. So, I shall begin, no? I admit, the secret I have to share could make you richer by far than you are today, noble Arimathean!"

"Please proceed, Zaccheus." Joseph could not help but smile at the energetic, enigmatic little man.

Not only slight, but uncomely as well, poor man. Surely loved by his Creator—but who else could find such an odd creature lovable? Yes, Zaccheus is very small, but the same cannot be said for his nose! And the bubble-like growth on its end, like the knob on a tiny door, is impossible to ignore.

As they sat, Joseph gestured for Zaccheus to enjoy the fresh goat cheese, new wine, and pomegranates attractively arrayed on a table at his side. Zaccheus' sons were led away by another servant for refreshments of their own, leaving their elders in privacy, save for Duca and his quill.

Zaccheus ignored the food and turned his full attention to Joseph. There was magnetism in the little man's stare. "Now, at last, I can return the favor to this most enterprising of Jerusalem's merchants!"

"Favor?" Joseph was confused. He did know of Zaccheus, particularly through his former occupation as Hebrew tax collector, but considered the man the barest acquaintance. He could certainly recall no favor he had ever done for him.

Zaccheus responded quickly. "Joseph, I can see you don't remember me well." He joked, "It is shocking, considering my princely ways, handsome looks, and imposing stature! They generally assure a powerful recollection!"

Joseph smiled, appreciating his visitor's self-deprecation. "I do indeed remember you by sight, honored guest, but I don't recall ever having the honor of doing you a favor. Tell me, Zaccheus, of what do you speak?"

"I am he who ventured into the crowd, awaiting Jesus some time ago. You came to my rescue, Joseph.

"Though I'm not much to look upon, and though people thought I was a mistake at birth, the fact is I'm a living miracle! First a despised publican, today I am an esteemed tanner by trade! I am proud to call myself a happy husband and father. And proudest of all to preach the word of our Lord to all who will listen! All by God's grace!

"Did you not recall Jesus' surprise at discovering me in the sycamore tree? I was taking notes as he spoke words of wisdom on that hot summer day in Jericho. In fact, Jesus complemented my determination to hear the truth he was sharing. I was the one in the tree, good man!"

Joseph pondered his visitor's story.

I was in so many crowds during Jesus' ministry. I ignored so many people, trying to remain faceless and discreet among the masses, never wanting to stand out as more than curious. I was a coward following Jesus.

Zaccheus continued. "Your stress is clear to anyone with eyes to see! It is like a millstone around your neck, Joseph! How could you forget the Lord ordering me to climb down from the tree in haste? Don't you remember how shocked

I was, that the likes of myself, a sinner and ruthless confiscator, could be singled out by such as he?

"When he invited himself to my house, I was stunned. No, I thought, no—I'm not worthy of this. And the crowds cackled on about my honor—insulting my treetop strategy, my stunted frame, my sinful life, and my unbeautiful self.

"But my perch—precarious as it was—allowed me to hear and record every precious word he spoke! It would have been impossible for me to hear or see on the ground, as tiny am I, and ugly as a boar! Why, the crowd would have trampled me! And...it was you, dear Joseph, who came to my rescue!"

Joseph laughed, now, for the first time since he had returned from his cell. Of course! Now he remembered. Duca had only taken a few notes. He chuckled as well, simply happy at seeing his master brighten.

"Yes, Zaccheus, I remember now!" said Joseph. "You were frightened—rightly so—and couldn't free yourself from the prickly branches. You were so terrified of the people and the distance to the ground; you sat paralyzed in the boughs. Then, when Jesus declared he wanted to visit your house—well, you were in quite a predicament."

"Exactly! You, powerful and noble man, were with some of the Sanhedrin—and of that entire crowd only you heeded my cries. The others laughed and taunted me. When I dangled from the branch, you reached up and helped me down with your strong arms. I could have been seriously injured—not to mention even more humiliated, if such a thing is possible! It was a kindness I will never forget."

Taking a deep breath, Zaccheus reached for the crafted goblet of fresh wine.

"You honor me with the refreshing nectar of our rugged land, to cleanse my palate and loosen my already overactive tongue. I must not be dry. The words I have to share with you excite me—and they will certainly help you with your healing!"

Zaccheus' tiny hands reached for the soft cheese and succulent dates, which he abruptly began stuffing into his not-so-tiny mouth. Suddenly, the little man's voice was stilled—although his eating could not be called quiet.

It was all Joseph could do to keep from bursting out laughing.

While Zaccheus munched greedily, Duca spoke further of their chance encounter in the city.

"Master, I listened to Zaccheus as he debated his peers in the market—even the allegedly most religious and wisest who gather there. While many in the crowd reviled him, his words touched my heart. It was as if he were speaking to my soul. Naturally, I thought of you. I knew he had a deeper secret to deliver."

Zaccheus made very quick work of a surprising quantity of food. He wiped his mouth daintily with a napkin, and cleared his throat noisily.

"Now I can speak without the distractions of the flesh!" Zaccheus said.

"So, if you are ready, Joseph—let us begin."

Duca reached for his quill, ready to capture whatever the little man had to offer.

"I became a believer that day in the tree.

"Before that, whenever I had heard about the Nazarene, I simply scoffed that one man could espouse forgiveness, love, eternal life in a kingdom to come—and even a better existence on this side of eternity! How could he forgive our treatment under the Roman yoke? And what about those self-proclaimed holy men, yelping that they had all the answers? What answers? How torn apart our poor people are, caught between the lashings of the Romans and the posturing of our priests!

"Then, my friend, along comes an itinerant, penniless preacher, with words and ideas radically at odds with both our conquerors and our know-it-all rabbis.

"And what did he recommend? The turning of the other cheek!

"How astounded I was by him! His message and his attitude toward these earthly authorities were contradictory. Given whom he was going up against, I could only surmise his time among us would be short.

"But then, as I clambered above in the branches of that tree, he saw me — and my life changed in an instant!"

Zaccheus reached for his drink, gulped it down, and then slapped both his hands on his thighs. He smiled broadly, remembering the most profound moment of his life.

"What did he say that influenced you most?" asked Joseph.

"So many things," Zaccheus replied. "But here, this is something he said to me personally that day. Do you remember these words? 'This day is salvation come to this house, for he is also a son of Abraham.' Remember, Joseph?"

"Yes, Zaccheus — I do remember that."

"Ah, but it seems you have forgotten its real meaning, Decurion! You see, most blessed man of Arimathea, much like you, I let my hard experiences in life make me bitter.

"And yet, I had much to be thankful for. I was a prominent publican, but my actions were shameful. My father arranged the position. He was so concerned for my well being, misshapen as I am.

"And I have a beautiful, tall wife. But of course she's been blind as a bat from birth! How her friends and family discouraged our betrothal, a beauty wedded to a loathsome beast! Yet Miriam saw herself as defective as well, and feared no other man would want her. And she has given me healthy, tall sons! Poor, sweet sons — despite their fine stature, they more closely resemble me than her.

"And yet I was in misery! And I passed my misery along in every way I could. I was unkind to everyone. I was selfish. I was hard and cruel in my position as collector of taxes. Why should anyone else be happy while I suffered so—a victim of my own birth!

"I was so conflicted, unsatisfied, self-conscious, and jealous—until I was touched by Jesus' words that day.

"How could he consider me a son of Abraham? Abraham, the patriarch of all the Jews! Abraham, most blessed and beloved of God! How could a legacy so magnificent dwell in my stunted heart and body?

"But Jesus' words struck me with the force of absolute, undeniable truth. That was the power of Jesus. He spoke simple truths that none could see—yet none could deny once they were spoken! The Torah promises that I'm made in God's image, like Him in spirit. Who was I to deny the word of Jesus! It was unthinkable. My heart was forever turned toward the light. From that day forward, I saw myself as I truly am—a Son of God!"

"You were most harsh on yourself, Zaccheus," Joseph consoled. "Truly, our lord Jesus helped you very greatly."

"Yes. But you assisted as well."

"Me? How?"

"The moment I came to understand that my name belonged in the same breath with Abraham, the revelation of magnificent greatness in me came alive and began to grow. I reflected on it in the midst of the mocking and murmuring crowd.

"And then, as fear flooded in, trying to wash away that divine teaching—there you were! Looking so serious and proud, you took my hand as an equal and gently ushered me into Jesus' entourage, heading to *my* home! I knew who you were, so famous has your caravan business been!

"You see, Jesus sparked hope that even I possessed the power of God within. And then *you* confirmed his words by treating me like a deserving prince, a person of worth—as much a man as yourself!"

"You give me too much credit, Zaccheus. We are all equal in the eyes of God."

"Perhaps, but this story should be a reminder to you now. Duca and Mary have described your downtrodden spirit since the departure of Jesus and your good wife's death.

"I am here to encourage you to enter each moment with praise and thanksgiving. Not merely because of all the blessings you have received in your life, but because of what you have *in this moment*, in the deepest depths of your heart!"

"And what's that?"

"You have magnificence inside of you! Just like me— you're created in God's image! If that is true for me it is certainly true for you! Would you ignore Jesus' wisdom?

"If God cares for even the lilies of the fields and the birds of the air, is He not so much more concerned for our well-being—our magnificence? After all, we're created in His image! If we can focus on this great worth within us, and not the circumstances around us, we'll grow as beautifully as those lilies of the field."

Joseph noticed something strange. As Zaccheus spoke, animated and joyful, he no longer looked repulsive. Not at all. In fact, there was something undeniably attractive and compelling, an inner glow and vitality that shone warmly, about the little man. It was the same power that Duca had seen in the marketplace that made the people crowd around and listen to his passionate words.

"Shame on us if we insult our Creator by being suspicious of our worth in this world! No matter how small I may be, or grief-stricken you may be—there is no excuse for it, Joseph! I had to rise up out of my life-long luxury of self pity, and you must do that as well. Don't let your self-imposed gloom snuff out the greatness God placed in you.

"And this magnificence is not in the past or future, but right here, in this priceless present and eternal moment... now! We have every single moment of our lives to savor our uniqueness and greatness!

"You will understand these secrets. They will heal you. And when they do, generous Joseph, you must pass them on. That is the task our Lord has given you!"

"You've worked hard to overcome your past, Zaccheus," said Joseph. "You have gained much wisdom."

"But so have you, Joseph! Unfortunately, you've forgotten. But that's all it is—you have merely forgotten! Surely you can remember and live again!

"Look how greatly you shone after Jesus was crucified. It was you and you alone, my friend, who found him a suitable burial place. Only you, of all men in Judea, were in a position to do so. It required courage, enterprise, sacrifice and great presence of mind. That quality, that greatness, is waiting to awaken in you this moment."

"But much confusion and suspicion still surrounds those incidents," Joseph reflected. "They have cost me dearly—I still do not even know how much."

"That is out of your control, Joseph! Trust in God! Don't try to force a different future than the one he has so magnificently planned for you! Open up to the greatness within yourself. Don't contemplate the ghosts of the past. God guarantees your greatness—right now, in this moment and in this moment only! All that is asked of you is to realize that magnificence."

Joseph smiled ruefully. "You mention 'now' and 'this moment' almost as frequently as Mary and the fisherman."

"The fisherman—Peter?" Zaccheus inquired.

"Yes."

"I do believe I know the man. A true disciple! Slightly larger and handsomer than myself—am I correct?" Zaccheus chuckled. "But the magnificence inside Peter ... is exactly the same as in me. And in you, good Joseph!"

"Might this not be just another beautiful, yet fleeting thought? Will it not leave my tortured mind as quickly as it entered?"

"Of course—if you have no discipline, and if you are selfish! But neither of those traits is in your nature. It should be far easier for you than most!

"But you make a good point, Joseph—it takes work. First comes knowledge. Understanding takes effort! You must practice every day. When you feel your mind drifting back to the old ways, stop whatever you are doing for a moment. Feel the blood pumping through your veins. Attend to your blessed breath as you inhale and exhale. Invite yourself into the blessed present!"

"Yes, I've felt that over the years," confirmed Joseph. "But my tribulations keep dragging me back."

"Yes, problems abound. Such is life. But don't let these matters distract you from the wonderful miracle of your life. The Rabbi cautioned us there would always be tribulations!"

"Jesus honored you as a son of Abraham. But my loyal eunuch Duca is an Egyptian—no son of Abraham. Can he share in this legacy?"

Duca looked up in surprise. His master's concern for him was a flash of the Joseph of old.

"Duca is a wise young man, Joseph. I believe he understands the miracle of his life. He has his own cross to bear after man's attempt to maim him, and deny him life's pleasures. His lack of knowledge of our ancestors need not preclude his individual power. As much as you or I, he was made in the image of God!"

Duca, diligently taking notes, felt a wave of pleasure at Zaccheus' words. Made in God's image! It was an attractive thought.

"Joseph, if you crouch down low enough, no force but the one inside you can lift you up! Rise up I say! The physical act of shaking off your doldrums will force your mind in the right direction. When your thoughts and actions are aligned with the all-powerful force inside, your regrets from yesterday and concerns for tomorrow will be dwarfed by— your enthusiasm!"

"Enthusiasm?" inquired Joseph

"Yes! After all, how do you think such an insignificant speck such as I can go about the city with boundless assertiveness, encouraging all I meet? It's my enthusiasm; or as the Greeks would say, *Intheos. God within*: that's the true definition of enthusiasm!

"And this understanding came to me first in the tree, and then after you came to my rescue!"

"Dear Zaccheus, I fear you've exhausted me with your brave insights," said Joseph.

"I shall take that as an accolade." Zaccheus sighed. "In fact, I must admit I'm feeling rather tired as well. This is a good sign that I have given my all to share the full secret! I will leave you, good sir, to rest and ponder what I have said today."

Duca arose, massaging his tired writing hand. Tiny Zaccheus followed suit, taking his last swallow of sweet wine.

Joseph wearily stood. "I do believe you've amply repaid any small service I may have done you, tax collector turned tanner. Please come back with your beautiful wife and strong sons for dinner. Duca will make the arrangements."

Zaccheus brightened once again at the invitation. "And then, when you are restored to God's favor, you will honor me with a history lesson on your stone menagerie!"

"If that day comes I will praise God with all my might. I have been broken and filled with doubt these many weeks. But I will carefully consider your words, my friend."

After Zaccheus' departure, Joseph took to his rest. As he contemplated all he had heard, he entered into the peace of the moment. His sleep was sound and restful.

By that evening, Duca had organized his notes:

Zaccheus' Supportive Secret:
Recognize inner greatness

- **What is inside of you is greater than anything outside.**
- **Allow the miracle of your body—its functioning, the blood flow, and the preciousness of each breath—to bring you back into the present.**
- **Replace self-pity with gratitude; marvel at the opportunity to tap the infinite potential inside you.**
- **Problems shrink to insignificance when met by your inner greatness.**
- **Recognize the magnificence in everyone you meet.**
- **Know that in the moment, if you have done your best, all is well. Be still.**
- **Have faith that results of your actions will be better than you had planned.**
- **Obsession with self fuels impatience. Impatience cultivates despair.**
- **Patience is a positive by-product of tribulation.**
- **Live patiently for others and not for yourself.**

Chapter XVI.

Feminine Intuition

Seconds after Zaccheus entered his house, Miriam appeared at his side to greet the little man.

"Welcome home, my love."

"Ah, my dear. It's good to see you again. No matter how quietly I try to enter, you always manage to know I'm home…yet I somehow never see you coming."

The beautiful woman embraced her husband.

"You've had a long journey, dear. You need rest and refreshment. You seem troubled— was your time with the merchant fruitful?"

"Yes, love. I believe I have been useful. Once again our Lord has used a broken vessel to aid in the rescue of another. Please, do let us sit. It's true. I am tired. Jericho seems further from the Holy City than I remember from my wretched days as a tax collector.

"But you're right. I can hide nothing from you. It's more than the journey. I've been thinking all the way home without ceasing. There is something vexing me. Something I very much want to ask you."

Miriam knew her husband well. "Take my arm, dear Zaccheus, and let us sit together. I hope you don't plan to ask me to take over the food shopping," she joked.

"You are the light of my life," Zaccheus said, smiling at his wife's kind good humor. He took both her hands in his. "Miriam, there is something I don't understand. In truth, I never have. It troubles me now.

"We both saw Jesus perform wonderful miracles, not the least of which was changing my heart. But for all the time we were with Jesus, why—why did he not restore your sight?"

Miriam lifted her head to face the setting sun on that warm, late spring day in the hills outside Jericho. Her sightless but shining brown eyes stared, focused on things unseen.

The silence seemed to speak to the beautiful woman.

Zaccheus finally interrupted. "What do you see, Miriam?"

"I see an impatient man sitting next to me."

They both laughed. "Dear Zaccheus, search your memory. I've done so on countless occasions. Remember how close we were to Jesus, so many times? How we witnessed his healing the lepers, giving sight to others?"

"That's exactly my point. Why not you?"

"It's simple, really. I never asked. And neither did you."

"No—but it was our hearts' desire."

"Yes, Zaccheus, but his teaching is quite clear: 'Ask and you shall receive.'"

"So...we have ourselves to blame?"

"Perhaps. But I wouldn't use the word 'blame.' Dear husband, may I confess something to you?"

"Confess? You are pure and good and have always been. I have nothing to fear from any confession of yours. Please, go ahead."

"Well, I wasn't exactly joking a moment ago. I *can* see, even in this moment."

"Your humor abounds, Miriam—but like so many things in this life it seems to be over my head."

She laughed. "Your stature, as much as you regret it, and my blindness, as much as it frustrates me—they're not important! The spirit gives birth to all form. The flower, its beauty and fragrance, was once merely an idea in the mind of God. At its proper time and place, it manifested.

"God has given me powerful intuition. It is sharp as the eagle's eye. It doesn't detect color or form, but it does something even better. It captures the essence of whatever comes before me! You, for instance—it's your glorious spirit I see with my mind's eye, that brightens my day and gives me hope."

"You equate intuition to sight?"

"Yes and no. It's not the sight you and I yearned to have Jesus restore. But never forget— I didn't choose to reach for the hem of his garment."

"Didn't you want to see?"

"Of course, I would love to see. But my spirit tells me now is not the time."

"How could you be so content in your blindness, darling?"

"I simply glory in your magnificence, and mine! I see greatness in us all—as I'm sure you reminded Joseph.

"Can you imagine my regaining sight as a young, impressionable woman? Perhaps it would have precluded our marriage. Blind, I joyfully committed to what I could see. Your spirit! Beautiful, handsome, gentle, intelligent, passionate, kind and generous—in spite of your questionable reputation and physical form.

"You've just returned from the Arimathean's. Recall your conversation with Joseph. I'm sure his spirit leapt at the thought of his inner magnificence, forgetting the fear and doubt surrounding him."

"Indeed."

"Well, he was restored by your spirit—by your essence. Not your form! There in the world of unseen Spirit; all that is before us now has its conception there. It lives in that world, and there I am content to dwell!

"My Zaccheus, you know me better than anyone; please don't be offended with what I'm about to say.

"Here's my heart: My spiritual sight shows me truths even you do not accept. Take the Sanhedrin and even the Romans—I know how they make your blood boil. You see the snarls on the faces of the High Priests, their self-righteous raised eyebrows, their every movement betraying how closed their minds have been to the miracle that stood right before them.

"But me? While I perceive what you behold, I also see they are in search of truth. They seek God. They have taught us our blessed Torah and share what they understand to be the teachings of the prophets. Like us, they're sinners—as the Lord proclaimed. But I see into their hearts because their flesh does not distract me. They're trying to do what they believe is right, as frightened as all of us about the times we face."

"Yes, Miriam, you're blessed to not see them strut into the Temple, so sure of themselves. They're hard to love and respect these days."

"And the Romans?" she continued. "Zaccheus, what you see with your naked eye is truly ominous and dark. Murderers, torturers, rapists, and robbers! But my blindness forces me to look for the deep-seated good in their success— the magnificence in all you spoke of to Joseph. And so I also see creativity, hard work and a drive to excel."

"You truly see what I cannot," Zaccheus confessed. "And while you'll have a hard time convincing me of their virtues, your words strike me as true and wise. But, my love—are you honestly content in your infirmity?"

"That's my confession, dear husband. I pray you forgive me for it. I tell you from the bottom of my heart: My blindness has become my strength. I glory in it."

Zaccheus dropped his head. He felt himself once again being filled with the recognition of his wife's magnificence, and his own. It was truth: Miriam's blindness had been much more of a blessing than a curse in both their lives.

Of course Jesus had not restored her sight. Perhaps one day she would see. But the time had not yet arrived.

Zaccheus closed his eyes, wishing he could see things the way they were in Miriam's world.

All I can see is the face of Jesus.

Chapter XVII.

Joy in the Morning

The sun came up. It broke through dark clouds that had been dropping cool spring rain on Jerusalem for days. Duca, hurrying to an unexpected summons, opened the gate slightly.

He was shocked and confused to see a lone Roman soldier. The behemoth of a man, fully armed with long lance and the tightly fitting, plumed helmet of a centurion, was unfamiliar to him.

"Duca of the house of Joseph?" the centurion asked.

"Yes," Duca said. His abdomen tightened. Roman visitors were never a good sign. Now less than ever.

"I am here on assignment."

"Please, state your business, Roman." Duca tried to give his voice as much confidence as possible, but the sight of the man's gleaming spear made him weak in the knees.

The imposing young man simply shuffled slowly to his left, revealing a tiny, black robed woman who had been completely hidden behind him.

"I've been requested by Mary of Magdala to escort this fine lady through the perilous morning hours. She has come to assist in the restoration of your master, Joseph of the Sanhedrin. Her name is Martha. She is from Bethany."

133

The man turned and looked back down the muddy road, as though fearing he and the woman had been followed. "May we enter?" he requested.

Still baffled, Duca agreed. They stepped through the gate. Once safely inside, the guard stepped back.

"By your grace, I'll remain in the garden," the soldier said to the unimposing little woman. "When your task is complete, call for me."

"Of course."

Duca, still perplexed, guided the frail but sprightly woman into the house. She clearly welcomed the warmth emanating from the large reading room, a few steps from the house's entrance. Dampness from the rain clung to everything.

"Martha is your name?"

"Yes, please take my robe, and I'll explain."

The woman looked all around, observing with squinted eye the home's abundance of appointments—the tapestries, the statues, the ornate candles.

"May I sit? The journey from Bethany has sapped the little strength left in my legs. The past month has seen me working day and night."

"Yes, forgive my rudeness. Please rest here in Joseph's study," said Duca, helping her to a comfortable seat close to the burning coals that warmed the room.

As the woman relaxed, she breathed a heavy sigh and smiled contentedly. It was good to be in such a safe, comfortable and warm place. She looked up at Duca, who was still obviously surprised at her unannounced appearance. Despite his surprise, the young man had a graciousness about him that reminded the woman of another young man—the minister from Galilee.

She smiled warmly at the servant. "Duca, will you please sit with me for a moment? I have much to tell you and Joseph."

Duca was confident that Mary of Magdala would not have chosen a rescuer without careful consideration. "Of course, good woman. Please forgive my uncertainty."

As Duca sat, Martha leaned forward.

"Joy abounds in my heart to be of service to Joseph of Arimathea. His tithing to the Temple, his support of Jesus' ministry and the sincerity of his counsel confirms his worth to so many.

"Let me explain why I am here. I am Martha of Bethany, widow of Simon, and sister of Mary and Lazarus. For nearly three years I've toiled to provide comfort to Jesus and his followers."

As the slight woman readjusted herself, Duca noticed her boney hands and tiny wrists, dark circles under her eyes telling of years of commitment and toil to make others comfortable. But then the servant took note of a mysterious smile, so peaceful, that seemed to come directly from the lady's soul. There was a glow coming from Martha, something he had seen at times in followers of the Rabbi.

"Good woman, forgive me. I'm taken aback by the peacefulness of your countenance."

Martha chuckled like a little girl, a reaction that surprised the servant.

"I am a living contradiction, Duca. Countless days of fretting and laboring over the well-being of my family and our possessions is clearly painted on my face. And at times it's still saddled on my back, almost too heavy to bear. But the seed of joy blooms in my soul in each and every moment. I have been transformed—and it's time for me to speak to Joseph so that I may share the change that has taken place in me! Mary of Magdala tells me he's sorely in need of a resurrection in spirit."

Duca stood up. He was excited, now. Each visitor had given his master some relief, and this woman surely had something worthwhile to share.

"I'll fetch Joseph immediately. His heart grows more open to such teaching with each passing day. He's been in prayer in his bedchamber. Warm yourself. I'll retrieve him—and refreshment for your tired body and generous soul."

Moments later a perplexed but hospitable Joseph shuffled into the study, his white tunic seeming to light up the dark room. After the guests he had received so far, he had come to anticipate these visits as a balm for his still-troubled spirit.

To Duca's surprise, a smile briefly crossed Joseph's face as he greeted the little woman as an old friend.

"I could have never imagined the industrious Martha would be a guest in my home! How could she tear herself away from her selfless chores to visit with a tired merchant?"

"Good man, much has happened since you last supped in my home. I fear you've become like me—the way I used to be. I have come to reprove you for that!"

Joseph stepped away and looked at Martha carefully.

"Truly, good woman—a change has come over you. You look happy. Forgive me for saying so, but is it possible you have grown younger?"

Duca returned with food and drink on a large wooden tray. Martha helped herself to a handful of red raisins and set them on her lap.

Before the servant could assume a comfortable position to begin his writing, the guest spoke. Her lightness and enthusiasm were in sharp contrast to Joseph's memory of her worried, anxious presence in the old Bethany house.

"Joseph, you remember me. Never smiling, sternly focused on the cares of the day—all to help my family and their loved ones. I suppose my husband's sudden passing, my motherhood denied, my love for my siblings, and the young Galilean's mission convinced me it was my destiny to work every moment—to earn acceptance through my labors.

"There was no joy in my life. There was a fleeting feeling of accomplishment at the conclusion of my chores.

But along the way I got so frustrated. My beautiful young sister Mary would drop everything to be with our guests. She hardly ever helped me, because she was so determined not to miss a word of conversation."

"Martha, you were an outstanding hostess," said Joseph. "And Mary helped by putting guests at their ease."

Martha played with the raisins in her hand, as if counting them.

"She'd always be at the foot of Jesus," Martha continued. "And our home was always teeming with his followers—yet it's so tiny. All would be intent on the Rabbi, while I toiled away by the fire. When their business was over, it was my lot to restore order to the whole disrupted household! I was the one who was left to do all the work. As the days and weeks passed, all feelings of satisfaction left me. I was being taken advantage of! That was my constant thought."

"I marveled at your energy—but I could see that you were careworn," Joseph said.

"And that's why I am here, Arimathean!"

"What do you mean?"

"To tell you—to show you—I've been changed by God! Joy overflows in me, in this moment. It powers my days; I fulfill my destiny now, as opposed to waiting for future rewards—rewards that can never arrive!"

"A transformation!" Joseph gestured to Duca, "These words must not be missed, scribe." Joseph chuckled. It had been a long time since Duca had seen his master laugh. "When Martha would speak in the past, everyone would jump. Her industry and intensity always commanded respect. But look at you now, my dear—what a different story you're telling!"

"It is as real as the springtime rain that graces our lands outside. And it all began with my brother Lazarus."

"Of course," Joseph said. "Lazarus was a miracle. Jesus healed his sickness. I'm sure that must have brought enormous joy to your heart, Martha. Duca, did I tell you of it?"

"No, master."

Before Joseph could continue, Martha spoke. "Ah, Joseph, you're missing some important details. You have heard that Jesus restored Lazarus to health. But even so, there were events—remarkable events—which you apparently needed to see with your own skeptical eyes."

"It's true, Martha. I have sorely wished for the confirmation. But please—tell me more about the change in you."

"Oh, Joseph, the suicide of worry, the deification of work, the resentment that so often accompanies those illusions, and the fatigue that follows in their wake—all these things were pulling me to my grave. And it was happening in the midst of so much wisdom and grace!

"You know, like all the others, I fell in love with Jesus' teaching of love, forgiveness, commitment to a cause, the kingdom to come, and everything else. Peter, Matthew, and Judas walked away from their livelihoods to be with him. But I was unable to do that. It disturbed me so that many chores and tasks remained to be done, and I felt they were calling to me and to my pride! I couldn't bear the thought that anyone might think me idle. How blasphemous to not be industrious, I thought."

"I have felt that myself," Joseph admitted as he poured his guest a glass of new wine.

"My dear Joseph, even after Lazarus was restored, my old worries still rose up! That's how strong they were. I fretted when my sister Mary offended my frugality by breaking of the vessel of perfume, just to bless weary Jesus. Oh—I, too, had believed in his mission. But let's be practical and not do stupid things! I scolded her cruelly for her generosity."

"So your transformation did not come all at once?" Joseph asked, as Martha thoughtfully sipped her wine.

"No, old habits die hard. But after Lazarus was restored—that's when the change bore fruit in me. That day, I was reminded of the gift of joy that should be opened in every moment.

"You see, I was angry at Jesus! Yes, I was seething with anger, although I kept it bottled up inside me. He had come too late to attend to my sick brother. Oh, his teachings were soothing, but his band of friends was always so irresponsible—including my sister and brother! Never on time, always smiling, forever blithely going on about fulfillment of the scriptures!

"But who made the meals, and poured the wine, and swept the rugs? Me! And then Jesus finally arrived—too late to help my poor brother! God's gift to the world? Too late!

"Yet when I approached the Lord, looking for exactly the right words to berate him for his tardiness, what did Jesus do? He said the strangest thing. He claimed he, himself personally, was the resurrection! What could he mean by that? I was stunned."

"What do you think he *did* mean?" Joseph asked.

"My tired mind was in a whirl! I believe he meant time as we know it is not that important—that it's a delusion. We allow it to pressure our thinking, and that is wrong. In what way did my sense of time—my belief that he was too late—entitle me to rail against Jesus? I used my perception that he had come too late to deepen my hurt and anger, until I was ready to upbraid God himself! Jesus too late? Oh, my foolish heart!"

"What else could you have thought, my dear?"

"Even without the miracle—I should have stopped, even though my heart was breaking, and asked whether what was happening might turn out for the good. If our hearts are pure and not made anxious by our burdens, responsibilities and fears, even that which seems lost can be found.

"I was certain I had lost my brother to death. But Lazarus was never anywhere, even for a second, but in the hands of God! If God willed him to live, my brother's earthly existence would continue! It merely required the touch of wisdom and belief. Jesus showed me! All is possible if our minds are not stubbornly set upon darkness. All things are possible when we allow the light to overcome our dark expectations."

"You are saying much, Martha," Joseph stammered. "Please help me understand. I had heard Jesus cured Lazarus. But you say your brother was sick beyond all healing?"

"My friend, it is much more than that. My brother was very dead. The stench of death was on him. He arose in full health at Jesus' command."

Duca's eyes widened.

"Days had passed since he breathed his last. He had been in the tomb four long days before Jesus arrived!"

Joseph and Duca stared at Martha in wonder. Joseph knew of Jesus' miracles, but to turn back death itself—a wave of emotion passed through the merchant as he felt the old hope rise up in him, the hope that Jesus was truly the Messiah.

"Joseph, I can see you are touched by hearing this. And you should be. But I have a confession to make. If I had not been transformed, I would be too ashamed to say it.

"Even in the moment of this most incredible miracle, I resisted!

"Jesus laughed when he whispered in my ear resurrection was imminent. Would you believe my first unworthy thought was of the aloes, rose water, and expensive herbs my sister and I had anointed his body with! Yes—Lazarus was going to be restored—and for a moment my diligent, worrisome, and selfish being lamented over wasted money! How despicable!

"I think Jesus knew my selfish thoughts! Now I even laugh at myself to think such a sick thought was mine. But then, it occurred to me—and my heart was turned."

"What?"

"That the selfish, petty thoughts were not really *my* thoughts. They were simply something my busy mind entertained for the moment. An old habit—surely so much easier to cast aside than death itself! And when I realized I could change, I was filled with joy. Oh, if only I could describe the feeling that overcame me in that moment! Then Jesus spoke the words and Lazarus arose from the tomb in full health! From that moment to this, I have been a new woman!"

Joseph covered his mouth as he realized the enormity of what had happened.

"Oh, Martha—Lazarus was truly dead, then alive?"

Martha nodded emphatically, "Yes, yes! And all the worry and concern that had plagued my whole life—that I held onto with such a white-knuckled grip—I let it go. It turned to joy, and full of joy I witnessed Jesus' great miracle!"

For a moment the room was filled with silence.

"Perhaps your joy was rewarded with his resurrection, Martha," Joseph said, his brows furrowed in thought.

"Exactly! And it's that same joy that *you* must claim— make it real in this place and time."

"Joy in my life?" asked Joseph.

"Such gladness!" Martha continued, "How could our ancestor David have survived without singing hymns of joy in the midst of chaos—much caused by his own hand? Has not our God spoken through the prophets about turning mourning into joy; that a fool hath no joy; that Jesus encouraged our joy to be full; that no man can take away our joy, but in our ignorance, we can surely give it away?

"On that day of my brother's resurrection, a miracle beyond doubt, I decided to never again allow anything to take away my joy. I fought a fierce battle in my mind that day to embrace the lesson. But thanks to Jesus I won! Even when Jesus was crucified, I would not give up the joy of my learning!"

Joseph darkened. "But look what *did* happen, good woman. Jesus died, I went to jail, his body vanished, my wife died, and your life and even mine is still threatened by the Romans and the Temple courts. A fine set of circumstances!"

"And Jesus' own resurrection, Joseph; you know of that, do you not?"

"I've been in Pilate's dungeon over the disappearance of his body. I want to believe. But I cannot make myself feel sure."

"For you and others who have not seen, it must be hard to believe."

"You saw?"

"No, but after what happened with Lazarus, how could I doubt it for a second? And I've been with those who did see our Lord risen—and in their eyes I see joy, peace, love, resurrection, hope and power!"

"I've seen that as well," Joseph admitted. "When Peter visited, he was a different Peter than the moody, bullying fisherman I used to know. And poor little Zaccheus has little to be joyous about, yet joy abounds in him like a prize colt. And then there is the Magdalene. She radiates joy almost more than all the others combined."

Joseph stroked his beard thoughtfully. Martha's words carried a great deal of force.

Martha seemed to sense the shift in her host's attitude. "Joseph—joy can arise during tribulations. Life will be difficult. Nothing good comes easily. But you can be joyful—no one but yourself can rob that from you. Even the darkest evil can teach us and ultimately turn to good! And every evil will surely pass!

"If you must look back, don't stare—merely cast a quick glance and be done! Let your glances back at terrible times prove that good arrived the next morning. Sometimes it takes a while. That is a joyful thought, is it not, Joseph?"

"It is."

Martha smiled at Joseph. Despite his misgivings, he returned the smile.

"Joseph, I call it the 'blessing of dismay.'" Martha laughed at his confused look. "When you don't understand and are confused and dejected, let that be your motivator to cultivate joyful thoughts. Even the worst can turn to good for those who believe.

"Didn't Jesus tell us to 'walk in the light, just as he is in the light'? Expecting joy brings joy. That's the secret of resurrection!"

"Joy brings ... more joy?" Joseph asked.

"Yes! Be joyous! When the grapes of your life seem crushed by the evils of this world, add the ingredient of joy to each moment—and those pressings may turn into the sweetest new wine!"

Martha held up her goblet and took a modest but grateful drink. Joseph was a host who was known for serving his guests well.

Joseph brightened. Duca looked at his master and felt a rush of pride. Surely, Martha's inspiring words were having an effect. And this was a guest Duca had not even been expecting. These followers of Jesus seemed filled with wisdom—wisdom he was gratified to be capturing with his quill.

"I shouldn't have to remind a merchant as successful as you to be patient. Don't anticipate the worst. With time, as you keep cultivating joy, you'll surely taste that new wine in the morning. And with it will come a love and peace you've never known."

"Martha, you have surely changed from the careworn, cross woman I once knew," Joseph said. "But have you given up on work entirely?"

"Of course not! But now I don't anticipate its completion. I realized I've always loved to work—so now I simply enjoy each moment of every chore. It's the journey, not the destination, that brings meaning to my life."

"Ah, yes, that's how I led my caravans," Joseph said. He had a faraway look, remembering the different man he had been in the not-so-distant past. "I gloried in every moment then—even when the desert winds did their best to scatter my camels far and wide."

"I am certain that approach helped you become a great man. How did you forget?"

"Perhaps...I stopped believing," admitted Joseph.

"Stopped believing in what?"

"In anything. Abilities, accomplishments, God, blessings—even the hope of the young Rabbi's message of joy, love, and peace."

"Well, Joseph, thanks to your Duca, here, your joy is being restored. It will draw more joy unto it."

Joseph bowed his head. The truth seemed so close. For a moment he was humbled.

"Of course you're right. I have much to be thankful for."

"But, Joseph, don't tarry. Be joyful *now*."

She arose abruptly, taking a last grateful sip of wine. Then her short arms reached for a handful of dates. "With your permission, I'll share these with my escort."

"Oh, my Lord!" exclaimed Duca. "Joseph, I forgot to tell you of Martha's guard. It is strange, indeed—more so now that I have heard her words. It was a lone centurion who ushered her here this morning through the shadows of the city."

"That is not exactly true," came a strong voice from beyond the veranda. The figure of the giant soldier could be seen through the veranda curtains where he stood. "I'm not what you perceive, honorable Joseph. In truth, I'm but a guard of the Temple, in Roman disguise. And I could not help but listen to this most enlightening conversation."

Joseph rose and gestured for the stranger to enter.

"Please, join us. And forgive our lack of hospitality." Joseph cast a brief, reproving look at Duca, who rose to get refreshment to offer the soldier.

"Thank you, but I won't be able to stay," the soldier said. "We have to return from whence we came."

"Is not your life at stake to be with a believer—even one as frail and womanly as Martha?"

"Yes, more so than you know."

Joseph and Duca exchanged bewildered glances. Martha nibbled a date, smiling and seemingly detached.

"I'll explain more tomorrow when I become your next instructor."

"Truly, sir, you leave us with mystery upon mystery! Can you not tell us more?" said Joseph.

"Tomorrow you will know all. For now, let me simply leave you this spear. It is a gift from a real centurion—one who knows you well. Tomorrow I'll tell you of my relationship with him and the secret I must share."

The centurion handed the spear to Joseph, who took it reluctantly.

Looking to Martha, the big soldier gestured for her to rise. "Dear lady, let us be gone while the morning is still young. I must put on another disguise before the sun sets this day."

Martha rose, and Joseph rose as well. They faced each other. Though he looked less troubled than he had in recent days, Joseph was serious—but the sweet, contented smile had never left Martha's face.

"Joseph, be joyous," Martha said. "Your adventure continues tomorrow. For now, I bid you God's love and farewell."

While Duca walked the guests to the front gate, Joseph stood transfixed, alternately looking after his departing guests, and then through the sheer curtains dancing gently in the damp morning breeze. The cold spear in his left hand glistened as the sun forced its rays through the scattering clouds.

Martha's Supportive Secret: Joy

- **Cultivate joy—count your blessings!**
- **Joy creates more joy.**
- **Work joyfully, enjoying the process without focusing on the results.**
- **Being joyful now guards against dark thoughts.**
- **When you glance back, choose moments that can feed your joy now, never staring at darkness.**
- **If joy is present even in times of trouble, even evil can be turned to a good.**

Chapter XVIII.

Come Forth!

The next morning, Martha was doing what she did every day as the cock crowed—sweeping the entrance to the modest home she shared with her brother Lazarus and sister Mary. But there was a difference. Until recently, she never hummed a joyous song of hope as she began her daily chores. Lazarus awoke with a smile on his face at the sound of her happy, lilting voice.

By the time the two siblings greeted each other with a holy embrace in front of the fireplace, Lazarus could not help but ask what so many others wondered about Martha. "My sister, you work more heartily than ever before. But now it's with song in your heart and smile on your face. Is it due all to what you've heard from the city?"

"You mean about Jesus?" she responded.

"Yes."

"Oh, dear brother—indeed it is. But you must know it all began with your return to us!"

Lazarus cradled a wooden cup of fresh water in both hands, sipping it carefully as a glow came upon his face.

"You see," she said. "Your own joy at your new life is a beautiful thing!"

"Martha, it was unbelievable, so hard to comprehend, even today."

"Oh, Lazarus—I can't believe we've never spoken of it. While we're alone, before others begin arriving, will you please tell me more?" Martha led her brother to the fire and bid him to sit.

Taking a deep breath, her brother recounted his time bound as a corpse in the tomb. "Martha, there was no time. Perhaps it was a day, maybe a thousand years. I'm not sure. And I didn't care. There was no concern for time. Few words were spoken, but the understanding was infinite."

"Lazarus, who was there? Did you see mother and father?"

He laughed, "Calm down, dear sister. You will most certainly find out for yourself one day, as we all will!"

"Excuse my impatience."

"Yes, I could see our beloved parents. They waved to me from afar. But it was Abraham upon whom I was transfixed. Yes, it's true! Abraham, Isaac, and Jacob. His garments flowed, his skin smoother than I could have imagined. A countenance of peace and contentment. Strangest of all, it seemed as if he knew my time with him would be short!"

"How could you tell?"

"Well, in words and attitude, his introduction of me to the others seemed to say, 'Lazarus, tell what you've seen to those not yet here. And know our God is truth. His kingdom has come, on earth, as it is in heaven.'

"With those words it seemed as if the distance between where I was at that moment, and where our lives are today— well, the separation simply vanished. It became all one moment, all part of the same eternity.

"The joy in my heart was indescribable. I laughed at all the times I had allowed fear to disrupt the peace in my life. How selfish and stupid I had been! I had the feeling I would get a second chance to live more abundantly."

Lazarus paused again, staring at the cup, soothed by its cool, smooth surface.

"And so I have!"

Martha reached for his hand, "Please, brother, continue."

"All were smiling. Our parents seemed to be able to comprehend my thoughts. There seemed no need for us to speak. Silence was all around me. Then I heard a voice as if a babbling brook was flowing through my very soul, cleansing me from my head to my feet. And it spoke words I did not at first want to hear." Glancing to Martha, he reminded her, "Words which I know rang through Bethany as well."

"What were they?"

"'Lazarus, come forth.'

"I instantly knew it was my friend calling. He was firm, and the utterance seemed to invigorate all around me even more, as if they had anticipated his gentle command. As the words echoed in the canyons of my spirit, they seemed to rain on all of us like a warm spring shower gently kissing even the most fragile flower."

"Everyone heard it, including mother and father?"

"Yes, every son and daughter of Abraham! As if what was to happen would usher in for them even more joy; that my return to life as we know it was part of a plan that they were privy to; that they would benefit from it as well."

"Were you feeling anything, brother?"

"Yes. I, too, had anticipation of joy that the adventure would continue—but back in the life I had known. There seemed no time or walls between where I was and where Jesus wanted me to be. There was no hesitation on my part to see the Master, to do whatever I had to do to obey his command.

"I had no time to say goodbye. Suddenly I could smell the cloth wrapped tightly about my face, almost suffocating me!" Lazarus laughed. "Yes, I tore that shroud off quickly enough!"

"Brother, how we shouted and praised God when you walked out of the tomb!"

"Yes, I remember. It hurt my ears, so sensitive they had become. But the first thing I remember was seeing his face."

"Yes?"

"Jesus smiled at me. He said nothing. He just smiled. That's the story, Martha."

"Oh, my! How long it has taken for me to ask you. To think the tomb can't hold any of us down any longer.

"How can the realities of our days here disturb us? How foolish I was all these years—me and you, such brooders we were! Only our sister seemed to savor every moment, and we thought her our problem child!

"The joy of your return persists, in the midst of my chores which I now truly love. I'm so glad I shared the secret of this joy with Joseph of Arimathea."

They stood and embraced.

Lazarus reminded his sister, "But let us not forget the Lord's words: 'In the world there shall be tribulation...'"

Martha interrupted, "Yes, but 'be of good cheer, I have overcome the world.'"

The sun had risen. Minutes later some of the followers of Jesus, hiding in the hills, entered the humble dwelling by the back portal.

Martha's day of joyful serving had just begun.

Chapter XIX.

Eyewitness

J oseph could not sleep after Martha's visit. It wasn't her teaching that prevented his rest. In fact, he had set aside her wise words for now.

What consumed him was the moonlight glinting on the sleek spear standing in the corner of his bedchamber.

Why did the centurion give his weapon to this mysterious Temple guard? Why is it now in my home? How could such a young guard be so bold to think he can teach me with his wisdom? Ah, but I must trust the Magdalene—the truth of her helpers' words have struck me like so many arrows. What will this young man add?

Joseph finally nodded off just before dawn, strangely content despite his misgivings. His rest ended a short time later when birds chirping just outside his window awakened him. Their divinely orchestrated music, inviting him to rise and greet the day, reminded the tired man of the miracle of creation. Though the sight of the spear troubled him slightly, he smiled, recalling Martha's joyful transformation, and the promise she had offered: that a resurrection in joy might still be possible for him. He had a glimpse of that joy now, wondering at his Creator's humor in employing innocent sparrows to awaken a troubled man.

On recent mornings, he had scarcely noticed the daily concert. Today, he allowed himself to enjoy the simple, cheerful song of his early morning guests. Their happy chirping reminded him there were always new lessons to be learned—and yet another visitor today to help him with his healing. Truly, there were blessings to count.

Duca had long been awake, preparing for the guard's arrival. As he sat anxiously on the single step to the villa's entrance, he saw something unusual coming down the road. An infirmed man, dragging his right leg, was hobbling up the muddy pathway leading out of the city.

This man appears so strong, yet he labors to gain ground. His caped head is downcast, never looking up. Yet he moves steadily, so he must know where he's going. He's already limped a long distance from the squalor of the ghetto.

As he continued to watch the man, Duca's face lit up with a smile.

How could a man so disabled manage to come this far? It must be the Temple guard, once again in disguise!

With hands on hips, Duca met the enigmatic traveler as he stepped up to the gated entrance. Blooming spring flowers that bordered the gate greeted the seemingly lame man—as did a smiling Duca.

"Apparently you've fooled the masses on your early morning journey," said the servant. "But I'm afraid your disguise cannot fool me as completely as the one you wore yesterday."

A youthful, handsome head appeared sheepishly from within the coarse woolen hood, like a shy, humble turtle poking its head into the fresh, sunlit morning.

"I am sorry to hear it, Duca. My safety is not confirmed until I enter! Nevertheless I am filled with peace and most happy to see you!"

"Most ingenious and most brave sir, I would likely never have guessed if I had not seen you yesterday—and had not been anxiously awaiting your arrival! You are most welcome here—please, do come inside. I am most eager to hear your secret, as is my master."

"Well, perhaps I really should be concerned," said the inscrutable man. "Particularly if someone I've met just once has so quickly unveiled my disguise."

"Don't trouble your peace, sir," Duca assured him. "The circumstances of my youth have compelled me to be aware of all around me. I've always lived with suspicion." He guided his guest. "Here, step forward. I have rags to wipe the mud from your sandals and ankles."

With his tattered robe removed, Mary's latest secret-sharer explained his impersonation.

"The Sadducees and Pharisees speak of the coming Messiah, yet they regularly ignore the diseased and poor. What better way to remain undetectable to those on the lookout for me—even if we were to come face to face in the markets!"

Finished with the visitor's sandals, Duca stood to face him. "You are very insightful. And as I said, despite your size you would have fooled me had I not been expecting you."

"Ah, but I have a further strategy, Duca," said the man.

"Which I would most love to hear. But please, wait and also tell my master. He eagerly awaits you on the veranda."

Joseph greeted his latest visitor with open arms.

"The Temple guard is back. But in a very different guise. It seems he has fallen far in the world in one short day. I'm puzzled—but this mystery makes me even more eager to hear what you have to share."

Duca detected a rare sparkle in Joseph's eyes.

"Although we do know one thing about you, mysterious sir," Joseph continued. "And we are prepared! Duca, I believe the kitchen was very busy before daybreak. Am I wrong in believing you wish to fetch your specialty for this poor, wandering beggar?"

Duca smiled. "Oh, yes, I almost forgot the roast lamb that's been prepared."

"Ah, good sirs," said the big man, a smile crossing his own face. "I must confess—that is my favorite food."

"Martha of Bethany has made it part of her life's work to feed many followers over the years," Duca said. "As you were departing yesterday she whispered a secret to me. She testifies that you have the appetite of a lion for a lamb."

Suddenly, the man's smile faded, and he looked vexed.

"Oh, but there is one small problem. My disguise requires a gaunt, starved countenance if it is to be effective—I'm still working on that part. I should fast, not feast."

"Sorry, friend," said Duca. "Your starvation must wait for another day. We can't waste a good lamb, can we, Joseph?"

This time, Joseph actually laughed. As Duca went to fetch the food with a light heart, Joseph reassured his guest and encouraged him to sit.

"Duca's preparation is not only succulent, but perhaps a bit sacrilegious. Wait until you taste the Persian herbs that accentuate the best lamb of the Hebrews!"

Joseph settled himself and focused on his guest. "Please, young man, I am ready for your mysteries to be revealed. Please, tell me about yourself and explain these disguises."

Although he had been gone but a moment, a beaming Duca returned, leading servants bearing new wine and the succulent, steaming lamb. They quickly spread the delicious meal before Joseph and his guest. The other servants did there best to hide their surprise at the strange beggar sharing their master's rich hospitality.

"Enjoy," Joseph added. "But speak while you eat if you can. I am eager to hear your mysterious secret."

Wiping his hands after cleaning them in the wooden water bowls Duca had placed on the table before him, the visitor leaned forward to begin his dining. It took but a moment for the young guard to break his fast.

Duca picked up his pen, and Joseph sat back in his seat of woven Spanish myrtlewood. He was ready for the next secret to be shared as the messenger smacked his lips over the first savory bite.

"My birth name is David," he said between swallows. "My father is the Rabbi of Nazareth. My devoted mother has gone on to be with our ancestors. I was schooled to follow my father in the workings of our synagogue. I studied the Torah day and night. Knowledge, understanding, and wisdom were all that my father talked about."

The guard—David—paused to consume another chunk. "And then I left him."

"You abandoned your family?" asked Joseph.

"Yes and no. My father taught me well. All those days with him in Nazareth, and here in the Temple in Jerusalem, convinced me I must constantly grow through the acquisition of knowledge.

"But then I became intrigued by a voice I heard, calling in the wilderness. It was speaking a message of repentance. It was a subject I knew of, but had not heard my father lecture about in any great depth. It was a voice unlike any other. His name was John the Baptist."

"Oh, my!" Joseph said. "John, the rebellious, wild cousin of Jesus." He looked to Duca to clarify the reference to the Baptist. "Duca, according to my peers in the courts and in the Temple, John's was an errant cry."

"According to my father as well," agreed David. "So much so that he became concerned for my very sanity. He arranged for me to go to the Holy City to enlist as a Temple Guard."

"But, David, how may I learn from this experience?" probed the merchant.

"Mary of Magdala has shared the secret of the power available to those who live in the moment—as she proclaims to all who will listen. Yet this precious knowledge that sounds so simple is sometimes difficult to achieve. My secret will help you keep returning to the priceless present moment."

"And the secret?"

"It is one you have most likely practiced on many occasions." The big man took a large bite of lamb, and sat back contentedly. "It is simply this: you must seek knowledge in every encounter, from everyone you meet. No doubt when you were brought low by circumstances, you turned your attention inward, and lost your habitual, genuine interest in others."

"It is true," Joseph admitted. "Although these visits are helping greatly."

"Yes, I'm sure they are. The knowledge you are gaining—thanks to the Magdalene and your faithful servant—is helping you come back into the present. And by seeking knowledge in each encounter in life you will surely be drawn fully into the moment. And you can also begin to tap the infinite power in and around all of us."

"In and around us? Which is it, young man?" asked Joseph.

"Both. Our scriptures say, 'Knowledge is power, and my people perish for a lack of it.' But it's not enough, Joseph. That knowledge must be tested—judged against other sources—to validate it. Once it passes the test, it gains power—the power of truth. And once we know something to be true, that knowledge begins to be converted into understanding."

"You seem much like a teacher yourself, son of a rabbi."

"I return everyday to the Proverbs and the Psalms of our beloved Solomon and his father, my namesake, David. And I do trust my father's counsel—because his source was the Torah. The Godly order shows that knowledge, confirmed as truth, converts to understanding. Every day my father reminded me: 'Seek first to understand.' At that point you're willing to stand behind that information and proclaim it to others!

"He showed me something else. Growing from knowledge to understanding requires a respite, a retreat, a reflection. The knowledge is a seed that has been planted. It takes time and patience to bear fruit. In the peace of an unhurried and undisturbed moment, understanding can steal upon one, sometimes in a surprising form.

"But there is more, Joseph! Because beyond knowledge, and on the far side of understanding, lies the greatest blessing: wisdom! Wisdom grows when understanding is tested and put into practice. Because it's rooted in experience, wisdom is skillful in its nature. This is why the wisest among us always seem so real—because experience has made their understanding reflexive and natural.

"Knowledge, understanding, and wisdom," David summarized. "They are the three stepping stones that can ford the most raging stream. And by the way, dear sir, I've heard you have long been known as a man who has followed this path many times in your life, gaining and sharing much wisdom. Your reputation is that of a man with a hunger for learning."

"It seems I've lost my appetite, and my way," admitted Joseph. "But why did *you* leave the rabbinical quest for knowledge to follow the rowdy Baptist?"

"Allow me to explain it in the terms I just described. The Baptist offered a new kind of information. While it was not entirely contrary to what I had learned, his delivery had urgency and a fury that was far different from anything I had ever seen. For my father and his friends, that made him an adversary to the established order. I considered it rather healthy."

"Healthy?"

"Yes. As I said, the Baptist was different. And what is difference but something one simply has not seen before? New knowledge! He aroused my curiosity. The rabbis' discomfort suggested willful ignorance on their part—a preconceived notion of how things ought to be. In my mind, confusion, disagreement and adversity should drive you into the moment to seek more truth! Nothing is a richer source of knowledge than that!"

"So what did you learn?" Joseph was anxious for more.

"I learned that this seemingly mad man was foretold in our ancient writings. And his task was to clear the way for *someone else* who would eventually follow him!"

"You're speaking of Jesus. You became a member of his sect, then?"

"Not directly. But after being assigned to guard the Temple, I had a surprising amount of time to study, and more freedom to pursue studies that personally interested me than when I was at the synagogue.

"My father heard I had shown an interest in the Baptist. One Sabbath he called me back to Nazareth to answer his fears about my alleged rebelliousness. I was in our place of worship when Jesus took hold of the scriptures and scandalously proclaimed he was fulfilling the promises of the prophets. My father and the elders chased him to the border of our town!"

"And how does this fit into your being here?" asked Joseph.

"If you must know, I also ran after Jesus as he departed from Nazareth—but my hope was to catch him to question his claims."

"Did you?"

Duca's head lifted up, as eager as Joseph for the answer.

"No. Sadly, I never was to meet him," answered David. "But my curiosity was aroused to a new pitch. Now I was hungry for knowledge! I continued to study and to listen to all who had heard him in hopes of gaining knowledge, turning it into understanding, then claiming it as wisdom to share with others—to become skillful with it.

"I was driven. How could my father, a teacher, seek to stop my pursuit of the truth? Why would he block me from listening to new knowledge from John the Baptist and the carpenter's son from his own village?"

Duca noticed Joseph was leaning forward, intensely interested in the young man's words.

"What's the answer?" Joseph asked. "What happened then?"

"Two things. My moment-by-moment concentration on gaining and testing knowledge gave me power and influence I had not had before. This was a surprise to me, but I welcomed it. The past was quickly fading, and I had no use for the future. My quest was for now. And in that search I found satisfaction, fulfillment—and freedom. As long as I remained present in the moment, I knew my quest for knowledge, understanding and wisdom could never be denied."

"The second thing that happened, David?" asked Joseph.

"A miracle. On the night of our Sabbath more than a month ago, a messenger from the Sanhedrin came to our guard chamber and commanded three of us to go, fully armed, to your tomb."

"You were one of the three?"

"Yes. I hardly knew the meaning of my assignment until we arrived at the garden. I didn't know of Jesus' crucifixion, so quickly did it happen. When it was explained to us, I saw our job that night was an important one."

"Why?"

"Because by procedure, if any guards were placed they should have been Romans, not us. Pilate was fearful of some kind of disruption from Jesus' followers and did not want to show himself inept. Caiaphas and the Sanhedrin, let alone

Vitellius and the other Roman officials above Pilate, all the way to Caesar himself, might have berated the procurator had any sort of untoward incident occurred.

"Using Temple guards was a brilliant solution. Just as the Pharisees had forced Pilate to condemn Jesus, so he forced them to take responsibility for the aftermath!"

"And?"

"Pontius Pilate had greater foresight than many give him credit for. What happened is the miracle that some predicted and others feared."

Joseph nodded thoughtfully. "If I know my friends at the Sanhedrin and in the Temple well enough, your failure to stop what transpired puts you in great peril."

"Well, that night I and my fellow guards did our job well, alternating sleep so that one of us was awake all the time. And it was I who was standing watch when the stone began to roll back."

"You—you saw someone move the stone?" asked Joseph.

"No," David quickly responded. "It simply began to move. And a light emanated from the opening—so bright and warm that it blinded me. For a moment I was frightened. But then, as the heat surrounding me seemed to penetrate my every pore, I simply fell to the ground, as if slain with a painless, hot thrust to my heart. But my eyes remained opened, not focused on the light, but on the darkened Holy City sleeping beyond the garden and down the hill."

"You did not see anything?"

"I saw only what was in front of me when I fell: the city. I sensed its people were lost, helpless, and doomed."

"And then?" asked Joseph.

"And then I heard a voice command me to awaken others with some kind of message—one at first I could not discern."

"Whose voice was it?"

"I don't know. Then I fell asleep.

"When I awoke I heard the voices of women approaching. The sun was up, and the other guards were gone. I was very afraid. I fled over the garden hill, only to be captured later by cohorts of the Court. They interrogated me with the other two.

"I told them the truth. Rather than punishing me, they gave me and the others gold to remain quiet. I don't know why. I have since heard they regretted their actions, and they seek us again."

"You took the money?"

"Regrettably, I did. But the money bought me time."

"Time for what?"

"I now have a purpose. Yes, I took their money to keep quiet, but I can't be silent any more. The sleeping, doomed city that night—I must share with its people what I've learned. And other cities. I must pass my knowledge, under-standing, and wisdom on. I'll give the money to the poor, change my disguise regularly, and await my final destiny."

"What do you mean?"

"The ancient scriptures are plain: 'The steps of a righ-teous man are ordered by God.' Every step I take ushers me closer to my ultimate reason for being. By being lost in the moment, I'm fulfilling that destiny now. As I search for more knowledge, I come ever closer to discovering that which I'll share with others—just as I've been doing with you."

"Yes. Much knowledge has been given to me these recent days. It has not yet turned to understanding, but I feel it stir-ring in me."

"Joseph, the brilliance that is your life must not be dimmed by your current sorrows. Continue to learn, to seek out the truth. Pursue it in every moment. Then pass it on to others. The Dead Sea passes nothing along. It has killed all that once inhabited its space. God forbid you should become a Dead Sea."

"David," Joseph said. "I come close to understanding how learning in each moment can bring power to all we do. I do have a strong memory of it in my own life. But the spear, good man, explain it to me, please!"

"Yes, Joseph. Forgive me. The lance is the gift of Longinus to you. You may remember him as the Roman centurion at the cross of Jesus who assured the Galilean was dead. If you were to have the body, Pilate had to guarantee the young rabbi was no more."

"How could I forget the young Roman? Duca, could we have done it without him?"

The humble servant slowly shook his head in silence.

"Yes," Joseph continued. "The soldier thrust his spear into Jesus' side."

"Well, that lance is now your possession," announced David.

"Why would I wish to possess such a vile weapon? Have my deeds been that harmful?"

"Joseph, give yourself more credit. You possess the spear now for several reasons. Longinus has become my friend. His life has been changed—he is a follower, Joseph! He wants you to know he's convinced his act of obedience was part of our blessed scripture's fulfillment. He wants to encourage you to believe equally in your own part, as you should in every moment of your life."

"But he's a Gentile, a true Roman. What does he know of the meaning of Jesus dying on the cross?"

"True, he knew nothing of our Scriptures. But in the days after Jesus' death, his heart ached. He sought after Jesus' followers—he was lucky to find the Magdalene. As she and others gleefully spoke of Jesus' bones not being broken and the mystery of the empty tomb, he sensed that his cold act had been preordained! When he heard of your plight, he believed a Decurion of the Roman Empire such as you, and one so close to Jesus' last moment, would cherish this spear, used to fulfill prophecy."

A silence rushed into the entire villa like a flood. The morning breeze vanished, as did the chirping of the birds. There were no ceremonial trumpets sounding from the Temple. Even the hum of the ancient city seemed to die down in the heavy air.

Joseph sat long, quiet in thought. Finally, he spoke. "My boy, you have given me much to think about. But, now I'm concerned. What will become of you?"

The man smiled. He seemed peaceful and calm, despite the danger he faced.

"Well, I'll have to start my fast again tomorrow. I'll change my appearance as often as I need to, buying time. I'll continue to study and listen to others, and share whatever knowledge and wisdom I have. I anticipate a call is coming to me from on High—to walk a different pathway in my life.

"Yes, this all I'll do unless the Sanhedrin sends me to an early grave."

"You don't seem at all afraid," Duca said.

"Fear invades my soul from time to time. I'm no different than any man. But I know it's not of God, and therefore I rebuke it. Then the peace we have experienced this morning rushes in."

David stood.

"I must go. Your hospitality has been most appreciated."

As Joseph stood, he stretched his tired muscles. The intense exchange had taken an emotional toll.

Joseph thanked David. "You have much at stake, and you risk all in the name of knowledge. Your father taught you well."

"Thank you, Joseph. What excites me most is not the knowledge—but the understanding and skillful wisdom that follows. This search keeps me firmly in the precious moment, just as Mary of Magdala said it would. She's taught me well, and I am most happy and honored to pass it on to you."

The three men embraced, and David left the villa, his tanned face absorbing the midday Jerusalem sun as he began to hobble down the muddy road back to the Holy City.

Duca worked all afternoon rewriting his notes for Joseph's review that evening.

The Tomb Guard's Supportive Secret: Knowledge, Understanding, and Wisdom

- **Knowledge is power.**
- **Use every moment and every meeting to gain knowledge.**
- **Test your new knowledge against what you know and believe.**
- **Tested knowledge becomes understanding.**
- **Freely share what you understand for the benefit of others.**
- **Skillfully shared, understood knowledge creates wisdom—and releases the power of God's knowledge into the world.**

Chapter XX.

Family Reunion

అుఖ్రుహ

After his return to the city, David decided to continue on the long journey to Nazareth in Galilee. His mind was full of thoughts of his aging father, and his heart yearned to see him again.

It had been almost three years since that fateful day in the cramped temple in his Nazareth when Jesus proclaimed he was fulfilling prophesy. David's conservative father and the others in attendance gasped at the young carpenter's boldness.

David could not forget Jesus' reading from the ancient book of the prophet Isaiah:

"The Spirit of the Lord is upon me because he hath anointed me to preach the gospel to the poor; he hath sent me to heal the broken-hearted; to preach deliverance to the captives; and recover of sight to the blind; to set at liberty them that are bruised; to preach the acceptable year of the Lord."

To add even further to the tension in the house of God, the upstart son of Joseph the carpenter sat down and calmly added, "This day is this scripture fulfilled in your ears."

Even I cringed when I heard him speak of prophetic fulfillment, thought David, as he limped toward Nazareth in disguise. *Because he was never around our hometown much, I had not befriended him. In fact, he was a mystery to us all. Then to do this in my father's temple? I can't forget how they chased him out of the building. I thought they would kill him there and then!*

But that was not his destiny.

David was exhausted when he finally arrived at the tiny hut behind the temple where his widowed father lived.

"Who is there?" asked the tired, nearsighted rabbi.

"It's me, father."

The rabbi rose up like a young man, surprised but pleased to see his son.

"Father, it is me, pretending to be another—but for a good cause. Our time apart has been too long."

They embraced. The Rabbi of Galilee knew nothing of his son's most recent adventure.

"These rags—what does it mean?" asked the old man. "Has the Temple removed you from your post? Now I'm concerned. Come, sit. I'll fetch cold water."

"Yes, father. We should sit. I have a most remarkable story to share."

As his father sat in concerned silence, David recounted the details of the empty tomb. His father knew well of Jesus' execution. His hometown was divided on Jesus' guilt as a blasphemer. But the case of the missing body was only being whispered about by some of the local Nazarenes.

"My son, your safety is at stake," concluded the rabbi. "You say the Temple has paid for your silence. But I fear they may repent their action. If all is as you say, your *permanent* silence is their objective—and if you do not intend to keep quiet, you are in serious danger, and there's nothing I can do to keep you safe."

"Yes, father. But I'm not seeking safety with you. I only wish to test my observations and conclusions."

"About what?"

"About what the scriptures have foretold. About what has just happened."

"Please, David—you and I have argued enough about this. Those arguments drove a wedge between us. Your precious mother died in sadness because of the division in our family. I will no longer try to sway you from your beliefs. But we should not engage in another useless and painful discussion. Not again."

"But, father, I've studied without ceasing—just as you have encouraged me over the years. My studies and my personal experiences have given me many priceless, precious moments of sacred awareness—a consciousness of the living spirit. I believe we may be seeing Holy Scripture fulfilled before our very eyes."

"And?"

"You should no longer ignore the preacher from our own town."

The elderly rabbi took a long sip of water.

"He has fulfilled prophecy."

The rabbi looked at his son and stroked his long beard thoughtfully.

"Father, just look to our Prophet Isaiah from so many years ago."

"Indeed," responded the rabbi quickly. "You are correct, son. That was so long ago!"

David looked at his father reprovingly. "But, father, as you have told me so many times, God's word is timeless."

The old man took a deep breath. "Forgive me, my son. Perhaps I'm getting old."

"Father, you taught me that Isaiah spoke of the arm of the Lord being revealed. He prophesied that the coming one would not stand out as handsome and powerful, but be more like a tender plant. You remember Jesus as a youngster. He was quiet and unseen."

"Yes, his mother Mary was a good woman, and Joseph his father—one of our most faithful tithers. The boy himself was quiet and attentive."

"Isaiah goes on to write how the One would be despised and rejected. He would be imprisoned, wounded, and then killed. He would die with thieves, yet be buried with the rich! This all came to pass, father! Jesus was condemned with thieves, never even accused of being a man of violence or deceit! And he was buried in Joseph of Arimathea's own tomb—you must admit that was a strange thing that came to pass!"

The father interrupted. Despite himself, he was getting caught up in the old argument with his son.

"Strange, yes. But I hope you don't base your belief he is the One, the Christ, the Messiah, based on this alone!"

"You're right, father. That would not be enough. But there's so much more. I have studied the scriptures line for line. Jesus fits every promise from Genesis to our minor prophets."

"The scriptures promised the Messiah would deliver us, David! We're still being persecuted! And he's dead. What answer did he have for us?"

"To believe in the Father. To know He's a loving God. To understand that we can be saved in this moment if we allow a new birth to come about. To be humble and to inherit the earth. To love, expecting nothing in return. To look to this day, not yesterday or tomorrow. To cast our cares on God, and not carry them ourselves. All of this he said and more!"

"David, I am so glad you are here. And I am proud to hear you're reading our scriptures daily. But I cannot forget the rebelliousness of that fellow, Jesus. You give him too much credit. And perhaps you've not asked the most important question of all."

"What is it?"

"Was he a liar?"

"Father, I've searched my mind, my spirit, and the scriptures for that answer."

"And what have you concluded?"

"After everything I read I became very nearly convinced. But after what I personally experienced at the tomb, I no longer had any doubt. How could I? Jesus is who he said he is!"

Silence engulfed the room. The rabbi stared at the dirt floor below him. David awaited a response. It finally came.

"And now he is gone. So how can I determine the ultimate truth of who he really was, my son? Go ahead, you tell me."

"Father, continue to search, with hope, faith, and love—not by being judgmental. Savor each moment of new learning like a succulent morsel of mother's finest fare after a week of fasting. When peace overwhelms you—when you have taken your fill—stop! Accept each day's revelation; embrace each day's teacher.

"Then take a step. Test the knowledge. If you understand it to be true, share it with others."

"But how will I know I've uncovered eternal truth?"

"You will experience profound peace in that moment. The peace of eternity. The peace of God."

"Have you spoken this way to others, David?"

"Many, father."

"And the result?"

"For me? Peace. For those I have spoken with? Only time will tell."

Chapter XXI.

A Widow's Lament

Duca found it hard to rise. Lying in his bed in the early dawn, it was not the latest secret that dominated the servant's troubled mind. It was the hefty spear David had left behind.

First, Mary returned the burial shroud my master provided for Jesus. Then David delivered Longinus' shining weapon, the one that pierced the Galilean minister. Two unmistakable symbols of the evil days Joseph is struggling to put behind him. What good, meaningful reason can there be to have these dark things? David's words confuse me.

Duca was finally roused by a violent knock at the front gate. He hastily draped a silk robe over his night clothing as he shuffled out into the gray dawn. An innocent-looking youth, breathing heavily, stood there with a small roll of parchment in his hands.

"Mary the Magdalene ordered me to deliver this note to you!" the breathless youngster exclaimed, looking over his shoulder as though frightened.

Duca quickly unfolded the coarse parchment and read the message silently:

Dear Joseph and loyal Duca: Your next visitor bearing a secret will arrive alone. Please welcome her. All have shunned her. I know her plight better than anyone. Remember, Jesus drove seven demons from my own body. I have been with her every day since the tomb was found empty. Her wisdom, if heeded, will settle your master into the moment and further return him to his destined call. She will appear from the darkness of dawn tomorrow, as the cock crows.

Duca thanked the messenger. Although he offered him refreshment, the youth shook his head and departed immediately, trotting back to the city as fast as his thin legs would carry him.

Later that day, Duca informed Joseph the next visitor would arrive in the morning. Joseph seemed disappointed at the wait, and humbly approved with only a nod — which suggested to Duca that progress was being made. Joseph wanted more. And he wanted it now.

The old cock greeted the next morning with a hoarse, tentative crowing that showed his age. Duca had been waiting at the gate since long before sun-up, and as the Magdalene's messenger predicted, just as the last crow faded, a tiny woman emerged from the early morning gloom. A heavy, oversized cloak accentuated her frail, stooped appearance.

She seemed to struggle under the weight of a cloth-covered object she embraced with both arms. As she shifted it to her left hand to greet Duca, she lost her balance, and Duca reached out to keep her from falling.

"Thank you, young man. You — you must be Duca," the woman stammered. "You know my new friend, the one who encouraged this visit."

"Yes, I've come to know the Magdalene well. Please come in. Welcome to the house of Joseph of Arimathea."

The woman shuffled through the gate and through the garden, looking neither right nor left. When they entered the vestibule, she strained to stand erect. She took a deep breath and spoke softly to her host.

"I enter humbly, with regret in my heart. I come with a lesson I'll share with anyone who will listen. My blessed mother taught me a powerful secret. I carry a heavy burden of guilt, because I was unable to impart its wisdom to my late husband. And it may have made a difference.

"I am Jude—widow of Judas Iscariot."

While Joseph had shared little with Duca about the ministry of Jesus over the years, the young Egyptian knew about Judas. As a successful merchant, Joseph was originally enthusiastic about Jesus' enlistment of the analytical Iscariot as financial advisor, treasurer, and business planner. Judas had been zealous in his anticipation of the liberation of his people. His support of the young minister from Galilee was aggressive and consistent. Joseph liked loyalty in a business ally.

But from the time of the final Passover supper shared by Jesus and his disciples, reports circulated of an altogether different Judas—a vile betrayer, selling Jesus to his enemies for few handfuls of silver.

And now Judas was dead—a suicide it was said—and he was mourned by none of Jesus' followers.

His widow would not normally be a welcome guest. Only Duca's ever-growing admiration for the Magdalene's judgment overcame his prejudice against the betrayer's widow.

"Woman, I'm mystified by your potential role in resurrecting my master's spirits. But I have faith in your sponsor."

"Faith will be sufficient. I will not disappoint. Joseph must not make the same mistake my husband did."

"With respect, I cannot imagine my master ever sinking so low," Duca said.

Jude shifted uncomfortably with her burden.

Immediately, Duca wished he had not spoken so coldly to the distraught, humble woman who had come to help his master. As if to make up for his lapse in courtesy, he asked, "May I take your package?"

"No. Thank you. I want to present it to your master myself," the widow said. "But you may take my robe."

Duca helped her remove the heavy garment, far too large for her. Then he led her into Joseph's library, where there was a warming fire raging. Although there was no visible smoke, Jude began to sneeze uncontrollably.

"It's the burning wood that tickles my nose, good man," she stated apologetically. "May we sit elsewhere?"

"The morning chill on my master's porch will not distract you?" Duca asked.

"If you'll return my husband's robe, it will continue to comfort me. Will the Arimathean object to our meeting outside?"

"Oh, no, Joseph loves the clean air at daybreak. He often spent mornings outside with his wife, God rest her."

Joseph entered, wincing slightly at the reference to his beloved Sarah. Still, he walked upright, with a firmer tread than he had in recent days, and as he looked at his latest visitor, he noticed her stooping, uncomfortable posture. She did not glow with happiness or enthusiasm. For once, Joseph was possibly in a better state than one of his rescuers!

"May the God of Abraham, Isaac, and Jacob be with you, woman, on this gracious morning."

"Master," Duca hailed him, "Your countenance has brightened, and your words brim with life. I'm pleased."

Joseph gave a sad smile and reached for the widow's hand. "Who has Mary sent today to aid this broken-down old caravan master?"

"Your honor, while I bring a secret to aid you, the miracle of rebirth appears to have already begun its work in your spirit. My faith is uplifted, for I still have much to learn myself."

"Please, dear lady, sit. Duca will bring honey, cheese, and warm bread for your comfort."

Jude seemed grateful to relax on the marble, open-aired veranda, although she did not smile. She placed her package on the small table beside her. Thankfully, the morning sun soon blessed their bodies with warmth. The day promised to be bright and clear, the recent rains a thing of the past.

Jude wasted no time. She looked at Joseph directly and began speaking.

"With the crucifixion and burial of Jesus my life ended—or so I thought. My husband was one of his disciples."

"Then I would know of him," Joseph said.

"Yes, you would. He was Judas of Iscariot."

Joseph's face paled. His recollection of the days of Jesus' ministry and Judas' support raced through his mind. And then the strange events seemingly foretold by scripture, leading up to Judas' tawdry betrayal of Jesus—ending with the Iscariot's grotesque suicide. It was a fitting end in the minds of many.

"Yes. I am Jude. His childless wife."

"Woman, excuse my dismay at your presence, but you must explain further."

Duca returned. Jude ignored the plate of cheese and hot bread, continuing her explanation.

"When my husband joined the Rabbi's followers, he was so excited. Every time he returned home he would read to me the Torah passages that foretold of the coming Sent One of Israel, who would give strength to our people and conquer the occupiers. I was convinced Judas' ability as a planner and money manager would surely support this great endeavor."

Joseph interrupted, "His belief in Jesus and his enthusiasm—they seemed genuine to you?"

"Indeed."

The woman was now wide-eyed, remembering her husband's initial involvement with the young rabbi.

"My Judas was so unlike the others. Not only was he from Judea, different from the Galileans, but his mind was that of a mathematician. The others in Jesus' group were mostly uneducated. Not that his intelligence was superior—but his analysis of the young preacher's purpose was more detailed and scripturally-based. He was a thinking man.

"My husband fully recognized the need for a leader to come forth to defend the Jews against the Romans. He was convinced Jesus was that person. In the early days, when he arrived home after weeks with the others all over the countryside, he could hardly sleep, so certain was his belief he was aiding the true Messiah.

"But all that changed when Jesus began to speak of his own demise so that others could live."

"Ah, in that respect, your husband and I had something in common," admitted Joseph.

"Yes, I know."

"How?"

"Mary of Magdala said you, too, had much planned for Jesus. My husband's hopes probably matched yours."

Jude paused to sip some water. Her shaking right hand reached for a small piece of cheese. She savored it, following it with more water.

"I feel so unworthy of your hospitality. But I believe you will value my teaching shortly."

"As perplexed as I am," said Joseph, "I'm confident your husband's life has a lesson for me. Please proceed."

"Judas' attitude—and spirit—changed almost overnight. I saw it and demanded he explain his turn of heart. Callousness overwhelmed him. I insisted he must address it.

"And so he told me. He said he had made a mistake. Jesus was not a heroic figure who would set our people free. There would be no prominent place for my husband. He was most bitter in his disappointment. I listened and tried to share the wisdom of the ages I had learned from my mother.

"I argued for Jesus with all the wisdom I had, but my husband's mind was set."

"What was that wisdom?" Joseph leaned forward in anticipation.

"Patience."

"What?" Joseph fell back in his seat, obviously disappointed.

"Just as I said. Simply patience."

"But how would that have helped?"

"I loved my Judas, but he never felt he was successful. He always had to do *something* to validate his worth. He would will himself to success!

"He could not see that it was this very willfulness that often prevented him from succeeding—or even understanding the character of true success. In his frustration he often aborted the process of bringing about the very things he was hoping for!

"He was an impatient man. I could not slow him down. He would not allow the natural rhythm of God to deliver what was coming to pass. He was so obsessed with his own proud destiny and how Jesus would help him fulfill it! In the end, he could not wait for the prophecies to unfold naturally. And so he tried to force the moment himself.

"He went to the Temple authorities. He gave the prophecies an unholy push."

"So...you admit he betrayed Jesus?"

"His impatience confused him," Jude said, her head hanging in shame. "He abandoned the one who had given him a sense of worth for the first time. During those three loving years, it was Jesus who cut through my husband's pride and self-delusion.

"All Judas had to do was wait a little longer. But his patriotism for the cause and his selfish anticipation of his own role drove him to report Jesus to the Temple authorities. During this period Jesus spoke plainly about all that would occur. The young Galilean made painfully clear that his kingdom was not of this world; that he was on a much larger mission than that."

The woman began to sob quietly as she put her knuckle to her mouth.

"But, good woman," Joseph said, "it's not a sin to be concerned about this world."

"My husband was an intelligent man. He knew we humans are three-part beings—mind, body, and spirit. And he understood Jesus' reference to a new world where the spirit would continue into eternity. He liked that.

"His problem was his impatience—he could not delay his own gratification in this world. That was it. Had he heeded my plea to let God find a way, and approached each day and moment as a gift, he would have seen the natural evolution of Jesus' plan. But no—he had to rush things. He jumped to conclusions out of fear and greed. He aborted his part of the plan, when all he had to do was have faith in God."

"And that's your lesson to me? Be patient? Can life be that easy?"

Jude composed herself. She took a bite of bread. When she had carefully chewed and swallowed the morsel, she began with great deliberation.

"No, Joseph of Arimathea. It's not that easy. But it is simple.

"You see, there is a huge difference between ease and simplicity. Simplicity does not imply ease—only clarity.

"It is a simple thing to walk from Jerusalem to Rome. You simply put one foot in front of the other. But it is by no means easy. The same is true for patience—waiting for God's infinite will to unfold without trying to force events to follow your own narrow will. It is very simple. But it is rarely easy.

"I'm told of your brilliance as a merchant, counselor, and member of the Sanhedrin," she continued, gazing out beyond the porch to the Arimathean's terraced gardens and bubbling fountains. Focusing on Joseph again, she added, "Yet it's being said among those who know you that your impatience has caused you to disbelieve what your own eyes have seen, and what your heart has always known.

"You've received some precious secrets, honored merchant. Others will be delivered as well. Fitting them all together is not easy. But each of them is simple. How much simpler can patience be? If you continue on this course of disbelief, of self-absorbed grieving, then you're making the same mistake my husband made.

"The difference is you are still alive to correct yourself."

Joseph raised a hand to halt her words. He thought long and hard before speaking.

"You're saying that like your husband I've jumped to conclusions. And thereby I am preventing myself from enjoying in the fruits of what is yet to come?"

"Sir," the woman said, looking at the merchant with sad, kind eyes, "If you know a thing to be good, and you've seen progress, then isn't it best to allow it to grow peacefully and in its preordained time—just like a precious baby in its mother's womb? Only at the perfect moment can the miracle of birth occur.

"Much of your tribulation since the days of the crucifixion is self-imposed. Sadly, your wife passed away in the midst of the already trying events. But your life did not end with Jesus' demise and the sudden passing of your beloved.

"Don't allow these losses to paralyze your faith, hope, and love."

"Woman, your boldness is refreshing," Joseph said. His brows were deeply furrowed. "But this secret is also very disturbing to my soul."

"Then I congratulate you, dear sir. Unlike my husband, you are receiving with the spirit of a learner."

"I thank you for your confidence. But I must tell you," Joseph objected, "I struggle with your notion of patience."

"Ah, just like my Judas. So learned, but always preferring the complicated to the simple. Please listen, Decurion." Jude leaned forward to make her point. "Must I remind you that this teaching was crafted from the blood of our ancestors?"

"Now confusion overwhelms me," Joseph said, leaning back on his chair.

"When I was a little girl, I was always running about. I asked my blessed mother how to develop patience. Her response was cold and honest: 'Tribulation.'

"Yes, my mother told me that suffering develops patience. But there is also an alternative. She went on to tell me of our ancestors who had suffered in enslavement, only to survive and stubbornly resist in the desert, displaying patience that passed all understanding.

"She called this their gift to us. Because of their suffering, you and I may not have to go through such trials to cultivate true patience—but we must heed the teachings of the ancient and wise.

"In the end," she said, "their patience, forged in the fire of suffering, is an offering for us, if only we'll heed it and receive it."

"Yes, I do understand that tribulation endured can bring patience," Joseph quietly admitted. "Perhaps I have been foolish and selfish to fight against what cannot be changed, when the lessons of the ages are so clear."

The woman's passion rose at this glimmer of understanding.

"People throughout Jerusalem need a Joseph of Arimathea. A strong, wise man who may not have all the answers, but who patiently waits and listens for them while helping those who need him.

"I believe it is nothing more than impatience that has driven you into your bedchamber—to the point where your Duca and Mary of Magdala fear your premature demise. It has made you disconnected, self-pitying, and unable to love. All because you cannot wait, just as my husband could not!"

"God help me, Jude. You are correct. I'm no different from Judas Iscariot."

"My friend, that will change," Jude said. "Starting today. God has eternity to teach you; there's no hurry to fulfill your destiny.

"Our scriptures tell us to wait on God. Don't sit like a vagabond by the road, but live in a state of readiness in the moment to do God's will. If you rush your Creator, you create an aberration of that which was destined to be yours.

"My husband loved the ancient words written by Isaiah and David our father," Jude said, folding her hands in her lap. She paused, and then quoted the prophets:

"'Be still, and know I am God.' My husband needed those words to calm himself from time to time. But he forgot them when his strength was restored. It was not a license to go ahead of the plan. Instead, Judas ran forward, forcing himself ahead of Jesus' strategy and forcing his God out of the moment.

"'The steps of a righteous man are ordered by God.' If only he had not dashed into a future God had not designed for him, he might still be with us today. His name would not be destroyed. And I would not be an outcast."

Jude unfolded her hands and helped herself to another piece of cheese and crumb of bread. Duca had not stopped writing.

"I will give these words much thought, widow," Joseph said.

Jude put down her food and gave Joseph a serious look.

"You think too much," she said.

"How can that hurt?" Joseph asked. "My worldly success fed upon my constant thinking."

"Joseph—my husband lost his way in thought. He was not thinking for the moment. His mind was oriented toward past memories and an imagined future reality. These thoughts betrayed him, leading him to become the betrayer.

"He obsessed over his plan to overthrow the oppressive Romans. The present was not where he wanted to be—he lived for an imagined future! With dissatisfaction feeding his impatience, despair overwhelmed him. What he wanted was not coming to pass soon enough, so he rushed to judgment.

"Judas saw Jesus become displeased with his obsession with finances and a material conclusion to this messianic mission. Unfortunately, he knew the writings so well, he began to believe he was the one foretold to abandon Jesus and become an enemy! He understood the form of the scripture, but not its spirit. The result of his arrogance? Horror."

"My woman, I know those same prophecies. Perhaps Judas was destined to betray!"

"Thou mayest," Jude quietly responded.

"What does that mean?"

She proceeded slowly. "'Thou mayest.' My husband, learned as he was, failed to recognize that God gave him choice. Judas may have fit the description of the foretold traitor, yet he need not have fulfilled that destiny. He had a choice! Thou mayest: words written by Moses to bring light to our free choice. My husband's lack of patience caused him to ignore that truth. He chose incorrectly.

"You may know, Arimathean," she continued, "that some of the followers felt Jesus saw the change in Judas. You're probably asking, 'Why did the preacher not shake some sense into my husband?'"

"It's true," Joseph said, nodding. "I have wondered similarly about Jesus. Personally, I am haunted by the fact that he would not heed my warnings about the Temple—and also that he never asked me to support him more openly, as I should have."

"Because Jesus knew his Father in Heaven intimately. Because choice is a free gift from above, given directly from the Creator to each individual. Jesus wanted Judas to make each choice as a free human being—not one in bondage to him. And the same applies to you, Joseph."

"I understand," Joseph said. "Deep inside, I think I've known that all along. But there's something about your message of patience that still bothers me. Many times, I have been forced to act in haste when the circumstances offered an opportunity or a challenge. Was I wrong?"

"Not at all. Urgency in business and life can yield good fruit, when it is based on being fully alive and aware in the present moment. But hurry that is based on worries about the past or fears for the future can compromise even the most sincere. Our obsession with tomorrow and yesterday obscures what is before us now. This, to me, is the definition of impatience.

"Recall some of the greatest achievements and revelations of your life. Looking back, wouldn't you say they manifested at a perfect time? Perhaps they were later than you wanted, but were they not perfect anyway?"

"Yes, it's true," Joseph nodded. "Many of the best moments of my life seem to have happened effortlessly—almost when I was least expecting them. I should be more patient. Ever since the events of the past month, I have been living in fear of an uncertain future, and regret over an unchangeable past. Indeed, nothing has unfolded as I'd hoped. These events have been too much for me to bear. They have surpassed my understanding. But I cannot disagree with you: they are surely part of God's plan. Patience might save my soul and my body, just as it might have saved Judas Iscariot. I can't control these events, but I, too, have a choice about how I react to them. You are correct."

"My call in life," responded the widow, "is to make sure other people like you do not make my husband's mistake. Then he will have not died in vain."

"You do a good deed, woman. But your heart is obviously still heavy. His actions will always be looked upon as infamous," Joseph said. "And it grieves me in the end that his worst fears were realized."

"His fears?"

"Well, after all," Joseph said sadly, "Jesus *did* die on the cross."

"Dear, Joseph, with all due respect, your decision to remain in your home since those terrible days has insulated you from a miracle unfolding." She paused to take a deep breath. "If you visited the markets, the countryside, or the courtyards, you would sense an impending event that will validate all the young preacher promised. Hiding here has invited the same darkness upon you that killed my Judas."

"Clarify, please," Joseph requested.

"A lack of patience flourishes in ignorance! You do not have current information. Get out of your palatial prison, dear man!"

"You speak of impending events. What events?"

"Seek and you shall find them in the city."

Joseph pondered. A small smile crossed his face. "You have aroused my curiosity, now," he said. "Perhaps I will go into the city."

"Good! That shows you are becoming interested in the present. And many would love to see you again. I would be very glad if my visit could have such a result!"

Jude rose, a look of contentment on her face. She looked at the object she had brought, still wrapped in cloth on the table next to her.

"Before I leave, I must fulfill one of my husband's last requests."

"What is that?"

Jude reached for the item and slowly unraveled it from its coarse linen cover. Joseph stood, clutching his chest. Duca had stopped writing and stood at his side.

"Master?" Duca inquired, hoping for Joseph to explain his shock.

"It's the cup, Duca. The grail. Good woman, my gift to Jesus has been found?"

"The cup that had been at the Passover supper," she said, holding it out to Joseph, "that you had made sure was at the cross. Mary of Magdala told me she had seen it filled to overflowing with the blood and water issuing from the young man's chest. That Holy Grail is now returned to the one who gave it to Jesus."

Joseph took the heavy goblet, stunned into silence for a long moment.

"Dear woman, I had retrieved it in the upper room after the supper. The group had left for the Garden of Gethsemane, and the women restored the room.

"It was left behind. The Magdalene knew it was my gift to Jesus. She gave it to me for safekeeping. I took it to the cross. I remember holding it up to catch the blood and water from Jesus' side. But then...nothing. I lost all sense of where it was, and thought it gone forever."

"It is a strange story, Joseph. My own husband, Judas, found it lying in the rain in the middle of the storm the day Jesus died. Later, Mary told me you flew to Pilate's to try to gain possession of the body. You must have dropped it on the way!"

"Incredible!" Joseph exclaimed.

"God works in strange ways," Jude nodded. "Judas recognized the grail immediately. Even on the verge of his own death, he thought it only just that you should have your goblet back. From afar he had seen all that happened at Calvary. Even at his lowest, Judas knew its worth to the movement and to its creator, Joseph of Arimathea. 'An

185

acclaimed merchant of metals in the Empire,' is how he described you.

"Judas' last command to me was to retrieve it and return it to the man who had been so faithful and so generous to Jesus."

Joseph looked away and softly added, "Not faithful enough. But, God willing, there is still time to make that right."

He bowed his head in relief at this gift that was such a blessed reminder of Jesus.

Jude smiled.

"My own spirit is lifting," she sighed. "I can see that from my husband's impatience—even from his profound and grave error of judgment, good has finally come. I trust patience will soon be with you, Joseph, and you'll take another step toward God's destiny for you."

"Jude, you've taught me bravely and well. With patience, even this Holy Grail is found. But now I'm concerned for your well-being."

"Do not fret. Even if my life ends in moments, in passing on the secret my husband refused to receive, my life is complete. However—I'm also sure Mary of Magdala is not finished with me. She says there are others to teach.

"Although I cannot imagine any I will feel better about teaching than the Arimathean."

Jude turned to Duca and requested his assistance to the villa's front entrance.

He smiled at her. "Of course, dear widow of Judas."

As Jude walked down the winding path away from the villa, Duca watched her every step toward the horizon of the city. As she disappeared in the distance, an odd stooped figure muffled in an oversized cloak, Duca felt moved to offer a prayer of thanksgiving.

But Duca had never worshipped any god. Not the gods of the Romans, the Egyptians, or the Hebrews.

God of my master, if you are truly Lord of the universe—I thank you.

Joseph continued to sit in the fresh morning air. Jude and the return of the cup overwhelmed him.

None of my riches compares to the value of the wisdom I'm feasting on. I must leave my domain and reenter the city, just as the widow instructed. While I have more to consider, my strength is returning.

And now, even this precious cup has found its way back to me.

Within hours, Joseph was reading Duca's notes.

The Widow's Supportive Secret: Patience

- **When in doubt, be still.**
- **Do not rush events. You may abort God's natural plan from unfolding as it should.**
- **If you have done your best in each moment, all is well.**
- **Do not fear results; have faith that God's plan is better than anything you could imagine.**
- **Tribulation breeds patience—and the wisdom gained from the tribulations of others is a gift one can use to learn patience without suffering tribulation yourself.**
- **Living for others fuels patience.**
- **Self-obsession fuels impatience.**
- **Impatience cultivates despair.**
- **Simplicity does not imply ease.**

Chapter XXII.

This, too, Shall Pass

Jude was undecided whether to return to her modest home just beyond the market in the city, or to proceed to the home of the widow Mary, where she knew she would find the Magdalene.

She was tired to exhaustion from her journey, and as she entered the bustle of Jerusalem at midday, she began to worry that she would again run into someone who would scorn her for her husband's failings. Her mind seemed to swirl with the market crowd. And as her thoughts intensified, so did her doubts.

Yes, Mary of Magdala has taken me in like a sister, sharing so many of the Master's teachings Judas never mentioned. And I have finally shared my knowledge with Joseph—I hope it does him good! The anticipation by the followers of coming revelation surely created a sense of urgency about this tiring trip. But I long for my husband—not the conflicted, frustrated striver he came to be, but the brilliant young man I married. Not the one who said 'goodbye' to me on the night of Jesus' execution. Why did he not heed my words? Why could he not have been just a little more patient?

Lost in her thoughts, unable to decide where to go and with her heart heavy with grief, Jude had taken a wrong turn.

Without consciously meaning to do so, she found herself trudging up a hill to a rock-strewn plateau perched not far from Calvary on the outskirts of the city. As she paused to catch her breath and wipe her perspiring brow with her heavy robe, a stunning thought paralyzed her:

These are the heights where my Judas ended his life! How did I end up here?

I can't believe he did such a thing! We had so many plans!

Yes, his enemies must have caused his death. How could he leave me? How can I continue on without him? He took care of my every need.

All Jesus' followers look upon me with suspicion. They wonder how I could respect the memory of Jesus, when it was my husband who betrayed the preacher! Mary of Magdala sincerely loves me. Not so many of the others. So accursed was she as a young woman, she knows my feelings more than anyone.

But who knows if I'll ever be as strong as her.

Jude inched closer to the unstable ledge of the limestone cliff.

I, too, can be in the bosom of Abraham and rejoin my Judas in the hereafter. Surely he misses me! I have no family to embarrass with my self-destruction. And I'm sure my God will forgive me.

The woman began to shake and moan. There were no passersby to console her. She was alone with her self-destructive, helpless thoughts.

Then the face of Joseph of Arimathea appeared in her mind's eye.

Her moaning stopped. Jude began to breath normally again. She looked to the horizon, at the beauty of the sun low on the purple, rolling hills.

Here and now, she was safe—if she chose to be. Here in the moment, she had purpose.

Patience.

Jude's grieving ceased; her body relaxed.

I must heed my own teaching! How can I rush to my death when so many positive things are happening around me? Would I not be a hypocrite, a false teacher if I were to violate that which I profess to have been the solution to my Judas' torment? Then the delivery of my secret to the world by the Arimathean would be totally compromised.

Surely he will teach the multitudes when he resumes his travels!

Jude stepped back to firmer ground. Her eyes filled with tears, clouding her view of the Holy City. She envisioned her husband's handsome face, smiling and at peace. Her breath was taken away, just as when they first met.

His message to her was as clear as if he were whispering in her ear:

"Even my deed, the one which the enemy meant for evil— that very crime of the centuries; it has been turned for good by the mind of God.

Be patient, my love. Allow all that has been ordained to happen. Step into God's will for your life. Only He will call you home, and that time is not now. Complete my work—the good work I began with Jesus and the eleven others."

Wiping her face with soiled hands, Jude quickly turned to rush back down the slope. Her destination and purpose were now clear: Arrive at the widow Mary's as soon as possible, find Mary the Magdalene, tell her of her tormented moments on the hill, and proclaim the power of the secret of patience to settle one into the precious moment.

Chapter XXIII.

Not to Return Void

Joseph paced back and forth in his bedchamber.

The widow's right. I must venture from this place. I've been enduring a self-imposed prison sentence. How dare I offend my God and scorn the plan He's designed for me!

Joseph stopped his pacing. He inhaled the lilac-laced air drifting across his balcony. Although the sun had barely risen, he sensed a presence below, a shadow perhaps. He stepped out on the edge overlooking his beloved garden.

"Is that you down there, Duca?" he called. "It is you, isn't it?"

"Of course, master." The servant looked up in surprise from his early morning harvest of herbs for the kitchen. He had not heard Joseph call for him with so much energy in many days.

"It's early, master. It is good to hear your call! What can I do to be of service?"

Joseph opened his arms as if to embrace his faithful servant.

"It's time, dear Duca! The moment has come for me to re-enter the world I fled. The widow's advice was worthy. I'm missing too much!"

Duca savored the moment, looking up and taking in the vision of his master as he had long known and loved him.

How blessed life sometimes is, he thought. He brushed his tunic clean.

"Master, I'm so glad! The Magdalene assured me this day would come."

Duca decided to take a chance.

"May I make a suggestion?"

"Duca, today I am inclined to grant any wish!"

"Then please, master—allow me to change our plans with our next guest. Instead of entertaining him here, let's venture out and visit his place of business!"

Joseph hesitated only a moment. He took a deep breath and smiled at his servant.

"You'll prepare the horses?"

"Of course, master! What a happy day! It seems so long since our last trip to our Holy City!" Duca said. He felt tears of happiness welling up in his eyes at the thought of Joseph once again venturing out into the world.

"Indeed, it was not long ago, though it seems a lifetime ago." Joseph said. "It was that dark afternoon of the crucifixion—when Nicodemus and I rushed, too late, to Calvary."

"Master, let's not think about that now. I can assure you this next trip will bring you only light."

"Will you reveal our next angel to me?"

Duca paused. "His name has not been given to me. I only know he's a young man of position and wealth. And I know where to find him."

Joseph could not wait for the ride to begin. Before Duca could finish his preparations, his master was out inspecting the horses.

Not many rode into Jerusalem. Even the wealthiest usually traveled on donkey or ass. Other than the occasional Roman chariot, the only vehicles to be seen were a smattering of two-wheeled carts piled high with goods and a few lumbering, oxen-drawn wagons. Even these generally only traveled to market and back, moving slowly along the road before dawn and at the end of the day. Joseph's fine Arab steeds were one of his most prized possessions, and they marked him as an extremely successful man.

The Arimathean was almost childlike as he stroked the mane of his favorite, Persian Prince, cherishing each moment with the majestic animal.

"It's been a long time since our last trip together, Prince. Ah, the day you became mine for more silk, gold, and metal than I thought I could afford!

"But my Sarah always believed there was never money better spent. My faithful friend, she always spoke of how I glowed in your presence—I think she was a little jealous of our friendship at times!"

Good creature, I should apologize to you. Your calling in life was to run like the wind, with thunder in your hooves and lightning in your legs; the fastest and most beautiful of your kind. But circumstances kept you in Jerusalem as my involvement with the Galilean grew, and we traveled less frequently.

How glad my Sarah would be to see me speaking to an animal whose only response is to stand at respectful attention. But so I do not become too sentimental and mired in yesterday, let me not forget how special it is to be in this moment now with this innocent creature.

My God is such a genius of creation!

As the Magdalene has taught, and as her friends have confirmed, it is good to be here in the warmth of this peaceful, present moment—without a thought of future or past!

"Ah, how I have neglected you, my old companion! But today you will carry me back into the world!"

Duca surprised Joseph, appearing before him.

"You're enjoying Persian Prince as in days gone by," the faithful servant said. "For this I'm grateful! Master, it's good to see you and the animal together again. I know he has pined for your companionship and your command."

"Yes, my friend, and I for his strength and respect."

"Master, as I review the secrets shared with you in these last days, I've gained many insights. But what I am seeing in you today is the value of a childlike innocence: To savor the moment; to be without cares, just as your Jesus taught. And, my Egyptian logic, taught me so well by our Greek friends, tells me the Prince, this innocent masterpiece, is relishing this instant with you as well."

"Duca, he could have been the champion of all."

"No doubt, master," Duca responded, "But to him, spending this moment with you is every bit as good as prancing after a great racing victory. You may regret that he did not race more. But to him, there is only this glorious moment—now. What might have been is irrelevant in his blameless world."

Duca smiled, charmed by a new thought.

"If the Prince could speak and you were to ask him what time it is, I am sure he would say, 'Master, it is now.'"

"Duca, of course!" Joseph laughed and fed the mighty animal a handful of sweet grass. "You are most certainly correct."

"He might even add, 'This time together is precious. It is good to see you. What we are doing now is more important than yesterday or tomorrow. It is all I care about!'"

Both men chuckled. It really seemed as though Duca was speaking for the glorious animal, and the Prince whinnied and nodded his head as if to agree.

"Master, he anticipates that his muscles will soon be tested! It's already invigorating him. And you, too, should be invigorated!" Duca added, "Because your next rescuer will remind you of another secret you have temporarily forgotten."

"Then you've already heard the secret?"

"Not really," Duca responded, as he tightened the reins and inspected the harness. "But Mary of Magdala has given me some hints. I am as exited as you."

Joseph allowed Duca to give him a leg up onto the mighty animal. Then Duca himself mounted a fine bay mare—not as fine as the Prince, but still a mount no other servant in Jerusalem could ever hope to ride.

Joseph would fully enjoy the journey into the city. Whether it was on camel, on horseback, or driving his personal chariot at the head of a trading entourage, the veteran traveler had always thrilled at the idea of rushing to the next destination. Although there was no particular hurry, as soon as the Prince was warmed up and the road was clear, Joseph allowed him to trot proudly for a while before breaking into a joyful gallop.

Joseph reveled in the powerful sensations of the ride. It was as if horse and rider became one, and the animal's brute strength invigorated his own muscles, used too little in recent days. Surely, he would be tired and sore tomorrow, but it would be the best kind of fatigue.

When the smoke from the approaching urban glut and the river's reek tainted the fresh, cool air, Joseph slowed the Prince to a walk. The merchant looked regal and almost young, and could not stop grinning from ear to ear.

For him, a new revelation was emerging: the closer he was to the heart of Jerusalem, the closer he was to rebirth.

The horses' hooves echoed against the stone alleyways. As pedestrians made way for the richly appareled and even more richly mounted merchant and his servant, Joseph remembered how this ancient Holy City could never hide its filth and poverty. Only the incense floating low above the narrow streets like a scented blanket could cloak the stink of waste coursing the streets and alleyways in the heart of the city.

"Duca," Joseph called out, "are we nearing our destination? This seems an odd part of the city for such a meeting!"

Above the chatter of the humanity and the clattering of the horses' hooves, Duca shouted out, "Unfortunately, we're almost there! I'm afraid there will be little protection at our meeting place from the smells and sounds of your beloved Holy City. Just a few more moments down the alley to the right."

"You said we were to visit a 'rich young man,'" inquired Joseph. "But the nearest palace is in the city's heights."

"Be patient, good master! All will be explained shortly."

Moments later, Duca pulled his mare to a halt. Indeed, there was no majestic edifice to be seen in this nondescript nook of Jerusalem. In fact, this section of the city was best known for its warehouses and places of business.

Duca dismounted and helped his master do the same, not giving Joseph a moment to ask another question. Within moments, the servant had given a coin to an intelligent looking — and grateful — youth to look after the animals, and the servant was hurrying up a steep, narrow flight of stone steps, pulling his master along.

When they reached the landing above the street, Duca turned to Joseph in tow, surprised to find him laughing.

"Were it not for my faith in the Magdalene and curiosity about the excited haste of my Duca," exclaimed Joseph, "I would have serious doubts about this inauspicious meeting place!"

Duca, out of breath, was also grinning. "Kindly wait here while I attend more fully to Prince, master. You'll be welcomed shortly, and then I will join you."

Joseph shrugged his shoulders and nodded like a child. He was willing, today, to accept this unique experience as it unfolded.

No sooner had Duca bounded down the stairs than a handsome, olive-skinned man opened the door to Joseph.

"Is this the Arimathean, whom I've not seen for almost three years? The wealthy merchant who has defined my standard of excellence?"

Joseph was speechless for a moment, not recognizing his greeter.

"I am Prochorus, known to familiars as the rich, young ruler. Today, please call me 'friend'—because I'm about to tell you a great truth!"

"Prochorus, if you're a friend of Mary of Magdala, and if my servant Duca has arranged this meeting, I already embrace you as friend."

The striking young man, attired in the latest foreign fashions, looked oddly out of place here. Truly, he did look rich, but this was certainly not the type of place Joseph would normally expect to find a man like him.

"I can see you're curious about my modest place of business. But you have the courtesy to remain silent. You're a gentleman, Joseph—but don't jump to conclusions. Remember the lesson of the old scripture writer: 'I was your friend, until I told you the truth.'"

"Yes," Joseph said, laughing. "The truth often does hurt. But I've been reminded it can set you free as well."

"Then free shall we be, good man." Prochorus turned and gestured for Joseph to enter through a drape of Persian lace. "For you will find only truth in my presence."

The interior, though not large, was an even greater surprise. Comfortable and richly furnished, Prochorus' offices were graced with objects that Joseph would have been proud to display in his own villa. The contrast to its ordinary Jerusalem neighborhood and rough exterior took a moment to get used to.

Before both men sat, Duca returned and introduced himself.

"I am most excited to hear what you have to share today," he said. "Mary of Magdala has spoken most highly of you."

"And she has spoken highly of you, as well, Duca," Prochorus said, looking the handsome Egyptian over with his sharp eye. "It is your dutiful service and love for your master that has made me enthusiastic about seeing both of you today."

The host made sure each was comfortable on the fine couches that graced the room, while a servant offered fresh, warm beer.

With all settled, Prochorus proceeded.

"I was once a spoiled publican, a ruler in the city. My family has riches from Judea, to the Spanish shores, and deep into Persia. We, like you, are importers of the finest products Jerusalem could buy. But it was in money changing and lending that my father and his partners excelled. To shield me from some of their abuses, my mother insisted I be raised on the Torah, so I spent my days in the Temple. My father's business kept him too busy to care. I then ventured into local politics."

Duca was already delighting in the conversation. The ride into Jerusalem had been just the type of breakthrough he had barely dared hope for. He joyfully spread his writing things before him, eager to capture more wisdom for his master.

Joseph seemed lost in thought. Finally, a look of recognition crossed his face.

"Of course—now I remember you! How could I have forgotten? Your stately presence, rich attire, and sincerity when you interrupted Jesus—almost three years ago! Your role in local government was well known, as was your family wealth. And you respectfully addressed the Lord, speaking proudly of keeping the laws."

"Yes, Joseph—that was me, indeed!"

"But when the Galilean instructed you to sell all you had, distribute it to the poor, and follow him, you took on a sorrowful countenance and vanished. Then Peter the fisherman reminded Jesus that he and the others had left all they had to support him. Jesus assured the big man he and the other eleven would be rewarded.

"With all respect, Prochorus, I have to admit I forgot about you from that moment on!"

Prochorus was curious. "Then how did you recognize me now?"

"It was the way Jesus reacted to your courtesy and sincerity that rekindled my memory. It seemed to me as I watched from several steps away that he appreciated it when you addressed him as 'Good Master.' And he seemed to recognize that you understood the meaning of 'eternal life.' Knowing Jesus since his youth, I can tell you how patient he had to be with Peter and most others to help them understand eternity. Then you showed up with full discernment!"

"And?" the host coaxed Joseph to continue.

"And then Jesus spoke about how difficult it would be for the rich to enter the kingdom of God!"

"Precisely," confirmed Prochorus. "I heard those words as well."

"Well, then, Duca and my rich young friend, why are we here?" asked Joseph. "You said I was to be told another secret."

Prochorus sipped his beer.

"Joseph, it is simply this: now you must hear the rest of the story."

"I'm learning to be patient," Joseph said, smiling as he willed himself to relax into the moment. "Please, continue."

"As you noticed, at first Jesus' words made me morose," said Prochorus. "It hit me hard in that moment. I have to sell everything I own? A monumental task—let alone having to convince my parents I was about to become one of Jesus' wandering followers.

"But as I reflected on what the Rabbi had said to me and the way he said it, my heart soon leapt with joy!"

Duca's interest was piqued, and he stopped his note-taking. Joseph leaned forward to catch the full explanation.

"By the time I arrived home, I was literally dancing with joy! Somehow, I knew I could do just what Jesus commanded. And yet I had no desire to become one of his full-time ministers. But I could sell all, or at least most, of what I had, and give to the poor, just as he commanded."

"But isn't that why you left sorrowfully?" inquired Joseph.

"Yes. But I was an idiot. Or perhaps I was in shock from the power of Jesus' words. Whatever the reason, in a very short time his wisdom swept over me. Jesus was right!

"Still, I felt I had far too many contacts, too much wealth, too much talent for creating wealth, and too much energy to follow Jesus as his thirteenth apostle. Instead, I saw a way to remain closer to the life I knew while working directly with the infirmed and impoverished—to help them prosper, gain respectability, and enjoy a long and healthy life."

"But I was there, young man," Joseph reminded. "Jesus asked you to join him."

"Yes. But I believe he also knew the power in those words and the nourishment they would provide me—seeds being planted that would grow into something surprising. He expected something would happen in my bosom; that the word would not return void. And he was right!

"Excuse me, Joseph, but I know everybody, including you, expected me to join his itinerant band right there. But Jesus spoke to *me*. And I believe he had a better plan—the one I am following today. He knew there are many ways to serve. He taught me with such patience and love!"

"Oh, Duca, there's that word again," Joseph said. "Will this be another lesson in patience, then?"

"Just the truth," said the young politician and businessman. "And while my secret is not directly about patience, I will ask you to be patient while I share this wisdom. After Jesus admonished me, I knew I had to go home and invent my own way to serve. I knew I had to change for things to change. I understood I had to act now—I had become so rich and complacent.

"Don't you see—Jesus was not rebuking me, but challenging me!

"And today, Joseph, I challenge you."

Today, Joseph felt ready to be challenged.

"How? What is the secret you're to reveal?"

"My secret is a joyful one! It is simply this: Always be open to change—then act! And do it for others!

"If you want a better future, invent it. Try something different to help others every day of your life. Discover your talents, try them on for size, develop them into strengths, and then make sure they help someone else. While I revere that group that physically followed Jesus through the countryside, I knew I could do exactly what the carpenter's son required of me, using what was mine. Indeed, God had already blessed me with much!"

"I believe my patience for this lesson will come easily, Prochorus," Joseph said. "All my life, until recently, I have reveled in new experiences. And I have been greatly blessed, as well. Of all my teachers, you are perhaps the most like me."

"Then listen to what I did next," the host instructed. "Remember I told the preacher I had kept all the laws?"

"Yes."

"Well, that means my family and I always tithed, giving the first fruits of all we had to the Temple."

"You have been faithful," complimented Joseph.

"Perhaps. But when I arrived home after speaking with Jesus, I decided from that day on, so blessed was I in worldly wealth, that I would no longer give just ten percent of my income to the Temple. No. Rather, I would give ninety percent—that's what I would provide to the poor and to the work of God. The original tenth would amply fund my life. Today I'm distributing all that I create and own to the poor and to God's ministry.

"And there's more," Prochorus added excitedly. "You see, in my political dealings and businesses, I've hired scores of those in need. Rather than give them a handout, I give them a calling to respond to, doing meaningful work in jobs I create for them.

"Can you see? We give what we have. My talent is creating and distributing wealth. God continues to inspire me with inventions to serve others in my businesses. I may not be with Mary Magdalene, Peter, and the other followers every day, but I am also giving my life to spread Jesus' story and plan.

"I consider myself a minister of works," the young man said. "I only keep an appropriate amount to continue to fund my enterprises.

"Yes, I still wear fine garments and live well. But I'm sharing all that I have with my fellow man. More importantly, I teach them how to live a better life—not by lofty words, but with practical deeds."

"You have given up much, Prochorus," said a transfixed Joseph.

"I gave up my rights to myself, my desire to always be comfortable and popular, and my notion that change must be resisted at all costs. But I gained much more! I look forward to change and new ideas now, because I know if they're of help to others, they must come from God.

"I'm creative and useful because my Creator is creative and useful. I'm making a difference by trying different things, every day of my life. I am now sick of the way I used to be—always more anxious about God's law than grateful for God's love."

"But God's law protects us from error," Joseph said.

"True, Joseph. But now, I'm not afraid of mistakes. I make them every day! I know I am flawed. My righteousness comes from living in the flowing, changing, selfless *spirit* of the law! I am wealthier than I have ever been! And do you know what is the greatest treasure of all, Joseph?"

"I would dearly love to know, Prochorus."

"It is eternity itself! As I delve into each new action, I lose all sense of time in the eternal moment. In each creative action, I'm reintroduced to who I really am. The outcome, as we say in business, is fulfillment—personally and materially!"

"I am humbled by your teaching and by your example," Joseph said. "It is much to ponder."

"Then perhaps you should ponder less and act more," said a serious Prochorus. "Doing overcomes depression. It draws us into a higher realm. Do something new now, and your sense of far-off destiny dwindles. Why? Because destiny does not dwell in tomorrow. It is right now, right here. Don't dream about the past or the future. Show your true nature and do something now!

"Make a mistake: step into the mud, bray like a donkey. You can correct a mistake. Correcting lethargy or inactivity is much more difficult—they are insidious diseases, errors that sap every bit of meaning from life."

Joseph suddenly felt defensive. Had Jesus been speaking to him, as well, three years earlier?

"Are you suggesting, young man, that I've been inactive over the years?"

"Of course not, my friend!" Prochorus said. "But you have been hiding in your villa since Jesus died. You thought it was the end of the story—but it was merely the beginning! I'm here to tell you that you have been missing the birth of a new world. So much has happened!"

"It's true. I have languished in my home, and I know that was wrong," repented Joseph.

"I'm not casting blame, Joseph. Others like you are sitting still, alone in grief, fear and confusion. But I'm encouraging action. Not frenzied acts of futility, but simple acts that serve others in our businesses and in the cause for which the Nazarene died.

"Good Joseph, your many talents are well known. I've been aware of your name since my adult years began. I encourage you to imagine you're an artisan, charged with rendering a detail for the Temple. It's a task that will require years of artistry. You know this work will never be completed unless you attend to it every single day.

"Yes, rest when you must in order to gain strength. But do not allow idleness to dominate your life. Enjoy your moments of rest—in the silence of those private places you may glimpse eternity. But when you're restored, step right back into the creative process.

"At that point you step into eternity! There you are being who you really are—your authentic self!"

"Young man, I've had glimpses of such moments over the years," Joseph said. "I have learned much from the friends of the Magdalene. Truly, I should make a serious plan for my re-entrance into the world!"

Duca was writing furiously, intent on not missing a word.

Prochorus smiled at Joseph and chose his words carefully. "Good Joseph, too much pondering, too much planning, would bring all my work to a halt. Yes, go ahead and plan, but move forward even as you plan! I believe God prefers imperfect action to planned perfection.

"Though you may be uncertain, by doing for others in God's name you become an instrument to a power well beyond your comprehension. Suddenly, you're no longer alone—and that is a true prize. Be open to the surprise your activity will bring you and others. Become something you have never been before!"

"You make me yearn for those days where my youthful energy knew no bounds, Prochorus." Joseph mused. "I fear age is creeping up on me."

Prochorus took a deep breath and nodded his head. "Don't be like the Israelites of old who fled Egypt, only to desire to return days later because they tired of the desert and the manna that was their nourishment. Know that you are where you are because of a divine design that is your destiny. You allowed your energy to be sapped because circumstances arose that ran counter to your own plans. Things changed in ways you weren't expecting. Good! Let those incomprehensible changes teach you that it's no longer your plan that matters, but God's.

"Joseph, this is how you built your reputation, your business, and your value to the Sanhedrin. Every day you made a new contribution—until the death of Jesus and all that followed.

"Suddenly, you were confronted by more change than you could handle. You became overwhelmed. But now it is time to embrace change, make new plans for your life. This will restore a youthful vitality to everything you do! Doing for others will never take away your energy. It will only add to it! And in the midst of change and new plans," he continued, "you will experience an almost childlike delight in your life and in your God!"

There was a long silence, broken only by the scratching of Duca's quill on parchment. Finally, Joseph spoke.

"Did you ever see him again?"

Prochorus did not hesitate to answer.

"Yes."

Duca looked up from his writing. Joseph felt his chest tighten in anticipation.

"And...what did he say to you?"

"It was on his way to the Garden of Gethsemane. The night of Passover. It was entirely by chance that I crossed his path. My bakery workers were supplying bread for the Passover suppers all over town, including at the inn where Jesus and his followers were taking their meal.

"I had not seen him since that day nearly three years before.

"He was clearly burdened. Our eyes met, and he stopped for a moment."

"And his words?"

"He said nothing to me."

"Nothing?"

"Not a word."

"Well, then, what did he do?"

"He smiled at me."

"That's all?"

"It was so much, Joseph. I could tell Jesus was walking with a heavy heart. But when he smiled, it was as if we were continuing a conversation in a bountiful garden that would last a lifetime and beyond. I felt such worth, confirmation, and joy. I knew in that moment, that by devoting myself to acting to benefit others, I had followed the command Jesus made to me almost three years earlier. He knew — somehow he knew! And with that smile he said to me, 'Well done, thou good and faithful servant.'"

A profound peace enveloped the small meeting room. Duca stopped writing.

Joseph bowed his head, lost in his own thoughts.

Prochorus discovered the spirit of Jesus' words and acted upon them. Me, I've followed the letter of the law, but overlooked its joyful, ever-changing spirit. I've over-thought what I should be doing, putting myself at the center of my concerns, and not others.

Lifting his head, Joseph looked Prochorus in the eye.

"I believe I would be afraid to give so much," he said.

"Of course," Prochorus said. "I can very well understand that. But Joseph—God gives seed to the sower. I sow, and the Almighty continues to refill my barns with more seed to give away!"

An unexpected laugh escaped from Joseph. "You can't stop your own success, can you, young friend?"

"No, Joseph, I can't. Just like your own stream of success over the years!"

Joseph sighed.

"But my trade routes, caravans, drivers, and partners have all dwindled to almost nothing since the tomb became empty."

"My hope is that by my example I've reminded you of the real origin of your wealth—and how you will resurrect it."

"That may be beyond my power, my young friend."

"Joseph, have faith. My family and I are engaged in many of the same businesses as you. I've assured Mary of Magdala and Duca that any additional business I've attained because of your misfortune will be returned to you when you are ready. And there are other relationships that have been stolen from you. They, too, will be restored in the fullness of time. Duca knows a little, although it is best for everyone if the details remain quiet at this moment. I will tell you I'm not working alone. You are cared for by many—and this is a gift you have earned through years of honest and fruitful labor. My Ethiopian colleagues are thrilled to be helping the 'Arimathean Man' as they call you."

"Prochorus—I am overwhelmed. Why are you doing this? Who are these people?"

"You'll learn soon enough. Pilate and the Sanhedrin are crafty, but they are a clueless bunch when it comes to trading. The routes are yours—whatever it takes, they'll be restored to you and your heirs."

"Ah, but now I don't have a family, particularly with Jesus' departure."

"You're wrong. Your family is huge. You have Duca. And you have the poor. Unfortunately, they are many. You and I must pass our blessings onto them. Mark my words, Arimathean—when the time is ordained, your business will be fully restored."

"I will do my best to be patient—and to practice trying new things to benefit others, as you have so eloquently shared by your words and example. I will do my best to not rush things, good Prochorus, but I must admit I am very excited by this news. Would it be wrong of me to ask when or how I will know the time has come?" asked a humbled Joseph.

"You will know. A voice will whisper to you: 'What about now?'"

The three men embraced. Prochorus promised he would keep in touch and continue his preparations to act on Joseph's behalf when the time was right.

They all marveled at the process of restoration that Mary the Magdalene had been orchestrating with Duca. And Joseph was grateful for his new friend—another wise rescuer who had the courage to tell him the truth.

Duca and Joseph took their time on the ride home. There was no galloping, only a mindful, restful ride on the strong, willing back of the Persian Prince.

The late afternoon sun felt good on Joseph's skin. He was more content and at ease than he had been for a long time, enjoying the simple pleasure of the slow, luxurious journey to his comfortable home.

All the way, as he marveled at the scenery, Joseph played and replayed Prochorus' hopeful, joyful words in his mind.

That night, Duca summarized the priceless teaching.

The Rich Young Ruler's Supportive Secret:
Embrace Change. Act for Others

- **For situations to change, you must change.**
- **Change requires new activity.**
- **Activity dedicated to others will not tire the doer, but will inspire and revitalize.**
- **Getting lost in new, selfless, creative action blesses you with a moment in eternity.**
- **Don't over-think. Procrastination invites delay, lethargy, and inactivity.**
- **Don't fear mistakes. You can always correct an error.**

Chapter XXIV.

Family Business

Not long after Duca and Joseph departed, Prochorus' assistant announced that his aging father was paying a visit. The young entrepreneur rolled his eyes indulgently, knowing full well the lesson on international business he was about to reluctantly receive. On the other hand, while his father was not a regular at the Temple and had been accused as unscrupulous by some, Prochorus appreciated his parent's business intuition and ability to generate wealth.

Not waiting for the servant to escort him to his son, the elder businessman casually sat himself down on Prochorus' plush sofa, clasped his hands in his lap and ordered the assistant to leave.

While hard of hearing and slow to travel beyond his palatial estate in the heights because of his failing vision, the old man looked regal in his finely woven multicolored robe and shining, imported leather sandals.

Staring intently at his son, he announced, "We have something to talk about."

Prochorus was amused. While he respected his father, he no longer feared the old man's authority.

"Dearest father, why aren't you at home with mother, counting your money, appreciating your flowers, sipping on the finest of wines, and nibbling those ever-helpful prunes I supply you with each week?"

"Son, I've been speaking with mother, and we both agree you're working too hard—and taking too little for yourself."

"Oh, I suppose you did not overindulge in your businesses over the years. Actually, father, I have always considered your prodigious activity as a wholesome example for me."

Prochorus called for his servant. "Fetch some of that warm beer for my father. It will calm his nerves."

"No, thank you," the old man responded. "That brew will put me to sleep, and then my trip will be wasted."

Prochorus laughed out loud. "Good decision, Father. I'm afraid the overnight accommodations here are not up to your standards. And I won't be traveling into my home in the heights tonight—I have far too much to do here."

"Seriously, son. I have wondered for a while why you live like this—spending all your time in these cramped offices and dingy warehouses. And while your wife and children have a nice enough place in the heights, your mother tells me they live very frugally. I thought perhaps you had secretly invested your profits somewhere. Now your mother tells me that after your expenses of doing business, you only retain ten percent of your income—with the full balance going to the Temple!"

"Mother is nearly right."

"That is absurd! What happens to you if your dealings fail? Think of all that money in the hands of those self-righteous religious zealots. Ninety percent to the Temple? Do you believe for a moment that they will come to your aide when misfortune pays you a visit?"

"Father—get your facts straight. The ninety percent is split equally between the work of God and the needs of the less fortunate. The temple only gets forty-five percent."

"Oh, now my brilliant son is giving away his money to the irresponsible poor of the ghettos! The lazy, tired, uneducated mistakes of the God of Abraham, Isaac, and Jacob. I think following that rebel Jesus has softened your mind. I hear he was not much of a financial manager."

Prochorus shook his head in amusement, although he was a little concerned for his father.

"The sudden redness of your face tells me you should calm your nerves, wise father.

"The funds to the poor are not handouts. I educate them in business. I encourage their religious teaching. I provide them with jobs. Basically, I finance their transformation to self-sufficient people. Hardly giving away money! I am simply a trustworthy employer and friend in time of need. Anything I ask, they do. Business thrives. More are employed. Our city has fewer poor. It is a better place for all to live. That's not such a bad return. Would you not agree?"

"Yes, I see you're giving them opportunities. Yes, I see this as good. Just don't let them take advantage of you, son. And ninety percent—really! This is extreme!

"Forgive me, son, for what I am about to say—but these empty sepulchers inhabited by dry bones you consider temples to our Father in Heaven—I really have a problem here. Oh, I am sure the Pharisees love when you toil to provide them with your nine tithes!"

"Four and a half to the Temple, father. You are usually so good with figures. Are you feeling well?"

"I can't fathom the percentage you let slip through your hands, Prochorus. I know these men. Only a few I would consider to be true servants of the Almighty. How could you work for them when they stand in their temples, swaying back and forth, pretending to be hearing our God? They're probably figuring how they're going to spend your hard-earned money!"

Prochorus laughed out loud.

"Stop, father, please! You're getting yourself far too worked up. I am sure your concerns have some validity. But have some faith in me! Just as in business, I immerse myself in every moment, and when contemplating the distribution of funds, I look at many variables. No one is taking advantage of me."

"Good. Because as you may know, while these are called temples of God, many operate as little more than family businesses. Even your precious Jesus disapproved. Remember when he got himself into hot water by taking a whip to the temple moneylenders? Not that I objected. They had an unfair advantage, in my opinion."

Now Prochorus fairly rocked with laughter.

"Dearest father, here's what you're missing. My wealth and yours, and our ability to generate it, is a gift from God. The money's not ours. We're nothing but managers for the Almighty. Giving takes nothing away from me. And be honest: our families will never want for a thing! And don't forget, father—neither of us will take a shekel with us when we've gone on to our final reward."

"But what about these prayerful unemployed who portray themselves as men of God?"

"You're being too harsh, you know. Yes, there are a few charlatans. But I feel certain devoted men lead the temples I fund. They pray for me, are open to God's voice, are servants at heart, and have their own harvest to sow. They help the same people I do. But unlike me, their focus is more on the spiritual lives of the masses. While I take care of the common man's physical and mental health, the rabbis I support focus on their relationship with God. That's what I look for."

"Oh, my hard-headed son. Just like your mother. I see your points, but so much you're giving away to those who sleep and tarry while you work—applying all your creativity and energy on their behalf!"

"Yes, but as I've learned, 'You shall know them by their fruits.' Once I give it away, it's up to the recipient to properly steward my gift. If they don't, no fruits will flourish in their garden. I have no interest in wasting God's money on those poor stewards. And I have made very few mistakes. But if I do, they are easily corrected!

"You and mother must be reminded of the most minor of our ancient prophets. Malachi made it clear: 'Bring all the tithes into the storehouse, that there may be food in My house, and prove Me now by it, says the Lord of hosts, if I will not open the windows of heaven for you and pour you out a blessing, that there shall not be room enough to receive it.'"

"Ah, my naïve son. It was so long ago that Malachi walked this world!"

"Father, God does not change. He is eternal, as is His word. The real gold you should seek in your latter years is belief in our Creator—as mother has instructed me since my youth. Seek His Kingdom, and all other things will be given to you. Look at my empire. And look at yours. I do believe my ten percent begins to approach your ninety!"

"Be gentle with me, Prochorus. I admit I have made mistakes. But my best decision was allowing your mother to send you to Temple and be responsible for you in my absence. I owe my life to her."

"Yes, father, you married well. But you owe everything to God, including my dear mother. All good things come from Him—including these precious moments we are spending together!"

Raising both hands in love, the father responded, "Oh, it has been a stimulating exchange, to be sure. You have always had a mind of your own. And as I have always told anyone who would listen, it is a very fine mind, indeed. But you should listen to your father. Come with your wife and my grandchildren to our home this Sabbath. Your mother and I miss you all."

"We'll be there. Indeed, on the Sabbath there's no room for business. And we'll rejoice in our rest with our families, just as the Lord did on the seventh day."

There was a knock on the door. A servant announced that the time was growing late, and asked if the old man was ready for the journey home.

"Has the time really flown by so fast?" the old man asked in genuine surprise.

"Father, there was no time. God was present with us in each precious moment. And when that happens, we are standing in a portal to eternity."

Chapter XXV.

Serving to Lead

The next morning, Duca gently knocked on the solid mahogany door of Joseph's bedchamber. While summer had not yet arrived, Jerusalem and the countryside glowed in the warmth of the early morning sun, and the light of a new day began to filter through the nearby city smoke.

"Is that you, Duca?" Joseph asked, reaching for his robe.

"Master, please forgive me, but I've just received a message from Prochorus."

Joseph pulled on the door's ornate bronze handle to greet his servant.

"He must have risen long before dawn to get a messenger here this early. Prochorus has so much energy," Joseph smiled. "He reminds me of myself as a younger man."

"Well, Mary of Magdala apparently delivered instructions to schedule your next teacher without delay. Now Prochorus requests our presence at our earliest convenience."

Joseph sat on the bench next to his bed, reflecting. "Our friend Mary seems even more energetic than the young ruler. Always such urgency in all she does now — what a pair the two of them make!"

Duca smiled. "Yes, they are always active. They have no hesitation caused by warring thoughts the way so many others do. They certainly practice what they preach."

"So—we must go now."

"You do not object?"

"Object? Duca, I feel I could deliver these secrets to others; my heart is so full today! Every instant I feel more alive as I seek to immerse myself into this idea of the moment. You have done well, Duca. The Magdalene and her friends have penetrated my spirit. I'm surrendering and accepting, recognizing the magnificence in myself and others, and delighting in the joy that can be found in every instant. I'm looking at each experience as a chance to learn, being patient—and now focusing on what I can do creatively to take advantage of change.

"In short, I could not be more eager to rise this morning to learn our latest lesson!"

"I hardly imagined, master, that you would have time to review my notes from our visit to Prochorus."

"Not had time? Duca, you should know better by now. You and Mary—well, you are crafting a new Joseph of Arimathea!"

"I don't think so," Duca sincerely responded. "We're restoring the old Joseph of Arimathea; the one conceived at the foundations of the world."

"You flatter your master." Joseph laughed. "But tell me. Who is the bearer of our next secret?"

"I'm not sure. It's someone who works with Prochorus."

"Another wealthy publican with rich parents?"

"Master, you are teasing."

"Yes, I am. The young politician and businessman was most sincere and honest, and has only himself to thank for his great successes. But our next teacher, what does he do?"

"I've heard he is a 'helper.' Indeed, I am told he's a steward—a servant of sorts."

"So be it, my friend," said Joseph. "I'm learning a new reverence for all who serve. After all, where would I be without my servant, Duca?"

Within an hour, Persian Prince and the fine bay mare were saddled for their second jaunt into the city in as many days. Although they didn't gallop into the city today, the journey seemed shorter this time. And although he was eager for his lesson, Joseph enjoyed the ride so much he didn't want it to end.

When the horses clattered up to the entrance of Prochorus' place of business, Joseph called out to Duca, "Here again?"

"Yes and no," Duca replied. "Today we go down into the cellar!"

As Duca dismounted and hurried to help Joseph, he was laughing.

"I know my master's thoughts. You have seen too many huts, shanties, and underground cellars from Jerusalem to Jericho to Joppa, and throughout the former lands of your people. But don't be concerned, Joseph. It's no ordinary cellar. You needn't worry about rats or spiders delivering today's message. This cellar has been turned into a dining hall—and I understand it's a surprisingly pleasant place."

Just as he did the day before, Duca rushed Joseph into the building, this time around the back and to a nondescript doorway bordering a dark, narrow alley. Although it was difficult to keep a low profile on their fine horses, it was well to not linger too long outside Prochorus' office. The servant knew all too well of the growing suspicion of those who followed Jesus.

Duca knocked loudly on the door, and in a moment a young woman in a soiled apron opened the door slightly, smiled at them, and politely requested their identity.

"The House of Joseph of Arimathea," Duca said.

"Gentlemen, you are most welcome! Prochorus and Stephen await you. Or I should say they will attend you once they've completed the serving? Follow me," she requested.

As they scurried down the cavernous stairwell, they were greeted with the appetizing perfume of crushed grapes, roasting lamb, and simmering chicken soup.

A dozen paces beyond the narrow passageway they could hear the clacking of wooden plates and metal goblets above the quiet chatter of people.

At the end of the passage they entered a low, large dining room. Though surprisingly large, the space was crowded with a motley group. Most of the diners seemed to be part of the faceless poor, homeless, and widowed of the Holy City.

There was Prochorus, resplendent in his fine attire, delivering a tray of new wine to one round table, while other servers were busy distributing chicken and lamb dishes. Additional attendants cleaned the rough wooden tables and laid out knives and spoons.

To the astonishment of Joseph and his servant, a familiar, hulking presence stood at the far end of the room, about to leave through a back door.

"Peter!" shouted Joseph.

The fisherman turned. On recognizing the Arimathean, he smiled and called out across the busy room, "Look what our Lord has ushered in. An old friend so hungry he would visit us in the cellar?"

They met in the middle of the hall and embraced.

"I see your restoration continues," Peter said.

"Very well, thank you! Or thanks to you, Prochorus and all the others. Perhaps you can explain this menagerie of humanity—and what I'm doing here with them?"

"Haw!" Jesus' chief disciple roared. "Just give in to the reality and enjoy it, Counselor of the Sanhedrin."

"Of course—I should have expected your answer, Peter."

"Good man, if I am not mistaken, you are here to listen to a secret Stephen has been asked to share with you. I have no doubt it will further draw you into the moment—and give you a taste of eternity, as well. Now, good day to you—and to Duca. I have a net full of souls to haul in, and I must be about my trade."

"Exciting days ahead?" queried Joseph.

"Yes. We're standing at the brink of death. Or possibly life. Who knows? It's all happening so quickly! We shall all know soon." Peter placed both his arms on Joseph's shoulders. "But for you, my friend, just learn the secret of this day and apply it. God willing, I'll see you in a week or so."

Joseph looked to Duca and then back to Peter.

"I am grateful to you both for the time you are spending helping me," he said.

"We need you, Joseph," said Peter. "We all believe we are spending this precious time wisely."

The fisherman departed.

Prochorus freed himself from his duties and found a place for his guests to sit.

"Over here, gentleman. Stephen will soon be with you. Here. Get comfortable. I hope you brought your appetites."

Joseph straddled the bench gracefully, not unlike his younger days mounting a horse or climbing upon a camel. Duca took note.

The secrets are taking hold. My master is regaining his mental, spiritual, and physical poise.

Prochorus did not sit. Looking across the room, he waved to Stephen to join them.

"Here he comes, Joseph. Your next counselor exits the kitchen."

When Stephen arrived at the table, Duca and Joseph respectfully stood, not knowing what to expect.

"Joseph of Arimathea and Duca of Egypt," Prochorus announced, "please meet the servant of all servants, Stephen

223

by name. I prefer to look to him as a steward, but he answers only to 'servant.'"

Before the three men finished respectfully greeting each other, Prochorus left to serve another table.

"Joseph and Duca, please sit," Stephen quietly requested. "I will as well, cherishing this time off my weary feet!"

Taking stock of the young man before him, Joseph was incredulous.

This fellow can't even be Duca's age. Has he lived enough to advise a man of my years? Ah, well, it is another chance to learn, and after all I've heard lately I won't question it!

While he was of normal height, Stephen's wraithlike frame made him appear almost frail. With small hands, slight wrists, and bony arms it seemed unlikely he could carry much weight—even the weight of a powerful new idea.

But as he spoke, his face began to glow, and his voice radiated inner strength.

"I've been counting the hours since Mary of Magdala asked me, through Prochorus, to share what I know with the austere, wise and highly reputed Joseph of Arimathea! It is a real honor to serve you, sir."

Joseph interrupted. "Young man, I am grateful. But I beg you not to assume I am wise just because of my age—any more than I should question your words because you have the face of a young angel. I welcome your own wisdom, however you have earned it. Despite your years, my recent experiences lead me to believe that your knowledge and understanding will flow from on High.

"Stephen, you're the eighth good person to walk with me on the path of my recovery. I'm deeply humbled at such attention and at the profound nature of the secrets. Your words will drive me further into the depths of the eternal moment, I know."

"Do you mind if we sit here in the midst of our patrons?" asked Stephen. "I must be available if my service is needed."

Joseph nodded his agreement.

Duca retrieved the blank papyrus from his leather pouch.

The bearer of the newest secret spoke.

"I have little right to assume the role of teacher of this subject—for I have only recently learned it myself. But its importance has been confirmed by Mary, Prochorus, several of Jesus' apostles, and the workers here this day. A year ago, I had never even heard of the Galilean. But then one day Jesus was speaking in the countryside, and what he said changed everything for me."

"What was it, dear boy?" asked Joseph.

"Jesus said, 'He who serves shall lead.' I even heard him command, 'He among you who is greatest, let him serve.'"

"You have a good memory, Stephen. I heard him speak these sentiments myself," Joseph said.

"He also disturbed many when he claimed, 'If you are not faithful in the little things, you will not be given authority over the larger ones.'

"The Magdalene knew how deeply I took these messages to heart, which is why she encouraged me to bring you this secret. She told me that while many heard what Jesus had to say about service, very few really heeded."

"So, you feel this part of Jesus' message spoke to you in a special way?"

"Honorable Joseph— while I encourage many of Jesus' followers to devote all their time to spreading his words, God has commissioned others like Prochorus and me to attend to the bodily needs of poor, the disabled, and the widowed. You see," Stephen blushed, "it was I who opened my young mouth one day to tell Peter, 'I think it's time you stopped fishing for fish.'"

"Not just a young mouth, Stephen," observed Joseph, "but brave as well!"

"In truth I was petrified to correct Jesus' most faithful follower. But when Jesus' body disappeared, some in the group were compelled to devote all their time to the ministry to keep it from expiring. Yet, they still had families to feed. Thus, it was only right for others to step forward to help meet their needs."

"This reminds me of Prochorus' secret. He spoke of taking action with creativity and urgency—even in the midst of change—all to help us focus on the moment and fulfill our destiny." Joseph turned to Duca, "Do I remember correctly, scribe?"

Duca glanced up from his writing and gave Joseph a concurring grin.

"Joseph," Stephen continued. "There's another part to the secret, and here it is: Service creates leaders. That's what Jesus meant when he said the least would be the greatest. Look at every moment as an opportunity to serve others, and you create a new kind of leadership."

Joseph squinted. "Serve and then rise to a position to lead, Stephen?"

"Not exactly, Joseph. Serving *is* leading. According to Jesus, they are the same.

"Although the way you are looking at it has merit as well. It is true that when you serve in the moment, you plant seeds of leadership. A baby becomes a young person, and then an adult. At the proper time, the servant will take on the mantle of a leader. But in truth, he is a leader in every single moment of service."

"Stephen, I will be frank with you. This is perhaps the most confusing secret I have heard so far. I have been a leader of people all my life. It was hard work, and at times I had to endure real hardships. But they served *me*."

"Yes, they did. But you earned their trust by hard work, competence, and a sense of commonality with them. You cared for those who followed you. It was your service to their needs that attracted their loyalty, not your ability to command.

"A man can compel a slave to do what he asks. But only a real leader can earn love, loyalty, and commitment. And only the most humble and dedicated servant can bring out the best in others.

"Joseph, you are already known as a just and honorable leader throughout the Promised Land of our ancestors, and well beyond to the deserts and plains of our enemies. Everywhere you have walked, your reputation as a leader went on before you! You've already seen this lesson work in your life."

"Indeed, I always dedicated myself to the welfare of those who were dependent on me. But I saw it all as my leading."

"As I've told others, your being *unconscious* of the Godly law that was in effect in your life has caused you to forget it. In other words, as Mary of Magdala has told me, because you did not fully know your value, you lost it.

"This secret today will make you *conscious* of that competence and restore it to your deepest being."

"But how does your wisdom relate to the power of the moment?" Joseph asked.

"Because it should be your constant point of focus. By looking at every moment as an instant to serve, by focusing on someone other than yourself, it is much easier to free yourself from worries about the future or regrets about the past. In the end, your destiny as a leader unfolds and is validated. And it becomes much easier to remain fully alive in the precious moment."

Joseph placed his hand on Duca's shoulder as his servant recorded the conversation. "Here we go again, my servant, another bright young mind races ahead of mine."

Duca slowly lifted his head to look at Joseph. A mischievous grin crossed his handsome face as he spoke.

"Choose your words well, master. If what our new friend says is true, then you might want to address me not as 'servant,' but as 'leader.'"

The three men chuckled.

"You have certainly led me on this journey, Duca. Proceed, Stephen," Joseph encouraged.

"The words of Jesus kept me awake for many nights. I had always felt promptings to direct the actions of other people. Even as a child, I would organize and lead the games of my small friends. Yet I'm young, not well connected, and unqualified—at least by the standards of the Sanhedrin. I was unsure where I might lead as an adult—in the Temple, in business, or in a social setting.

"The idea of 'serving to lead' hit me like a thunderclap. It was simple and so obviously true! So, I simply started helping anywhere I could. That was how I was able to 'lead' Peter. Because it had nothing to do with me, and everything to do with what was practical. It was what God wanted."

"Tell me," said Joseph, "How did the big man react to a slight fellow like you piping up?"

"He has not given an answer yet. No one has. But I have faith that he and others will be led by my sincere and selfless suggestions. They know about serving as a seed of leadership—because that is what our leader, Jesus, did."

"What do you mean, Stephen?" asked Joseph.

"Remember when Jesus' washing of his twelve friends' feet caused such a commotion? How he served the multitudes with a couple of bushels of bread and fish? Helped the woman of ill repute before her accusers? And I would not even be speaking to you had he not served Mary by casting those demons out of her in dusty Magdala."

"Did you witness any of these acts of service?" asked Joseph.

"Only the potential stoning of the adulterous woman."

"And?"

"Jesus knelt down before her, very much like a servant. He wrote something in the dirt. He said something to the men. Immediately after his comment to her judges, they dropped their stones and scurried away. His service to her quickly manifested into his leading them all!"

There was a long pause. Then Joseph said, "Stephen, I do not mean to question your teaching, or the teachings of Jesus—but I feel I know many who serve who do not lead."

"That's true. But that merely means they do not choose to lead!" Stephen paused. "We are all capable of leading, but some of us are content to follow. It is even possible to be a leader one day and a follower the next. Leadership in the moment is a possibility in each of us, because we are made in the image of God, as the Torah teaches us. It is embedded in us from creation—a part of our very design. Service holds the seed of leadership. But if we do not wish to lead, we never will. It's our choice. And choice is also a gift from God!"

"So while we should all serve others, even in doing that, some of us may refuse the responsibility of leading?"

"Yes, Joseph. But don't stray from the core of this truth: When we serve, we can also lead. Either way, the benefits to us and to others are as numerous as the stars in the sky. But if we do not serve at all, we miss out on the most powerful method to help us embrace the moment—along with an opportunity to express the God that is in each of us.

"The God of Abraham, Isaac, and Jacob was and is the ultimate leader as well as the ultimate servant of man. Did he not create the entire world and all its bounty for our benefit?

If we are crafted in that glorious image of complete generosity, how dare we not serve in each moment? Then in that moment of service we can take on the joyous responsibility of leading others! In that moment we become who *we* really are. In that moment we pass through a door and enter into eternity. We become the person God had destined us to be."

"Stephen," Joseph said. "For so young a man, your wisdom is as clear and refreshing as a rushing mountain stream."

"I thank you, honorable member of the Sanhedrin. Indeed, when God's spirit comes over me, my words flow like a bubbling spring. Still, many caution me to speak more guardedly because the times are so uncertain."

"Stephen, I have no uncertainty in this moment—I want you to continue," Joseph encouraged. "I thirst for more of this water!"

"Oh, forgive me, my friends," the Stephen exclaimed. "You must be more than thirsty. I have been a poor servant— I must fetch you some food."

Duca quickly responded, "Don't worry, Stephen. Before my master and I hurried to hear this wisdom, we had some fruit and nuts at the villa. Besides, the midday hour is still hours away."

"That is true," Stephen agreed. "But Martha of Bethany has given us her special recipe for lamb—and there may be none of that fare available when your stomachs summon help."

"Does Martha frequent this place of service?" asked Joseph.

"Oh, no. Her service is in Bethany where so many of Jesus' followers are hiding in the hills around her home. Talk about serving to lead! Martha has scores eating joyously out of her hand—partly because of her excellence as a cook, but mostly because of her loving labor for others."

"A great woman, indeed," Joseph concurred. "Truly an example of both a servant and a leader."

"So, no food, gentlemen?" Stephen asked again.

"Perhaps later, Stephen," answered Joseph. "For the moment, I am only hungry for more of this knowledge."

"Then I am happy to serve it up." Stephen paused to collect his thoughts. After a moment, he continued.

"Ah, yes—I must share something else about this secret. It is about pain."

Joseph frowned. "I feel I may know something about this. I have felt much pain since the loss of Sarah and Jesus."

"Of course. So perhaps you already know that while effective leaders do not inflict pain, they often endure it. Serving others has its benefits, but if you choose to lead, to be the best leader, you must never stop serving your followers— even when it hurts. Did we not see that with Jesus?"

"I am sad to say I saw more than you know, young Stephen," Joseph added, as he dropped his head.

"As I combed the scriptures after hearing the Rabbi teach, I read how our Creator gave each of us dominion over the creeping things of the earth. As I pondered that truth, I saw an abuse," said Stephen.

Joseph interrupted. "Do you mean the innocent creatures of the world suffer under our rule?"

"It's about more than animals, Joseph. Too many of our people—especially the ignorant and irreverent like the Romans—take dominion over fellow men. That's not what the teaching states. We must not dominate people; we must serve and lead them."

"Stephen, you must forgive me. But nearly all the leaders I've known—other than Jesus—were assertive, self-centered, physically imposing, and often distant from their followers. They were hardly servants at heart. Indeed, this leadership idea is a slippery fish."

Stephen nodded thoughtfully. "I know, Joseph, it's hard to define leadership. This frustrated me, too. Then God whispered this in my ear: 'Don't be confused by leadership. It is as difficult to describe as beauty. Elusive—but you will know it when you see it.'"

"So, should I throw away all my old ideas about what it takes to be a leader?" Joseph said.

"Joseph, I remind you again. Do not be distracted by nattering questions. If you keep it simple you won't have to over-think what you do. Jesus made it simple: "Serve and you shall lead." That is the core."

"Stephen, thank you much for this lesson. But there is something I'm curious about. You must tell me more about Peter. Harking to a little angel like you seems out of character for him. You telling him to turn his back on the countless fish waiting to be netted—it seems like advice he would scoff at."

"Interestingly enough, Joseph, when I tapped him on the back to tell him what was burning in my spirit, he did what he usually does. First, he put those big hands on my shoulders and gave me a stern look, straight into my eyes.

"Then he smiled."

"What did he say?"

"He said, 'Stephen, you make a lot of noise for a waving blade of grass! With the grip I hold on you right now, I could flip you into the sea—which is filled with fish bigger than you.' Then he continued, 'But, honestly, I welcome your counsel because it's the same my mother-in-law has been giving me since she met Jesus. Seeing the needs of the ministry before I did, she has been encouraging me to leave my business and devote all my time to the former carpenter. And now you are saying the same thing.' In the end, Peter assured me he would consult with the others about what I had recommended.'"

Joseph asked, "Did he say anything about surrendering?"

"Ah, yes. He spoke of accepting the reality before him and surrendering to its wisdom."

The Arimathean looked to Duca. "Peter also is doing what his secret commands: Surrender and accept. He is a good fellow!"

"Still stubborn, though," added Stephen, laughing. "I must admit!"

"Have you told him that?"

"No, but the Magdalene has! Peter respects and cares for her, but he has resisted her place in the movement. I don't think it's even conscious on his part. But after our talk about serving to lead, he could not ignore how much Mary embodies that very secret. He has slowly welcomed her into the group more formally. And with his humble surrendering and service to others, the strength of his leadership is becoming more obvious to all than ever before."

Even though the hall was overflowing for the midday course, Joseph felt as though he was resting in a private, peaceful, contemplative place. The grateful diners spoke softly, and despite the quiet, contented murmur that filled the crowded space, there was an overall sense of space and silent fellowship.

Joseph closed his eyes, letting the good feelings penetrate his being. He allowed the moment to linger, and Stephen watched silently. The merchant recognized that this latest secret was seeping deep into his spirit, and it was almost as if Duca and Stephen could see it happening.

Finally, Joseph opened his eyes and smiled at the slender rescuer and faithful servant.

"I have recorded everything," assured Duca.

"Then all is well," said Joseph.

Stephen smiled. "May I hail Prochorus to bring us some food?"

Joseph sighed, "No, thank you. Let this bounty go to those who need it much more than we do. We should rise and take our leave. We have work to do back at our home. Your wisdom will be transcribed for the future.

"Although a part of me would like to stay here and do some serving myself!"

"One more moment, please, Joseph?" Stephen asked.

"Of course."

The slight servant leaned forward.

"So that you do not forget, I offer three final thoughts:

"First, do not allow your memories of any person define who you think they may be today. With God's help, we can all be reborn in surprising ways.

"Second, do not cramp your own leadership potential by minimizing yourself, being negative, or dwelling on your weaknesses. Have respect and love, not just for the ones you are serving, but for yourself as well.

"And lastly, develop another leader by sharing this secret. This way the gift is forever being given.

"I encourage you to let these final three ideas guide you. You are a natural leader, Joseph. You always have been. If you become conscious of your gifts I know you will be of great service and lead many—finding your destiny and highest self in each moment!"

Understanding that the talk was completed, the three men stood.

"Go in peace, Joseph. I am honored to have offered this small service on your holy journey to become who you really are."

"And what is next for you, young counselor?" asked Joseph.

"I will continue to act as steward here, serving all. And I'll continue to pester Peter and the apostles to allow Prochorus and the rest of us to take care of their families, the widows, and the poor. My God promises limitless opportunities for me to serve.

"But that is in the future—and we no longer worry about that, do we? We belong to the moment now."

"Well, my son, continue to speak the truth. But be careful, for many hate the truth."

Stephen quickly added, "I would gladly die for God's truth."

Joseph nodded and took Stephen by the hand. "I can see it in the happy, contented look on your young face. And surely you have shared an invaluable truth with me today."

Duca led his master out the dining room and down the corridor to the steep steps leading up to the roadside entrance.

Not a word was spoken until they had returned to the estate of the Arimathean. By evening, the secret had been recorded.

The Slight Servant's Supportive Secret: Serve to Lead

- **Service ushers you into the moment.**
- **Service builds the trust that is essential to leadership.**
- **Service will reveal your highest destiny and truest self—unleashing your leadership potential.**
- **Leadership is a choice. It is possible to lead in the right moments and follow in others.**
- **The best leaders don't inflict pain—but they must be willing to endure it.**
- **Don't limit others or yourself; develop other leaders.**

Chapter XXVI.

Choosing Your Words

As Joseph and Duca left Prochorus' building, a massive black man entered by the back door. It was the scarred, statuesque Ethiopian merchant. Stephen had never seen the man, but a long hug between the powerful visitor and Prochorus made it clear the young ruler knew him well.

"I hope you're hungry, my friend. I assure you your first visit with us will be an unforgettable gastronomic experience."

Prochorus escorted the man to a vacant table, gesturing to Stephen to join them.

"Stephen, meet my friend: Tarek, the Ethiopian."

The slight servant bowed. As he rose, he found himself enveloped in a crushing embrace that nearly made him faint.

Tarek finally relinquished his grip with a huge smile. "I hope your rich associate hasn't confused you, and I've not squeezed the last breath from your bosom. I can tell you're an intelligent young man. Perhaps you wonder at an Ethiopian with an Egyptian name? Let's sit, eat, and talk."

"I am honored — but, Prochorus," Stephen said, "I should order the dishes for your friend."

"No, Stephen," said Prochorus. Waving to the kitchen door, he gestured for others to serve the table. "Please relax. I just want you to talk to Tarek. This is the best service you can render now."

Surrendering to the moment, Stephen took his place at the table.

"Tarek was an Egyptian slave, traded to the Romans and sent to the Coliseum to perform as a gladiator," Prochorus explained. "As you can see, he bears the marks of encounters with lions, leopards, and the most treacherous Roman athletes on his body—his scars are a veritable map of the Empire.

"But his real scars are the ones you cannot see."

Tarek sat calmly, carefully watching for Stephen's reaction. Stephen looked at the hulking man and smiled.

"Then you are surely one of us," Stephen said. "And I am eager to hear everything Prochorus has to tell me of your life and reason for joining us today."

"You see, Tarek—just as I told you," Prochorus said. "Stephen is not only the servant of all, but his discernment prepares him for leadership as well."

Several servers delivered mounds of lamb and chicken, and the Ethiopian looked them over approvingly.

"It is good that you will tell my story, Prochorus," Tarek said. "I think this food will keep me busy for the next little while."

"Stephen, Tarek is assisting me in restoring the Arimathean's routes. He won his freedom in Rome as the greatest gladiator of all. Today he provides security for his enterprising associates from Jerusalem to the Nile. In his work, he had never met a more trustworthy man than Joseph of Arimathea. When the Sanhedrin and associates of Pilate approached him to take part in the plan of absconding with Joseph's routes and relationships, he contacted me."

Prochorus paused to gesture that Tarek begin his meal.

Stephen suggested the three pray.

Tarek looked up with a blank stare.

Prochorus clarified with a smile. "Good Stephen, our friend Tarek doesn't know the God of Abraham, Isaac, and Jacob."

Looking to his Ethiopian friend, Prochorus continued, "Tarek, Stephen and I pray for your long life, good health, prosperous dealings, and ultimate acquaintance with your Creator. But today, eat up and be at peace."

Although confused by Prochorus' strange blessing, Stephen accepted it as he accepted all things, and restarted the discussion of Joseph.

"The Sanhedrin and Pilate are in unholy alliance against the righteous Arimathean?"

"Yes, Stephen, but that's not the reason I asked Tarek to join us. I simply wanted him to meet you. In the realm of dealing with all types of people, his wisdom knows no bounds. When I spoke of your courage in serving while also leading others to new thoughts, he insisted he meet you when we convened again.

"Yes, he and I will discuss Joseph's businesses privately later. But Tarek was moved by the spirits that guide him when I spoke of you."

Tarek swallowed a mouthful of succulent lamb, made from Martha's special recipe, and sighed appreciatively before speaking.

"Young Stephen, my good friend Prochorus believes you are destined to lead. He feels your service shows a special understanding of your Jesus. I know little of your rabbi, and care less.

"But I do know a thing or two about the crueler side of life. And Prochorus also says you have a tendency to say whatever you feel in the moment. I am alive today because of my skill at properly speaking when spoken to. Therefore, I bring you a warning."

Stephen's eyes widened at this, and Prochorus patted his hand in reassurance.

Tarek continued. "Words are cheap. Deeds matter. If you are to truly lead, choose your words carefully. Don't be so confident that all you say comes from the mind of your God. Take care that it is not *you* always opening your mouth, but rather the Wisdom of the Unseen. Respect even the despicable.

"And hope they return the favor." The Ethiopian returned to his seasoned lamb.

Stephen looked to Prochorus, taken aback at this teaching. He was suddenly afraid to open his mouth.

"Say what is on your mind, Stephen," Prochorus said.

Stephen took a deep breath. "But Tarek, I believe my words are those of a servant—honorable observations as God orders me to speak."

"I don't doubt your sincerity, Stephen," said Tarek. "But I'm convinced of your naïveté. If you wish to serve properly, ask more questions. The answers you'll receive will be your signposts, guiding you as you proceed.

"When others start asking *you* questions, you have begun to lead."

"With all respect to you and my sponsor Prochorus, from what source do you speak?"

"From my own source. Prochorus knows the story well. For years I could barely talk at all, I was so mentally and physically debilitated. But in my silence I served. All the while the abuse continued—especially in Egypt. But I was strong. Finally, I ended up in Roman arenas, venting my frustration in physical form. My deeds spoke for me. The crowds and the leaders came to love me—and my silence particularly captivated them.

"When I finally began to speak, they listened. Ultimately, my freedom was won, and today I'm dining with you both.

"Prochorus tells me you are special. I can see that. But if you do not choose your words with utmost care, your listeners may some day stop listening to your flow of wisdom. By all means continue to serve to lead—but fewer words will carry more weight. Then all will know your tongue is anointed with God's inspiration—not simply your own self-interests."

"Tarek, I do understand. And I have certainly been free with my thoughts. But please tell me—how will I know when the words are mine, and when they're my Creator's?"

Tarek contemplated as he continued eating. He appeared to have all the time in the world. Prochorus awaited his response patiently. Stephen leaned forward in anticipation.

The big man put his knife down. He reached across the wooden table with his scarred, massive forearms. He took Stephen's boney hands and they vanished within his ebony grasp.

"You will know, Stephen, by the response of your listeners. If you speak and there is no response, be silent. Let that sacred silence teach your listeners.

"You will learn from it as well."

"That strikes me as a difficult task," admitted Stephen.

"Perhaps. But the key is to always be aware. Aware of where you are, to whom you are speaking, and why. Be conscious of that moment."

"Your words remind me of Mary of Magdala," Stephen said.

Prochorus explained her role in the Jesus movement to the Ethiopian.

"This Magdalene must be a smart woman," Tarek said. "Her wisdom matches the logical thinkers I've met in Egypt, and even some Romans, as emotional as that lot can be."

The three sat for a while, silently pondering Tarek's words while he continued enjoying his meal. Finally, when he was finished, he looked directly at Stephen once again.

"When you speak too much, you announce loudly what you don't know. When you listen, you learn. You also discover what the speaker doesn't know. This is nourishment for leadership.

"I believe you are destined to lead, Stephen. You're sincere. Choose your words carefully, and all will be well. In the meantime, I hope your physical well being is as much a concern for your God as it is in my mind."

Chapter XXVII.

Other Worlds

Joseph slept later than usual the next morning. As Duca peeked into the room at the cock's first crow, he saw the papyrus notes he had inscribed strewn across Joseph's bed. Duca was gratified. The plan for the Arimathean's restoration was working.

Duca decided not to disturb his master's rest.

An hour later, as the sounds of the waking city could be heard, Joseph called from his bedchamber.

"Duca, Duca, I've overslept! Are we late for our next appointment?"

Having just disposed of the ashes from the library's fire, the servant hastily finished washing his hands and rushed to Joseph's bedchamber.

"Don't fret, master. Today we rest and reflect. But tomorrow and the next will have us returning to the city, if you are still willing. Then on the third day, you'll receive your final guests here.

"Then all the secrets will have been delivered!"

Joseph sat upright in his bed.

"You know how eager I have become for these teachings, Duca. But I wonder, am I being sufficiently patient, as

I have been taught? Is it possible we're rushing these final lessons?"

"It's wise of you to ask, master. But there is a reason for our haste. Word comes from Mary and others that tensions are rising. At first the authorities believed that the followers of Jesus had scattered and the controversy of the empty tomb would fade along with them. But then came other news."

"What was it, Duca?"

"Master, I beg your forgiveness. But the Magdalene insists I withhold that information until the last secret is delivered. She urges you to be patient in this matter."

"If Mary of Magdala appeals for my patience, I'll most certainly heed her. I've placed myself in the dark for almost fifty days now. I can endure being ignorant for three more."

"Good," Duca responded. "Then tomorrow the horses will be ready. We shall travel just beyond the eastern gate of Jerusalem. There in the rolling hills is a tiny conclave of shepherds. We'll call on a petite woman and her brother."

"Old friends of yours?"

"It's Mary who's acquainted with the man. The woman is his sister. They're twins. It's her house. Her brother, a master builder, will be working there to shore up a shed that's starting to lean."

"A master builder reinforcing an old shack?"

"Ah, you are most observant, master! My understanding is that he has missed his sister's companionship since Jesus' last days. His visit there is convenient for us—and is part of his disguise."

"Was he close to Jesus?" Joseph asked.

"Yes, master. The next secret will come forth from the one known as Thomas—Thomas, the Twin."

Joseph shook his head.

Thomas. The pessimistic, over-serious, negative over-thinker, who just happens to be a building genius, will be visiting his sister? Another Galilean who had no problem dying for a cause!

But this one always needed to know—and to share—too much!

Joseph smiled ruefully in recollection.

Hard to believe Thomas carries a valuable secret for me. But I suppose I could say that about most of the wise rescuers who have come to my aid! I must remain humble. My precious moments of revelation are fast dwindling, while those who have brought them to me have become even more enigmatic!

Duca noticed his master's odd smile, and wondered what was going on in his mind.

"Master, does your thinking take you out of the moment, or bring you into it?"

Joseph laughed out loud.

"You might say I'm marveling at the creative genius that assembled this motley gang of counselors, Duca. I credit the Magdalene for her skill at orchestration—and the God of Abraham, Isaac, and Jacob for having such a sense of humor."

"You know our next rescuer, master?"

"Oh, most assuredly! My wager to you, young Egyptian, is that Thomas will not smile once during our visit. His approach is always to teach by asking stern questions! If we arrive with a bright countenance, he'll surely darken it with his seriousness. I suppose he's one of those whom men describe as 'too smart for his own good.'"

"You may be in for a surprise, master. Mary assures me a change has overtaken your friend Thomas—a change of spirit and mind."

"Of course," Joseph apologized. "How short-sighted of me. I've seen how the others have been transformed. God forgive me for doubting that Thomas, too, is capable of change.

"I well remember how ready Thomas was to die with Jesus that day in Bethany when the Rabbi restored Lazarus. Yes, he was a man with many questions—perhaps too many. But once satisfied with facts, I cannot deny that Thomas could be loyal, even to death."

"So," continued the servant, "let us rest today in preparation for the next three. Tomorrow we visit with Thomas. I myself am most excited now!"

The next day in Jerusalem seemed like midsummer. The dusty roads just beyond the city contrasted with the gentle, green slopes dotted with innocent sheep.

Persian Prince trotted the road proudly. Joseph, happy and confident on his back, felt his own strength had nearly returned. After nearly an hour's ride, Duca pulled back on the reins and brought his bay mare to a halt at a neat cottage. Joseph followed suit on the Prince.

A small, perspiring woman with a warm smile welcomed the richly outfitted horsemen. As Duca helped Joseph slide from his saddle, the woman introduced herself.

"I am Elizabeth, twin of Thomas. I'm honored that the great Joseph of Arimathea graces my abode."

"Oh, good woman," Joseph quickly responded. "I'm the one in debt. My heart is leaping in anticipation of listening to one who values knowledge as much as your brother. I'm hungry for yet another revelation."

"You'll find him more remarkable than ever, Joseph. While Thomas remains a thoughtful and serious man in these challenging new days, he's doing something that was foreign to him in the past—he's smiling. I knew him from the day we both were born, and I'm as surprised by this as anyone!"

Duca and Joseph followed the woman around the tiny cottage.

"I'll fetch some fresh spring water for you. I'll bring it to you by the shed over there," she pointed. "As you can see, the master builder is propping up my donkey's stall!"

Thomas was so enthralled in his work that he didn't notice his guests drawing near. Duca coughed loudly to get his attention as the builder bent over a tough beam he was working with a plane. Startled, Thomas recoiled, and then turned to face his guests.

Seeing Joseph's lined, gentle face, Thomas smiled so broadly that a sunny glow seemed to engulf him.

"Joseph of Arimathea! May I embrace the one whom I respect above all, save the Rabbi? To think the Magdalene would choose me to deliver a secret to one as distinguished as a judge of the Great Sanhedrin!"

"Thomas, is it really you? I feel your warm and sincere welcome is not deserved by one who's been hiding in a dark room for almost two months. To be frank, I would have expected something more like, 'Where were you when we needed you, Joseph, the Trembling?'"

"No! Not now, Joseph! Now I am simply overjoyed to see you out in the world again! And so much of it due to your faithful servant, Duca!"

All three men laughed and embraced.

"Although you managed to startle me, I have been expecting you," Thomas said, producing three squat, three-legged stools and placing them in the shade of the small outbuilding. "Please sit. As much as I'd love to seek advice from you this day, wise Joseph, the Magdalene has asked me to share a secret with you. And I do have much to share.

"As you know, these times are overwrought. Things are happening."

Elizabeth arrived with cool water and fresh dates, and then left the men to themselves.

"Joseph, when I heard of your condition, I pleaded with Mary that I might serve you. I had so often been mired in the past and in the future—always blind to the moment before me. I was so conflicted because of my obsession with truth, facts, details, evidence—I imagined I drew power from the most insignificant specks of knowledge."

Joseph smiled. "I remember well, Thomas."

"Well, that changed in an instant."

"An instant?"

"Yes, in one moment. The Lord did something that changed my world."

"Was it something he said?"

"No. It was what he did."

Duca wobbled on his precarious wooden stool, struggling to make notes with the papyrus perched on his knee.

"Gentlemen," he pleaded, "your indulgence, please. Speak more slowly so I have time to write down the words. I suspect this secret has the potential to change the world, in addition to restoring my master!"

"My heartfelt thanks, young man," Thomas said. "Such praise emboldens me! And I might be able to do something to help your writing, as well!"

The master carpenter brought a small log used for chopping firewood and placed it in front of Duca. He put the smooth tray Elizabeth had used for dates on top of it.

"Not your regular desk, Duca, but surely a better platform for a scribe than his boney knee!"

"I thank you for your generosity, Thomas," Duca said. "Now I can be certain I won't miss a word."

"Joseph, you knew me well. I was always either seeking or offering words of explanation for anything and everything that happened to Jesus and our band. I always worried, always anticipated the worst that could happen. Often was I lost in the jungle of my own pondering. But our friend from Galilee even found use for someone like me—so burdened by facts and so unburdened by faith!

"In retrospect, I was not the smartest member of our group."

Joseph tried to hide his smile, and Thomas laughed out loud at his own admission.

"No one will ever approach Jesus' patience with us," Joseph offered, kindly. "Nor could any hope to match his insight. We have all fallen short."

"So true, Joseph. But here's what happened to me," Thomas proceeded. "It was only four weeks ago. We were all frightened—in a frenzy to make sense of everything that had happened. I had the most questions. Mary Magdalene had spoken with Him after the crucifixion; Peter, John, Mark, and some of the rest had, as well.

"Me? I was absent, searching for answers in all the wrong places. When I would see one of the followers and hear of their stories, I would get autocratic, then distant—and even attack their credibility! I was an ass, pure and simple. I allowed facts and intellectual prowess be my gods.

"No one knew what to do with Thomas the Twin!"

"Thomas, I didn't know you were struggling so much," admitted Joseph. "But now I recognize it—because I labored similarly."

"Here's the secret revealed to me," Thomas announced. "It's simple to grasp, but not easy to practice. It is this: The moment before us—the one that God gives to us—is all we have. To distance ourselves from it with our minds is to reject this holy gift.

"So, to immerse yourself in this moment, simply listen to whomever you are with; observe their every move; get into their world.

"How blessed I was to learn this in the presence of Jesus himself!"

Thomas took a moment to allow his words to sink in.

Duca continued with his notes.

Joseph waited for more.

Silence flooded in. The sound of sheep munching on grass just beyond the shed could be heard faintly. The wind passing through the frail lean-to filled their ears. Elizabeth could be heard in the small home, cleaning wooden pots. The hum of the city in the distance was now discernable. No one felt a need to speak.

Thomas and Joseph were in a moment of revelation and contemplation that had no place for past or future events. It was a simple, timeless instant to be savored.

After a long while, Joseph broke the silence, speaking reverently, but with a slight note of hesitation in his words.

"Thomas, my spirit approaches understanding. And my body confirms your words with a peace that passes understanding.

"But I cannot seem to help myself—my sinful mind is stubborn."

"Don't worry, Joseph. It's only because Jesus was standing right in front of me when he did what he did. There was no more room for doubt."

"And he did what?"

"He showed me his wounds—his hands, his side, and his feet."

Joseph stood up from his seat, seemingly in a daze, unsure of what he had heard. Duca ceased writing and began to stare into the placid hills.

Silence.

"When?" asked Joseph.

"When he visited with us."

"Thomas. Please understand my difficulty! I have the spear that pierced him. I have the cup that filled with his blood. I was outside the tomb as his dead body was anointed. Thomas, I have in my possession the shroud that wrapped his body!"

Thomas responded with a soft, understanding voice.

"You and I are so much alike, Joseph. You want facts. Not truth."

"This is so hard to grasp, Thomas,"

"Facts are not truth, Joseph. Not the real truth. Not the hopes, the dreams, the intuitions, and the visions that fill our souls. You, like me, need to touch to prove existence. But here is the real truth: everything we see and touch today was birthed in the unseen world—the invisible Kingdom of the Spirit.

"This is the truth that matters—not the syllogistic, over-thought points of a Greek logician!"

Joseph sat down again, still wide-eyed with shock.

"Unlike me, perhaps because of your years of successful trading," Thomas continued, kindly, "you can at least claim to want the other kind of truth for the sake of a practical end result. At least you have always sought after knowledge that would help you make sensible decisions. My vain temptation was to seek endless, tedious, empty knowledge for its own sake!"

"In truth, Thomas, I always thought of us as being similar," Joseph said.

"Not quite, Counselor." Thomas reached to place his hand on the older man's shoulder. "I just wanted the facts. You wanted to do something with them. We are different. That's part of the secret."

"Yes, I understand our different worlds, Thomas. The Magdalene told me of her meeting with Jesus after his death. I have tried to believe. But I want to hear *you* tell me. How...how did he come to be in your presence after the crucifixion?"

Sweat stood out on the Arimathean's brow, and he leaned forward with both hands together, as if praying.

"That is a question that will be asked by many for centuries to follow. But please understand what he did first. And please—take a cool drink, Joseph, and rest back on the stool."

"My heart is kicking like a colt," Joseph said.

Duca put down his writing instruments and brought his master some water.

"Just as mine did when I saw Jesus," Thomas said. When Joseph had finished his water, Thomas continued.

"Listen how Jesus behaved, Joseph. He entered the room. He ignored those who already believed or who had already encountered him in those impossible days.

"He walked right up to *me*. He walked past everyone else. His sights were set only on me.

"He came to my soul at the exact location it was in. He entered my world of evidence, facts, observations, axioms, rules, and laws—and delivered all of them to me in a moment, right then and there!

"He demonstrated his existence the way I had to see it. He showed me the brutal facts—the holes that were punched in his mortal body. As he moved into my world, I realized how deeply he understood me. In his compassion to understand me and honor my behavior and my way of living—despite my wrong-headedness—I was able to embody the reality of his presence."

"Thomas, he was there *in the flesh?*"

"I touched him, and I immediately understood."

"The others?"

"They did not need the evidence I needed. Perhaps they possessed more faith. I was simply a different sort of man. Jesus knew that and respected it. Getting into my moment, my world, my space, helped me come to my own realization, my way.

"In his compassion he ignored my selfishness. Because of that act of love and understanding, my agenda vanished. Now, I'll always belong to him.

"Joseph, I know his physical appearance dominates your thoughts. But please—pause for a moment to learn the real secret."

"How can I?" Joseph was struggling to believe the enormity of these miracles.

He took a deep breath. Then something softened inside as the secrets urged him to be present in the blessed moment.

Duca and Thomas waited patiently, seemingly aware of the process he was going through. Finally, he was ready to hear what Thomas had to share.

"I must grasp this secret. Yes, teach me, Thomas. Undo my awful consternation. I beg of you."

"All will be revealed, dear brother," Thomas answered, "Just don't race ahead of the teaching.

"On that day, in the presence of many, Jesus came into my analytical world. He set aside his mission to the entire universe to address my own individual obsession with details. Here was a man on assignment from the Great Almighty himself, with a map so ambitious I could only be the smallest dot on it. He was literally driving history to a set of cosmic conclusions prophesied by our most anointed ancestors.

"Yet Jesus took the time to slow that series of cataclysmic events down to recruit my heart! With an objective put in his hands by the Creator of the Universe, he paused to persuade me—in the only way a man like me could be persuaded!"

"The secret, Thomas? Speak!"

"Listen carefully, again, Joseph: Appreciate the *kind* of person you encounter in the moment. Approach them with respect for their thoughts, their orientation, their inner spirit, and their usual behavior. Maybe they are an analytical fact-finder like me, or a results-oriented driver like you, or a visionary dreamer like our wonderfully expressive friend, the Magdalene. Or perhaps they are one who lives to love others, like the amiable servant by your side.

"Regardless of their world, observe it, respect it, and enter into it. In this way you will gain their attention, respect, and trust. By entering into their spirit you become one with them in their hearts—and lead them on to greatness in their own destinies."

"But how?"

"As I said, it's simple—but not easy. You must be flexible and adaptable. Versatile, if you will. You must learn to approach people humbly, with more interest in them than in yourself.

"In my case, it meant that their thoughts were more important than my own thoughts. I needed to become a loving servant in my heart, just as Jesus had to each of us."

"How exactly does one do this?"

"Lovingly watch each person's behavior and see what matters to them. Observe how they behave during times of difficulty. Try to understand what is important to them, and speak to them using words and values they already understand."

"But Thomas, are you saying I should abandon my natural behavior and beliefs—to make myself over in the image of others?"

"No. You get to keep being a businessman, Joseph! Don't leave your world of interests and habits. But others will surely appreciate your world better if you first respect theirs. Remember, none are better than you, but neither are you superior to them."

"So I should move into the moment by focusing on where others come from and how they like to behave," Joseph said.

Thomas looked at the busily scribbling servant and smiled.

"Duca, you and Mary have made much progress with the Arimathean. He is a good student. I think he's beginning to understand!"

Duca continued with his note-taking while answering.

"Yes, the best of the Joseph of old is re-emerging, and along with him I get glimpses of an entirely new Joseph. I perceive that my master has arrived on a shore from which he will never go back."

Duca dotted the page with his quill as if to emphasize that he had caught up with the conversation. Then he looked up at Thomas.

"Thomas—forgive my impertinence, but may I make an inquiry about my own self?"

Thomas smiled. "Certainly, Duca."

"Well, you characterized me earlier as being primarily interested in relationships with other people. But I don't believe we've ever met. How can you claim to know me, or know that my world is more about people than about facts, dreams, or results?"

"Duca, Mary described you very vividly to me as a man to whom relationships and service are all-important. If what she told me is accurate, you overflow with concern for others and their well-being—with minimum conflict. Believe me, your inner nature is often quite apparent to others."

Joseph interrupted.

"The lady from Magdala is most astute. But I fear I am slower to grasp this moment-enhancing secret as quickly as you younger men."

"Do you have a specific question, trader?" asked Thomas.

"A thousand, master builder! I can see how this approach would be useful in the presence of one other person. But I'm dying to know how Jesus dealt with the diverse group he assembled. Do you know?"

Thomas stood up to stretch, knowing his student was now fully engaged.

"It's an excellent question, Joseph. I can't authoritatively say what was in Jesus' mind. And none of us will ever match

255

his ability to see to the heart of every person. But here is how I've come, through his example, to approach others.

"First, I examine each person I am with. I ask myself: are they like me, always asking questions? Or do they simply tell what they know, the way our assertive friend from Magdala does?"

"Ask or tell? That's a hint?"

"Yes. If questions flow, we know that person likes to direct by asking. It's very unlike Mary, who shows her strength by making statements, seldom asking any questions. Her behavior is dominated by telling. That's what you have in common with the Magdalene. The question is, what do I and Duca have in common—since we both usually tend to ask rather than tell?"

"Please, continue," said Joseph.

"Well, Duca and I *are* alike because of our penchant for questions," Thomas added. "But we're still different. Duca is more emotional than I. I am more controlled. In your case relative to Mary, you lack her open, visible emoting—but you are both most forceful in your behavior."

"I can see those differences," Joseph admitted. "And they require alternate approaches to make the other person feel respected and understood?"

"Yes, Joseph. You're getting it," affirmed Thomas. "I am sure you have had similar experiences as a trader. Surely you proceed differently with Pilate than with a date merchant in the city."

"Very true. But this seems different, somehow," Joseph said.

"Yes. You must appreciate that this secret requires time and practice. But for now, rest assured: The more you open yourself up to the world of others, the more deeply you will enter into the eternal moment."

"Thomas, you've changed from your days as a negative worrier obsessed with detail," observed Joseph. "Your arguments are most convincing. We must come back together so I may learn more.

"But now, while these thoughts nestle into my brain, please give me more clues to help me paint the picture of others' worlds."

"Of course. Stressful times are a good indicator. Analytical me and amiable Duca both react the same during tense times—we flee. He acquiesces, whereas I merely vanish. He reluctantly agrees with those around him, while I fly away to find more facts.

"On the other hand, you, like Mary, usually fight back when under pressure—although this recent episode apparently broke down your usually great strength. But generally, I am sure you assert your autonomy—while Mary simply attacks whoever is in disagreement!"

"I've heard that about her," agreed Joseph.

Thomas' eyebrows rose.

"You should've seen her with Peter when he seemed offended she had been chosen to encounter Jesus before anyone else! She was insulted, reminding the fisherman how he had denied the Lord's friendship to some accusers on that horrible night. She even hinted that his faith was insufficient. Thank God she took control of her emotions and apologized to him. Who knows what he might have done!"

"Oh my, this is all too much. You're filling my head with these interesting habits of the mind while something unfathomable has happened that I must understand!"

"And what is that?"

"You must tell me more about Jesus' appearing to you, before our time together today ends. That's what I most long to know."

"I will soon, Joseph. I cannot today. In a few more days, but not now."

Thomas noticed the look of disappointment crossing the merchant's face.

"Don't let impatience take over, Joseph. I understand your pragmatic need to drive to an end result. I can assure you the assumptions you made in Jesus' youth, despite your doubts, were all correct. Joseph—I believe you're about to see your wildest hopes confirmed!

"For a long time, you were on the road to revelation. You fell off only because you witnessed the horrible event firsthand. Then you encountered Pilate's so-called justice — from the bottom of a dank, cruel cell. Then, to cap it all, you suffered the sudden passing of your wife.

"Naturally, you attempted to respond with what had always brought you success in the past: your orientation to results and reasonableness. But that response was woefully inadequate to the dreadfulness of the situation. It broke you. It sent you into seclusion, and there you stayed.

"Believe me, good man, there's a day coming when the Spirit of God Himself will enter your world and confirm who you are, giving you power to continue to fulfill your destiny."

"When, Thomas?"

"Mary and her guest will reveal that to you in a couple of days."

Duca halted his note-taking and took a deep breath of the warm air. He caressed his cool wooden cup with both hands and enjoyed a drink of refreshing water.

Thomas smiled at Joseph.

The merchant smiled back—but it was a weary smile.

"I'm exhausted," admitted Joseph. "But once again, I will follow instructions; this time because a new Thomas has promised me my questions will be answered in my way. But who will explain to me what is happening when these future events transpire?"

"It will be the Holy Spirit of God. He understands your world and mine better than we ever could. He will walk through the doorway of your world, just as I'm suggesting you step into other people's worlds. After all, it is He who revealed this secret.

"You will see the essence of this secret unfold, just as it did for me when Jesus walked directly to me in front of all the others."

The three men paused thoughtfully over their empty goblets, each perspiring in the late morning heat. As they rose and embraced, Thomas assured Joseph he would see him in a short while.

They could sense in the stillness that there was a growing urgency in the moment—the uncanny quiet of a world about to be turned upside down.

Before retiring that night, Joseph studied Duca's notes.

The Doubter's Supportive Secret: Enter Their World

- **Speak to others as they wish to be spoken to.**
- **Focus on what is important to them—and how they can be encouraged to achieve their destiny.**
- **Some are doers—people who like to achieve and to lead.**
- **Some are thinkers—who approach every situation with perspective and distance.**
- **Some have expressive, artistic personalities—they live by spinning off creative energy.**
- **Some are naturally social—they do their best close to people, and by communicating.**
- **Some show feelings, while others control emotions.**
- **People react to distress differently:**
    - **A cold questioner gets lost**
    - **A friendly companion acquiesces**
    - **A driving caravan leader becomes autocratic**
    - **An artist attacks**

These are telltale pointers to their worlds.

- These behaviors are not good or bad—but unless we acknowledge that we all function and reason differently, we will never understand one another.
- Versatility in entering others' worlds builds understanding that leads to trust.

Chapter XXVIII.

Many are Called,
but Few are Chosen

Thomas completed his repairs to the donkey stall later that afternoon. Then he sat down wearily on his three-legged stool. While the temperature was as high as a midsummer day, it was not the physical labor that weighed him down.

It was anticipation of the immensity of the task before him.

Thoughts began to flow into his mind.

What I know must now be shared with all the world. How can this be done? I must recruit a building crew and set out to where the Lord needs me most. I'll lead with my trade, and tell the story as well.

I can't tarry. I don't have time to attend the gathering in Jerusalem with the rest f the followers! Now is my time to go to the ends of the earth to teach and tell—just as I've done with Joseph.

Elizabeth interrupted Thomas' dour thoughts. She plopped down in the hay beside him, wiping a damp lock of raven hair off her brow with her sleeve, marveling at how summer seemed to have arrived so early.

"Thomas, so much is changing. Even the weather seems to be following an unfamiliar schedule."

"Indeed, sister. And an unfamiliar future plagues me now."

"Thomas, are you thinking too much again? I know you better than anyone. Remember—it is said we held hands as we entered this world."

"Ah, yes, my twin." Looking upward as if conversing to God, Thomas said. "She knows when my pondering holds the promise of change—and when it's simply useless thinking. I thank you, Father, for my sister."

Smiling at her, Thomas reached for the plate of dates and goat cheese the pretty girl had placed at his side.

"It's also fine if you say 'thank you' to me once in a while," she teased.

Savoring the food, Thomas continued. "I think the Lord would have me fulfill my destiny now. I feel a pull to the Far East. The story of the Man from Galilee is unknown there. My building skills and my men will finance our travels. My words, God willing, will attract the masses to hear."

"That plan's not new, Thomas. Why your consternation?"

"I feel I must go now."

"Before the moment proclaimed in the Holy City?"

"Yes. I've seen Him, spoken with Him—and now I'm ready to sacrifice everything. I don't need an emotional gathering of friends to spur me onward. It's a person like Joseph who should be there. There's still so much for him to see and learn."

"Well, isn't this a surprise! My old brother has returned."

Elizabeth rose to make her point.

"Try to remember your secret—delivered just this day, Thomas doubter! Are you too wise to learn when all gather together on that day? Now you judge *their* readiness to go forth? They should be present for the event, but not you?

"Thomas, you make me angry! You have all the answers, and they don't?"

Thomas raised his hands, taken aback by his sister's passion.

"Elizabeth—you know the change in me more than anyone!"

"But why? Why would you not heed the One you respected so much?"

"Who?"

"Was it not Jesus himself who commanded you all to remain in Jerusalem? You told me yourself! It was on the very day He walked up to you directly in that cramped room! He talked about a promise from the Father. He talked about a new baptism—one not of water but of the Holy Spirit.

"Practically speaking, my good, analytical brother, I don't think you're ready to go *anywhere* yet!"

"How can you say that? Since His last supper with us I've relived the last three years in my mind constantly. Then He appears—and speaks only to *me* in that crowded place. I think I *am* ready to go now and spread His gospel."

"But His command was to wait in Jerusalem. Not to go out now! And I know why!"

"Why?"

"Because you'll need strength of mind, spirit, and body which you don't possess yet. For that matter, no one on earth has that power, because according to Jesus, it's the power of the Holy Spirit that's to come upon you.

"The future will be much more treacherous than you think, Thomas. And only that power from on High will pave the path for your destiny—and all of our destinies."

"Oh, so you're going out to proclaim his story as well?"

Shaking her head, Elizabeth turned her back on Thomas, and then abruptly faced him again with pointed finger.

"You'd best search that cluttered mind of yours, brother! Because you missed it all if you think what Jesus represented was just for a few!"

"Calm down, Elizabeth. Please. Yes, I need you to show me my reflection. Yes, you have reminded me! He did make it clear His message is for 'whosoever will.' And, I do recall He spoke of all of us being empowered on that coming day."

"And didn't He also proclaim that only at that point you should go into Judea, Samaria, and to the outer bounds of the world? Well?"

"Sister, I stand corrected, but ..."

"No buts. There's no reason for you to rush the process. See, I am right. I perceive you've been thinking too much. And like the hardheaded, tense thinker that you used to be — and claim you have stopped being — you planned on escaping too soon. Keep it simple, Thomas! Follow His instruction regarding this gathering! Makes sense, doesn't it?"

"Ah, my sister. Just like me — ends her reasoning with an assertive question."

"Well?"

"Perhaps."

"No perhaps, Thomas! Besides, I'll be with you. And we'll be holding hands just as we did when we were first born — and just as we did when John the Baptist dunked us in the Jordan River. I think it would be proper we be holding hands during this new spiritual baptism, however that comes about."

"How charming," Thomas reacted, sarcastically.

"*Charming*? Stop it *now*, Thomas. It is simply obedience to the One you'll soon risk your life for. And yes, it would be proper. Our parents would smile at our continued love for each other and our obedience to the Higher Power."

A welcome breeze caressed Thomas' perspiring face.

Then something happened. Elizabeth dropped her head in prayer—and it was as if the warm wind blew away all the doubts coursing through Thomas' mind.

Suddenly, there were no thoughts rushing through Thomas' head. None at all. Simply a peaceful moment.

Then a small voice seemed to whisper to him from within: "Obey."

It would please my Lord for me to be present. Finally, his "Doubting Thomas" would learn from a realm beyond touch, hearing, taste, or smell.

Thomas rose and reached for his sister's hand.

"Twin, let's refresh ourselves and be off to the Widow Mary's. Perhaps today is the day for this new baptism."

Chapter XXIX.

Agape

T he late spring moon was full, shedding the only light Joseph would see for at least the next two hours. Yet he was fully dressed, lovingly brushing a sleepy Persian Prince with his own hand. Even Duca had not yet arrived to prepare the horses for today's ride.

The Magdalene's written instructions, delivered just before Duca and Joseph had retired the night before, were short and simple:

Arrive at the house of Mary the Widow before sunrise. The days are racing to the moment of transformation. The Romans and the Sanhedrin are keenly aware of our increased activity. You must arrive in darkness and wait until sunset to depart.

Mary the Widow was the wife of Clopas and mother of young Mark. Though elderly, she was exceptionally strong and sensible. Her home on the outskirts of Jerusalem—on the road to Bethlehem—had become a refuge to many of Jesus' followers who had yet to flee the Holy City for the woods and hills.

While it was but a short walk from the city gate that welcomed travelers from across the region, it was off the main road, and its walled perimeter was smothering in pomegranate trees so thick the house was virtually invisible to passersby.

The home was orderly and well kept, in spite of the recent volume of transient visitors. Respect followed her wherever Mary the Widow ventured throughout the area. The believers knew her as one of the four woman witnesses at the crucifixion of Jesus. It was also in the upper room of her house that Jesus presided over his final Passover meal with his apostles, just before his arrest in the nearby garden at Gethsemane.

Joseph had mixed emotions about the proposed meeting site. Over the last three years he and Nicodemus had been guests at Mary's several times. But the memory of the days that immediately followed the Passover dinner in her home still weighed heavily on Joseph's heart. And the Arimathean's initial enthusiasm for the handcrafted cup he had fashioned for Jesus' last gathering had turned to bitter sadness. While the cup was now in his possession, it was supposed to be the Galilean's for life.

And its purpose had been to hold new wine—not the young preacher's blood.

Even though it was dark, Duca and Joseph approached Mary's home in a roundabout way to avoid the earliest predawn traffic heading to market in Jerusalem.

As they reined in the horses in the familiar courtyard of the home, Joseph was wrestling with thoughts. Unfortunately, some were not his own.

The secrets have given me strength because they impel me into the moment. Yet, it's so difficult to ignore the recollections that attack my mind as we approach the widow's house. So that I may be fully prepared to take advantage of this teaching, I must review the secrets.

Duca helped Joseph dismount.

"Duca—leave me here for a moment to be alone with my thoughts. I will sit under this pomegranate tree."

"Very well, master."

Joseph seated himself under the tree and closed his eyes, reviewing all he had learned in the past days and willing his troubling thoughts to cease. As he did so, time seemed to stand still, and he felt the power of the secrets working on his behalf.

It seemed only a moment had passed when Duca placed a gentle hand on his shoulder.

"Master—excuse me for disturbing your thoughts. The next to last secret will be delivered to you shortly."

Startled, Joseph looked at his servant.

"Were you sleeping, master?" Duca asked. "I fear you were awake most of the night."

Joseph smiled and reached out his hand for his servant to help him up.

"Duca, I hardly slept at all last night. But no rest is possible with my heart pounding in anticipation like a young child."

"Watch your step, master. Mary the Widow will be awaiting our arrival. I smell the early morning fire, and I see that her home is well-lit."

From the depths of the new day's shadows, the elderly hostess appeared, holding a rope tied round the neck of a sleepy donkey.

She embraced Joseph without a word.

"I know your thoughts, dear wife of Clopas, my loyal friend of old. Your silence speaks your disappointment in my absence since Golgotha."

Turning to Duca, Joseph added, "I surely wandered like Mary's lost little donkey. Thank God I, too, have recently been lassoed by my rescuer friends."

"No, no, Counselor, I never doubted your intentions," said Mary. "Just seeing you restores my faith in our God. He is still on the throne.

"Prayer changes things, Joseph. Your safety and healthy countenance bring joy to my heart. I know all about your recovery. I assure you this day will provide more divine healing.

"On the other hand," she said, "While I would never dare compare you to a donkey, I do have to scold my little friend here for drifting from time to time."

A hearty laugh issued from the Arimathean as he and Duca followed the widow across the cobbled courtyard to the house.

The solitary rooster of the yard cried out announcement of a new day. As Mary of Magdala had planned, all three were safely in the building moments before the rising of the sun.

Cheese, honey, fresh water, grapes, pomegranates, and nuts awaited the guests. Mary seated the two men near the open hearth, each with a small table to support a wooden plate for their breakfasts.

Joseph spoke first.

"Your son Mark is one of my favorite young men in Jerusalem. His potential for the cause was always plain to me."

"Yes, Joseph, he's a good boy. You will see him today. But as with all of us, his life has changed. His innocent youth has fled like a bird—out of the cage and far from his old mother's bosom. The good news is that our God is ready to use him. Mark will arrive later with the others."

"Doesn't he live here?" asked Joseph.

"Oh, yes. But like so many who have become my sons and daughters since the passing of the Lord, they depart at varying times of the day and night. We can't let the authorities find us all under the same roof at once."

"I understand your fear," Joseph said.

"No, good Arimathean—it's not fear. It's merely sensible strategy until the time we are to be gathered together.

"That moment is coming soon."

"I sense that as well," commented Joseph. "I am eager to hear your secret, Mary. Have you shared it with your son?"

A grin made Mary's wrinkled face look suddenly youthful.

"Gentlemen," Mary said. "I'm not the one to reveal any secrets. Keeping order in this depot of humanity during these indescribable days is work enough for me."

"Mary's been so helpful to the followers over the years," Joseph explained to Duca. "She has treated Jesus' mother Mary like a daughter. Mary of Magdala would probably not be alive if it were not for this industrious widow."

"You give me too much credit, Joseph. I know my place. I'm a worker. I simply do my work."

"There's enough wisdom in *that* fact to qualify it as one of our secrets," observed Duca. "I am honored to be in your home, ma'am."

As he reached for the water and morsel of cheese, Joseph asked, "So, Mary. Who is my deliverer today?"

"Your teacher will be John," she answered. Not looking at her guests, she took a handful of pine nuts for nourishment.

"One of the Sons of Thunder," Joseph thoughtfully recollected. "He and his brother were prized followers of the Rabbi."

"Well, yes," the widow agreed. "But young John has been doing less thundering and more thinking lately."

Joseph needed no explanation. "I'm sure the horror at Jesus' crucifixion took its toll, maturing him immeasurably."

"Yes, it did," Mary agreed, "But the responsibility of caring for Jesus' mother is what I believe dominates his thinking and doing these days."

Joseph nodded his head with concern, as Duca prepared to record the conversation to come.

"I heard the Rabbi myself, making the request from the cross," confirmed Joseph. "'John is to be as a son to the young mother.' Her well-being is his assignment for the rest of her life. It's an immense responsibility."

The widow nodded. "As well as being an immense gift."

The slamming of the wooden gate outside beyond the courtyard startled the visitors.

Mary arose, peering into the dimly lit morning.

"Well," she said, "You can ask young John himself shortly. He's here."

A frail, handsome, somewhat effeminate young man respectfully entered the home.

As Joseph and Duca stood to greet him, thoughts and questions raced across the Arimathean's mind.

Could this be the brash, self-centered, and zealous brother of James—the same one who seemed more concerned for his position in Jesus' assembly than the work to be done? Mary the Widow is correct. He seems pensive now, peaceful, yet curiously focused in his countenance; surely more mature.

I'm convinced his secret will touch my very spirit.

John embraced Mary, informing her that her son Mark would return home by midday, having just left for the inner city.

John greeted Joseph as an adolescent in awe of a man whose worldly and spiritual assets he appreciated and respected.

"Good Joseph, I'm pleased to see you well. The Magdalene and the others are encouraged by your reappearance and renewed strength."

John then embraced Duca, as if the two were old friends.

"And this is the faithful servant Duca, without whom we would not be here today—and without whom Joseph's contributions to the world would have ceased with the missing body!"

Somewhat embarrassed, Joseph responded, "John, I see a heavenly change in your being. You seem simultaneously at peace ... and on fire!"

Duca had found a stool for John, and the young man pulled it close to Joseph.

Mary became serious.

"Yes, I and my own son Mark marvel at how John has grown. All the credit goes to Jesus and John himself. But the events of the last month have caste John's own destiny in bronze."

"Let me say this, good people," John said. "The events that commenced upstairs during Passover in this very house: the arrest of Jesus in the garden, Peter's denial of him while I stood beside the mighty fisherman, the Rabbi's command from the cross that I must care for his mother, his horrific death, and then his burial and departure — all this has permeated my spirit to birth the secret I'm about to share with you, Joseph."

The merchant remained silent like a studious schoolboy.

Duca was ready, writing instrument in hand.

Mary stood again.

"I'll leave you all here to your discussion. But I suggest the privacy of the upper room. By midday, this space will be like Prochorus' dining hall in the bowels of our great city."

John prepared to depart for the room upstairs, but Joseph bowed his head in contemplation.

"May we stay here?" the Arimathean asked. "If others arrive, we'll move as John sees fit. But the upper room awakes too many memories for this tired caravan master."

"So be it, sir," confirmed John. "My message is short and simple. We won't be bothered by the flock that will return here later. With all their nighttime travel, I know many are still sleeping. We may very well be done by the time they appear."

The young man began his teaching as he played with the ripened grapes Mary had left for the men.

"The most powerful force in the world is love. It's been misunderstood and even abused. But in its purest form, it can change lives and alter history. Creatively, it can be employed as a weapon. It can be perverted if not properly wielded and expressed. But when it's right, love is the perfect essence of God. It is the most powerful force in the world!"

Joseph sat up. "Yes, John, but love can take many forms, each as different as night and day."

"Indeed, Joseph. As young as I am, even I have wrestled with its several manifestations. Its power can be seen most clearly in each expression. There is that affection between a man and a woman that can be erotic. Without the sanctity of a marriage agreement," John grinned, "young men like Duca and me can be naïve fools about that type of love."

Duca spoke while writing. "Oh, how little you know, John, especially about my walk in love. I was once quite angry about it. But no longer."

Unperturbed, the servant smiled to himself while continuing, "And my master assures me my life is less complicated and troublesome as a result."

"Continue, John," suggested Joseph. "Duca's story is both blessed and tragic, but he often bears his challenges with more grace than his master."

"Forgive me, Duca, if I have assumed too much," John said. "I will continue.

"In addition to that power between the sexes that conceives new life, there's another form. It is the love that emerges from men and woman living and working as brothers and sisters with their own kind—not unlike that love which emanated from Jesus' followers."

"I understand that," said Joseph.

"And the natural love of a father or mother for a child should be most obvious," continued John. "Even the simple animals of the barnyard express that affection.

"But the most powerful aspect of love, the kind that accentuates all you do and ushers you into a timeless realm, is another kind. It is known as *agape*."

"Ah, that wonderful Greek word," Joseph said.

"Then you understand the power of giving and expressing love for someone or something without expecting anything in return?" John asked.

Joseph was slow to answer.

"Yes, I understand what I've heard in the Temple. But I've found love of that nature is not as popular as the others."

"Indeed, Joseph, common sense would not birth such love. But it is at the core of the secret."

"John, I can see this will be a prized teaching," commented Joseph. "On the other hand, I confess such agape love has been fleeting in my life—if I have experienced it at all."

"Of course. I understand," assured John. "I'm sure you remember how my brother, my mother, and I clamored for Jesus' support to elevate us to high positions amongst his followers. Yes, we loved the Nazarene, the Man from our Galilee. He was wonderful to us in so many ways—his honesty, his kindness, his profundity.

"But our intent in loving him was selfish. We expressed our fondness for him initially to gain status for ourselves. We were self-interested and shallow. Our love for him was saddled with our own pride.

"On the other hand, Jesus demonstrated affection, respect, concern, and interest in each of us. All he wanted for his love was to know, as our leader, that we were learning from him—and that we would go on to teach the same lessons to others."

"Even as a youth he was concerned for others," Joseph reminisced.

John raised his right hand. "And then he began to speak of how his death was imminent, and that according to our great Hebrew traditions, that would be the ultimate expression of his love for us."

The men sat silently for a while, pondering the immensity of Jesus' sacrifice.

"John, you're mature beyond your years. Many times I encouraged Jesus to minimize that teaching because of its provocative and violent nature. It was too final, too controversial for me to accept—that somehow his death would give us life.

"He rebuked me. Sometimes, he told me God asks us to pay what seems to be a heavy price at first."

"Joseph, I didn't understand him, either. If I had, I probably would have left the group with my brother. Why bother with a leader who intends to leave you? But Jesus spoke truly. What he predicted came to pass. His ultimate sacrifice took on a spiritual dimension that made it the most powerful standard of love. He became the personification of *agape*. And I have since seen its rewards."

"John," Joseph interrupted, "like so many of the other teachers, now you're moving too fast for me."

"Forgive me, but I'm simply describing a love that expects nothing in return in order to usher us into the moment. While our Hebrew writings remind us of the debt owed for our indiscretions and sins, Jesus lovingly paid the ultimate price on our behalf, seeking nothing in return. He set a new standard for love—and that standard will change our world. Because of him, we can live our lives in the moment in the same spirit of love."

"But love of what?" asked the older man.

"Love of everything—the person in front of you, no matter how unlovable. The air you breathe, no matter how much you take it for granted. The opportunities before you, no matter how spoiled so many of us have become. Your enemy, no matter how threatening. The widow's dopey donkey, no matter how dumb. The doubting and negative Thomas, no matter how picky he becomes. And yes, even the late, Great Herod—no matter how evil!"

"Forgive me, my boy, but I can find nothing practical here. The Rabbi's example of paying for our debt, I understand. I can see how that might have an eternal ramification. But what good can it do to love the unlovable?"

"Dear businessman, it is simply this: If you enter each moment with appreciation and love—regardless who may be in your presence—you enter into the present. When you do this, time melts away, and you pass into eternity. Love releases you from timely constraints.

"If there's someone before us we're convinced we should hate, our *agape* love for that person, accepting and embracing him as a child of God, transforms the universe."

"But if I were to encounter the despicable Herod, John— how could I possibly love him?"

"You would simply love him! Save your spite for what he represents, does, thinks, or imagines," John responded forcefully. "Remember Jesus screaming at Peter when the big man objected to the Rabbi's announcement of his imminent death? You recall that, don't you?"

"Yes."

"Don't you see? Jesus was not rebuking Peter, but the spirit of ignorance and selfishness that lived in Peter. Yes, the fisherman was putting his big foot in his even bigger mouth again. But the Lord wasn't scolding the person of Peter— and certainly not hating him. It was the backward spirit of Peter's comment that Jesus couldn't accept.

"And how about the demonically possessed Gadarene man?" reminded John.

"I've heard that story," concurred Joseph. "Wasn't it after you all almost perished in the raging sea?"

"Precisely. And when we arrived safely on the shore, immediately after our monumental lesson on faith as Jesus calmed the sea, this crazy person shows up! You can't love a wild man, right?"

"Hardly."

"But Jesus did. He ignored the drool, blood, dirt, disease, and sickness on the man, and spoke to the *spirit* of his infirmities. In fact, he forced the spirit to make itself known! To our great dismay, all these garbled voices rushed out of the poor soul and began conversing with our leader."

"Amazing," said a transfixed Joseph.

Duca was not writing a word. He had to listen to the entire story.

John proceeded, "So what did Jesus do? When the demons responded, 'We are Legion, because there are so many of us,' the Rabbi commanded them to depart. And they did just that, fleeing into some swine squirming in the mud nearby! Those pigs then threw themselves off a cliff and perished!

"The unlovable Gadarene man came to his senses, and peace and tranquility overwhelmed him. Jesus' love disarmed the demons. They simply dissolved in the omnipresence and power of love.

"When you show love in the face of the unlovable, it's a way of turning of the cheek—a teaching the Rabbi was often criticized for. But by refusing to recognize the existence of the despicable form, it is robbed of its power.

"The secret for you, Joseph, is this: By addressing the spirit and root of the ugliness in this man, and not the man himself, Jesus demonstrated an effortless power that chased the problem away. And witnessing that expression of love brought us all into the eternal moment."

Joseph asked, "But how can you say this was an eternal moment?"

"My friend. A crazy man became serene in the wink of an eye! Now, *that* was a miracle to many of us. And miracles can't happen without a power from above. When Jesus expressed agape for that poor fool by addressing the spirits in him and not the man, the infinite power of God manifested right before our eyes.

"This secret is incredibly practical, caravan master. Because when you express love without expecting anything in return, something good always happens. You unleash power that's beyond understanding. With that power, you can change others, yourself and the world for the good.

"You can't get any deeper into the moment than that."

"Oh, John," Joseph sighed, nodding his head. "I think I'm grasping this secret. To love this way chases away any pride, envy, lust, insincerity, or vanity I might have. Because such love is God-like. And God *is* love. Therefore that moment becomes eternal, because God is eternal. Whatever happens then is God's own will happening—not ours."

John smiled and took Joseph by the hand. "Joseph of Arimathea, you now share the secret."

"John, I most humbly thank you for your patience in sharing it." Joseph took a deep breath. "But please—this secret about agape is so powerful you who should write it down even further. Yes, Duca is preserving the message, but this is extraordinary good news! I urge you to share it with the world in your own words."

"In due time, Joseph."

The widow reappeared with refreshments. Then an odd couple bounded into the room, seemingly familiar with its surroundings.

"I think we've arrived at an auspicious moment, my beautiful wife!" the diminutive man exclaimed to the statuesque, raven-haired woman standing hand-in-hand with him. "I perceive a man not simply reformed, but rather transformed to fulfill his imminent destiny!"

Joseph jumped up to embrace Zaccheus.

279

"You little bundle of enigmatic energy—how is it with one of my favorite teachers?"

"All is well with me—but you! I can see you've come far since our day together!"

"It's true, dear Zaccheus. You and the other wise counselors have created quite a change in me!"

"I'm honored, dear Joseph. I'm ready for a change myself—and I perceive a big one is coming upon us. But please, good sir, let me introduce you to my beloved wife."

Zaccheus presented his blind spouse Miriam. She was every bit as stunning as he had described when he visited Joseph and Duca at the Arimathean's estate.

"I know, Joseph, your thoughts are saying, 'The little man's fortune is beyond imaginable!' And you are correct. Of course, Miriam's infirmity is my blessing."

"Don't listen to him, honorable Counselor," Miriam said. "His strength, kindness and faithfulness to me, my children, his business, and the Lord make him good enough to keep around. At least for today."

All laughed as Zaccheus embraced John and Duca.

Calling across the room, Zaccheus added, "Mary, we don't wish to bother your guests any further. With your permission, we will go to the upper room."

The widow gestured to the stairs, and the little man and stately woman ventured up. Before he was at the top, however, Zaccheus stopped, turned around, and called out to John.

"Good evangelist, don't forget to remind the Arimathean to learn to love himself! After all, there's magnificence in him, as in each and every one of us!"

Everyone smiled. John and Joseph nodded. Duca appreciated the reminder.

Indeed, that teaching of Zaccheus is surely in concert with John's this day. How disobedient to our God we'd be

*not to love the greatest of His creations. How disrespectful to
not love what He loves.*

*And how could we love anything at all if we detest
ourselves? We would have no love to give. I know—today I
know!—I've fled that selfish loathing of myself.*

Thanks to God for sending his angels!

"By noon, more than one hundred followers will come
together upstairs," John explained. "We'll be joined by
Peter, the Magdalene, Roman and Temple guards in disguise,
Prochorus and many of his workers, Stephen, Jesus' mother
Mary, and a group from Bethany led by Martha and Lazarus.
And many I don't know as well."

Duca seemed confused. Joseph's spirit was not settled as
he asked, "But for what purpose, John? Is it safe to bring so
many together in one place?"

"We were told by Jesus himself to wait in the upper room
for instructions."

"Instructions to do what?"

"We don't know. But we eagerly wait for that moment.
Knowing our teacher, I can only surmise it will be another
example of *agape*," John concluded, rising. "I should go
upstairs before the guests arrive. I would like to spend some
time in prayer."

Duca and Joseph rose as well. They bid their farewells as
John assured Joseph, "I know, that I know, that I know—you
will return soon to the upper room yourself."

"I must contemplate your secret first, John." Turning to
his servant, Joseph said, "Duca—perhaps we should proceed
home."

"Excuse me, dear master, but the day is young. Mary
of Magdala has instructed us to return only after sunset."
Turning to John, Duca asked, "What do you suggest?"

"Please, stay here so Joseph may greet the arrivals. It
may tire him, but it will reveal how much the world has

changed since the crucifixion. I'm sure they'll all have stories to tell."

"As exhausted as it may make me, if the Magdalene has ordered it, I stay." Joseph smiled, adding, "Besides, it will give me a chance to see all my old friends."

"But, master," Duca cautioned, "your concern for your reputation, now that the return of your business has been promised—might you not be at great risk if you are seen by the wrong person?"

"Duca, it's time every follower knows that I knew Jesus before any of them—save his mother and Joseph, my cousin. God's destiny for me is unfolding, and it no longer allows for petty concerns for myself. Today will be like no other— neither the past nor the future matter.

"Yesterday *is* a long time ago."

"You're correct, Joseph," agreed John. "But no moment will compare to that when we're all together in *agape* love and total agreement.

"Then something truly special will come upon us."

At sundown, Joseph and Duca mounted their well-rested horses and carefully headed out on the roundabout way back to Joseph's villa. The traffic was dense all the way as pilgrims entered the holy city to celebrate the Jewish harvest festival of Shavuot, commemorating the day, fifty days after the Exodus from Egypt, when God presented Moses with the Ten Commandments.

Joseph had enjoyed meeting many of his old friends as they arrived at the widow's house. In fact, many of the visitors shared stories with him that left him nearly speechless. Indeed, the Arimathean was now fully aware of nearly all the miraculous events that had occurred since he laid Jesus in his own tomb, over a month before.

Duca could not wait to transcribe and summarize his notes. He felt a strange urgency, a sense that big things were about to happen. The warm late spring breeze in his face gently reminded him change was in the wind.

The Evangelist's Supportive Secret: Agape

- Love every moment and every person, regardless how unlovable.
- God-like love that expects no return—*agape*—is the most powerful force in the world.
- In agape, God facilitates miracles and provides a portico to the eternal moment.
- Agape can disperse un-Godly forces from the person or situation being loved.
- Agape eradicates selfishness, envy, jealousy, greed, lust, intolerance, and self-pity from the giver.
- Find many reasons to love yourself, just as God loves you.

Chapter XXX.

Long Life

By the time Duca and Joseph departed, young John sat exhausted in front of the fireplace. So many had already greeted him on their climb to the upper room. But John was not prepared at that moment to join them.

His heart was heavy. Although he hadn't shared it with the Arimathean, he was almost constantly troubled by Jesus' command that he care for the Rabbi's youthful mother, Mary.

I know it was the request of the Lord, even as he perished on the cross. But why did he choose me to be his mother's protector for all the years to come? Although her husband is dead, could not Jesus' step-brothers care for her? She's so young herself. Must I leave my own family and forego a normal life?

The Widow Mary was cleaning up her cooking area in preparation for joining the others in waiting upstairs, when she noticed John sitting alone by the fire with knitted brows, lost in thought. Her mother's heart alerted her of John's contemplative state.

She knew too many thoughts were invading his mind. She wiped the sweat above her mouth and on her nose, and then toweled her hands clean.

Slowly shuffling to John, she sat and leaned forward in the young man's direction. "Your heavy heart is too much for so young a boy," she said.

John only shrugged his shoulders.

"I know your concerns," she continued. "Caring for a grieving mother is an assignment you don't necessarily cherish."

He nodded.

"So what are you to do with this request of Jesus?"

He shook his head—no answer.

"Dear young John—even I shuddered when I heard Jesus speak those words from the cross to you and his mother Mary: 'Dear woman, see here is your son! See, here is your mother!'" I knew how impossible it would have been for my son Mark to take on that call. So, I, too, as a mother, pondered how you were to accomplish this task."

"How can I do this?" John lamented, looking to the Widow for wisdom.

"You can't."

Startled, John quickly responded, "But I must!"

"You're correct."

"Mary...with all your wisdom, I thought you could help me."

"I can, John. Your answer is right before you. It is in the lesson you just shared with the Arimathean," she said, patting the young man's knee. "It's a*gape*, John. Only through God's love can you care for Jesus' mother until she joins him in eternity. Expect nothing in return, knowing you're obeying—and *not* sacrificing. The notion of sacrifice will drain your mental, physical, and spiritual strength. But loving obedience will be like breathing in a holy breath. It'll give you strength in this world, and eternal life in the Kingdom to come."

"How so, good woman?"

"Because it's promised. It is proverbial: 'Honor your mother and father, and God will give you long life.'"

"But she's not my mother."

"She is now."

"But how will I do it? That's the question."

"John. You are living in the future and it is causing you stress. You have piled all the coming years on your shoulders in this moment. Who could possibly carry so much at once? Stop and take a breath.

"Can you handle the burden that is placed on you in this very moment?"

John pondered a moment as he noticed his own breathing. "Yes, of course," he finally answered. "I'm just sitting here talking to you."

"And so it will be in every moment. Just keep reminding yourself to stay present, and rejoice in agape love in every one of those moments. Don't forget the prophecy was *for you*. Trust Jesus' wisdom. He was giving you a gift, not a burden!

"How could you forget he said only you, John, will have long life? The other apostles will never see their latter years. Judas is already gone. The reward for the others? It will be martyrdom. He never hid that from them.

"Your prize is time; not only to take care of his mother, but to teach the most powerful secret—agape love.

"Don't you see? You're on a special assignment from on High. And it comes with a double blessing: Honoring Mary as a mother will fill your life with agape, and Jesus' promise assures no man will harm your body. John, you are gifted … and blessed.

"But you do need help. Have faith that you will receive it soon. Don't be impatient. The strength will come, but not from your mortal mind and body.

"And it will come soon."

Chapter XXXI.

As If

For Joseph, the next day did not begin until noon. All morning, he stayed in bed reviewing his copy of the secrets. Knowing only one more was coming, he was delighting in his recovery.

I must correct Duca when he speaks of my restoration. It's no longer a restoration, thank God. To return to what I was would be less than what my Lord would require.

No, I'm not restored—I'm transformed by the wisdom of the ages, the events of these past fifty days, and by the love of my friends. Yes, I'm a new man, totally transformed!

While Joseph contemplated his journey since the death of Jesus, he gratefully inhaled the fresh air drifting through his laced drapes, ushering himself deeper into the moment.

He enjoyed these moments without thought, becoming more common everyday, when he simply existed, allowing his mind, spirit, and body to accept the gift of the present.

A peace he could not define rose up from the deepest caverns of his heart. He knew who was doing this. It was the great God of the universe, the One who lived within him. Joseph smiled, knowing that his Creator foreordained the adventure of each moment.

"Great caravan leader, Decurion of the Empire, Judge and Counselor, respected by all—most of all your humble servant—when *will* you begin this day, master?"

Duca's light-hearted impatience accompanied a tray of new wine and warm bread, as he pushed open the heavy door with his worn sandals. The servant set the breakfast beside Joseph's bed.

Joseph laughed at his servant's entrance.

"Thank you, Duca. I'll begin now! I'm famished," Joseph replied. "My spirit feasted on visiting with old friends at Mary the Widow's home yesterday—but my belly was empty by the time of our departure. I think she needed Jesus on hand to multiply the loaves and fishes one more time! The poor woman ran completely out of food."

"She is a great hostess, Joseph—but we were far from her only guests, were we not?"

"What an amazing day it was," Joseph said, as he reached across the pillow for his wine. "I have to wonder—how could today's teaching match yesterday's, or any one of those before?"

"Well, good master, first of all, the secret will not be delivered to you until just after sunset. My assignment is to return to the Widow's to escort our last rescuers here under the protection of darkness."

"Indeed," Joseph emphasized, "I understand the need for safety, now that I know all that has occurred."

"Yes," Duca confirmed. "Tonight will be the safest time to conclude your restoration."

"Not my restoration, dear Duca! From now on, we call it my transformation! And I have no doubt it will certainly be sealed this evening!"

"I agree, Joseph."

Duca looked down at his hands, thoughtfully.

Joseph knew his servant had something to say, and he remained silent in anticipation.

"You know, master—even I've been changed."

There was nothing more to be said. For a long time, the two men remained silent, taking time to let everything that had happened sink into their spirits.

Joseph ate his breakfast with gratitude, while Duca gathered up the notes and tidied the room. There was no need for conversation. It was good enough to be together—one supporting the other, reliable and predictable as the sun rising in the east each morning.

Finally, Joseph gazed into the sunlit day and sighed. Then he smiled at his faithful friend and asked, "And who will reveal the last secret?"

Duca smiled back. "I was wondering when you would ask me that! Master, tonight the Magdalene returns with a friend—your oldest friend!

"Nicodemus has been commissioned to give you the last secret!"

Joseph bowed his head as he felt tears rising. Looking up with shining eyes, he breathed a sigh of relief.

"Oh, Duca—I was afraid our friendship had floundered. I was so confused by Jesus' crucifixion, then his disappearance, and so mournful at my Sarah's passing; Nicodemus and I have not spoken a word since he and Mary rescued me from Pilate's God-forsaken jail cell! I simply couldn't bear to have him see me so low in spirit."

"Be encouraged, Joseph. Mary of Magdala assures me your fellow judge can't wait to see you. He's heard the reports of your renewal."

"Only the best of friends could forgive me for my actions."

"Don't be so hard on yourself, master."

"But you don't know, Duca. You don't know what happened when Jesus was laid to rest. And in those moments I know I disappointed Nicodemus."

"He never mentioned it, Joseph."

"Of course not. But I know it hurt him."

"May I ask what happened in the tomb?"

"It lays heavy on my heart, Duca. I could not enter my own burial place. Nicodemus and the ladies cared for Jesus. They anointed him, preparing him in haste lest the Passover begin. Nicodemus was so dutiful as he wrapped Jesus in the shroud. My friend and the ladies and were so caring.

"But me? I could only look away and pace the entrance impatiently. I couldn't lift a hand. I couldn't touch the body.

"I was angry—mad at God Almighty, mad at Jesus, mad at myself! No plans in all my life ever turned out so disastrously. And this was my cousin's young son! I had counseled and broken bread with him in private! I was disappointed and confused.

"There were times in the tomb when I could see Nicodemus needed help. He looked at me questioningly. But I looked away. I believe it was my worst moment in life outside that tomb. I wanted answers, and couldn't get a single one. I'd never been involved with a failure before— and this, my first, was monumental.

"For a while that afternoon, as the storm raged all around, I felt I was on a mission from God. I burned with desire to get possession of Jesus' body and get it to the tomb at all costs. But once we got there, once it seemed we could get Jesus entombed before sundown, everything changed. I simply collapsed—I no longer even cared. I'm sure Nicodemus will never forget my apathetic look.

"But inside, I was brimming with frustration, self-pity, and self-loathing.

"Worst of all, in my selfishness I missed the opportunity to touch my young friend, and wish him well as he passed to the other side. I couldn't even look at his body!"

"But now, Joseph?" Duca probed. "Things have changed, no? The secrets and the full story have restored and transformed the forlorn Joseph of that night, haven't they?"

"Yes, yes—I am so blessed today, Duca." Joseph admitted. "But I hope Nicodemus has forgiven my egotistical attitude that evening, and my unavailability since.

"You know," Joseph continued, smiling sadly as he remembered his friend, "Nicodemus and I spent so many exciting, stimulating hours discussing the teachings of the itinerant preacher—coming to the realization of who he really was. And then my fellow conservative, soft-spoken member of the Great Sanhedrin became a zealous follower. He was so taken by the Man from Galilee! Had I not held Nicodemus back in my own lukewarm restraint, he might very well have ended up hanging on a fourth cross next to the Nazarene. What a turn of events and beliefs!"

"Joseph, I'll see the dinner is properly planned for this evening, and then with your permission I'll travel with extra horses to retrieve Nicodemus and Mary Magdalene. I will travel just after sunset to avoid detection. You should be ready to break bread as soon as I return. When they're finished delivering the final secret, I'll return them to Mary the Widow's."

"Duca, shouldn't they remain overnight?"

"I suggested that to the Magdalene—but she insisted the time is short for the moment Jesus prophesized. She and Nicodemus are to depart for the upper room immediately after the teaching."

The day passed slowly for Joseph as he read the Torah, reviewed the secrets further, and spent hours in prayer and contemplation.

I do believe I was better at living in the present when my caravans streamed across our world. And now I sense my prayer, study, and reflection is preparing me for yet another trip. My God is telling me my adventure is just beginning. But please, oh God, allow me to forget my recent stubborn, selfish foolishness.

I must look only to this day!

When Duca appeared with Mary of Magdala and Nicodemus, the stars had risen over the stone-strewn hills in the west.

Joseph embraced his oldest friend. There were no tears.

As they looked deep into each other's eyes, they knew their lives had changed forever. Nicodemus' honest face was lit up with a warm smile as he cherished the visible proof of Joseph's transformation. Both men were excited as Duca led them and Mary to the stately dining room.

Warm lentil soup, partridge, figs, bread, and goat cheese represented the fare for the evening. For a while, nothing was said of the final secret. Joseph was too curious about his guests' experiences since the crucifixion, and their knowledge of the upcoming instructions from Jesus that were on all the followers' minds.

Mary was patient with Joseph's questions.

Nicodemus did not seem as troubled about the last seven weeks as Joseph thought he would be. But his friend did wish to relay the secret as soon as possible.

The Magdalene agreed.

"I know the events we've described have piqued your interest," Mary began. "But without the last secret, your true appreciation for what has happened since the Passover, and even before that, will diminish over time. The cares of the world will steal your enthusiasm. While what has occurred in the last couple of weeks will change our world, you must be prepared to do your part.

"And this last secret is critical."

"Then delay no longer, good woman," said Joseph.

Mary nodded to Nicodemus to proceed. While only a few years older than Joseph, his easy smile showed him to be a man who had found what Joseph had not: total contentment.

Nicodemus raised his arms as he began, as if praising the God who had ushered him to deliver this message.

"My good friend, you must act, in each and every moment, as if everything you have believed from your child-hood, all you've represented to others, and all you hope to be, is coming about.

"You must demonstrate complete faith that God's will for you is unfolding as you speak and as you breathe—no matter where you may be. By acting as if God is directing your path as the scriptures promise, you'll make your destiny infallibly real."

Duca pushed away the wooden plates and goblets so his writing space would be adequate. Mary rested her hands on the table, ready to hear Joseph's reaction. Nicodemus grate-fully raised a goblet of wine to his smiling lips.

"Nicodemus," Joseph said, "I remember a time when Jesus delivered a simple yet profound teaching to you. It was under the shadows of darkness in the garden. You, the most judicious of all the Pharisees, had insisted on visiting him at night so as not to cause scandal. Remember when he told you that you must experience a new birth, a rebirth from above, to even *see* the Kingdom of God? You and I met early the next morning to discuss the encounter—and it took me all day to explain the meaning of his message.

"Now, my old friend returns and delivers a secret more complicated than anything Jesus ever taught! I know I'm aging. I suppose what I'm asking, Nicodemus, is this: can you please translate your message into terms I can fathom?"

"Oh, Joseph, don't feign ignorance," said Nicodemus. "Do you forget the many years we've spent together? Yes, there were times when I needed you to explain Jesus' plan for full life on earth and in the kingdom to come. But once the revelation touched my spirit—as you well remember—a change swept over me, and there was never any turning back. I agree, though: I could not have fully understood without you.

"And that's the point, Arimathean! You've done so much to help others open our minds—yet you seemed to close yours to everything as soon as Jesus died. Yes, I was shocked by what appeared to be your self-absorbed apathy in the tomb. It was confusing, because I knew if it were not for you, the young man would have been left to rot with criminals.

"You became so distant, missing an eternal moment of gazing on the Master, the one we had both risked much to follow—the one who had accomplished his mission. This woman beside me was there, in your own resting place, gently attending to his body, while you were impatiently pacing at the entrance, as if awaiting a late arrival of one of your caravans.

"But, Joseph, I still love you. Your life had been so effi-cient, so successful up to that point. I can hardly imagine your disappointment that night.

"So now I assure you: the secret I present today will complete your return to the correct path. The path God put you on when we were little boys in Arimathea. As foretold in the old writings, you must act as if each moment holds God's will for you. Give up your despair and stop pretending your dreams may never happen.

"I am only sorry I could not share this secret with you at the tomb. Because I now realize that despite what was happening, God was still in complete, eternal, unshakable control."

"You have been gentle with me, old friend."

"Just walk in God's destiny, Joseph. It is unfolding moment by precious moment. Have faith each step you take follows a grand, Godly map created for you in Heaven.

"You've been acting as if all is lost, not happening as designed. I saw your wandering begin at the tomb—but at the time, I didn't have the wisdom to help you.

"And for that, I apologize to you."

"No, Nicodemus. The fault is mine," Joseph said. "I know I hurt you deeply by not helping care for his body."

"There is no need to look to the past. Think of the blessing of this moment, dear friend! My secret is that you must always act as if you are walking in His presence and faithfully following His plan. Only our faith pleases God. This is the revelation of the action step of faith."

"Action step of faith, Nicodemus?" Joseph asked. "Then I should act as if I believe, even when I have doubts? Is this not being false?"

"You complained that I complicated the principle of rebirth Jesus presented to me so simply that night in the garden. You were right to say so. His truth was simpler than I was willing to let it be. My confusion stemmed from trying to make it much more complicated than it was.

"But my secret right now is just as simple.

"Need I remind you that until our ancestors walked in faith, God's plan would not unfold? It took them forty years to go forty miles to the Promised Land because they did not act as if God was leading them! Confusion filled the void created by their lack of faith—and God's plan for them was delayed.

"It was the same with you. With your faith shattered by the crucifixion and confused by the empty tomb, chaos set in. If you had calmly reflected on all you knew at the time about our God, about Jesus' life, and about his promises, you would not have slipped into despair these last fifty days. Your businesses would still be flourishing, and you'd be working and praying alongside us night and day!

"But you forgot what faith means. Faith is like stepping on the stones to cross a steam. You aren't sure what will happen. But you are confident that your God, your mind, your spirit, and your body are prepared for wherever that step takes you. Had you been stepping in faith since the crucifixion, you would not have sunk into despair. Instead, you would've been walking on water!"

Joseph raised his hands. "So, if I simply recalled my beliefs, added my faith in God's scriptural promises, and acted as if all were still well—despite what my eyes had seen—I would never have fallen into my stupor at all?"

"Precisely."

The Magdalene interrupted. "Joseph, Nicodemus is not implying that each of us understood this secret from the beginning. But, by taking faithful, confident steps in each moment, rather than bounding anxiously into the future, or crying as we creep back to the past, our faithful steps will align us with God. The challenge each of us faces is not succumbing to feelings of pessimism."

"But sometimes our plans do go awry." Joseph said.

"Our plans," Mary replied. "But never God's. Just because we cannot see the grander plan, we're wrong to conclude that we're alone, that God has departed from us. We must walk through those awkward moments, and then take another step—leaping forward or backward. And if we stray off course, our way will be corrected over time. God will guide us. We must not try to guide Him!

"Also," Mary continued, "remember that mistakes are part of the lesson we're learning. When we suffer, our suffering will either guide us to our final reward or it will make us stronger. So when things go wrong, glory in your infirmity! Believe God's will prevails even when circumstances seem bleak. Have faith that this, too, shall pass—and it will!"

"Mary, I apologize to you as well. You did such a service in caring for Jesus' body that horrible day."

"Please, Joseph. That is past. My hands were trembling as I anointed him. I could not think of anything at that point, let alone your inner conflicts.

"I knew he was dead, but with every touch I felt as if his life was entering mine. There was so much energy in that small place. Nothing mattered but that moment. It was eternal."

No one spoke for a time. The air was heavy with a profound stillness. Even Duca could not lift his pen.

Nicodemus pointed at Joseph. "Joseph, I look at you now and it's hard for me to imagine. How could you forget all that had happened to you? How could you forget the miracles of your life—the countless blessed moments of your existence? Jesus would not have been alive at all if not for you! Did you not tell me that your late cousin, Joseph the carpenter, nearly accused Mary, his betrothed, of falling into carnal sin with her pregnancy; that he was about to order her stoning until you convinced him to hold back his anger?

"Then Joseph had a dream that confirmed that Mary's conception was not in sin, but rather from on High. And who ushered them to safety after Jesus was born, when the murderous Herod was killing babies throughout the land?

"It was *you*, Joseph of Arimathea, who used your influence to speed Joseph, Mary, and the baby Jesus to Egypt and safety.

"And then during the young boy's adolescent years— wasn't it you who sponsored him on many of your caravan expeditions so that he might learn more of the world, its people, and how it all worked? And without you, no educated, successful, religious, and law-abiding member of the Temple would've tolerated Jesus as long as they did. Had it not been for *you*, I might have even joined with those who put him on trial!

"And finally, those tense moments we spent buying all the aloes and myrrh for the body, and your purchasing the most expensive of burial cloths for him—what caused you to forget these deeds?

"*I* was frightened with the quick conviction of Jesus by our peers—while you seemed on a mission." Nicodemus' voice pitched higher. "*You* faced Pilate, astonishingly gaining possession of the body!

"Then we put him in the tomb you'd carved out of limestone on the hill—the tomb reserved for you. I wanted to be at your side because of *your* strength. You were acting as if you had been commissioned by the God of Abraham, Isaac, and Jacob to do these very things!

"We were part of a supernatural moment, when the dimension of time had no place. Because of *you*, I was a part of that moment that gave us a glimpse of eternity.

"So you see, old friend, you've had every reason to act as if all that has happened since Jesus' arrest was part of a master plan. All along, you have played a vital, intimate role. If there is a God, how could He be more pleased with you?

"But unless you add this final secret to propel you into the moment, even the provocative events you heard about yesterday will not sustain you.

"It sounds so odd to the unbelieving mind: Always act as if things are working out the way they should—and they will! Yet it's true."

Duca was writing as quickly as he could. Mary's eyes had not left Joseph.

Joseph reached for a goblet of water. He gazed into the fire, roaring to warm the damp, late spring night.

Then Joseph looked at the Magdalene. He smiled.

"So, Mary, you wanted to be here so my Pharisee friend wouldn't overcomplicate a simple, but profound, secret?"

"That would have been the case before the Passover," she said. "But with what Nicodemus and I and others have seen, touched, and heard since then, I had faith he could've delivered the secret alone.

"But I did want to make sure my intelligent and worldly friend from Arimathea didn't over intellectualize this secret.

This is uncommon sense—as are all of the other secrets. And, perhaps just as important, I wanted to see you reminded of the amazing role you have played, since even before the day Jesus was born!"

"How could I forget after all those years of knowing Jesus?" Joseph reflected. "How could it have taken his entire life, his death, and then all this to convince me of who he was?"

"Joseph, stress, fear, and fatigue make cowards of us all," she reminded. "'Act as if' ... is the secret. And don't forget its miracle is in your mouth."

"In my mouth?"

"Yes, actions do speak louder than words—but your words will paint your world. You can change that world both by your actions and your words. Be careful with each."

"Well, Mary, in the end, my friend Nicodemus has done well. I see how I've allowed my faith and hope to wane. But after having reviewed the secrets daily—thanks to Duca's faithful recording—I now have a disturbing question for you both."

"And what is it?" the woman asked, as she daintily dipped her bread in the soup.

Joseph worded his question with care.

"Isn't this secret of 'acting as if' a step out of the moment and into the future? Aren't we doing the very thing we set out not to do?"

Mary responded quickly and firmly.

"No. I see what you're getting at. But the answer is no. When you act in the present moment as if God's destiny is being fulfilled in your life, there's no dimension of time. Why? Because your destiny is like a seed, planted deep in your soul. You aren't looking for a specific outcome. Only believing that it will be the best thing that God—not you— can imagine.

"Can we see the seed planted in the ground that will bring forth more figs like the ones we enjoy tonight? The seed may be invisible to us, but God's economy is at work. It will grow. Only a fool would dig it up to inspect its progress.

"At the moment prescribed by God, the fruit will appear. At that point we'll pick it and enjoy it.

"Acting as if God's plan for you is unfolding waters that divine seed in you. Lust for the end result will abort the natural process. Belief that it is happening exactly as it should chases away anxiety. And it puts the timing into the infinite hands of your Creator."

Joseph grimaced. "I have not been able to act in this way for many days. Everything seemed to have fallen apart, and it was far beyond my understanding to imagine how my life might ever be put together again."

"It's true that circumstances may do a powerful job of obscuring God's plan," Mary admitted. "Think of Lazarus coming back from his own tomb! How could anyone have imagined his destiny? But Jesus knew God's will, and at the proper moment—Lazarus came forth!"

"So Jesus simply acted as if resurrection was possible," Joseph said, knitting his brows.

"Yes, Joseph. We don't all have Jesus' faith, but think of the many miracles we 'act as if' will come to fruition. No one can see a baby at conception, but with certain signs, the mother believes it—and the miracle of birth takes place.

"Lazarus lives, babies are born, and figs grow—as does God's plan for you!"

A peaceful smile slowly spread across Joseph's face, and he bowed his head in gratitude.

He was not thinking. He was simply basking in the moment.

Finally, the Arimathean spoke.

"Oh, my God, I receive this secret. The profound simplicity of this idea—it will surely add power to each moment. Yes,

I've had glimpses of this secret during my selfish life. But now, the idea is sustaining itself in my spirit."

Joseph raised his head and looked at his guests with deep gratitude.

"Mary and Nicodemus, your patience this night with my ignorance is a gift I'll always cherish."

"There is something else, Joseph," Mary said, "which required my accompanying Nicodemus here tonight."

Nicodemus nodded in agreement.

"Proceed, good woman," Joseph said. "My heart leaps in anticipation."

Mary of Magdala stood, reached for an over-ripened fig, and wandered to the fire. She stared into the jumping flames, slowly enjoying the sweet fruit. The men waited patiently.

"Joseph," she said as she slowly turned to him, "all that we've shared tonight, and the other secrets before this, will fall to waste without action. Remember, faith is an action word, and only faith pleases God.

"It requires careful, faithful practice of *all* the secrets to escort us into the precious moment. Only then can we make our true contribution and fulfill our destinies.

"Because of this, I have a question for you, Joseph of Arimathea."

"I'll do my best to answer. Please go ahead."

"What will you do now that you are restored?

"I'm more than restored, Mary. I'm changed."

"And your answer?"

"Well, first—I now truly believe, with all my heart, that Jesus was who he said he was. And I'm deeply humbled by your reminder of the parts I have played—many without even realizing it—in God's grandest plan.

"Given all of the secrets, I know the time for action is near.

"What is my first step, my friends? My heart tells me it's to be fully engaged again in my businesses and the ministry of Jesus. I will not lead another caravan, but I'll give my assistance to Prochorus and put my talents to God's work.

"I must admit to you both, however, that I have a burning expectancy in my spirit. I feel something wonderful is about to happen that will direct my path," he laughed. "But I have no idea what it will be!"

Mary responded. "Joseph, you and Nicodemus have both expressed the same feeling—as have more than one hundred of the followers. I believe it's true, because I feel the same way.

"All I know for certain is that we are to gather in one accord in the upper room in Mary the Widow's house, awaiting a clarification. Some grow impatient, while others are feeling pregnant in the spirit."

"Yes, Mary," agreed Nicodemus. "That's the feeling—like a birth about to happen."

"Mary?" Joseph humbly asked.

"Yes, Joseph."

"Perhaps I might wait there in the upper room with you. I don't need to know why. It's enough for me that Jesus asked it. It will be an act of faith, and a chance to apply the precious secrets you have so generously shared with me."

"When, Joseph?" the Magdalene asked.

"Duca and I must first get my affairs together, and then I shall proceed to the Widow's."

Mary smiled softly. She crossed the room and put her arms around Joseph in a loving, spiritual embrace. Then she spoke softly in his ear.

"What about now?" she asked.

That night Duca accompanied Joseph, Mary Magdala, and Nicodemus to the home of Mary the Widow. After everyone was settled for the evening, he hurried back to Joseph's villa to consolidate his notes, working late into the starry night.

Nicodemus' Supportive Secret:
Belief Creates Reality

- Act as if God's plan is unfolding in each moment, and it will become real.
- Do not allow temporary setbacks distract you from the truth: God's seed of destiny will emerge in the fullness of time.
- Do not dig up seeds to check their progress.
- Practice faith until it is stronger than fear, lust, doubt, and anxiety.
- Do not anticipate God's results—his imagination is far beyond your own, and anticipation takes you out of the present.

Chapter XXXII.

Reserved Seats

J oseph of Arimathea slept peacefully on a bed of hay, carefully put together for him by Duca, in the donkey shed at the home of the Widow.

He awoke, fully rested, at the first sound of the cock strutting in the courtyard.

Nicodemus had made his bed in the hay as well. The two old friends opened their eyes and looked at each other at the same moment. Like boys on a camp-out, they were filled with excitement for everything the new day promised to bring.

"It's today, my friend," muttered Joseph to his shed-mate. "I can feel it. The time is now—the time you and the others have been awaiting has arrived!"

Rubbing his eyes, Nicodemus sat up and observed, "You seem most confident, Decurion. I like it."

"Well, we're awake, thank God. We are healthy. I'm not sure what will happen next, but in this moment I am filled with joy."

"Joseph," Nicodemus said, rising with surprising ease. "I can't tell you how glad I am to see you back to your old self—making a drama even of waking up in the palace of Mary's broken down, wandering ass!"

"Not such an inappropriate bed, the way I've been acting lately," Joseph said.

Nicodemus laughed out loud and gave Joseph a hand up. As they chased the hay from their robes, Joseph smiled. "I remember my cousin Joseph telling me it was in a stall like this where he and his wife Mary welcomed Jesus into the world."

"Oh, dear Joseph—now you compare our scratchy night here to an event as meaningful as Jesus' birth? The only similarity is that we've been about as stupid as the sheep that accompanied the shepherd boys on the hills outside Bethlehem!"

Both men laughed again. They felt young and full of life.

"Yes, Nicodemus, maybe we're dimwitted as lambs—but with God as our Counselor, we've survived to witness this day!"

Rolling his eyes, Nicodemus gently patted Joseph on the back, encouraging their exit. "Before you wax as religious as some of our friends in the Sanhedrin, let's go inside and make our way upstairs. We want to find seats in that upper room."

"No problem," assured Joseph. "Peter guaranteed stools for the two old fools."

"The fisherman has changed," Nicodemus said, shaking his head at Joseph's giddy silliness. "He's been corrupted by thoughtfulness and planning."

"Wait until later today," added Joseph, a bit more seriously. "From what I know—from what I've learned since the Passover, and from what the small voice in my spirit tells me now—today is the day our Peter takes charge."

Chapter XXXIII.

That Day

Wh
hile the day was still very young, the upper room was
packed with people.

The younger men had stacked empty wooden crates to the low ceiling, maximizing the space for sitting and standing. The more senior followers sat quietly, while the walls were lined with younger men, women, and children.

Standing in the corner of the hot, cramped space was Peter.

Reminds me of a net of bountiful fish. We've been here for days, but this looks like the biggest catch.

Thomas entered with his sister, squeezing in amongst the crowd, trying to find some breathing space.

"Well, Elizabeth" he whispered. "It seems the smells of all the world have congregated in one place. This is too close for me. From the finest perfume to the most rotten fish! I pray the Lord not tarry."

"Stop complaining," she ordered.

Joseph, sitting near the middle of the room with David and Nicodemus, leaned over to speak to his old friend. "I wish Duca was with us."

"If anything happens today, we'll tell him," assured Nicodemus. "Otherwise, he's welcome to my seat tomorrow. I don't know if I can stand another day of this."

David promptly rose, allowing Mary the Widow her proper place in the front of her room.

Zaccheus was making sure his beautiful Miriam was comfortable in the swelter.

"Dear, just sit quietly and breathe slowly. I'll observe for you. It's most unbelievable. The only things not in this room are the animals. Though I've called some of these characters worse in the past."

Prochorus stood at the top of the stairs. He and Stephen gently ushered each new arrival into position.

Jude, the widow of Judas, sat nervously next to Mary of Magdala.

"Dear lady, relax," the Magdalene suggested. "You deserve to be here as much as anyone else. See that handsome Roman man over there? He thrust the spear into Jesus' side. Forgiven and enlightened, he doesn't look back on his past. And you don't have to carry guilt for your husband, either."

As Martha of Bethany entered, a sudden hush fell over the assembly. Her brother Lazarus was behind her. The more recent converts looked upon the resurrected man as profound validation of their newfound faith, while the rest saw Lazarus as the ultimate confirmation of Jesus' awesome connection to God.

The silence that accompanied Lazarus' entrance remained unbroken. Shoulder to shoulder and knee-to-knee, the followers sat and stood so close that every one was in physical contact with another of his spiritual brothers and sisters. There was no movement. Only the soft, almost inaudible breath of more than one hundred true believers in perfect accord. Everyone knew the time had come for absolute quiet, and almost as one they settled fully into the moment at hand.

A sliver of golden sunlight penetrated an opening in the roof, revealing a universe of dust motes dancing and glinting in the thick air. The unearthly hush commanded reverence.

All in attendance obeyed.

Although the door was firmly closed, a warm breeze appeared from nowhere. And while each felt it equally—as if it were blowing directly onto their skin—it went unheeded at first.

Peter was perplexed. The balmy air heated his entire body, but his arms would not respond to wipe his perspiring brow.

The wind rose, and still no one moved. No one spoke. All were rooted to the spot, wedded to a moment that seemed to be unwinding into eternity.

With each passing moment, the wind rose higher and higher, until each person in attendance felt as though it was passing completely through their bodies. Still, no one stirred, as the superheated wind erupted into a furious gale that only the people could feel.

The stray wooden plates and utensils strewn on a table near the entrance did not move. The splintered, cracked crates did not budge. The loosest garment lay still. Not even the dust in the air moved in the utter, eternal stillness.

Yet the people could feel themselves buffeted by the storm's overpowering strength—blowing away their fears, doubts, inadequacies, and any thoughts of the future or the past.

When the group began to realize that they were all experiencing the same thing, the silence was broken. Many closed their eyes in prayers of thanksgiving. Some cried, while the laughter of others filled the air.

Some felt the urge to dance, while others fell to their knees or went prone on the floor. There were those who claimed seeing balls of fire crackling at the heads of all, while others saw nothing at all. A controlled frenzy ensued; peaceful joy collided with childlike astonishment. Words of praise to a manifest God rang out in unknown languages; others could only cry, "Halleluiah."

Above the controlled commotion and sounds of exaltation could be heard the loving revelation of young John, words with the power of a melodious thunder rolling in from afar.

"He had to leave so the Holy Spirit could fall upon us all this day!"

Everyone seemed to exit the room at the same instant. Time was irrelevant. Within a moment, the upper room was empty, and those in attendance were now in Mary's yard, pouring out through the shielding pomegranate grove and dancing, shouting, laughing and singing their way into the heart of Jerusalem.

It is recorded that approximately one hundred and twenty followers of the young Rabbi from Nazareth squeezed into Mary the Widow's upper room on the day of the Jewish harvest festival of Shavuot, commemorating the day, fifty days after the beginning of the Exodus, when God gave Moses the Ten Commandments.

Today, the event is known as the Feast of Pentecost— fifty days after the Passover.

Some time during that day, the world outside the stone home was turned upside down. A spiritual and physical event occurred in that room that birthed a surge of power into the minds, bodies, and spirits of all in attendance.

They did not walk calmly down the stairs to Mary's kitchen, out into the courtyard, and all the way into the heart of Jerusalem with decorum and dignity. Rather, like little children released to play and frolic in the fresh air of God's creation, they bounded, stumbled, and leaped, overjoyed at the eternal freedom they had found.

Thousands of celebrants in the Holy City that day were witnesses to the unbridled enthusiasm and joy streaming from the group. Tourists and city-dwellers alike froze in their paths as Peter hopped onto a porch overlooking the cobbled street. His powerful frame and masculine presence paled compared to the commanding voice that came forth from his heart. While he spoke with his own voice, it is recorded that every listener heard him in their own tongue — whether they spoke Peter's native Aramaic, Hebrew, or the dialects of visiting Persians, Arabs, Greeks, or Romans. As the people marveled at the miracle, the uneducated fisherman delivered his moving account of the young preacher who was crucified, died, and was buried.

But it was the rest of the story that captivated the crowds. They were stunned as they heard the tale of life after death, and the promise that it was available to all who would listen.

According to some accounts, three thousand new converts were baptized before sunset, moved by the same Holy Spirit that touched and transformed the followers of Jesus.

On this day, over two thousand years ago, a new church was born.

It was an edifice without walls or windows, whose structure arose from the very bodies of its members.

An unseen power had embraced the one hundred and twenty, and by the end of the day, they were joined by multitudes in a revolution that continues to the present, precious moment.

Chapter XXXIV.

Lessons Learned and Secrets Shared

*P*eter visibly assumed the role of leader of the fledgling church. Thousands would flock to see and hear him during his lifetime. While his countenance, words, deeds, and attitudes were a mirror held up to Christ, he always reminded others he was just a stubborn fisherman who argued too much with his mother-in-law.

It became obvious to all that *Peter* had *surrendered* to a new life, *accepting* what he had been taught and had seen. He simply walked with the belief his God was always with him. His following became so strong that the Romans jailed him on several occasions. He eventually traveled to Rome—where the authorities ordered his death by crucifixion.

His only request was for his body to be nailed upside-down.

He believed he was unworthy to die like Jesus.

In the end, *Peter surrendered* himself to his Creator and the Romans, *accepting* his final fate with dignity and humility. It was his finest *moment*. He was *present* in it totally, *submitting* to that instant, knowing he was destined to see his friend in eternity.

Today, *Saint Peter* is revered by millions of Roman Catholics around the world as their first Pope. His body lies in peace somewhere in Saint Peter's Basilica.

The Fisherman's Supportive Secret: Surrender

- **Surrender to whatever you believe to be the highest good.**
- **Surrender concern for results to whatever you have surrendered.**
- **Submit to the present, focusing totally upon it, with no selfish, illusory thoughts of the past or future.**
- **Accept reality—it is the plan of God unfolding.**
- **In surrendering, there is no room for worry. Relax, for all is progressing as it should.**
- **Childlike joy and increased energy will be the signs of successful surrender.**

Zaccheus' life thereafter was hardly recorded. Tradition has it that he lived to an old age, surrounded by his beautiful blind wife and ebullient children.

His favorite message of *magnificence in each human being* has been chided over the years by the most cynical. But his belief always focused his attention on the *now*—even with the least worthy. This made his *moments* full of laughter, smiles, joy, and the thrill of discovering God's design in all.

It was a hot, humid summer afternoon, not so very long after the events of this story, which ushered *Zaccheus* and many others to an even higher level of consciousness in God. Peter was walking quickly through the crowd, followed by many, when he suddenly stopped.

His giant shadow had enveloped a beautiful blind woman. It was *Zaccheus'* Miriam.

At that instant she received her sight.

As she, her boys and others about her danced in thanksgiving, tiny Zaccheus fell to his knees.

In his mind he could hear the words of Jesus echoing: "I must go away that the Holy Spirit visit with you. You will do more than even I have done."

To the end of her days, Miriam told anyone who would listen that she had married the most handsome man in the world.

Zaccheus' Supportive Secret: Recognize Inner Greatness

- **What is inside of you is greater than anything outside.**
- **Allow the miracle of your body—its functioning, the blood flow, and the preciousness of each breath—to bring you back into the present.**
- **Replace self-pity with gratitude; marvel at the opportunity to tap the infinite potential inside you.**
- **Problems shrink to insignificance when met by your inner greatness.**
- **Recognize the magnificence in everyone you meet.**
- **Know that in the moment, if you have done your best, all is well. Be still.**
- **Have faith that results of your actions will be better than you had planned.**
- **Obsession with self fuels impatience. Impatience cultivates despair.**
- **Patience is a positive by-product of tribulation.**
- **Live patiently for others and not for yourself.**

Martha of Bethany, the sister of Lazarus, had not prepared any food for that fateful day in Mary the Widow's home. When she arrived there early with her brother, she apologized to Mary. Both sensed it was not an issue; that manna from above was about to feed those in attendance in the moment and for a lifetime.

What *Martha* did not forget to bring was her *joy*—her pure love for the *moment* that she experienced regardless of circumstances. After the monumental event that occurred in the upper room that day, she and Lazarus danced into the streets. Even for the *joyful Martha*, it was the first time she had ever danced.

For the rest of her long life, *Martha* continued to *joyfully* welcome all to her house in Bethany. Her culinary skill continued to attract believers as well as doubters. But there was no doubt in her *joyful* daily service to her resurrected brother, her beautiful sister, and the cause of Jesus.

On her deathbed, *Martha* smiled and said, "When I get to the other side, I look forward to my eternal chores—to serve others in *joy*. There will be eternal *joy* in each and every *moment*. And that *joy* will be infinitely beyond anything I've already experienced during my journey in this world."

Martha's Supportive Secret: Joy

- **Cultivate joy—count your blessings!**
- **Joy creates more joy.**
- **Work joyfully, enjoying the process without focusing on the results.**
- **Being joyful now guards against dark thoughts.**
- **When you glance back, choose moments that can feed your joy now, never staring at darkness.**
- **If joy is present even in times of trouble, even evil can be turned to a good.**

David the Temple Guard was able to survive in Jerusalem thanks to his many clever disguises. Even Joseph did not recognize him in the upper room when the powerful student of the Holy Scriptures sat himself between the Arimathean and Nicodemus.

His fate after what became known as the Day of Pentecost is not documented. However, Joseph would not ignore the *knowledge, understanding, and wisdom* he had gleaned from his constant, moment-by-moment study in his plans for his own future.

Legend has it that within a few short weeks after the wondrous event at the Widow's house, *David* would be with Joseph every day of the Arimathean's life, joining him in his traveling adventures until the merchant's last breath.

David was not at his father's side when the Rabbi of Nazareth passed away. The old man was alone, still awaiting the coming of the Messiah.

The Tomb Guard's Supportive Secret: Knowledge, Understanding, and Wisdom

- **Knowledge is power.**
- **Use every moment and every meeting to gain knowledge.**
- **Test your new knowledge against what you know and believe.**
- **Tested knowledge becomes understanding.**
- **Freely share what you understand for the benefit of others.**
- **Skillfully shared, understood knowledge creates wisdom—and releases the power of God's knowledge into the world.**

Jude, the widow of Judas Iscariot, *patiently* and quietly waited for that *moment* when power fell upon the followers. Daily she ministered to those tarrying in anxiety, sharing the secret that one must not be tempted to rush to assume about impending events. She convinced all who would listen that if her infamous husband had practiced *patience* to abide into the precious *moment,* then he, too, would have witnessed to the miracle of the upper room.

Never once did she speak of her moment of suicidal insanity. There is no record of her life in history.

The Widow's Supportive Secret: Patience

- **When in doubt, be still.**
- **Do not rush events. You may abort God's natural plan from unfolding as it should.**
- **If you have done your best in each moment, all is well.**
- **Do not fear results; have faith that God's plan is better than anything you could imagine.**
- **Tribulation breeds patience—and the wisdom gained from the tribulations of others is a gift one can use to learn patience without suffering tribulation yourself.**
- **Living for others fuels patience.**
- **Self-obsession fuels impatience.**
- **Impatience cultivates despair.**
- **Simplicity does not imply ease.**

Prochorus, the rich, young ruler, amply fulfilled his promise to Joseph. He credited the giant Ethiopian, Tarek, for restoring the Arimathean's routes. It seems after a short conversation, the most famous gladiator in all of Rome convinced an uncharacteristically trembling Pontius Pilate that Vitellius Caesar, Tarek's biggest fan in all the Empire, would not be pleased with the Judean Governor's unholy conspiracy with the Sanhedrin to steal an innocent man's business. Pilate then quietly returned ownership back to Joseph.

When Jerusalem calmed down a bit after the Day of Pentecost, *Prochorus* performed the first of many *acts* that consumed him for weeks in joyous *moments* of visioning, strategizing, and planning new and exciting revenue-producing *ideas.* He recruited multitudes of the poor and less fortunate to work within the giant enterprise that was to evolve.

Most importantly, *Prochorus'* daily commitment to generating witty notions and inventions spawned his greatest service to Joseph—suggesting a replacement to take over the aging merchant's leadership role.

It was not difficult for him to convince Joseph to make his surprising but imminently qualified selection an equal partner.

Some present-day students of international trade claim many of the world's most profitable importing and exporting companies are spin-offs from the ventures of *Prochorus,* Joseph, and the partner they named shortly after the Pentecost.

The Rich Ruler's Supportive Secret: Embrace Change. Act for Others

- **For situations to change, you must change.**
- **Change requires new activity.**
- **Activity dedicated to others will not tire the doer, but will inspire and revitalize.**
- **Getting lost in new, selfless, creative action blesses you with a moment in eternity.**
- **Don't over-think. Procrastination invites delay, lethargy, and inactivity.**
- **Don't fear mistakes. You can always correct an error.**

The Pentecostal experience convinced Peter and Jesus' other apostles to heed the call to formally enlist seven men of good character and reputation to look after the business of the growing band. In addition, this new group would oversee the care of and distribution of food to widows, the poor, and other followers of Jesus.

Since *Stephen* had already performed these chores in his pledge to provide *service,* he was chosen as the first of this group. The faithful servant quickly assumed a leadership role as his example inspired the other six—of which *Prochorus* was one.

The more he *served* others, the more *Stephen* grew in power, strength, faith, grace, and ability. The grace and wisdom he had gained in the upper room propelled him into each *moment.* He eventually complemented his daily work of *serving* in the dining halls and in the highways and byways with his own preaching.

Eventually, with Joseph and Nicodemus no longer active members of the Sanhedrin, *Stephen* was called before the Council. He was accused of slander, blasphemy, and abuse in his frequent telling of the story of Jesus' life. *Stephen* answered the charges with *carefully chosen* words of boldness, courage, truth, and passion—recounting in a few strong strokes the Hebrew history from Abraham to Jesus. With his unabashed proclamation of Jesus' divinity, *Stephen's* role as a faithful *servant* dissolved, and his destined *leadership* qualities began to overflow for the world to see.

Enraged by his confident, yet angelic delivery, his accusers dragged him to the outskirts of the city.

There he was stoned to death, the first martyr for the truth of Jesus.

The Ethiopian Tarek was present at the stoning. He cried, knowing *Stephen* had spoken words that had attracted the wrath of the self-righteous. On the other hand, in his heart the big Ethiopian knew *Stephen* could not have remained silent—and that he had spoken well. Indeed, Tarek understood that the young *servant* listened to a different Spirit, one the former gladiator did not know.

Eyewitness accounts say Stephen was so focused on his mission in that *moment* to declare Jesus as the Christ, that he stepped into eternity well before his physical body ceased to function. There are those who believe he never felt the pain of one stone, so transcendent was that *moment* of ultimate *servitude*.

Today he is often referred to as Saint Stephen.

The Slight Servant's Supportive Secret: Serve to Lead

- **Service ushers you into the moment.**
- **Service builds the trust that is essential to leadership.**
- **Service will reveal your highest destiny and truest self—unleashing your leadership potential.**
- **Leadership is a choice. It is possible to lead in the right moments and follow in others.**
- **The best leaders don't inflict pain—but they must be willing to endure it.**
- **Don't limit others or yourself; develop other leaders.**

Thomas the twin was amazed at what he saw, heard, and felt as a heavenly wind swept through his very being in the upper room at Pentecost. He never doubted that God's Spirit *entered his world* with fire and might as real as the many buildings he had built from Nazareth to Jerusalem. That afternoon, he heard his friends give witness to the life and teachings of Jesus in languages in which they had never spoken. With his sister at his side, he saw the miracle of God's plan come forth from the lips of those he had once called fools.

As the two of them received their Baptism in the Holy Spirit, Thomas and Elizabeth were holding hands.

There is evidence that *Thomas* wrote of his experiences with Jesus and his apostles, although Christian authorities in later centuries question the authenticity of his authorship of what became known as The Gospel of *Thomas*.

What has been documented, however, is that "Doubting *Thomas*" later traveled *into the worlds* of other cultures, demonstrating his genius by designing and building noble edifices for the wealthy and wise. He also preached the Gospel of Jesus with sensitivity to diverse audiences, speaking to them the way *they needed to be spoken to*. He traveled as far east as India, where he established churches believing in Jesus' message, mission, and messianic role.

In the end, while *Thomas entered effectively into each moment* of his life by *observing and honoring the behavior and culture of those listening to him*, his ultimate fate was martyrdom for the cause he supported. He was pierced by a spear that instantly sent him to his eternal reward. His own wound was not unlike the one in Jesus' side that *Thomas* touched, convincing him of the resurrection. Legend has it that his body is buried in India, a country some say would have never considered Christianity had it not been for a *versatile* builder by the name of *Thomas, who respectfully* presented its cause to this foreign culture.

The Doubter's Supportive Secret:
Enter Their World

- **Speak to others as they need to be spoken to.**
- **Focus on what is important to them—and how they can be encouraged to achieve their destiny.**
- **Some are doers—people who like to achieve and to lead.**
- **Some are thinkers—who approach every situation with perspective and distance.**
- **Some have expressive, artistic personalities—they live by spinning off creative energy.**

- Some are naturally social—they do their best close to people, and by communicating.
- Another difference: some show feelings, while others control emotions.
- People react to distress differently:
      A cold questioner gets lost
      A friendly companion acquiesces
      A driving caravan leader becomes autocratic
      An artist attacks
These are telltale pointers to their worlds.
- These behaviors are not good or bad—but unless we acknowledge that we all function and reason differently, we will never understand one another.
- Versatility in entering others' worlds builds understanding that leads to trust.

John, who in his youth was one of the "Sons of Thunder," grew into the more docile sobriquet "Apostle of *Love.*" Jesus' command from the cross that the handsome, almost feminine young man be responsible for Mary, the Mother, cast his adult life in stone.

The excruciating death of his mentor matured *John* beyond those not blessed to be eyewitnesses. The nailing, the suffering, Jesus' cries to God the Father, his last breath, Longinus' spear into his side, Joseph's frantic attempt to preserve the dripping blood in the cup—all these events were tattooed onto *John's* spirit.

The advice of Joseph of Arimathea that *John* write down his *secret of the power of love* did not go unheeded. The Gospel of *John* in the Holy Scriptures, as well as several epistles written later in life, are often recommended to new believers as essential readings to be studied in one's early days of becoming a Christian.

In addition, when banished to the rocky island of Patmos near Greece by the Romans, *John's* recording of his many visions became known as the *Book of Revelation*. This apocalyptic creation has become the most literary of all writings considered heavenly inspired. John's use of metaphors, pseudonyms, and frequent descriptions of dreams and visions has provoked and challenged countless interpreters to this day.

In the end, *John's* leadership of the struggling Church of Jesus Christ in the first century was essential to its preservation. His *love* for Jesus and all the followers was evident to everyone who came to know the last surviving original apostle. His every *moment*, even with the newest convert, was full of the *secret he had learned to assure that every moment of life was a maximum opportunity to experience the eternal—agape love.*

As Jesus had predicted, and as Mary the Widow had reminded him, *John* died of natural causes as an old man on Patmos.

Saint *John* is still referred to today as the *Beloved* Disciple.

The Evangelist's Supportive Secret: Agape

- **Love every moment and every person, regardless how unlovable.**
- **God-like love that expects no return—*agape*—is the most powerful force in the world.**
- **In agape, God facilitates miracles and provides a portico to the eternal moment.**
- **Agape can disperse un-Godly forces from the person or situation being loved.**
- **Agape eradicates selfishness, envy, jealousy, greed, lust, intolerance, and self-pity from the giver.**
- **Find many reasons to love yourself, just as God loves you.**

Nicodemus and Joseph rushed down into the streets with all the others, burning with an all-consuming fire that recreated the energy of youth in the old friends. Standing together as Peter preached and others spoke in unfamiliar tongues, the two members of the Sanhedrin were speechless.

With child-like wonderment the two Counselors remained wide-eyed until the sun set that night. They spoke not a word.

As the crowd dwindled near the gate to Bethlehem, they embraced and cried, somehow knowing they would never see each other on this earth again. Their sharpened spirits had been instructed by God to begin *to act as if* all they had studied and believed from their youth was coming to pass. And as highly gifted men, they were now responsible to *step into eternity by acting out* their respective destinies, *now*.

The life of *Nicodemus* is left to tradition. A Gospel of *Nicodemus* has been distributed over the centuries. The Christian authorities have never made it a formal part of Holy Scripture. His departure from the Sanhedrin is most likely fact, as the religious Pharisees and Sadducees of that elite court were zealous in prosecuting members of the new movement.

On the other hand, each day throughout the world someone reads the account in the Gospel of John where a certain man among the Pharisees, who was a ruler, leader, and Hebrew authority, visited with Jesus under the cover of darkness. After confirming with Jesus his belief that he had, indeed, come from God, the visitor's questioning heart is answered.

Jesus says, "I assure you, most solemnly I tell you, that unless a person is born again, anew from above, he cannot ever see or know or be acquainted with and experience the Kingdom of God."

The caller on that fateful evening was *Nicodemus*. From that day on *he acted as if* Jesus' words were the inspired utterances of God, and with Joseph of Arimathea by his side, the two men began a dangerous walk of conversion in the midst of disagreeing peers.

Without *Nicodemus'* help, Joseph could not have buried Jesus. In the end, the two gallant men represent to all people today that with courage, conviction, passion, and a belief in the eternal, there is no evil force that can hold power over one's life.

Neither man saw the other again after the Day of Pentecost. They *stepped into eternity by acting out* the respective missions delivered to them by God.

Nicodemus' Supportive Secret:
Belief Creates Reality

- **Act as if God's plan is unfolding in each moment, and it will become real.**
- **Do not allow temporary setbacks distract you from the truth: God's seed of destiny will emerge in the fullness of time.**
- **Do not dig up seeds to check their progress.**
- **Practice faith until it is stronger than fear, lust, doubt, and anxiety.**
- **Do not anticipate God's results—his imagination is far beyond your own, and anticipation takes you out of the present.**

Mary of Magdala could not stop smiling on the Day of Pentecost. Every *moment* of that day a glow was visible on her face. She had become so *joyful* at her fate since being healed by Jesus. She remained silent until the Spirit of God manifested in the form of the mighty wind in the cramped upper room. Then her intimate *knowledge* of the person of Jesus, her firsthand experiences with his life, death, burial, resurrection, and final *instructions* burst forth in words of hope and faith to everyone outside who would listen.

Provocatively beautiful, the red-haired *Magdalene* attracted much attention around Jerusalem in the coming days, weeks, and months. Her destiny had become clear to her: *stay in each moment*, watch, listen, and feel for God's direction. Use the *wisdom* of the ages. Peacefully *act out* her commission to bring the Gospel of Jesus Christ in word and deed to the world.

The *Magdalene* took no pride in the transformation of Joseph of Arimathea. Rather, she was awestricken to be chosen by God to orchestrate the delivery of the secrets to the oppressed Counselor and businessman. She no longer felt unworthy to participate in the most monumental events in history. Jesus had taught her early that the unmerited favor of God was available to all who opened their hearts and minds to Him. Everything that happened to her, and everything of worth she accomplished in her life, she credited to the grace of a loving God.

With women playing a secondary role in the early church, *Mary of Magdala* at first seemed to be content to assist in the mundane chores of serving the followers. But the flame burning in her soon became evident when she informed her friends she would be traveling north to share what she knew about the life of the Man from Galilee. With a caravan-like entourage organized by Joseph, she set her sights for Rome and Gaul, far from the Hebrew culture of Jerusalem.

Traditions and legends about the *Magdalene's* later years have become prolific. Most agree modern-day France, then part of Gaul, was as far as she traveled on her missionary journeys. There she preached in a land where women had already been granted more rights than in the Holy City of Jerusalem. Many miracles were ascribed to her, particularly in the area of female infertility. So mystical was her fame that current researchers, feminists, theologians, and even novelists depict her relationship with Jesus as closer than scriptural or traditional references imply.

In the end, however, it was the *moment* she was set free from a multitude of demonic spirits that has the most influence on those who study her life today. Cryptic recordings beyond the Gospel accounts of her exorcism report how she could never forget that *instant*. In a flash, all thoughts of envy, jealousy, self-pity, avarice, greed, lust, perversion, and murder left her. Like a rushing, swollen river departing her mind, body, and spirit, all the evil forces that had polluted her life were forever swept away. Only a profound, pure, silent peace entered the void in her at that *moment*. As she sat upright in the dusty road, her body that had been torn and abused was now whole. Her nails were no longer caked with the dirt, skin, and blood from the backs of ravaging men. For the first time in her life, she could smell the wildflowers growing along the byway. The delightful chirping of birds filled her ears. She could hear herself breathing; even sense the current of blood rhythmically gushing through her veins. The mangy dogs that had been circling her, awaiting her death, now whimpered, longing for the touch of her soft hand. The air was clean, pure, and heavenly, giving her a holy breath that signaled her life had been restored. The sun gently caressed her face and body like no man, its heavenly essence continuing to heal her to her very core.

In each of her enemies still curiously lurking in the shadows, awaiting a final outcome, she saw only *magnificence*, the good even they, themselves, had yet to discover. She *surrendered* to the young preacher, *accepted his act* of healing, and experienced immediate *joy*, *understood* beyond her mortal mind. She *patiently cherished each moment* of her newfound tranquility, sensed her mind filling up with *Godly inventions*, had immediate *compassion* for all in attendance, and overflowed with a *love* she had never experienced before.

She arose with a new power lifting her to her feet and gazed upon her rescuer.

He smiled at her.

From that moment she began *to act as if* she was worthy to serve her God, wherever and however her destiny would be revealed. She had arrived in a *moment* she never knew possible—a *moment* in which she was awarded a glimpse of eternity.

Yes, *Mary the Magdalene* had assisted Duca in the transformation of Joseph of Arimathea. But in her simple belief in the *power of the moment*, which began at Jesus' healing of her soul, she discovered secrets to living that others would later confirm. Her notoriety in popular culture today is miniscule compared to her courage to follow her true path when efforts to stop her were legion.

Mary of Magdala died and was buried in France. Today she is venerated as a saint by millions. Even those churches over the centuries that refused to recognize her as an honored leader at the time of Jesus, today acknowledge her profound role in crafting an example for all women who would respond to the Gospel of Christ.

The Magdalene's Foundational Secret: God's Gift of the Present

- **Live humbly and fully in the present moment.**
- **The past and the future are unchangeable and uncontrollable illusions.**
- **The present offers a glimpse of God's eternity and escape from the dimension of time.**
- **A feeling of peace and timelessness will show you have entered the present.**
- **Living in the present takes work and practice.**
- **Knowledge is not enough—understanding and wisdom must follow.**

- **The power of focus will be released to allow for your magnificence to be revealed...in the now.**

Chapter XXXV.

Man of Mystery

❦

*J*oseph *of Arimathea* watched Nicodemus step slowly into the dark shadows of Jerusalem on the night of Pentecost.

The full moon reassured him. Joseph no longer feared for his safety, but he knew his prompt return to his estate was essential. Duca was patiently awaiting his master's report on the happenings in the upper room.

For the first time in years, the aging merchant stepped into a trot. The cool, late spring air refreshed his soiled face. A smile overtook him as his mind's eye was entertained with a scene from long ago, when he ran after Persian Prince in the Arabian Desert. The majestic horse had playfully departed from the caravan, as if complaining that his destiny in life as a champion racer had been aborted to lead a rich man's plodding convoy.

Joseph picked up his pace to a run that would on any other day surely have killed him. But the idea of sprinting into the eternal moment with such a refreshing, youthful act was irresistible.

The *Arimathean* had no fear of running out of breath and dying. He was assured his health was guaranteed—secure in his mission for the balance of his time on earth.

For the next week, *Joseph* recounted his entire life to Duca, particularly the time he spent with Jesus during the young preacher's adolescence. The servant marveled at the role his *master* had played throughout the Rabbi's life, from his wise counsel to Jesus' stepfather, all the way to his night-time visits with Nicodemus.

He confirmed what Duca had always believed—that it was indeed the young Jesus who healed Duca when they both were in their teens. *Joseph* recounted finding Duca's near-dead body in the desert, believing he might have to bury him there, until the dying eunuch was restored after his cousin's young son laid hands upon him.

Duca respectfully waited for Joseph to complete his tale of the servant's rescue. Then he quietly revealed his most recent epiphany.

"You know, master, as I've been transcribing the secrets and contemplating them, I remembered a strange fact."

"What, Duca?"

"The secrets—I've heard the secrets before."

"When?"

"In the desert."

"From a voice in the desert?"

"Yes and no."

"Tell me."

"It was Jesus. When we spoke, he used such simple words—but in a very short time he delivered the same secrets to me as I lay close to death."

"Are you sure?"

"Yes. In fact, now more than ever I can see he possessed the wisdom of the ages, even as a young man."

Both men spent much time reviewing and discussing the secrets. They marveled at the efforts of the Magdalene and her motley crew of teachers to transform an old caravan master's heart. And they were in awe at Duca's recollection of Jesus' teaching in the desert.

"What a chronicle it is," Duca said, pondering the secrets and *Joseph's* report, spanning some thirty-three years. "What do you suppose the future holds for the two of us?"

Without taking a breath, his *master* revealed the plan.

"When the power of God's Spirit swept over us in the upper room, a sirocco of scenes whirled through my mind," Joseph said. "The event left indelible imprints in me that I'll cherish until my final day. My instructions were clearly delivered from the throne room of grace in heaven.

"First, my loyal former servant, we'll meet with Prochorus to seal our business relationship. It will be your duty to assume my executive role—as an equal partner with the rich young ruler and me!"

Duca stared at his master in disbelief. He was speechless.

"From our villa here in Jerusalem I envision that you'll eventually lead the greatest trade organization this world has ever seen. And in accordance with the *God-inspired strategy* of Prochorus, you'll employ the poor and uneducated to drive this worthy worldly venture. In the end, your workers will grow in prosperity and wisdom. And the churches will receive the first fruits of the venture to finance their own worldwide reach."

"Am I worthy of this, master?"

"It is God's will, Duca. I'm certain of it! You now know the full story of Jesus. You've witnessed its most climactic events. You have the secrets, and you have the *knowledge* of all I've taught you since your youth. Most importantly, you *now have the truth!*"

"And your role, master?"

"No, Duca. Not master. From now on you'll call me Joseph!

"I'll advise you and Prochorus from afar. I've made the following arrangements: David the Temple Guard will arrive here in disguise in seven days. The centurion Longinus will accompany him. You and Prochorus will summon the best of my former laborers, as well as the poor, to assemble the caravan with full provisions, horses, water, and all I may need to *venture into God's will.* My belongings will be few — clothing for northern winters, two copies of the secrets, the Torah, the hymns of David, the teachings of Solomon, and my most prized possessions."

"Mast—Joseph—you must be specific. I can only guess the value of all you own—I would hesitate to select your most prized possessions."

"The burial cloth of Jesus must be carefully wrapped and will be forever guarded by David. Longinus will conceal the spear. And I shall transport the cup—the Holy Grail I fashioned for Jesus."

"And will you reopen your northern routes to the shores of Spain and into the Greek isles, master?"

"No. The caravan business is for you and Prochorus to drive. Your revenues will help fund my mission. But I *now go forth* to tell the story of Jesus, to spread the secrets, and to make sure that every man and woman in the world may find *freedom in the truth.*"

The night before his departure, Joseph had a dream.

It's so good to be lying here with you again, Sarah. I know I'm dreaming, but I'll believe I'm not. You're alive again, my partner for life, my best friend, confidant, and lover. Oh, the wonderful life we had together.

Speak to me, Sarah.

You smile, yet you don't speak. But I won't complain lest you leave my bedchamber.

It's true, we had no children, but we enjoyed so many young people. There was Jesus. He was so special to us in his early days.

And then there was our Duca. He's grown to be more than I thought God had planned. In fact, I know he now believes. That was always our hope, but I was so involved in our busi-

ness and the Court. It was you who loved him like a mother. It was you who were always so patient with me.

Sarah...you're leaving? Please don't go. You seem so peaceful. May we embrace one more time?

Your kiss on my cheek is so soft. It's so gentle. It tickles my senses, and I smile.

Joseph awoke. His eyes remained closed. He still felt Sarah's familiar kiss on his cheek.

As he slowly allowed his eyes to open to the new day, his hope was that her kiss would not vanish. It did not.

Rather, a butterfly that innocently danced on his face continued to prolong the precious moment.

Joseph's dry, leathered face relaxed, and its many wrinkles seemed to almost vanish. He detected a sweet fragrance he had never smelled before. It was the scent of eternity and omniscience. Now it anointed his whole body. His Creator spoke to him of the years he had pursued this butterfly of life—its peace, contentment, and fulfillment always so fleeting. But now, the dainty visitor tarried, prolonging the sense of Sarah's presence.

Joseph's revelation was that at the end of a journey of striving for God's will, "try not" was the message—"just be and do."

The lilies of the field waved in his mind's eye, basking in the sun, never toiling.

I've entered the moment. I'm in my destiny. No longer will I chase the butterfly. He'll simply be here when God wants him to be.

It's time for me to rise.

The cock crowed louder than ever the morning David, Longinus, and dozens of workers arrived at Joseph's estate for the caravan's departure. The plan was clear and simple: David would ride the first horse, leading the entourage. The Holy Shroud of Jesus would be firmly strapped to his back in its own pack.

Persian Prince would be next, tethered to David, ready for *Joseph's* mounting at his discretion. Longinus would be at the back of the line, guarding the rear, armed with the spear that pierced Jesus. The staff members were all followers of Jesus, knowing well their chores would not be dedicated to trade, but rather to the building of churches.

Duca embraced *Joseph* as the *Arimathean* kissed Persian Prince.

"Have *no fear*, young Egyptian," Joseph said to his servant. "What the enemy meant for your torment when they tried to rob your manhood many years ago has been turned by God into a blessing. You are one of the finest and most complete men I have ever known. Your children will be as many as you employ. You will help the downtrodden masses find self-worth and credibility in their work. They'll follow your example, and they *will* find God.

"I'll speak with you by messenger frequently, only advising you when God dictates. I'll spread the secrets, as will you. I will only return to die in my bed, in my beloved Jerusalem."

"You're sure of this venture, *Joseph*?"

"*I know, that I know, that I know—it must be now*. I owe this transformation to you. I've been so blessed to have had you in my life."

"But, Joseph—I was only being a servant."

"Indeed you were! And because you *served*, you *led* me to the truth."

Joseph turned to the Prince. Speaking to the animal, he said, "Well, my friend, our *destinies are finally fulfilled*. I will apply what I know to the spreading of the Gospel, and you can run, and lead, and carry your old owner in our shared destinies. And my servant Duca standing beside me here shall direct our businesses.

"Prince, you, Duca, the Magdalene, and her friends have taught me well—*what about now?*

There is no better moment to fulfill God's plan in our lives!"

The horse stood at attention, not even blinking. The *moment* was frozen as all three recognized its *eternal value.*

Tradition and legend tell us *Joseph* and his entourage traveled through Rome and Gaul before finally arriving in Britain.

Eventually, the wealthy merchant and Counselor became known to church scholars and the ages as "The Mystery Man of the Bible." All four Gospels of the New Testament record *Joseph's deed*—acquiring Jesus' body and placing it in the family tomb reserved for the rich man.

After that act, *Joseph of Arimathea* vanishes from history.

In fact, David the Temple Guard and Longinus the Roman centurion remained at his side for the rest of his days. With their help, the *Arimathean* created churches throughout the British Isles. He was named a Bishop in the fledgling church.

Joseph's forte was teaching discipline to young men. Not only did he instruct them in the fundamentals of Christianity, but he also blessed them with the secrets he had learned. *Joseph* mentored many in managing their daily affairs, as well as the business ventures they continued during their ministries.

Joseph's rumored possession of valued relics from Jesus' life meant David, Longinus, and other guards had to fight off a constant flow of marauders and thieves in search of the priceless pieces. Joseph's near-death experiences during such robbery attempts always reminded him of his destiny to finish his work in the northern part of the Roman Empire, and then to return to Jerusalem to die. Amid these recurring attacks, he continued to counsel Duca and Prochorus as they leveraged their businesses to new heights of profitability and influence.

Joseph was alone with Persian Prince when the *magnificent* animal breathed his last breaths.

"I've been blessed with your companionship for many years, Prince," Joseph said. "Your stately *presence and patience* with your *master* have taught me well. I know the *time is now* for your passing into the kingdom of the other world, but I assure you that the words of Jesus and my ancestors are true—your spirit and mine will meet again. Then you and I will ride into the warm sunlight together, the wind caressing our faces, the Lord on his own white stallion.

"The *joy of that moment will be infinite*, because we'll no longer be in a race, but simply in a point in time where *nothing past or future will matter*. It will be a just reward for us both as we live in the *eternal bliss of that moment*. We've been there in times past, but my ignorance would often quench that delight. Thank God *the secrets have driven me into the moments* with you, and thank God there will be countless others we will share in eternity."

Not long thereafter, Joseph requested that David and Longinus escort him back to Jerusalem. The churches were growing. Persian Prince had gone home to his reward, and *Joseph* knew his time on earth was ending.

When he arrived at his estate, Duca, Prochorus, many of their workers, and dozens of the followers of Jesus greeted him. Joseph spoke with a youthful enthusiasm to them all, reporting the good news of the progress in the north.

The next morning, Duca found his *master had passed into eternity.*

The last will and testament of *Joseph of Arimathea* was executed by Prochorus and Duca. The faithful servant received his *master's* portion of the business, on one condition—that Duca weekly distribute at least seven copies of the secrets.

When this request was read, Duca and Prochorus exchanged smiles—because they had commissioned dozens of writers over the years of *Joseph's* absence to duplicate the lessons. In fact, Thomas the Twin had reportedly distributed many copies as far east as India.

Another document left by *Joseph* was not to be opened until after Duca's death.

After the will had been read, Duca asked David what had become of the Holy Shroud of Jesus, the spear, and the Holy Grail.

The guard lamented they had all been stolen. He related that Joseph's only comment when learning of their fate was that they now belonged to the ages.

Late on the night of Joseph's passing, David called for Duca and handed him a napkin. He whispered into the eunuch's ear in the presence of several workers. Duca accepted the cloth from the guard.

It became his most prized possession.

Chapter XXXVI.

The Richest Man in the World

D uca lived to a ripe old age. In the end he was managing the distribution of many copies of the secrets every month.

Twenty centuries later the secrets are still being shared with whoever will listen.

Upon Duca's passing, Prochorus administered his burial after reading the final document left behind by Joseph. The servant was to be laid to rest with Joseph and Sarah. A third place had been reserved for Duca. A sentence on the wall of the burial chamber declared the following:

The richest man in the world is not the one who has the most, but rather the one who needs the least...and gives the most.

Joseph authored the inscription on Duca's sarcophagus:
Duca of Egypt
Servant, Leader, Friend, Believer
The Richest Man in the World

The cloth given to *Duca* by David was the burial napkin of Jesus.

Just before he died, *Duca* explained the napkin's significance to Prochorus. He had learned about the Hebrew ritual from the studious Temple Guard, David.

"This cloth had been folded in the Holy Shroud. As was the custom, it had covered Jesus' face.

"It was the Magdalene who discovered it on the stone ledge in Jesus' empty tomb that morning. She promptly placed it with the burial cloth, eventually returning it to Joseph, who had originally purchased the material. When she saw Joseph in the streets outside the upper room after the miracle of Pentecost, Mary of Magdala knew it was time for her to reveal the meaning of the napkin to him.

"She related that the way it was placed on the ledge conformed to the Hebrew tradition: when a dinner guest is about to leave, he folds the napkin in a certain way if he has been served well.

"From the manner in which this cloth was found, carefully folded, Jesus had communicated, 'Thank you—I will return.'"

The burial tomb of Joseph, his wife, and Duca cannot be located today. However, legend has it that another tomb can be found.

It is considered by many to be the original site hewn out of limestone by Joseph of Arimathea for his own use, only to be given to Jesus for his burial.

That tomb is—and will forever remain—empty.

THE END

ABOUT THE AUTHOR

Joseph Rocco Cervasio is a versatile, engaging, and charismatic corporate executive with high energy and passion. A combination of entrepreneurial challenges, as well as corporate projects in public companies, has tested and proven Mr. Cervasio's visioning, strategic planning, inspirational leadership, business results, communications, and organizational and talent development competencies. His design, writing, delivery, and execution of business planning processes and learning curricula, the completion of detailed financial analysis, and the astute monitoring of the market place have resulted in revenue growth, performance efficiency, cost reduction, profit enhancement, and record-breaking associate opinion scores.

Today, Joe shares the wisdom of his experiences in his writing. His first novel in 2004, *Bad News on the Doorstep,* is a fictionalized memoir that has attracted a cult following all over the USA. While Tony Award-winning Broadway play "Jersey Boys" followed as the real-life depiction of many of Joe's characters, *Bad News...* is Cervasio's nostalgic look back to his own growing up in the Fifties in New Jersey.

In *Now or Never: The 11 Secrets of Arimathea,* Mr. Cervasio leaves behind the streets of Jersey in 1959, to escort us into the markets and back alleys of Jerusalem at the time of Christ. Lessons for life are depicted in 11 specific Secrets that are delivered to the "Mystery Man of the Bible," Joseph of Arimathea. Joseph's rescuers are some of the most interesting and enigmatic characters found in Holy Scripture, ... including some attractive fictional personalities as well!

His corporate, teaching, and writing accomplishments have allowed Joe to become an acknowledged keynote speaker, moderator, and guest lecturer for such groups as the American Resort Development Association, the New Jersey Association of Directors of Athletics, The Coccia Institute, The Juvenile Diabetes Research Foundation, and the National Association of Newspaper Advertisers. He has been a guest lecturer at Cornell University, the Harvard Business School, Montclair State University, Penn State University, Seton Hall University, Caldwell College, and Manhattan College. Leadership, Team-building, and Performance Secrets are his most demanded topics.

Mr. Cervasio continues his company, Diversified Global Strategies, that was founded to coach high level executives, develop strategic planning for Fortune 500's, lead executive searches for professional sales and marketing executives, as well as to coordinate speaking, consulting, and training engagements relative to his business and writing achievements.

Over the years, clients and employers have included Marriott Vacation Club International, Prudential Realty Associates, Guardian Life Insurance Company of America, Boise Cascade, The Rank Group of England, Bluegreen Corporation, and the Berkley Group.

Joseph Cervasio holds a BS in Organizational Behavior from the School of Industrial and Labor Relations at Cornell University. His MBA, concentrating in Management and Marketing, was earned at the Stern School of Business at New York University. He resides in Nutley, New Jersey with his wife Maria.

Breinigsville, PA USA
15 December 2009
229259BV00001B/66/P